GIRLS AT THE EDGE OF THE WORLD

GIRLS AT THE EDGE OF THE WORLD

LAURA BROOKE ROBSON

DIAL BOOKS

Dial Books
An imprint of Penguin Random House LLC, New York

First published in the United States of America by Dial Books,
an imprint of Penguin Random House LLC, 2021
Copyright © 2021 by Laura Brooke Robson

Dial & colophon are registered trademarks of Penguin Random House LLC.

Visit us online at penguinrandomhouse.com.

Library of Congress Cataloging-in-Publication Data is available.
Book manufactured in Canada
ISBN 9780525554035

10 9 8 7 6 5 4 3 2 1

Design by Cerise Steel
Text set in Dante MT

To Mom and Dad,
Who taught me snark and courage
in equal measure.

BEFORE we start, we must come to an agreement on something: All stories are about the ocean.

Oh, yes. I insist.

I could tell you of characters—a beguiling maiden with the pull of the moon, a volatile king with the ire of a tempest. And of plots, I could tell you about the boy searching for his love, or the girl searching for lost treasure, or the man searching for fame and glory, and what does the ocean do but search? In the crevices of canals and the sheer edges of cliff sides and the ground floors of city apartments where a better-behaved ocean would not intrude?

But the best argument, I believe, lies in the fables that follow.

Now. Let us begin.

—"Introduction," *Tamm's Collected Fables*

WHEN the land settles solid beneath my bow, I leap over the ship's rail and lay my back flat against pebbled shore. It is gloriously still; I have forgotten how not to sway with the sea.

I rouse myself to stare at my New World—cliffs clothed in wind-bobbed grasses, trees pining skyward, blood-red wildflowers I will name, in time.

This earth is reborn pure for my taking, crafted as my kingdom, and so it will stay until another reckoning floods us anew.

—*Captain's Log*, Antinous Kos (1189 PKF Edition)

The Harbinger Year

Storm Ten: Ice

Storm Nine: Blooming of the Trees

Storm Eight: Wind

Storm Seven: Swarm of the Insects

Storm Six: Heat

Storm Five: Exodus of the Birds

Storm Four: Panic of the Livestock

Storm Three: Exodus of the Frogs

Storm Two: Blood

Storm One: The Flood

1

NATASHA

Twelve hundred years ago, a man who should've drowned didn't. He was a fisherman, some say. Others claim he was a king. Others keep shaking their heads. He was a god.

As the story goes, there was a year of storms, called the Harbinger Year. Ten storms, each with a new horror to accompany it. The last storm brought the Flood. Water, the whole world over, killing every plant and animal and person that didn't make it to a ship in time, and plenty that did. The Flood lasted a year, and when the waters receded, the world was made anew.

There are others who survived, but they didn't write down their stories. And this was an important story. This was a story that could teach us how to survive a Flood. Survive anything.

So we forget the others' names and stories, and we remember Antinous Kos.

Nine years ago, a woman who shouldn't have drowned did.

She was clever and beautiful and in a constant, losing argument with the inside of her head. Before she went, she told me stories. Never Kos's story. The rest of the world told that one plenty.

Instead, she told me fables. Of kind kings and brave princesses.

Of ice palaces. Of girls she once called her friends, girls who knew how to fly.

When I was four or five, I realized the last kind of story wasn't a fable. She'd been part of them: The Royal Flyers, the girls who performed high in the air on the silks. When she was a flyer, she met kings and queens, lived in a palace, spun herself up in fabric where the water couldn't reach her.

The other flyers told her to leave when they realized she was pregnant. She never flew again. When I was nine, she drowned in a canal.

My mother's story isn't one anybody wants to remember, because it's not a story of how you survive. It's a story of how you don't.

I grip my silks, suspended in an arabesque fifteen feet above the floor. The other five flyers are at dinner. Their silks sway gently in the drafty studio—far below me, the fabric is tied in fat knots to keep it from trailing against the padded mats and wooden floor. Across from the wall of mirrors, a rectangular window nearly as high as the ceiling beams, at eye level from the tops of the silks, shows a plum-dark sky and the diluted glow of a tired gas lamp on the street below.

The door flies open.

"Have you seen Pippa?"

I spin to see Sofie cross the floor in three frantic bounds.

"Not since rehearsal ended." I pause to frown. "But she should be in here with me. Her elements were a mess."

"She's not in our room." Sofie cranes her neck up at me. Her eyes, heavily lidded, are wide with worry. The flimsy lighting makes her skin look gray, near translucent. She never took off her practice full-suit, a uniform that covers her in tight black fabric from ankles to collar to wrists. "Her things are gone."

"What?" I slide a few inches down the silk.

"Her books, her trunk, her shoes—"

My feet hit the floor. "I don't understand."

Sofie shakes her head. "She didn't come to dinner, so I went looking for her. But then I saw all her things missing. If she's gone someplace, why didn't she tell me?"

I hurry to the bedroom shared by all the other flyers. It was my bedroom from the time I was nine until I became principal flyer. The five beds are in varying degrees of the usual disarray. Wardrobes with the drawers spilling open. Books and hair ribbons and at least one poorly hidden wine bottle.

Pippa's bed is neatly made. Her side table is bare.

I turn to Sofie. "Is she with Gregor?"

Sofie plucks at Pippa's quilt. "Why would she bring all her things to go see her"—Sofie's face pinches—"sweetheart?"

When I leave the bedroom, Sofie keeps close at my heels. "I already tried to find Madam Adelaida," she says.

I knock on Adelaida's door anyway. After a moment, a petite housemaid cracks the door. Bulky gowns spill out of her arms.

"Miss Koskinen." She gives an awkward curtsy and drops a chemise.

"I'm looking for Adelaida," I say.

"She mentioned the Stone Garden, miss, to have a talk with Mariner Gospodin."

My heart beats faster. Gospodin—the Righteous Mariner who oversees Kostrov's branch of the Sacred Breath—is one of the busiest men in the country. In addition to leading Sacred Breath services every morning—which reminds me that I haven't gone in nearly two months; never mind that the flyers are supposed to go every Saturday—he's King Nikolai's most trusted advisor. I don't think Gospodin is the type to drop in just for tea. If he's meeting with Adelaida, they're discussing something important.

I turn on my heel. Sofie hangs back a moment, then jogs to catch me.

"Wait, wait." She hooks her elbow through mine. "What are you doing?"

"I thought you wanted to find out where Pippa went."

"I did. I do. I mean . . ."

Sofie and I turn a corner, leaving behind the part of the palace meant for flyers and flying. The rest of the palace is more imposing. Marble tiles the floor. Tapestries, lurid battle scenes stitched in turquoise thread, line the walls.

"I'm just afraid of interrupting them, is all," Sofie says.

"I know," I say, "but do you see an alternative?"

Sofie is quiet.

Six months ago, just before my seventeenth birthday, Storm Ten hit. People have a funny way of insisting everything's going to be all right. *No, Natasha, it's not Storm Ten*, they said. *There won't be another Flood for hundreds of years.* Adelaida told me I sounded like my mother. Paranoid.

But it was Storm Ten. It rained from sunrise to sunset, leaving the canals bloated with jellyfish and the streets puddled with sewage. Then everything froze. We started hearing reports of snow all over the world, even in places that never dip below freezing. Some people kept saying the Harbinger Year wasn't supposed to start for another eight hundred years. They didn't believe it had already begun. Why would they? It takes a special kind of cynic to accept that the world is trying to kill you.

I'm that kind of cynic.

By Storm Seven, after locusts and mosquitoes descended over Kostrov like a plague, no one could deny it. The Sacred Breath suddenly reported that they'd discovered a new interpretation of *Captain's Log,* one that proved this Flood would come eight hundred years early. But we didn't have to worry. The Sacred Breath and the king and the ocean's love would protect us.

Madam Adelaida told me otherwise. There was only one thing that would protect me. The same thing that had protected me all these years since my mother died. Being a Royal Flyer.

Kings came and went, but where there was Kostrov, there had always been the Kostrovian Royal Flyers. When Roen laid siege to New Sundstad three hundred years ago, the Royal Flyers kept practicing. When a cholera epidemic swept across the country, the Royal Flyers stayed put. And now, when Kostrov sinks and the country takes to the sea, we will stay right where we belong: among the royals, in the court, as we always have.

The girls who remain in our ranks when Storm One hits will join the royal fleet. The ones who don't will fend for themselves against the Flood.

I can practice fourteen hours a day. I can practice until my blisters burst and my hands bleed.

I can't practice enough to keep Adelaida from letting someone else go. From letting Pippa go.

"Pippa's so good, though." Sofie chews her bottom lip. "Maybe she looked a little sloppy in rehearsal today, but it was just one day."

We reach the Stone Garden in the palace's center courtyard and weave through the labyrinth of imposing sculptures and miniature canals. The wheezy light of the gas lamps cuts the fog and reflects along the wet path.

"I don't see why it's your business to have an opinion on my girls."

I recognize Adelaida's husky growl.

Then, in response, a confident, deep voice. "Everything's my business," it says. "No need to get ruffled."

"I'm not—"

Adelaida and Gospodin materialize through the fog. When Adelaida sees me, she purses her lips. Gospodin blinks away his shock and dissolves into an easy smile. While Adelaida's appearance is a meticulous construction—eyes tightly rimmed in black pencil, feet bound in narrow heels—Gospodin's handsomeness is lazy, windswept, and warm.

"Go back to the studio," Adelaida says.

Sofie clamps her hand around my wrist. I've never seen her challenge Adelaida before, but if anything might give her the courage, it's losing Pippa.

"Where's Pippa?" I say.

Adelaida's jaw twitches.

"Her things are gone," Sofie says.

Adelaida scowls, and Sofie bites her lip.

"Did you make her leave?" I say. "Why didn't you tell me?"

"Should I let you handle this?" Gospodin asks, his chin tilted toward Adelaida.

"No." Adelaida points. "Studio. *Now*."

Sofie flinches. I stand stubborn for another moment.

"Come on." Sofie tugs my arm. "She'll tell us later."

Reluctantly, I follow her out. "Did you hear what they were talking about?"

"I don't know." Sofie pauses. "Homilies?"

"They were talking about us," I say. "Why would Gospodin have an opinion on *us*?" I scan the hallway, nervous someone might overhear. It's empty. "I want to figure out what they're talking about."

"How do you reckon you'll manage that?"

"I reckon I'll manage fine."

"Oh," Sofie says. "Are we going back into the garden a supersecret Natasha way?"

I shush her.

A tapestry of a bear hangs adjacent to the library. When I was eleven and keen on the idea of spying on the royal children while they played board games, I discovered that the tapestry hides a crawl space.

I pull the fabric aside and drop to my knees.

"No way," Sofie says. "Wait, do you honestly expect me to fit through there?"

I press my stomach to the ground and begin the long scoot across the dusty floor. "You're not required to follow me."

Sofie, of course, drops to her knees and follows me. "I thought we were friends, but all this time, you let me believe there were only three hidden passages in the palace."

Actually, I know of eight, but I'd just as soon keep some for myself.

After a couple of feet, we pass an air vent that looks out onto the library. It's empty and dim. I keep crawling.

A couple stuffy moments later, the passage ends at the top of a tall stone wall in a dark chamber. I hear water splashing below.

"Sofie?"

"Yeah?"

"There's a four-foot drop ahead, so be careful."

"What? How am I supposed to manage a four-foot drop?"

"Um." I wriggle my torso into open air. "Inelegantly."

Once Sofie and I are both firmly on the ground, our feet submerged in about six inches of water, I squint around the room.

"This way."

"Where are we?" Sofie asks.

"Underneath the garden. Now, shh."

Water trickles through a metal grate overhead, leaking from one of the fountains into this tunnel, to be recycled again and again through the dozens of miniature canals and bubbling sculptures across the gardens.

I hear a scrap of conversation and lift my hand. Sofie's sloshing walk slows.

I rise on my toes and peer through a grate along the upper wall of the passage. Water dribbles over the lip, but above that, I can see Adelaida's and Gospodin's legs. They're facing each other. Gospodin's posture is relaxed.

Sofie rises on her toes beside me.

"Have you talked to King Nikolai?" Adelaida asks.

"Of course. He'll be sad to see them go, but he's rational. He understands we're in a time of difficult choices."

"And his councilors—"

"Understand as well," Gospodin says. "I'm sorry, Adelaida, I am, but the decision is already made."

Sofie glances over at me. She mouths something, but I can't make out what she's asking. I shake my head.

Adelaida lets out a long, thin breath. "So you want me to replace Pippa?"

"That's the pregnant one?"

Sofie's hand catches mine. She squeezes so hard I think she might break my finger bones. I try not to let this information sink in. Eighteen years ago, my mother had to leave the flyers because she was pregnant; her life unraveled and threatened to take mine with it. And now, Pippa. Pregnant.

I shake Sofie's hand away.

"Yes," Adelaida says. "I tried to get her to stay as long the festival, but she wouldn't."

"Inconvenient," Gospodin says.

"Selfish."

"Replace her as soon as you can. These days, we need all the public support we can get."

"You're not scared of a few Brightwallers scraping together an uprising, are you?" Adelaida asks.

"I'll worry about them. You worry about the flyers."

They start to walk away. Sofie and I have to hurry down the passage, ducking our heads next to different grates to stay in earshot.

"And, Gabriel," Adelaida says. Her voice is taut.

"Hmm?"

"I'd like to remind you that I've been a member of this court longer than even you have. I have a legacy. As long as Kostrovians walk this world, flyers will remain, I assure you."

"Art is an asset," Gospodin says. "I'm not arguing with you."

"Without me," Adelaida says, "no one can train the next generation of flyers when the Flood passes. I'm the only one who can rebuild the Royal Flyers. I will take my place on the royal fleet."

Gospodin pauses.

"I want you to guarantee it," she says.

"Adelaida," he says. "You're a vital part of the court. You'll be on the fleet."

"Good," she says. "Good, I know that."

"Of course." The space between their feet shrinks slightly; I imagine Gospodin putting a large hand on Adelaida's shoulder. "Many breaths."

"Many breaths."

I feel Sofie's gaze on me the moment the feet disappear, but I can't drag my eyes away from the space where they stood.

"Natasha?"

I swallow. I can hear my heart beating in my skull.

Again, quieter: "Natasha?"

Slowly, I face her. A rectangle of light runs slanted across her eyes, bisecting her nose. Her damp hair clings to the sides of her cheeks.

"I must've misunderstood something," Sofie says.

"I don't think so," I say.

"Why is Adelaida worrying about training the *next* generation of flyers?"

My throat feels dry enough to crack. "They're not taking us on the royal fleet when Storm One hits. They're going to let us drown."

2

ELLA

I'm going to kill the king of Kostrov.

I didn't grow up dreaming of murder. Murder found me. We're getting along nicely.

Though I have not technically killed anyone yet, my enthusiasm makes up for my lack of experience. When I go to sleep, I think about killing Nikolai. When I wake up, I think about killing Nikolai. When Maret and I drank our tea on the nauseating sail to Kostrov, we discussed, in whispers, all the ways we'd like to end his life.

As Nikolai's aunt, Maret brings to the table all the knowledge an aspiring assassin could want. Court structures and palace rhythms. As a nameless little nobody, I bring the sneaking and killing part of things.

I'm going to kill the king, and I'm not going to feel bad about it.

Here's what I grew up dreaming of: A farmhouse next to my brothers'. The smell of my mother's bread baking. The girl who sold flowers in town and always wore a bloom in her hair.

But my brothers and my mother and the flower girl are all dead. Washed away.

There was a time when I didn't spend every waking moment thinking of Nikolai. I spent every moment thinking of his sister, who loved me and devastated me and left me alone in this forsaken, flooding world.

But Nikolai killed Cassia.

So I'm going to kill Nikolai.

He's the most heavily guarded person in Kostrov, so I'm going to die doing it. But what does that matter as long as he's dead?

Maret didn't smile for weeks after Cassia died. Not until we stepped off the ship and into Kostrov. The moment that smile crossed her lips, I felt something between us fracture. The pain of losing Cassia had bound Maret and me together. Smiling in a post-Cassia world was expressly forbidden.

When Maret's feet settled on the uneven stone bordering the harbor, she took a big breath of air and held it in her cheeks. She let it out in a puff and spun to look at me. "Kostrov, Ella dear."

I gazed around the city. New Sundstad—*The only place in Kostrov worth going,* Maret said on our voyage—was a paean to gray. The ocean was the color of pigeon feathers. Sooty buildings tilted out of the ground and creaked into each other.

"To be in a city again." Maret hefted her large handbag industriously. "I don't think we'll miss rustic old Terrazza one bit, will we?" Smile.

I didn't answer, caught up in the voices echoing across the harbor. I hadn't anticipated that hearing so much Kostrovian all at once would feel like a goat kicking me in the stomach.

A man named Edvin with hair blonder than I'd ever seen on an adult met us at the door to our new apartment.

"Sorry," he said, unlocking the door. "It's not exactly a royal accommodation. A high ceiling, though, like you asked."

"You're a doll, Eddy." Maret swept inside and tossed her handbag on an exhausted pink sofa.

Through the window, I spotted an equally dismal apartment across the narrow street. I took a careful step onto the pale floorboards.

Edvin's eyes roamed my body. They snagged on the tattoo curling around my wrist. I pulled my sleeve lower.

"Oh, Edvin, this is Ella. I mentioned her in my letter?"

I gave Edvin a hard stare. Maret mentioned Edvin to me too, on the voyage here. She told me she had a few friends from her palace days who could help us. *They'll get us clothes and a place to stay, but nothing too fancy,* she told me. *We'll have to be terribly inconspicuous.*

Edvin's cheeks were splotchy pink. "Cassia's . . . friend?"

Maret set a light palm on my shoulder. "The very same." Then she enveloped my hand in hers and pulled me to the edge of the room. "Look how big. We'll push the sofa to the side and there will be plenty of space for the silks' rig, yes?"

When Maret smiled, she looked more like Cassia. They have the same coloration—the blond hair, the bright eyes—but their faces are nothing alike. Cassia had round cheeks, an upturned nose, a pouty smile. Maret's face is adult and angular and sophisticated. Cassia was more beautiful, but I couldn't say why. Sometimes, I think I must be remembering wrong because she can't possibly have been as beautiful as she is in my head. But the thought that I would misremember any details about Cassia is too unpleasant to bear.

When I didn't respond, Maret tapped my cheek with two fingers. "Look lively. We don't have much longer to wait."

~~~

But three months have passed. It feels like all we do is wait.

Every morning, I go to the silks. Edvin set up the rig in our living room on our second day here. Four wooden beams form a pyramid just short of the ceiling. A pair of long red fabrics hangs from the vertex of the beams. Edvin even managed to track down a book that explains all the different elements I could ever want to learn. I'm short and light and have climbed a lifetime's worth of trees, so I thought I would find some natural-born talent in myself.

But the silks hurt when I began to practice. Then again, all of me hurt, and at least this was a hurt I could control. And while my insides stayed numb and my head stayed foggy, the pain of over-stretched forearms and tightly wound feet ebbed. I acclimated.

I got better.

Maret is a royal through and through; she wants to be out in the city, being admired and discussing politics with people who matter. But her supply of Kostrovian allies is thinner than she led me to believe. Sometimes she dons an inconspicuous olive cloak and ventures out with Edvin—who I think is a scholar at the university, and maybe an old lover—but most days, she paces the apartment, flipping through copies of political treatises and news clippings about the Flood. If anything she reads is too insulting to the crown, she'll mutter that Nikolai is a disgrace to the family and hole herself up in her bedroom for the rest of the day.

By the time Maret manages to pull herself out of her own head around dinnertime, I've usually worked myself so far past my physical limit that I'm lying on the floor with the silks dangling above me. If I haven't, she makes me show her what I practiced. She checks the book, corrects my form if my body doesn't match the illustrations.

When I speak to her in Terrazzan instead of Kostrovian, she clicks her tongue.

"You won't get away with that in the palace," she said the last time I did it.

"At this rate, I won't ever get to the palace," I said. "You're sure there's no news on the next auditions?"

"None of the flyers have left," she said. And then, "But if no one leaves by the next storm, I might have to arrange for one of them to take a nasty fall into one of the canals."

"That's a joke, right?"

She let out a loud breath through her nose.

Three months of practice. Three months of Kostrov. How many more months do I have? How many more months does anyone have?

The thought strikes me while I'm hanging upside down in the silks on a day when Maret's gone to see Edvin. I prefer these days. Maret is, if not motherly, then like my aunt, making sure I find something to eat every day and letting me ask questions about Cassia that I didn't get to ask when she was alive. But auntly or not, I don't like it when Maret paces around me. It's like being trapped in an apartment with an increasingly bored lynx.

When Maret throws the door open, though, she's as giddy as she was on our first day in Kostrov. I'm so startled by the change in her that I almost lose my grip on the silks.

"It's time." Maret kicks the door shut with her heel and flings her cap across the room. "The flyers have an opening."

I unwind myself. "Now?"

"Edvin just brought me the rumor. One of the flyer girls dropped out."

I run my hands down the silks. "Did you push her into a canal?"

"For seas' sake, Ella. No, I didn't push her into a canal."

"Oh," I say. "Great news."

"Are you ready for the palace?" Maret says.

"I'm ready," I say.

Maret gives me a smile that shows each of her shining teeth. "Nikolai," she says, "will never expect you."

3

NATASHA

Pippa's departure is the worst-kept secret of the crane season festival. On the morning of the festival, I summon a gondola to ferry the silks to our stage in the Wharf District. Three different times, strangers stop me—leaning over bridges as I glide through the water—to ask after Pippa.

I've been a Royal Flyer since I was nine, but I'll never get used to the way people act like they know us personally. They've read our names; heard rumors from flying instructors who trained us as little girls; laughed over sticky tavern tables about which of us is prettiest. So on the third of these interruptions, when a barrel-chested man stops setting up his festival booth to ask if Pippa's truly pregnant, and if the father is that redheaded palace guard, I growl.

"Shove off!" my gondolier says. He slaps the flat of his paddle against the water, spraying murk. The gondolier gives me an apologetic smile. He paddles once, twice. "But is Gregor Lepik really the father?"

The other flyers arrive as a team of hired men finish setting up the rigs and silks along the waterfront. Five jewel-toned fabrics swing from wooden beams.

I rub my cold hands against my legs. It doesn't feel right to do this without Pippa. But then, nothing has felt right since I overheard Adelaida talking to Gospodin. The other Royal Flyers cluster around her at the stage. I've been trying unsuccessfully to catch Adelaida alone for the past two days. I'm convinced she's avoiding me.

Adelaida surveys each of us in turn. "It's noon now. Be back by two for warm-up."

Ness, who joined the flyers just a few months ago, claps her hands. Her round cheeks are wind-blushed. "All right then, girls. Into the festival?"

I hang back, watching Adelaida as she stalks to the edge of the stage, snapping at the violinists. They share a weary look.

"Natasha?"

The flyers—Ness, Sofie, Katla, and Gretta—wait at the far end of the stage.

"Are you coming with us?" Ness says. She rocks forward on her slippered toes.

Sofie tilts her head. Her mouth is a stubborn line. "Yeah, Natasha," she says. "Come on. We can share a baked apple."

If Adelaida has been avoiding me, I've been avoiding Sofie just as methodically. She wants me to tell the rest of the flyers what we overheard. But I can't; not yet. I know how they react when they're nervous. Ness loses the rhythm. Katla throws her hands in the air and sometimes quits for the day. If they realize we've lost our spots on the royal fleet, our performance will fall to bits.

Besides. I'm still holding out hope that I misunderstood Adelaida and Gospodin.

It's not as though I've seen the roster for the royal fleet, but the flyers have always been entwined with the royals—why should that change now? It would be like leaving all the guards off the ship. Guards protect the royals' safety, but we protect their culture. Their history.

"Oh, let's just leave her," Sofie says. "She probably wants to practice anyway. We should look for Pippa." Sofie turns to go, pulling Ness in her wake. Gretta—at fourteen, our youngest and most sullen flyer—hesitates, frowns, then follows them.

Katla hangs back. She crosses her arms.

"I'm waiting to talk to Adelaida," I tell her.

Katla doesn't budge.

"You can go," I say.

Her face is impassive.

I shoot one last look at Adelaida—still berating the violinists and acting very much too busy for me—and sigh. Then I trudge to Katla, matching her pace as she heads down the street and into the heart of the festival.

"You have bags under your eyes." She nimbly sidesteps a puddle. "Your face is all purple and splotchy."

I scowl. "Your face is all purple and splotchy."

"Why aren't you sleeping?"

"Who says I'm not sleeping?"

"Tasha. Come on."

We stop at a jagged point of street. I think it used to be connected to something, maybe a pier, but it's been bitten by storms. Now the stone crumbles straight into the ocean.

I avoid Katla's gaze, staring pointedly over her braided crown of hair to watch the festival unfolding. The smells of peat smoke and caramelizing mushrooms and spicy wine warm the wind. The crane season festival was my favorite celebration as a little girl. It's a spooky affair, held on the equinox to celebrate the last days before the snow comes.

The other three flyers wait in front of a pushcart with a festive orange awning. They pay while the peddler exclaims at their costumes, handing them rye toasts dripping with jam.

Sofie catches my eye from a distance. She holds up her toast in a gesture of cheers, but her mouth doesn't so much as twitch toward a smile.

"What's going on with you two?" Katla says. "Is she mad about Pippa?"

"No," I say. "I mean, maybe."

"But you didn't know."

"No, I would've warned you. And Sofie." I finally meet Katla's gaze.

Her mouth bows. This expression is Katla's default. Suspicious, downturned lips. Her heavy brows knitted. We're both fair-skinned, Katla and I, but her hair is dark and thick. Mine is thin and dry from too many aggressive buns. "You're all mixed up because of the weather today," she says.

I glance at the sky. "You know, given the new standard for bad weather, I think I'm okay with cloudy."

"It's worse today," Katla says.

A shard of sunlight manages to clip through the haze of clouds. "I'll take your word for it. Hey, is your family coming today?"

"I hope so." She turns and squints in the direction of the boglands. "I haven't been able to ask, though, with the schedule Adelaida's had us on. She's got to let up soon."

I follow Katla's gaze. Through the fog, I spot a few silhouettes, a few glimmers of red—the sides of distant barns and cottages.

Families like Katla's, who have lived in the boglands for as long as anyone can remember, are called Brightwallers. When the Sacred Breath crusaders from Grunholt landed on our shores three hundred years ago, they were—as the story goes—struck by the garish, brightly painted buildings. That vivid shade of red, the kind tailor-made for a snow-nestled barn—that's Brightwall red. It was good sense to paint the buildings red. The paint comes from the copper mines on the other side of the boglands, and it helps weatherproof wood. It also makes buildings easier to see through our famously heavy fog. But when the Grunholters got here, they acted like all those red walls were childish, somehow—a tasteless design decision from a people who didn't know how to paint a house white.

The name stuck. Katla calls herself a Brightwaller, but I hear it thrown around like an insult just as often. Most of the Brightwallers live outside of New Sundstad, in red-painted cottages in and beyond the boglands. Technically, it's not illegal *not* to be part of the Sacred Breath, but it *is* illegal to be involved in any other religion. And since some Brightwallers still worship old spirits and sing hymns in ancient languages, they all get treated with suspicion.

I'm startled out of my thoughts when a hand, small and cold, snatches my wrist.

"Got you."

My breath catches in my throat. Then I laugh.

I turn to see a waifish girl, too young for even the littlest troupes of flyers. She's dressed in a big wool coat. She jangles a pouch of coins in front of my stomach.

"Why, you're not a bog spirit," I say.

She grins. "Pay up, 'less you saw me coming."

"I did not," I say. "You're very sneaky." I pat the sides of my costume for pockets that aren't there. I turn to Katla. "Did you bring coins?"

She's already handing one to the girl. "It's like you didn't even remember which festival this was."

During the crane season festival, children slink around trying to frighten wealthy-looking Kostrovians. They're meant to keep you on your toes, stop you from getting snatched by something really awful, like a bog spirit. Of course, most Kostrovians don't really believe in bog spirits and their folkloric ilk. But it makes the children happy, and it makes me happy, and besides, all the spirit nonsense is just an excuse to give a hungry child a coin.

The girl vanishes in a current of bodies. The festivalgoers are winding away from the water.

"It's not time for Nikolai's speech, is it?" Katla cranes her neck.

"Let's watch."

The more I turn Gospodin's words over in my head, the more I snag on what he said about Nikolai. I wish I could remember it exactly. Something about Nikolai and whether or not he knew about the flyers being kicked off the fleet.

I set off at a quick pace.

The crowd flocks to a pair of podiums surrounded on either side by dozens of flags and twice as many guards.

"A few people heckle Gospodin and he's suddenly tripping over guards," Katla says.

"*A few* might be an understatement." I stand on my toes. "There are a lot of guards, though."

At the seal season festival, a group of two dozen Brightwallers took advantage of the distraction and looted one of the grain stores full of fleet provisions. They left a message in Maapinnen, an old language Katla had to translate for me—*sing as the sea*. That's become the rallying cry of the people, particularly Brightwallers, who don't think they'll be allowed on the fleet. The people trying to sabotage it. I'm not sure what the phrase means, but I guess the attack was enough to scare Nikolai and Gospodin. Today, the bloated force of guards scans the crowd with suspicion.

When Storm Ten hit, people demanded answers from Nikolai and Gospodin. Rumors spread that the royals were building a ship, and only a dozen of the city's most important citizens would be allowed on board. We teetered perilously close to an uprising.

Then Gospodin and Nikolai told the city they would construct the biggest, most durable fleet money could buy. They'd fill the ships with food and drinking water to last the year of the Flood. And when the waters receded, whoever accompanied the royal fleet would have a hand in building the New World. Gospodin made it seem like any good citizens, any devout followers of the Sacred Breath, could be on the fleet. Anyone could dream of joining it. And others could stock their own ships. Assuming, of course, they had enough left over after the tithes to add anything to their personal stockpiles.

Now Kostrovians follow the Sacred Breath more diligently than ever. But there are still only three completed ships in the fleet, despite promises that more are being made. The country is pinched by rationing, especially after the locusts that followed Storm Seven and the devastating heat following Storm Six. It's worse for families like Katla's. She comes from a big family with plenty of mouths and not enough food. But, every month, a collector shows up to ask for rations: wood, coin, peat, water, flour. Everything the royal fleet needs. "A tithe for the common good," Gospodin calls it, even though the good isn't half as common as anyone might wish.

But still, everyone hopes. This was a lesson I learned quickly when the storms started coming. You think everyone will panic, but they don't. They put their heads down, find new routines, and hope. It's too hard to conceive that your life might be distilled down to a statistic: just one more dead body.

I thought I was too smart or too cynical to fall for it. But I hoped right along with them, thinking I'd be part of the royal fleet, thinking there was no way the flyers wouldn't survive. I'm still falling for it, I realize. I'm still hoping.

The noise of the crowd around me fades. Nikolai and Gospodin climb the stage, Nikolai in black-and-gold regalia, Gospodin in white. If Gospodin is a pearly cloud, fair-haired and beaming, Nikolai is hidden in his shadow—his frown is as dark as his hair.

"He looks like he's getting teeth pulled," Katla says. "Not that I blame him. I'd probably look that way too if I spent all my time with Gospodin."

"Katla!" I say. When I see her sly smile, I realize she's just trying to provoke me. I bump my shoulder against hers. "Doesn't Nikolai *always* look like he's getting teeth pulled?"

"I've never understood why people think that whole brooding thing is attractive," Katla says.

I glance at Nikolai again. The dark lashes; the geometric angles of his cheeks and jaw; the almost bored stillness to his face that disguises whatever he's actually thinking. I can hear more than a few people whispering about him, our young and mysterious king. Katla might not get the *brooding thing,* but she might be the only one.

But it's more than that. For me—for plenty of Kostrovians—Nikolai is a symbol of home. I've watched him grow up while I've been busy doing the same. He's seventeen, same as me, and I first saw him up close when we were both nine. He was thin and brooding even then. As other royals die, fight, commit treason, abandon Kostrov, Nikolai has been a constant. What I feel when I think of Nikolai—this sense of place and home—is what I imagine the most devoted followers of the Sacred Breath feel when they think of Gospodin.

Gospodin leans against his podium and smiles broadly. The crowd angles forward to hear.

"Happy crane season," he says.

The crowd erupts. Katla jabs my side with her elbow. She gives me a look that says *I don't approve of their unbridled love for this man, and I want to make sure you aren't caught in the enthusiasm.*

I shrug. I might not be a devout follower of the Sacred Breath, but I like Gospodin well enough. Unlike Nikolai's stodgy councilors, Gospodin laughs warmly and often. While most men of his influence hide behind stone walls, Gospodin spends his time with the people, offering food and sermons.

I rise on my toes to get a better look. Nikolai's eyes flit across the crowd, searching, and finally settle on me. My heart thumps. The weight of his gaze —like I'm an anchor in the chaos—settles on my shoulders. Nikolai allows himself the smallest smile—a twitch at the corner of his lips.

"To begin," Gospodin says, "I want to share some good news. As you may have seen, the first three ships in the fleet are completed, and construction is well underway for the fourth. We've also secured a trade with Grunholt. Our peat for their lumber. Soon, we'll have ten new ships to add to the royal fleet."

An excited whisper ripples through the crowd.

"We are," Gospodin says, "as always, servants of the people, and servants of the ocean. We will continue to build and acquire ships until every deserving Kostrovian has a place. And now, a moment of history."

Gospodin launches into a winding story about Antinous Kos, the father of the Sacred Breath, and his first year after the Flood, tenderly nurturing the wheat seedlings he brought from the old world. I think it's supposed to be an allegory for patience. It's not a virtue I possess, so I don't listen too closely.

I scan the other figures near Nikolai and Gospodin at the podiums. When Nikolai announced his engagement to Princess Colette just before Storm Ten, I started seeing her violet-clad officials flanking Nikolai's councilors. I don't see any today.

I lean toward Katla. "Where are the Illasetish?"

Her eyebrows draw together.

When Nikolai finally begins to speak, I strain to hear. His voice is quieter than Gospodin's. Steady, but quiet.

"After much discussion with my councilors," he says, "I have called off my engagement to Colette, princess of Illaset."

The crowd gasps. It's all very dramatic. Gospodin's lips twitch in a pleased little smile.

Nikolai shifts his weight. "We have decided the spots on the royal fleet would be better used to protect deserving Kostrovians, not the Illasetish."

My heart leaps into my throat. When was this decided? What does it mean for the flyers?

"*Captain's Log* teaches us that the earth will be unrecognizable after the Flood." Nikolai glances at Gospodin. "Illaset has not prepared as well as Kostrov for the coming seasons. With their farmland disappearing, they have nothing to give us. If Illaset can't offer weapons, or food, or ships, the union isn't a favorable one. We wish the best of luck to our Illasetish friends in the face of the coming storms." He takes a deep breath. "As such, Mariner Gospodin and I have decided that instead of Princess Colette, a Kostrovian girl will be the next queen."

The crowd starts to buzz, and Gospodin looks more pleased than ever.

Gospodin offers us a winning smile. "Nikolai will make his decision in three months' time, on his eighteenth birthday, after the bear season festival. Think of your own sister, your own daughter, wearing the queen's crown. She'll be the mother of the New World. She could be among us today."

Katla scoffs loudly. A few festivalgoers shoot her dirty looks. To me, she says, "They're just trying to distract us from the storms."

"I don't know," I say. "It sounds like something out of *Tamm's Fables*. Like 'The Girl Who Married the Whale King'?"

"Yes, well, Nikolai is a human and not a whale, and I don't imagine he's going to marry a girl in a dress sewn by sand eels."

Gospodin caps off the occasion with a triumphant declaration that we Kostrovians are terrifically brave, and thanks to our enduring belief in the Sacred Breath, we are all quite safe indeed. When the crowd finally starts to disperse, it's time to warm up for our performance.

"He's so smug," Katla says.

"Seas, Katla, be quiet. He's just doing his job."

She shrugs.

"Let's get to the stage," I say. "Before Adelaida starts yelling for us."

I turn too fast. My arm jostles a shoulder. I spot the girl I've hit for just a moment. The moment lasts long enough for me to meet her eyes, to see the high bridges of her cheekbones, her olive-toned skin, and the dark curls spilling out of her hood.

She tilts her head at me, as if we know each other, but—I think I would recognize her, if I'd seen her before. I open my mouth.

Then I hear a murmuring. It's not the girl. She looks up too, her chin high, eyes searching.

Katla grabs my wrist. "Hear that? We have to go."

The murmurs are coalescing into words. All at once, I make it out: *Sing as the sea.*

A clump of mud—or a peat brick, maybe—whizzes through the air. It comes from somewhere so nearby that I duck, cover my head with my arms.

More mud. Raining around us. All of it directed toward the podiums, toward—

Nikolai and Gospodin are covered in it. Huge brown splotches stain Gospodin's perfect white uniform. The guards swarm in front of them, holding up their hands, but the mud-throwers stop as quickly as they started.

Katla pulls my wrist hard. "Come *on.*"

Between the shoulders of two guards, Gospodin's eyes find me. My breath catches. His gaze narrows. Head tilts to the side.

I try to shake my head, try to look bewildered. I didn't throw any mud.

Katla finally manages to tug me away. I remember the girl with the cloak, but she's already gone. We reach the edge of the chaotic crowd, squeezing through to where the street widens out again.

Katla curses under her breath.

Did Gospodin think I had something to do with that? I've lived in the palace half my life. I might not be diligent about attending Sacred Breath services, but I'm loyal to the crown. I press a hand to my cheek and find it mud-splattered.

"What was that about?" I say.

"More of the peat harvesters got arrested last week for skimping on their tithes," Katla says, her voice low. "I guess they're trying to make a statement."

"Well, maybe if everyone stopped sabotaging Gospodin and Nikolai, the tithes would ease up. The fleet's supposed to have room for all of us."

Katla lets out a disbelieving laugh. "Even with ten ships from Grunholt, you expect half a million Kostrovians to fit on fourteen ships?"

I look down. "No."

"Come on," she says. "Adelaida really will be yelling for us now."

I feel foolish. "Right behind you."

4

ELLA

I decide I like the tall red-haired flyer, even though she jostles me in the crowd. Her resting face is a scowl, which I heartily approve of. But when Nikolai announces his marriage scheme, her attention sharpens. Maybe I shouldn't like her after all.

Then people start throwing mud. It suits Nikolai, being covered in mud. He should wear it always.

I turn and squeeze back through the throng as fast as I can. I'm planning enough illegal activities. I'm not about to get arrested for a crime I didn't commit.

It's crowded in Kostrov. Too crowded. We went to plenty of festivals when I was a child, but none made me feel so claustrophobic. Not just because there are so many people. It's because of the way Nikolai and Gospodin talk. They make me feel slimy. Lied to.

Did I ever hear a speech like that at a Terrazzan festival? I don't think so. I can't remember ever seeing the Terrazzan Righteous Mariner in person, but then again, I'm not sure I could even pick him out of a crowd.

My family went to Sacred Breath services once in a while, but our farm was a two-hour walk from town. My parents were stoic, dutiful types. They planted and hoed and baked and cleaned, and I never heard them complain. But when it came to Sacred Breath services, they always had an excuse not to go. I thought it was because they didn't like being inside, didn't like staying still, didn't like trying to corral my uncorralable brothers.

It didn't occur to me that *I* might be the reason they weren't going until I was fourteen. I found them murmuring over mugs of spiced cider in the kitchen, their heads bent, hair mingling. When they noticed me, my mother looked angry and my father looked sad.

"What?" I said.

Neither of my parents was much for wasting time.

"Brigida Barbosa," my mother said. "The girl who sells flowers on the corner of Vine and Main."

I tensed.

"Apparently," my father said, "she was caught with a girl traveling through from Cordova. They were both branded as sirens."

My stomach went tight. "Branded?"

"As a warning," my mother said. Her cheeks were flushed. I could see, then, that she was gripping the edge of the counter, and even that wasn't enough to keep the tremble out of her shoulders. "To *men*."

My father covered her hand with his. They both looked at me for a long moment. None of us said anything. Not about sirens. Not about Brigida Barbosa, who always gave me a daffodil, no charge, when we walked down Vine Street. Not about the way I tucked the bloom in my hair and kept it there until it wilted. We all just looked at each other.

We never went to another Sacred Breath service.

Maret catches me as I reach the fringe of the crowd and pulls me to an alley between a cobbler and a postal office. There's a poster advertising their need for *fit young men for postal runner job—no insolence. Kostrovians only.*

"What are you doing?" Maret's cheeks are flushed pink.

"Well," I say, "currently, I'm wondering why delivering mail is too difficult a task with which to trust my countrymen."

"What? You know what, never mind. I meant at the speech."

"I wanted to watch."

"That's not what I'm talking about," Maret says. "I saw you slinking toward the Royal Flyers. You nearly knocked one down."

"I would never slink."

I did slink toward the flyers, of course. I've spent enough time training to be one of them that I was curious. Besides. I liked the scowl.

Maret lets out an exasperated breath. She pats her head and tucks a loose curl back under her hat. I wonder if being unobtrusive is hard for her. She's just so glamorous. Cassia once told me that before Maret's exile, she had a closet of dresses in every color I could imagine. When I said I could imagine earwax yellow, Cassia assured me Maret had such a gown, with snot-green satin heels to match.

I, on the other hand, am dressed in a formless black cloak disguising a formless black dress, and I wouldn't have it any other way. The cloak covers the siren tattoo on my wrist, and I can't ask for more than that.

"The mud," I say. "Did that ever happen to you?"

"Of course not," Maret says. "The people loved my father. They loved me. Though I can't say I'm surprised this is what people think of the crown now that Nikolai's in charge." She makes a sour face. "And all that about the fleet. Big enough for every deserving Kostrovian? I don't believe it. Nikolai and Gospodin have no idea what they're doing." She glances around the alley, like she might've spoken too loudly, but it's just us and the smell of dead fish.

Maret hates Nikolai and Gospodin both. Nikolai was the one who exiled her, but he wouldn't have done it without Gospodin's say-so. She's always been clear that it's Nikolai, not Gospodin, we're focusing our attention on. After Nikolai, Maret is next in line for the throne. She figures she can take care of Gospodin once she's in the palace. And, if I'm being perfectly honest, I just can't muster the same hatred toward Gospodin that I feel for Nikolai. Nikolai was the one Cassia hated. The one she ranted to me about. To her, Gospodin was just—an inconvenience. A thorn. Only dangerous as long as he was working with Nikolai.

"It's good news," Maret says, "Nikolai calling off his engage-ment. Princess Colette wandering in and popping out an heir too quickly could've ruined our plan."

I nod. Personally, I'm wondering how likely it is that Nikolai would ever marry a common-born Kostrovian girl. If he's any-thing like his aunt Maret, I'll put the odds at roughly never. If he's like Cassia—Cassia, who didn't see *poor* and *Terrazzan* and *orphan*, Cassia, who just saw me—

I shake the thought away, because Nikolai is nothing like Cassia.

"How was your first glimpse of him?" Maret asks.

I roll answers around in my head, but I can't make myself say any of them, because I don't know quite how to put to words the feeling that lives in my stomach. It's so far beyond hatred that I can't describe it in Kostrovian. The almost-right word for it exists in Terrazzan.

"I would like," I say finally, "to see him dead."

Maret smiles approvingly. "That's the spirit, dear. Shall we go watch the Royal Flyers?"

I nod, but my head is already far from this place. It's in a dark room with a knife in my hand, the whisper I've held in the back of my throat for months, finally voiced aloud. It's my breath against his ear—*This is what you get for killing your sister.*

5

NATASHA

When Katla and I get to the stage, Adelaida is coaching Ness through a tricky bit of choreography, ignoring the growing crowd.

I grab Adelaida's sleeve as Ness spins on the silk above us. "I need to talk to you."

Adelaida's whole face purses, lips and nose and eyebrows. "You have mud on your face. Ness, if you don't lock your knees, you will fall and break your neck and have only yourself to blame."

"I'm doing it!" Ness says.

Soft laughter burbles from the crowd behind us. I press my index fingers to my temples. "Adelaida, please."

"Not now."

"What Nikolai said about the spots on the royal fleet—"

Adelaida holds up her hand to silence me. "After the festival."

"You promise we can talk?"

"After," she says firmly. "Now warm up."

The ground in front of the stage is clogged with bodies thin as cheatgrass. Faces—smiling. Hands—mud-fingernailed, holding loose sheathed umbrellas and bags of festival splurges, warm bread with soft edges.

Behind them, under an awning of blue fabric, are the faces I know. Guards, councilors, Gospodin, Nikolai. None of them smile; none hold umbrellas or bags.

Nikolai catches me looking at him. He tilts his head sideways in silent greeting. Gospodin glances over at the young king, and then to me, and when his eyes narrow, I feel like I've been strapped to a scholar's dissection table. Does he think I threw that mud? Does he know I overheard his conversation with Adelaida?

"Flyers," Adelaida says. "In position."

The orchestra begins to play. I wrap my silks around my ankle. I stretch my hands up, then I'm climbing, rising into the rhythm of a performance I know forward and back. Before I was a flyer, the crane season performance, *Bog Song,* scared and enthralled me in equal measure. The music is full of creaky violins and jangling bells. As the principal flyer, I play the role of a little girl who gets lost in the bog on a cold crane season night. My role is the most difficult and the most important, and I can't afford a single mistake. I keep glancing out at the audience, my eyes seeking Adelaida, Gospodin, Nikolai.

If the flyers are going on the royal fleet, this performance matters.

If the flyers are getting left on Kostrov to sink, it means nothing.

With a deep, slow breath, I twist into a hip key, pressing my nose to my knees and holding myself suspended in the air while the other girls climb at my sides.

Katla is climbing perfectly. Sofie is a half-beat behind, but I can't scold her the way I would in practice. Gretta and Ness have managed to find something of a rhythm, thank the seas.

The stage feels uneven with only two bases instead of three. Pippa and Katla were my two wings as long as I've been principal. Now Sofie flies in Pippa's place.

I wonder if Pippa is out there. I wonder if Sofie found her before the flight. I wonder—

The music swells, and I nearly miss the cue. I spin out of my hip key just in time. *Focus, Natasha.*

Twist, flip upside down, straddle, flip back up. Separate the silks and fan them apart. Hold the position. Not much longer before we're through. One and two and three and—

The bird appears out of nowhere.

One minute, my gaze is flitting between the crowd and my hands. The next minute, my entire field of vision is consumed by a feathered body, eight feet long from wingtip to wingtip. The bird blinks its amber eyes, startled, and then its feathers brush my arm.

My hands shudder around the silk, and then they release. I release. The silk, suddenly free of all tension, bounces like a spring.

My world spins. The audience, then the rig, then the sky above me. My back hits the stage.

Above me, the crane—I see now that it's a crane, long-beaked and black-winged—warbles as it flies for the horizon.

The music screeches.

The crowd is silent. I gasp and I sit up so fast, my head pounds. Above me, Gretta and Katla are still moving through their elements. Ness stares at me. Sofie slides down her silk recklessly fast.

Keep going, I want to say, but I can't find the breath to do it.

Sofie hits the ground and kneels beside me.

Then the crowd stops being so silent.

It begins with a whisper. A concerned murmur here, there. Then a giggle, a laugh, a guffaw. Scattered applause; scattered jeers. Adelaida, from the edge of the stage, hisses, her voice so thin and angry that I can't understand what she's saying.

Sofie presses her hand to my shoulder. "Tasha, are you okay?"

I tell myself not to look at the crowd but I don't listen. Some people stare openly. Most of those underneath the blue awning are averting their eyes, as though they can't stand to be part of my humiliation.

Sofie shakes me. "Tasha. Natasha."

This must be what it feels like to drown.

I don't look at Sofie. "Get back on your silk."

She hesitates.

I can still feel the way the silk sprang out of my hands like a living thing. I can still see the bird's startled eyes.

"Get back on your silk," I tell Sofie again. When I try to haul myself up, my left wrist sears with the burden of my weight.

But I have to fly. *I have to.*

Tears sting my eyes as I climb, clutching the silk with my feet to relieve the burden on my wrist.

Another bird flies overhead, narrowly missing the top of the rig. Then three more; five more; a flock so large, I can't count all the sets of wings.

Cranes. Heart-faced barn owls. Jewel-feathered bee-eaters, and a dozen other species whose names I don't know. As they pass overhead, they shadow the city like dusk has fallen.

All the eyes that clung to me find the birds instead. And then, as the birds head for the city's edge, all those eyes find the sea. A pillow of cloud, as dark and smooth as a seal in water, balloons from the horizon.

Storm Five, *Captain's Log* says, begins with the Exodus of the Birds.

The word *storm* starts low, in mutters from the crowd, and begins to pulse around us.

Adelaida crosses the stage in swift steps. "Off the silks. All of you, now."

I drop the five feet straight to the floor, my wrist burning as the impact shakes through me. Katla catches me before I can fall to my knees.

"Come on." Katla loops her hand around my waist.

The crowd bubbles with unfurling umbrellas. The musicians rush to get their instruments in cases before the rain starts. I glance back to the blue awning, expecting to see Gospodin shouting consoling words at the masses, but the awning is already being packed away.

"Back to the palace." Adelaida's eyes sweep across us. "Leave the silks. Go."

Sofie grabs our cloaks from the edge of the stage. I put mine on as we begin to run, holding the hood over my head with my right hand as we go. Gretta and Ness lead. Katla and Sofie stay close at my sides.

We keep to the seawall, crossing slanting cobbled bridges and watching the angry ocean, the seething sky, still blotted by the shadows of birds. It's not the safest path, but it's the least likely to be congested with fleeing crowds. The streets have transformed in a matter of minutes. Carts lie abandoned in the streets.

"Are you okay?" Katla asks.

"We'll see," I say. I press my wrist to my stomach.

A wave smashes over the seawall.

It thunders against the stone and shoves through the gaps in the railing. The water slaps me to the side so hard, I nearly fall. Ness tumbles into a puddle. Sofie scoops her up. We keep running.

Then the sky unhinges, like a canal lock opening above us. In the distance, a bird shrieks.

Within moments, I'm drenched. When the hem of my cloak snags on the rickety rail of a bridge, I let go of the fabric. The wind carries my cloak into the ocean.

We run until the Gray Palace cuts a silhouette through the rain. The pointy-topped windows gleam like a row of bared teeth. Water drips from the snouts and antlers of a bronze menagerie, broodily watching from tower turrets.

By the time I fling myself at the palace wall, my slippers are disintegrating off my feet.

A guard stands at the entrance to the flyer door. He throws the door open and shouts something, but the rain washes the words past me. My head pounds.

The sky erupts with a claw-slash of light. Thunder booms.

"Tasha." Katla grabs my good wrist. "Come on."

How many more months?

"Natasha." Katla tugs at my arm. "Get inside."

How many more days?

6

ELLA

My family died in Storm Ten. Storms Nine and Eight and Seven, I had Cassia. Storm Six was my first in Kostrov, and I spent the whole of it hidden in Maret's apartment.

This is the first storm I've felt on city streets. It's the first time I have felt the terror of being trampled, the smell of sewage rising out of the canals. If I didn't have a job to do, I would leave New Sundstad tomorrow. No one ought to die in a city like this.

When Storm Ten struck, I was too busy grieving to realize what it meant. That the Flood was coming. After my family died, I got a job waiting tables at an inn near where my family's farm had been. That was where I met Cassia and Maret. They were traveling through town—running away from Nikolai's men, I later learned—and I was wiping their table down. Cassia looked up at me over the top of a pint of cider. She smiled, so sharp, so clever, like she already knew everything there was to know about me. I lingered by their table because they were speaking Kostrovian, which reminded me of my father, who taught himself—and, in turn, me—languages from places he'd never been and would never see, just because he thought it was the sort of thing people ought to do. So I listened to their Kostrovian. And Cassia saw me listening. She said, "You understand everything we're saying, don't you?" I nodded, and she said,

"Well, we need a translator. So sit down and tell us your name." By the time I sat, I was already hopeless. That's how I loved her: quick as a snake bite and twice as painful.

I found out she was a Kostrovian princess the next morning. They'd spent the night at the inn, where I'd started spending all my nights—I had nowhere else to go. I caught them arguing, in hushed Kostrovian, and I put the pieces together. Maret thought it was ridiculous to let a stranger join them while they were running from Nikolai's men. Cassia thought I had a funny smile. *Funny?* Good funny or bad funny? I was busy wondering if I'd mistranslated when they spotted me. I asked them point-blank if they were royals. Cassia, in answer, opened her wool coat and showed me a brooch pinned to the inside flap—an insect, studded with diamonds and pearls the size of hazelnuts.

"It's the ladybug," Cassia said. When I just blinked at her—*the ladybug?*—she said, as though it should've been obvious, "The symbol of Kostrovian royalty?"

So I went with them. Of course I went with them. They were royals! They were a family. And they wanted me around.

Storm Nine came a few days later. The rain was just as bad as Storm Ten, threatening to flood fields and burst dams. But afterward, the trees. Blooming and blooming and blooming. And that was how Cassia made me feel. Like I was growing again after the grief had shrunk me small.

Wandering through those blooming trees, tacking sideways from one Terrazzan town to the next, Cassia slipped a bright orange poppy behind my ear. Maret held a hat to her head as she craned her neck, looking skyward.

"It really was Storm Nine, wasn't it?" Maret said.

"Obviously," Cassia said.

I'd heard rumors, but there were always rumors. Whenever a bad bit of rain hit, everyone called it the start of another Harbinger Year. But my parents never believed in that sort of thing. Neveses didn't panic.

"You know the first book of *Captain's Log*, don't you, Ella?" Cassia asked me in that lush copse of trees.

I hesitated. "Remind me which part you're talking about?"

To Cassia, Maret said, "They're not as devout in Terrazza. You know that."

My face warmed. I still wasn't sure what Cassia and Maret believed—whether my uneven devotion was a bad thing.

Cassia waved her away. "I'm talking about the part where Kos insists that a Flood only comes once every two thousand years. He never gives any reason *why* a Flood can only come that often. He just says 'It is known.' But the Sacred Breath doesn't want anyone to poke holes in their book, so they're trying to convince everyone that this can't be the start of the Harbinger Year. You know, if I were queen, I'd send all those stodgy literalists to the bottom of the sea. Maybe Kos made a mistake. Is that so bad?"

"Stodgy literalists are the lifeblood of Kostrov," Maret said. "Stodgy literalists and a petulant child king."

"For now," Cassia said. She said it emphatically, which was the way she said most things. I couldn't have disagreed with her if I wanted to.

Over the next few months, I let her build a future for me. We'd go back to Kostrov. Reclaim her throne from her brother. Tell the country the truth—the Flood was coming, and we'd be ready. We'd do all the things countries around the world were slow to do: Stockpile food and water, ready ships. And then, when Storm One came, it wouldn't be the end of the world. Cassia and I would be on the same ship, rising above the waves. Surviving. Discovering the New World. Things I don't care about anymore.

Nikolai didn't just take Cassia away from me. He took my whole future.

When we get to the apartment, Maret fumbles with the key. She shakes her head and laughs. Water has sneaked a few of her curls out of their confines and plastered them to her face. Her cheeks are bright. Her lashes are long and rain-dazzled.

"You must think I'm acting the fool."

I shrug.

She finally manages to get the key in correctly. "It's just—aren't you excited?" She steps inside and takes off her hat. "We don't have much longer to wait."

While most everyone else counts the storms to the end of the world, Maret counts to the beginning. She wants to seize the crown as close as she can to Storm One. Too late, and the royal fleet will sail away without her. Too early, and someone else may come along to topple her reign. But if Nikolai dies at just the right moment, and Maret, as the only obvious heir left, arrives to take the crown and calm the country, it will all be hers. She will control the fleet. She will control who lives, who dies, who drowns, who breathes.

Most people are worried about ever seeing the New World. Maret wants to own it.

"Ella?" Maret says. "Come inside."

The water is fiercely cold on my skin. It's not unlike the way the silks hurt when I began practicing—painful enough to remind me I'm still alive.

If I closed my eyes and nose and ears and all I knew was the feeling of raindrops bursting on my skin, I could be in Terrazza again. I could be with my family. I could be with Cassia.

Maret snaps her fingers. "Out of the rain, now, before it eats you up."

I would like that very much.

7

NATASHA

I huddle with the other flyers in the hallway that connects the studio and our bedrooms. No one says why we've chosen this place, but I think we all know. There are no windows in the hall. In here, we can't see the storm.

Sofie, Ness, and Gretta play five-hundred sweep with a deck of tarot cards. Katla stretches, her legs out in front of her and her nose to the floor. My hamstrings burn just looking at her.

I'm a few feet away, having already wrapped and rewrapped my wrist in a length of bandage three times. I do it again anyway, holding the fabric tight in my teeth.

"Do you think they'll still call it crane season after the Flood?" Ness says.

"Why wouldn't they?" Gretta asks.

"Well, there won't be any cranes left," Ness says. According to *Captain's Log,* all the animals that didn't make it on board a ship in the last Flood died out, except for the sea life. When the waters receded, the birds and bears and bees were all new varieties, born from the seafloor and emerging with the land. "Oh, but maybe Mariner Gospodin can bring a crane on the fleet. As a cultural symbol."

"Can you imagine if you got thrown off the royal fleet to make room for a crane?" Gretta says.

Sofie catches my eye. I look away.

"I wonder if Pippa made it back home," she says.

"It's her own fault for getting kicked out," Gretta says. Sofie swats her with her cards.

"I'm sure she's fine," Ness says.

"No," Katla says, "your family is probably fine. Your rich friends are probably fine. Pippa is in plenty of danger."

Ness's round mouth bows. "I'm just being optimistic."

"Funny how obscene piles of money can make a person optimistic."

Ness glances around like she might find an ally among us, but no one springs to her aid. She's the only one with a merchant father and a terraced manor in Heather Hill.

In the end, she just ducks her head to her cards. Her curls hang over her face. "Mean."

"My father said the men at the university are making progress on an evaporator," Gretta says. "For the fleet. That's good news for our drinking water."

"Really?" Sofie says. "I heard some of the guards talking about it at breakfast, and they said they couldn't taste the difference between the seawater that went in and came back out."

Gretta makes a face. "Well, they better hurry. I don't want to drink grog for a year."

We're all quiet for a moment.

"You know what I wonder?" Gretta says. "Where did Adelaida go?"

Where, indeed. Adelaida's bedroom door is attached to this hallway. Yet another reason to sit here. But I haven't seen her since she waved us away from the stage. She promised me we could talk after the performance, but now I'm dreading the conversation.

She'll say I wasn't focused. She'll point out that none of the other flyers got so spooked by the birds, they fell from their silks. She wouldn't demote me, would she?

Oh, seas. What if she dismisses me from the Royal Flyers entirely?

"I bet she was just helping gather our equipment," Ness says.

"Those silks are ruined," Katla says. "Abandon hope."

Ness fans out her cards and collapses them together again. "Then maybe she was helping the musicians."

Katla snorts. "Because it's so like Adelaida to be charitable."

"Do you have to be grumpy all the time?" Ness says.

Katla nods, her hair dusting her knees. "I am contractually obligated."

Gretta taps her cards against the floor. "Sofie," she says. "It's been your turn for five minutes. Play already."

"Oh! Sorry."

Outside, someone screams. We all flinch.

Katla unfolds from her stretch and comes to sit beside me. She takes the bandage and finishes tying it. "Stop fidgeting."

I glance over at the other girls. They're immersed in their game. In a low voice, I say, "Are you okay?"

"I'll check on my family in the morning," Katla says.

"Sorry," I say, because I can't think of anything more useful.

I've visited Katla's home a dozen times in the five years we've known each other. It's small but cozy, full of peat smoke and cooking smells and the chaotic laughter of younger siblings. The house is squished into the mud at the edge of the boglands, and the last time I was there, during deer season, water was seeping through the cracks in every stone.

If there's any benefit in being alone, it's having no family to worry about.

The flyers are the closest thing I have to family. Sofie, Gretta, Ness, with whom I've trained with and laughed, and most especially Katla, who's flown by my side since we were twelve. When Katla smiles at me in her most Katla of ways—pursed lips, no teeth, hardly even a smile, really—my heart squeezes.

I know I need to tell her—all of them—what Sofie and I overheard. But I have to talk to Adelaida first. Make sure I haven't misunderstood.

Outside: thunder, wind, another scream.

That scream belongs to someone. Someone's father or son or brother. Probably someone with work-chapped hands and rain-soaked feet and, if he's lucky, a house full of peat smoke. He screams for help.

The guards won't invite him into the palace. The servants will wince and murmur, "Pity," but they won't go against orders. Not when their families could starve without a month of palace wages.

The scream is piercing.

I can only worry about so many people.

So I take my heart and I put it in an iron box.

I tell myself that the man wasn't going to survive Storm One anyway.

And unless I am selfish, neither will I.

8

ELLA

The morning after the storm, the street gleams dewy. The sky is an innocuous white, cream on its way to butter. It was a short storm this time—just long enough to last the night. When a pigeon lands on the windowsill of Maret's apartment, it tilts its head to the side and stares at me.

"Aren't you supposed to be gone by now?" I say.

It ruffles its feathers, taking offense.

I find a note from Maret on the little table in the kitchen.

With Edvin. Getting a present for you. Happy practicing!

A present? I trace the loopy letters with a finger. My own handwriting is cramped and tiny, like the letters are insecure. Maret's handwriting looks like Cassia's, and probably all other royal people ever: smart, loud, unafraid.

I set down the note and open a kitchen cabinet. A chunk of bread. A potato beginning to sprout.

When Maret and I first made our plan back in Terrazza, I assumed she had a few more friends with a few more coins. One would think the title of Disgraced and Exiled Aunt of King Nikolai would hold enough clout to get us better snacks.

I take the bread and tear a begrudging chunk with my teeth.

The pigeon stares at me through the window.

"This bread," I tell it, "tastes like despair."

The pigeon takes off. Perhaps it doesn't speak Terrazzan. I keep watch out the window, but I don't see another bird all day.

I practice on the silks, the Royal Flyers' performance my inspiration. The way they moved their arms smoothly, never betraying the spurtive effort of lifting one hand off the silks and pulling themselves higher. The elegant points to their toes. And the climbs. I understand now why they're called flyers, because while I've been practicing on an indoor rig that takes me only six feet off the ground, they soared.

And I heard my first flyer's name, whispered and giggled and muttered. Natasha Koskinen is the one who fell. The tall one with the excellent scowl. I flinched when her body hit the ground.

But when she hauled herself up again, hurt or embarrassed or exhausted—I couldn't tell from the iron set of her face—she was impossible not to watch.

Even before the fall, the audience was chattering about what an unusual performance it was, what with only five flyers. Once the storm hit, it became a performance I'm sure Kostrov will never forget.

Well, at least, not until Storm One. After that they will be mostly dead, so perhaps they'll forget then.

Maret returns at sunset with a splotchy pamphlet in her hands—the paper probably on its umpteenth round of recycling—but she carries it like a treasure.

I'm upside down with the silks yanking my legs in a straddle that could be a very effective means of torture. Maret pulls the paper tight in front of me. It makes a satisfying *pop* as it goes flat.

"Snoitidua reylf," I say.

"Oh, for goodness' sake, Ella."

"It's very taxing to read a foreign language upside down."

Maret turns the paper back to face her and clears her throat. "'Flyer auditions. Girls age fourteen to twenty. Must have prior flying experience. Recommendation from director required. Contact Adelaida Folkat for audition window.'"

I flip right-side up. The blood rushes pleasantly back to my legs. "I don't have a recommendation from a director."

"Edvin has a cousin," Maret says. "He asked her for a favor. Fortunately, she's not all that fond of Adelaida, and so they won't have occasion to talk. I remember Adelaida, you know. From when she was the principal flyer."

"Anything I should know about her?"

Maret pauses and thinks. "Once," she says, "I saw her push one of the younger girls into splits until she screamed." She brightens. "But you have lovely splits, so I'm sure you're fine."

"She sounds horrible. Perhaps we'll get along."

"I set up your audition and everything. Tomorrow at two in the afternoon. So rest up until then."

I unwind myself fully from the silks and slide to the ground. Maret is already turning away, humming one of the songs from the festival performance.

"Oh!" She turns back. "I almost forgot." Maret opens her shoulder bag and rustles through it. She pulls out what I think for a moment is a clock. It's a circle of glossy wood with a glass face and a single long hand. But instead of numbers around the edge, it has words: *Dry, Fair, Showers, Stormy.*

"Is this my present?"

"It's a barometer," Maret says. "Press the button at the bottom of the hand."

I do. The device clicks and the hand unlatches from the barometer's face. When I pull it loose, I realize that it has the heft and sharpness of a dagger.

"Isn't it clever?" Maret says. "No one will blink at a girl with an innocent interest in keeping track of the weather."

I set the knife back on the barometer. It clicks into place.

"If anyone caught you with a gun," she says, "you'd be in the dungeon by lunch. But a barometer? That'll work."

What she doesn't say is, *After everything with Cassia, I figured you wouldn't want to use a gun.*

"Thank you," I say, and I mean it.

Maret and I have been going over our plan for months. By now I know it so well that I'm afraid I'll start reciting it in my sleep.

I'll ingratiate myself with the flyers and the guards. Even Nikolai himself. When Maret was my age, a teenage princess in the palace, she and her brother—Nikolai and Cassia's father—spent many a bored hour with the flyers and the young guards, playing cards and lounging in the gardens. According to Maret, everyone is so busy drinking, laughing, and flirting that I'll be able to slide right next to Nikolai without anyone thinking anything of it.

And then I'll stab him.

I know I'll get arrested or killed. But I'll get Cassia her revenge and Maret her throne. And I'd rather die this way than at the hands of the Flood.

But first I need to make it into the palace.

"What if I'm not good enough to get the spot?" I ask.

Maret turns around slowly. "Why would you say that?"

Because there are girls out there with real recommendations from real directors. Because little Kostrovian girls grow up watching the Royal Flyers and dreaming of being in their ranks.

"Just a question," I say.

"Come now," Maret says. "You've become an excellent flyer."

But what if I don't become a Royal Flyer tomorrow?

Not long after her exile, Maret tried to plant a guard in the palace to spy for her. He was discovered and executed within days. Then, two years ago, she attempted to use a cook. The cook met the same fate before he even got the job.

All those palace positions, Maret told me, were scrutinized carefully. The Captain of the Guard interviewed everyone himself. Had people watched and trailed. Didn't hire people who had nothing to lose.

But the flyers report to a different leader.

According to Maret, Adelaida cares about finding the best performers, not the most patriotic Kostrovians. The flyers get to flirt with royalty instead of being trampled by it. Part of the court, but never seen as political.

Maret knows that men suspect other men but not pretty young girls. She knows that if she wants a spy in the palace, the spy has to be a girl on the silks.

If I don't become a Royal Flyer, Maret's plan evaporates. And so does mine.

She drags her finger down the silk, not quite holding it, like she doesn't want me to see her doing it wrong. "You were plenty strong before you started training, and now you're stronger. You have practiced every waking hour of every day since we arrived. But most of all, I know you will become a Royal Flyer because you want it more desperately than anyone else in New Sundstad."

"But—"

"The other girls," Maret says, "want to be Royal Flyers because they want a wealthy royal councilor to notice them and promise to love them forever. Someone to buy them a ticket to the royal fleet. But what do you want?"

My voice is sticky in my throat. "I want to kill the king."

"That's right," Maret says. "And so you will."

9

NATASHA

Adelaida wakes me up by throwing a shoe at me.

I sit with a start and rub my shoulder. She leans against my doorframe, arms crossed. A second shoe dangles from her index finger.

"You wanted to talk?" she says.

"You threw a shoe at me!"

She frowns at the shoe that's come to rest on the ground beside my bed. "I figured the slippers you were wearing yesterday were ruined from the rain."

"So you decided to attack me with a new pair?"

"Ah, yes, here lies Natasha Koskinen, bludgeoned to death by four ounces of satin. Get dressed."

"Last night," I say, "where did you—" Adelaida shuts the door on her way out. "—go."

My new slippers and I meet Adelaida in the studio ten minutes later. I'm freezing in a charcoal-gray full-suit with a gauzy skirt. Adelaida is laying peat briquettes in the fireplace. Her cat, a lumpy creature named Kaspar, winds around her ankles.

The light streaming from the window is thin and pale. From outside, I can hear the *drip, drip, drip* of leftover rainwater streaming off the eaves.

"Maybe tomorrow you could wake me up with a new cloak," I say. "I lost mine."

The fire sparks. Adelaida stands and brushes off her knees. "You're very demanding. And on today, of all days, when I did not even have a serving girl offer to light the fire for me."

"Perhaps," I say, eyeing the cat, "the serving girls are stretched a bit thin checking on their storm-terrorized families this morning."

I stoop to pick up Kaspar. He's quite possibly the stupidest cat to have ever lived, and despite Adelaida's impatience for foolish humans, she's rather fond of Kaspar.

"Well," Adelaida says, "that's very selfish of them."

"Seriously?" I say.

"Don't blame me," she says. "I'm cranky when I'm cold." She scoops Kaspar out of my arms and holds him to her bosom. Her eyes latch on my wrist. The bandage is still snug with Katla's knots.

I can feel my heart beating in my throat.

"So." Adelaida's gaze meets mine.

"It was that bird. Acting all strange because of Storm Five."

"You were distracted."

"The bird was huge! Adelaida, you know I'm too good to have fallen like that."

"Your arrogance is inspiring."

"But it wasn't my fault."

"Sure it was," she says.

Tartly, I say, "Well, you're the one who trained me. So."

"I trained you well and right," she says. "Enough to stay on those silks. But you were always free to fall. That much was up to you."

"Please, Adelaida."

She watches me through squinted eyes. I have to fight my instinct to look away, to cross my arms over my stomach. My teeth clench. Kaspar bats at her chin, and her nose wrinkles.

"No," she finally says. "No, you probably wouldn't have fallen if not for the storm. But you did fall, and even before that, it was as bad a festival performance as I've ever seen you give."

I gather a breath. "I overheard what Gospodin said. About the fleet."

She bends down and releases Kaspar. He bounds away, bumping his head against the mirror as he goes. "How much did you hear?"

"We're not going on the royal fleet, are we?"

"It depends," she says, "what you mean by *we*."

I ball my hands into fists at my sides. "What do you mean? You promised I'd be safe. How could you lie? I thought you were my—"

But what is Adelaida? Not my friend. Not my confidante. And though Adelaida knew my mother, flew with my mother, she's never tried to assume a maternal role. In the end, I suppose, she's just my director. She cares about me because I'm a good flyer.

"I wasn't lying to you," she says. "As far as I knew, Gospodin intended to take you on the royal fleet."

"Gospodin? Not Nikolai?"

She waves a hand. "Gospodin, Nikolai. Same thing. I thought we'd *all* be included. And we're not the only ones. Midway through seal season—around Storm Six, I think—a few of the big merchant families started talking to each other. Seems just about everyone who's ever had so much as an afternoon tea with Gospodin thinks they have a spot on the royal fleet. But there's not enough food. Not enough supplies. Not with the storms and the fires and the insects and the famine. Someone had to go."

My mouth is dry. "So they took the Royal Flyers off the roster."

"If you were Gospodin, would you rather say no to a powerful merchant with enough money to feed the fleet for a month? Or a bunch of *dancer girls?*"

"He called us dancer girls?"

Adelaida busies herself with the silks as we talk, spreading out the fabric and checking for holes. "We have neither enough food nor enough ships for this Flood."

"What about the ships from Grunholt?"

"A lie," she says. "Or rather, a feat of optimism. Gospodin *talked* to the Righteous Mariner in Grunholt about securing more ships, but they need them as badly as we do. Everyone does. We should've had a failsafe Flood plan all along, but no—*Captain's Log* said Floods only come every two thousand years, so why would we stock up on grain and ships eight hundred years early? Stupid. The only countries that might actually be prepared for this are non–Sacred Breath countries, and they're all too busy feeling clever to consider helping us."

"We have months left, though," I say. "We can make more ships."

"Fine," Adelaida says. "Assume we have a thousand ships. What about our food stockpiles, so generously destroyed and plundered by discontent citizens? What about all the fresh water we don't have?"

I feel like I could melt into the floor. "But . . . all the rain."

"Yes. All the rain they have painstakingly collected, only to realize that sewage has been spilling out of a cesspit and leaking into the collection basin. Personally, I love the idea of drinking only wine for a year, but the livestock might not be terribly happy."

I let out a slow breath. "Okay," I say. "Okay." My mind is spinning through ideas, and none of them are good.

"You're panicking," Adelaida says. "You're a panicker. See, this is why I didn't tell you about Pippa."

I dig my nails into the heels of my hands. "Don't you feel guilty? You're really going to sail away without us, not a care in the world?"

"Ah. That's where you're wrong." She drops the silk, fully inspected, and locks me in a steady stare. "You heard Gospodin. You heard what he told me."

I strain to remember. "That you shouldn't worry, because of course you're part of the fleet?"

"And," Adelaida says, "did you believe him?"

I turn the memory of his holy voice around in my mind. "I don't know."

She nods as though this admission pleases her. "Well, I'm not altogether convinced that Gospodin will let me on that fleet when the time comes."

"Do you want me to offer my condolences?"

"No," Adelaida says. "I want you to marry Nikolai."

My laugh is sharp and loud even to my own ears.

"I'm serious," she says.

"You believed that speech?" I say. "I thought this was just a big scheme to keep everyone distracted before the Flood."

"It's a scheme to do precisely that," Adelaida says. "And at the end of that scheme, who do you think Nikolai would rather end up married to? A girl from Southtown he's never met? An aristocratic girl with too many international allies? Or the principal flyer who's spent the past eight years in the palace, flirting with him and befriending his guards?"

My face heats. "I don't flirt with Nikolai!"

"That dinner? Last bear season?"

The palace hosted a royal gala just before Nikolai announced his engagement to Princess Colette. I may have noticed Gregor chatting with Nikolai, so I may have made a point to say hello to my good friend Gregor, and Nikolai and I *may* have talked for a few minutes. Nikolai greeted me by name and asked how my shoulder was doing, since the last time we'd seen each other—at one of the guards' card games—I'd been icing a sprain.

He had a subtle smile. I was so busy noticing it that I didn't even realize Gregor had slipped away, leaving us to talk alone.

I cross my arms. "That wasn't flirting."

"It was something," Adelaida says.

I'll admit to being intrigued by Nikolai—he's young and powerful and attractive enough—but I can't imagine myself as queen. Kissing him? Sleeping with him? And the politics? Seas. My father was a palace guard I never met, and my mother was a disgraced ex-flyer. I'm not exactly an eligible princess.

"Even if Nikolai agreed to it," I say, "Gospodin never would."

"Well, good thing it's not Gospodin's decision."

I almost laugh. "Nikolai trusts Gospodin more than his own family. You don't think he'll get his council on this?" Two years ago, Nikolai; his sister, Cassia; and some of the councilors hatched a plan to oust Gospodin from the royal council. They thought the Sacred Breath was getting too much power over the crown. But at the last minute, Nikolai switched sides. Told Gospodin what was happening. Nikolai's councilors were executed; Cassia, exiled. She was hardly the first royal to be shooed out of Kostrov, but I was shocked anyway. I always thought of Nikolai and Cassia as two halves of a pair. Isn't that what siblings are? But in the end, Nikolai trusted Gospodin more.

"Well," Adelaida says, "maybe Gospodin will see the wisdom in choosing a girl like you. If it's an uplifting rags-to-riches story he's after, you're as good a choice as any. The people know you. They've watched you perform for years."

I shake my head. "What about my mother?"

"What about her?"

"Isn't she a"—I wince, feeling like a traitor—"blemish on my candidacy?"

"Yes, but she's been dead so long, who can really remember?"

"Gospodin, probably," I say.

Adelaida exhales through her nose, nostrils flaring.

My mother grew up in Our Lady of Tidal Sorrows, an orphan raised by the Sacred Breath. They gave her the name Tatiana Kosen. *Kosen,* one of Kos, as all orphans are. But she privately renounced Kos's *Captain's Log* and read Tamm instead. The fables are hundreds of years old, telling stories from before the Sacred Breath conquered Kostrov. When this land was called Maapinn and we had clans and chiefs instead of noble families and kings. She dreamed of magic; memorized fairy tales; plotted maps to faraway kingdoms. She squirreled away money until she could have flying lessons, and she practiced until she could be a Royal Flyer.

When she got to the palace, she took a name out of Tamm's fables: *Koskinen.* Sigrid Koskinen was one of the girls from one of the stories, who rowed a boat down a river to the center of the world, to a cave where it never flooded and ancient beasts roamed.

Kosen means "one of Kos." *Koskinen* means "one of rivers."

Kosen. Koskinen. A three-letter change. Just one syllable. Hardly a difference at all.

But also. An erasure of her connection with the Sacred Breath. A betrayal of those who raised her, some of whom took it personally. The biggest difference in the world.

And then she went and had a child with a man who wouldn't marry her. Our Lady of Tidal Sorrows wouldn't take her back, and she wouldn't have gone if they had. She worked whatever jobs she could find. She raised me in bursts of manic attention and clouds of absence.

And then she handed me to Adelaida, walked off the edge of a canal, and never came up for air. Her final sin: Refusing to endure Kostrov any longer.

She didn't get a funeral. Apostates never do.

But I still have her name. Her hair. Her affinity for flying. Her copy of *Tamm's Collected Fables*. And unlike her, I will survive.

"Gospodin," Adelaida finally says, "might be hard to convince."

My mother knew Gospodin from her time as a Royal Flyer. She didn't keep her views about the Sacred Breath quiet.

"Impossible," I say. I remember the way he looked at me at the festival. The narrow eyes as mud arced over my head.

"And yet, you're thinking about it."

"If I married Nikolai," I say, "do you think I could bring the other flyers on the fleet?"

"Only one way to find out. Now, I don't know about you, but there's no way I'll make it through audition prep without whiskey. We can put it in our tea." She takes a few purposeful strides toward the door before I shake myself and manage to catch up.

"Hang on," I say. "Just like that? We're moving on to auditions?"

"Well, we can't perform with only five flyers again. It was atrocious. Auditions are tomorrow."

I shake my head. "We still haven't talked about Pippa."

Adelaida lifts a hand. "What's there to talk about? She got pregnant. I told her she'd have to leave when she started to show, and she chose to leave sooner rather than later. That's how the Royal Flyers do things. You, of all people, should know that."

"But what's the point? The new flyer will only be with us for, what, two seasons?"

"The Royal Flyers need to maintain some semblance of normalcy. The longer you're in the palace, the better your odds of enamoring Nikolai. There's no one better poised to abduct his heart than the principal flyer."

"That sounds oddly violent," I say.

"Love always is."

10

ELLA

Maret spends the morning of my audition preparing me. She twists my curls into a braid that wraps around my head like a crown, the same style the Royal Flyers wore at the festival. I shut my eyes and draw the palace maps in my mind. I imagine walking down the long hallways. Turning a corner and seeing Nikolai, haughty, his crown glinting on his head.

My stomach is a knot. I'm a nervous eater—my mother could always tell I was anxious when the pantry would go intriguingly empty—but Edvin hasn't yet brought our usual weekly delivery from the market.

Maret tugs at the sleeves of my black full-suit, procured by Edvin. "A little short, but if you mind the cuff, no one can see the tattoo."

Next, she stuffs a letter in my cloak pocket. "You can drop that at the postal office in the Wharf District before you head to the palace for auditions. I have an old friend in Illaset. Now that Nikolai has reneged on his engagement, I think the Illasetish might be keen to see a change of leadership. You remember the postal office?"

"The one that said they wouldn't hire anyone who wasn't from Kostrov?"

"You're very hung up on that." She straightens my cloak. "There.

You're ready." She sets her hands on my shoulders. "You look like a flyer already, dear girl."

I can feel my heart beating in my stomach. After so many months, I'll finally see the place that made Cassia. And meet the boy who ordered her death.

"Remember. If anyone asks, you trained with Luda. Your parents were Terrazzan, but you moved to New Sundstad as a girl. You live on a no-name street in Southtown."

I nod.

"You're an excellent flyer," she says. "Don't look so nervous."

But she looks as nervous as I feel. We both know how important my audition is.

"I don't want to disappoint you," I say.

"You're not doing it for me," she says. "You're doing it for Cassia. And the crown." She wraps me in a brief hug. Squeezes. "The crown is everything. I wouldn't trust anyone else with this job."

Then she wishes me luck, and I'm off.

My path through New Sundstad winds. Some of the stone bridges have crumbled, leaving one the choice to hire a gondolier or keep looking for a dry route. Since I don't have any money, I walk on.

A tangy smell settles over the street. I press my sleeve to my nose. Just when I think I can't take the stench any longer, I turn a corner and see a gray animal carcass sprawled across the path.

It has a pale, distended belly and a flat face. Three men in smart wool coats and brimmed caps lean over the body. One holds a knife, slicing open the creature's blubbery middle. Another holds a pen, scribbling notes. The third holds his nose.

"It's a bay porpoise," the man with the knife says. "Look at that coloration."

"Are you daft?" the pen-and-paper man says. "He's a seal-nosed porpoise. Where are the Skaratan scholars? They'll tell you."

"I'm going to be sick," says the nose-holder.

I wince at the porpoise of indiscernible species. He deserves better.

Once I'm upwind, I can breathe again, but the porpoise isn't the only remnant of Storm Five. Overhead, silhouettes of birds pebble the sky, but the city is nearly barren of them. Whole streets are so flooded that I can't walk through them. Roofs have caved in. The canal water teems, carrying a current of branches, boards, children's dolls, men's work boots, glass bottles, a pair of spectacles, a sodden copy of *Captain's Log*.

When I reach the Wharf District, I see the line for the postal office before I see the actual building. I drop Maret's letter in a mail slot inside as a woman argues with the postal clerk behind the counter.

"No letters from Grunholt? Are you sure? But my sisters are there. No, I'm sure they want to reach me. Well, when do you expect the ship from Grunholt will arrive?"

At least, when I left Terrazza behind, I didn't leave anyone to worry about.

I hurry back into the damp square of the Wharf District. My stomach is roiling more fiercely than ever. I pass a girl about my age, long-limbed with a pretty smile, and all I can think is, *Seas, I hope she's not auditioning.* I don't know what Maret will do if I don't get the spot. I don't know what I'll do.

A cluster of people stand in the shadow of Our Lady of Tidal Sorrows, and when I turn my nose to them, I catch a smell so lovely that I almost forget the odor of dead porpoise.

I take a few steps closer.

It smells like honey and warmth.

In the door of Our Lady of Tidal Sorrows, a woman stands by a table stacked with cloth-covered loaves of bread. My stomach grumbles monstrously.

I take another step. Glance around. When no one stops me, I slide into the queue.

The seashell façade of Our Lady of Tidal Sorrows looms over me. Nearby, one of the windows is smashed. Bits of glass still scatter the stone beneath. As a pair of men walk by, one elbows the other and says, sourly, "Brightwallers."

A man in all white is scrubbing paint from a wall near the window. I don't recognize what's written there. I know three languages, but not this one. It's almost Kostrovian, but—

The person in line behind me jostles me forward. I drag my gaze away and keep walking.

When I reach the front of the line, the woman greets me with a broad smile. She wears a modest white cloak and her hair in a subdued knot.

"Many breaths, friend," she says.

"Is the bread free?"

She waves me closer. "A gift from the Sacred Breath. Come."

I shamble forward, transfixed. When she tugs back the cloth, revealing row upon row of beautiful, steaming loaves of rye bread, I think I'm liable to soak them with my drool.

I reach out. The woman lifts up a loaf but doesn't give it to me.

"It's easy to be afraid during a storm," she says. "Even I found myself as frightened as a child when the thunder started booming."

Seas. She knows she has a captive audience. I try to give her a polite degree of attention, but my eyes keep flicking back to the bread.

"So," she continues, "during Storm Five, I lit a candle and returned to one of my favorite passages in *Captain's Log.* The sea chose to spare Kos during the last Flood. When we read his words, we read a guide on how one must act to earn the sea's favor. Compassion. Patience. Hope."

"Um," I say. *Bread bread bread bread bread.* "Yes. Completely."

"Kos dreamed of a golden age," she says, "when society was pure and no longer required the cleansing of the Floods."

My stomach rumbles again. "I couldn't agree more."

"Though the consequences of the last Flood were high, think of the benefit. It allowed Kos to spread his message." She smiles with lots of teeth. "The next Flood will bring a New World even more beautiful than this one."

And then, finally, blessedly, she extends the bread toward me. I stretch out my greedy, greedy hands.

But my sleeve inches up my forearm, putting the tattoo on display. A swirl of hair; vacant eyes; a woman's torso; a fish's tail.

"Oh," the woman says. *"Oh."*

I yank my sleeve over my wrist.

She pulls the bread back to her stomach. "A siren?" Her eyebrows come together, and it's not empathy that follows the flash of disgust. It's pity.

The crowd stirs behind me.

She waits for me to explain, but there's no point: She's already decided she knows all she needs to.

I drop my hands to my sides.

"Oh, dear," she says. Her cheeks are pink. I would like to tell her to stuff her secondhand embarrassment up her holy ass, but I don't feel safe in this crowd. "Perhaps you ought to run along."

I turn in a hurry. I collide with a body twice my size in every dimension. The man's hair is long and thin and dirty, and I can see his scalp through it.

"Excuse me," I say, but he doesn't move.

I clench my hands into fists and go around him. I've only made it three steps when he says, "You're too pretty, you know."

I turn slowly. Back toward him. His eyes are on my sleeve.

"To be that way," he says.

I grit my teeth until I think they will break. But I say nothing. I walk away. My vision threatens to blur with the memory of Cassia.

Too pretty, he says.

The sea is pretty too.

By now that man should know what the sea is capable of.

11

NATASHA

When we have to cut an audition short for the third time because the girl can't do a cross-back straddle, I glower at Adelaida. "Have these girls ever seen silks before?"

"I need more whiskey."

Adelaida and I sit on the floor with our backs against the mirror. We started the day standing. We lost that kind of willpower after audition twelve.

"I hear some of the studios are losing girls," I say. "No one wants to send their daughters to flying practice when they're worried about drowning, I guess."

"Well, that's a lovely excuse for the gross incompetence we've seen today."

A guard escorts in our twentieth audition. The girl is even taller than I am, with close-cropped blond hair and broad shoulders. She introduces herself; her name doesn't register.

Ten seconds into her clumsy climb, I'm staring at the bottom of my teacup. A few dark leaves are drying to the porcelain.

I want Pippa back. The other girls are off visiting her now, making sure she managed the storm. Gregor passed Pippa's new address on to Sofie, and I wish I'd been allowed to join the party. But as principal, I have to sit with Adelaida, hour after torturous hour.

The girl grunts with exertion as she attempts to tilt herself sideways into a hip key. The silk tangles on her foot.

"Thank you," Adelaida says. "But that's really quite enough."

"Wait," the girl says. Her voice is fast and thin. "Please, let me try again."

"We're very busy today," Adelaida says.

But the girl tries again anyway, and yet again, her foot catches the silk. She lets out a frantic, animal whine.

Adelaida calls for the guard.

"Wait, wait," the girl says. "Please. I know how to do this. I promise."

The guard puts his hand on her shoulder.

"Please," she says, eyes wide and desperate. "This is my only chance."

My cold, dead heart gives a hollow thud. The guard escorts her to the door. I pull on the neck of my full-suit, my breathing tight.

The girls who come here think they're auditioning for their own survival. But we can't even give them that. Maybe, when we turn them away, they'll try to marry Nikolai instead.

In the brief respite between auditions, I say, "When can I tell the girls?"

"About?"

"The truth. The fleet."

"You can tell them just as soon as you'd like the Royal Flyers to completely fall apart."

"That's not fair," I say. "I don't want to lie to Katla. To any of them. And besides, Sofie already knows. It's only a matter of time until she stops keeping it a secret."

Adelaida sets down her teacup. A vein in her neck is bulging. "Then make Sofie understand why the rest of the girls can't know."

"Do you really think they'd fall apart?"

"Of course," Adelaida says. "And you do too. That's why you didn't tell them before the festival."

I tip my head back against the wall. "Seas."

Adelaida snaps her fingers in front of my face. "Come on. We have three more hours to go. Pretend you care."

"Fine." I set down my teacup and get to my feet. I bend all the way forward, stretching until my palms flatten on the floor. "Who's next?"

Adelaida checks her list. "A girl from Luda's studio." She makes a face. "I'm not fond of Luda."

I unfold and examine myself in the mirror. My reflection looks back at me with sympathy. "What's the girl's name?"

"Sounds foreign," Adelaida says. "Ella Neves."

12

ELLA

A dark-haired guard escorts me through a blue door at the back of the palace, inconspicuous if not for the men with guns on their hips standing in front of it.

The small, unadorned vestibule on the other side is nothing like the grandeur that Cassia promised me. I have to assume they save the good bits of the palace for the royals.

The guard pushes through another door.

It opens onto a massive studio. I've never been under such a high ceiling. The silks that hang from the beams are vibrant and so endlessly long that my hands itch to climb.

I recognize Madam Adelaida and Natasha Koskinen from the festival. Madam Adelaida is a broad-shouldered woman, like my mother was, with brown skin and a blocky jaw. She sits at a wall of continuous mirrors, Natasha standing beside her. Without makeup, Natasha looks younger than she did at the festival. Even when her body rotates to me, her gaze hugs her reflection in the mirror, like some vanity keeps her transfixed.

If it is vanity, it's hard to blame her.

Her eyes land on mine. They're an indecisive shade of green-brown. Her skin is pale and freckled. She's as vulpine a person as

I've ever seen, with burnt-orange hair, a long neck, and a sharply pointed chin.

"Have we met?" she says.

"No." I watch her with my breath held in my mouth for one, two, three seconds.

Natasha keeps frowning at me. "Well?" she says when I haven't moved in a beat too many. "Climb the silk. Try not to fall."

"We're not supposed to fall?" The words are out of my mouth before I can think better of them. Natasha's mouth bends into a bridge. Madam Adelaida laughs, sharp and surprised.

"I think we can agree," Madam Adelaida says, "that there's no such thing as a good fall." She puts a hand on Natasha's shoulder. "Cheer up."

Natasha doesn't look cheered.

I set my cloak on the ground and double-check that my sleeves are snug around my wrists. I walk to the silk. My fingers twitch around it.

I put one leg on either side of it. Raise my hands above my head. Lift a leg, hook the silk, twist. Catch the slack. Pull myself up. Again.

The silk is serpentine around me. I know I should be demonstrating my ability to do fundamental moves—*Look, a footlock! Aren't I competent?*—but this silk, this studio, the knowledge that I'm being watched and evaluated on months of hard work, makes me hungry for so much more than that.

I catch Natasha's eyes far below. She says something quiet to Adelaida. Adelaida scratches her neck vacantly.

I knit myself into an S-wrap.

I've only ever been able to practice wheeldowns on a short stretch of silk, just enough for two rotations. Now I have feet upon glorious feet of fabric, and my body is greedy for it.

My legs fan out. I take a breath.

I spin, and the studio spins around me. My split legs parallel the silk. My hands move fluidly over the tail of the fabric as it streams out behind me. And then, just before the ground surges to meet me, I hook my knee around the silk and stop.

Adelaida's and Natasha's faces are level with mine.

They don't look bored anymore.

Natasha takes a step forward. "Can you do an infinity salto?"

Can I do an infinity salto, she asks.

Fifteen minutes later, my arms are trembling but my lungs are giddy. Every breath I take seems to pull air deeper into my body than I knew possible.

By the time Madam Adelaida tells me I can go, I'm sweaty and alive.

"We'll release the name of the new flyer tonight," Madam Adelaida says. "You can check the Wharf District for the posting."

I collect my cloak. A guard walks me out. On the street, it's misting. A smile keeps bubbling to my lips.

For the first time since Cassia died, I feel like I did not die with her.

13

NATASHA

"You saw it, didn't you?" I say in the echo of the closing door.

Adelaida tilts her head to look at me. "The tattoo?"

"Yeah."

She lifts a shoulder. "I don't particularly care." A pause. Suspicious eyes. "Do you?"

"No," I say, too loudly and too quickly. She traps me in a narrow gaze. "I'm just worried about Nikolai's reaction. Or Gospodin's."

"You know as well as I do that Sofie probably deserves that mark."

"Deserves?" Does anyone deserve to be branded?

She waves her hand. "You know what I mean. If Gospodin has a fit that she's a siren, we'll just tell him we're helping an unlucky girl heal her brokenness."

The word enters my stomach, invasive, and settles there. "Brokenness?"

"Seas, Natasha. Semantics. I'm just using the words the Sacred Breath would use."

I wonder how it happened. I wonder if someone held down her forearm and pricked her skin with a needle as she wept; I wonder if she fought; I wonder if she stood perfectly still because someone told her it needed to be done.

"She was the best we've seen all day," I say.

"By a lot. My apologies to Luda."

"She seems . . ." I pause. "Hostile."

Adelaida snorts. "You just don't like her because she made fun of your fall."

"Yes, and?"

"You'll make her do lots of pull-ups and she'll know not to tease you anymore. We'll get her a full-suit with very long sleeves. She can do a perfect wheeldown, and that's really all I can ask of the sorry lot we've seen today."

There was something in the way Ella looked at me, like she could see straight through me. I recognize her. I can't say from where.

Instead, I say, "Fine. Welcome to the Royal Flyers, Ella Neves."

14

ELLA

When Edvin brings us the news, Maret throws her arms around me.

"I told you," she says.

Edvin stands by the door, hands clasped in front of his hips. He's sporting half an inch of pale stubble and bags under his eyes. Maret invites him in for a celebratory toast, but he shakes his head.

"I'd better get back to the university. The infighting is only getting worse."

I frown at him. "Infighting?"

"It means fighting between colleagues," he says.

My jaw twitches. "Why is there infighting?"

He swats the air like my question is a buzzy fly. "A division about whether or not we should follow the birds on their exodus to see where they're going. Most of us think they all drop dead somewhere over the ocean. That's what *Captain's Log* indicates. But it's so like the ornithologists to stir up trouble." A pause. "An ornithologist studies birds."

"A criminologist studies why people get murdered," I say. "Three times out of ten, it's because they were condescending."

Maret claps her hands. "Lovely anecdote, Ella!" She grabs Edvin's shoulders and steers him out. "Off you go. Thank you for the news.

Bye-bye." When we're alone again, she turns the full radiance of her smile on me. "You're a terror, aren't you?"

"Only sometimes."

Not at Our Lady of Tidal Sorrows this morning, when I couldn't summon a word of self-defense. I consider telling Maret about the incident, but I don't want to be comforted. I don't want someone to smooth out the edges of that moment, to tell me it's okay, because it's not. I want that moment to feel like barbs on my skin.

I don't need Maret to boost my morale. My morale will be just fine once I kill Nikolai.

"You'll have to be careful, but you already know that," Maret says. "Keep watch for the men who assassinated Cassia. They might recognize you."

I nod.

"And remember, we have time. We've only just passed Storm Five. So ingratiate yourself. Snoop. Figure out where Nikolai goes, and when, and if you could ever meet him there with your new knife. And you'll come back and report what you're learning, yes?"

"I will."

She lets out a big breath and pulls me to her chest. I'm surprised how much my body relaxes into the maternal embrace. But Maret's not my mother. I don't need embraces any more than I need morale boosts or reassurances.

"I'll miss you," she says. "You're the dearest murderess I've ever known."

I step back and she drops her arms.

"The newest Royal Flyer." She shakes her head. "Sleep up. You have a big day tomorrow."

When I lie in my narrow bed, I splay my hand across the scratchy sheets. It's the last time I'll sleep here. From now on, I'll live in the palace, in the halls where Cassia grew up, under the same roof as her killer. I'll see the big library she loved; the garden full of rocks and rainwater; the thermal pools and their clouds of steam.

That's where I'll live. That's where I'll die.

I flip over onto my side and stare at the wall.

Sleep never comes.

15

NATASHA

With the auditions over, my thoughts drift back to a dark place. I still need to tell the girls what I overheard. The new flyer—Ella—probably thinks she just secured herself a place on the fleet. I'll have to tell her too. I hope they don't all quit.

I'm sulking through dinner, mashing my fork against my potatoes and watching them squelch through the tines. Is marrying Nikolai really the only way I can survive the Flood? Half of Kostrov will be trying to get his attention. I'm ashamed of how little thought I've given survival plans to this point. I was *so sure* the flyers would be on the fleet. Now that certainty makes me feel childish and naïve.

Gretta is the only other flyer at dinner. If she notices I don't want to talk, she doesn't let on.

"I just don't see why they had to leave without me," she says. "I would've gone to see Pippa, if they'd invited me."

We're sitting across from each other at a long, empty table in the kitchen. While the benches are usually packed with bodies, most of the guards and servants, if they're not on duty, are probably checking in on friends and family, like they always do after a storm. I wonder if some of the sober faces here have already checked.

I poke at my bowl of potato mush. "Is there fish in this?"

Gretta makes a face. She hasn't touched her food. The head chef, René, uses us as test subjects. Though it's hard to complain about a warm meal, given the state the country is in, I got tired of René's creative cooking when I was twelve. Gretta has had even more time to get sick of it, having eaten in this kitchen her whole life as the daughter of the Captain of the Guard.

Gretta leans across the table. "So. The auditions."

"You're glad you missed them, trust me."

"Have you announced the new flyer yet?"

"Adelaida should be posting it now."

Gretta's eyes are wide. "Tell me."

"She's good. Not very polished, but strong."

"How strong?" Gretta says. "Sofie strong? Or only Ness strong?"

"Have you considered being ten percent less competitive?"

"Is that how you got where you are?"

I cross my arms. Gretta mirrors me.

Of all the flyers, Gretta is the one who looks most like me. Not in coloration—her skin is light brown and her hair is dark, but we're both made of long lines. Stretched limbs, fingers. Her build means she has the same strengths and weaknesses as me in the silks—hands that can reach but narrow hips that can't keep the fabric secure.

What I most see of myself in her is fierce determination to be more. To be the best. At any cost.

Now that I'm principal, I don't have to fight my girls for solos. But I'm not proud of the way I pressed myself not just to be good, but to be better than my friends, on my way here.

I don't think Gretta would ever sabotage me. But I doubt she was heartbroken to see me fall.

"What's her name?" Gretta asks. "Whose studio is she from?"

Before I can answer, the kitchen door opens. Katla, Sofie, and Ness come through in a waft of laughter. Their cheeks are pink with evening air. They have cloaks slung over their shoulders.

Ness waves. When they sit, she eyes my bowl. "Ooh," she says. "Is that good?"

"No. Want some?"

Ness takes a forkful. "Oh," she says. "My."

"Pippa says hi," Sofie says. Her eyes are brighter than I've seen in days.

"I hope she marries Gregor," Ness says. "He's Nikolai's favorite guard. I bet if they're married, she can come on the fleet with us after all."

I catch Sofie's gaze over the table. Her mouth tugs to a frown.

Katla's eyes sweep from me to Sofie and back again. "Tasha? I need a moment in private."

"Wait," Ness says. "I want to hear about auditions. What do you two have to talk about so secretively?"

"Hip key climbs," Katla says. "Eat your slop."

In the hallway, the smell of seafood and peat smoke fades. Katla crosses her arms.

"Remember that time my full-suit split right down my ass before the seal season festival?" she says.

I smile faintly. "Yeah."

"And you ran all the way back to the palace to get me a new one so that Adelaida wouldn't get mad at me?"

"The flyers should run more. It really is a good exercise."

"You did it because you're my best friend," Katla says.

"It feels like this story is going to have a moral," I say.

Katla exhales loudly through her nose. She says nothing as a pair of manservants pass. When they open the door, the kitchen belches smoke at us. Once it closes again, she says, "Right before we left, Sofie pulled Pippa aside and told her something. Sofie wouldn't tell me what."

For a moment, I consider *not* telling her. But that's ridiculous. Too selfish, even for me. I'm just afraid. Afraid she'll think I've failed her, failed the flyers. Afraid she'll think there's no point being in the flyers anymore and leave.

I can't be principal flyer of a group that doesn't exist.

A surge of panic. I should tell Katla. I *have* to tell Katla.

I wipe my palms, sweaty, on my thighs. "We're not going on the fleet."

A pause.

"*What?*" Katla says.

I shift my weight. Pause to let a guard into the kitchen. He gives us a suspicious look. "Adelaida said there wasn't room. I should've told you right away, I know—but we had the festival, and then I was in auditions, and—I'm sorry."

Her expression hardens. "You're right. You should've told me right away."

I flinch. No one takes honesty more seriously than Katla. "I'm really sorry."

"Whatever," she says.

"But I'm going to figure something out," I say. "That's what I do, right? That's what I always do. I figure something out. Adelaida and I are—"

"Yeah," Katla says bitterly, "I have a lot of faith that *Adelaida* is going to come up with a plan to keep us safe. What's she going to do? Marry Nikolai?"

Katla must see something shift in my face.

"No," she says. "Adelaida wants to get *you* to marry Nikolai. Doesn't she?"

My mouth is dry. "She suggested it. But it's a crazy idea. Right?"

"It's ridiculous!" Katla says, too loudly. "Nikolai would never marry you!"

I'd be lying if I said that didn't hurt a little. "Like I said. It's a crazy idea."

"I'm sure he and Gospodin are doing all sorts of negotiations with the most powerful families in Kostrov," Katla says. "Probably brokering trades, or something. I bet the girl he marries is the one who can add the biggest ship to the fleet."

"Right," I say, feeling myself deflate. Seas. Was I actually starting to believe I stood a chance?

"I can't believe Adelaida would keep this from us," Katla says. "Actually, I can't believe *you* would keep this from us, but I love you, so let's move past that and get to the point. What are we going to do? I have half a mind to quit just to spite Adelaida."

"No," I say quickly. "Please. It's not like our odds will get better if we leave the flyers."

"Then what do you expect us to do?"

"What's your family planning to do?" I ask.

Katla's lips purse for a moment. "They've been stockpiling food since the day after Storm Ten, but do you have any idea how much food it takes to feed a family for a year? How big a ship you need for all that drinking water?"

I'm ashamed to say, "Um . . . No?"

"They were counting on me," Katla says. "I was stupid enough to believe that I could get them onto the fleet too. Stupid, stupid, stupid."

I take her shoulders. "You're not stupid. We all thought—well, never mind. But we'll fix this. I'll fix this."

She tries to shake me away. I can tell she's slipping into a dark place. When she starts to retreat from us—long silences, cold shoulders—sometimes it takes weeks to get her back. We need to do something. She needs hope. So do I.

"Let's go to the harbor," I say, feeling reckless.

"The harbor? Why?"

"We can't fight this if we don't know what we're up against," I say. "Let's go look at the fleet. Let's buy our own ship! Let's do *something*."

"I really don't think—"

"Nope," I say, pushing Katla down the hall. She's not going to the dark, hopeless place, and neither am I. "Come on."

Ten minutes later, we're hunching against the ocean wind. I have to keep Adelaida's cloak, which I stole, clenched in my fist so it doesn't blow up to my hips.

When the masts of the royal fleet ships rise into view, Katla points. "Look at the gates," she says.

Guards and iron gates surround the dock that leads to the royal fleet. Four huge ships bob there. One is still under construction. I can only make out the names of two: *New Paradise* and *Rain Reckoning*.

"Let's go over," I say.

"I'm pretty sure the message the gates are trying to send isn't 'Please do come say hello!'"

I wave her away and march to the dock. There, a pair of older guards—not the pliant young ones who are all too eager to cooperate with flyers—stand in a growing pile of cigarette butts.

"This dock isn't open to the public," one of the men says.

"We're flyers," I say.

They don't look impressed.

"*Royal* flyers," I add.

"Neat," one of them says.

I stand on my toes to get a better view of the ships. They're big. Very big. And we're small. Surely we could tuck ourselves in a cozy cupboard somewhere?

"Can you tell us anything about the ships?" I ask.

"Classified," one of the guards says. "We're going to have to ask you to leave."

Katla's eyes narrow. "Classified? How can the ships be classified? Isn't it a matter of public safety?"

The men just cross their arms and go back to smoking.

"Come on," I mutter, grabbing Katla's arm. "This isn't getting us anywhere."

"Where are we going?" Katla asks.

"Finding someone more useful."

We do find someone more useful. A man with sun lines in his dark skin climbing off a narrow boat stacked with fishing nets.

"Good evening," I say, trying on a merchant's firm but cordial tone. "We have some questions about the ship market."

Katla mutters something about how embarrassing I am, and I ignore her.

The man raises his eyebrows. He takes a long time to respond, just in case his skepticism wasn't clear from his eyebrows.

"The ship market," the man says.

"Right. How hard is it to buy a ship these days?"

"Look," he says, glancing around the harbor. "You can't go around asking to buy a ship. It raises eyebrows these days. We're all supposed to be doing our parts, you know? Keeping fish and peat and rye coming in to build stockpiles for the Flood. It's not illegal to buy a ship, but to supply it with enough provisions? You'd have to be awfully familiar with the black market. And have Heather Hill–deep pockets."

"So you don't have your own provisions for the Flood?" I say.

"I don't have my own provisions for next week," he says.

I point at the massive ships bobbing behind their guarded gate. "So, when the Flood hits, do you think you'll be able to get on the royal fleet?"

Katla grabs my wrist. I realize, after it's out of my mouth, that it was probably a stupid question. I really have been too naïve about the Flood.

But the man doesn't look annoyed. "Rumor is, they're only taking a hundred and fifty people per ship."

"But they're huge!"

He shrugs. "Takes up a lot of space, storing that much food and water. And livestock. And clothing, jewelry, fine art—"

"Fine art!" I say. "Don't bring fine art, bring me!"

The man barks a laugh. "Fine art doesn't need ten barrels of drinking water for a year at sea. But I take your point."

"Surely the ships need crew, though," Katla says.

"Sure. Any of us would love to get hired. Failing that, plenty of folks are stockpiling their food as best they can, but it's hard to scrape together much after the tithes take their chunk. But idealists are always going to try. They might last a season. Or maybe they think they'll find some unsinkable island somewhere." He sighs. "But I'm more of a realist."

"So what are you going to do?" I ask.

"Drown, probably."

"Hey," Katla says. "Us too!"

And that's that.

We're mostly silent on the way back to the palace. It's late enough that I should fall into bed, but I don't think either of us will sleep well.

"I'm going to figure something out," I say when we reach the door.

Katla shrugs against the wind. "Seems pretty hopeless to me."

I close my hand into a fist and rest my head against it. Adelaida thinks I can be queen. Is she right?

Do I have any other options?

"We'll all have a meeting," I say. "Not—not tomorrow morning. The day after tomorrow. I just need some time to think. Figure out a plan. And then we can get everyone together and tell them the news."

"Of our inevitable death?"

"Right," I say. "Of our *seemingly* inevitable death."

Katla gives me a long, pained look. "Don't lie to me again," she says. Then she goes inside.

I wait by the door a moment longer. Shut my eyes.

The ocean howls.

16

ELLA

I arrive at the blue door with the dawn. A guard lets me inside, but when I reach the studio, it's empty. I fight the urge to run through the palace until I find Nikolai. Instead, I do a slow lap around the studio, touching each fine silk in turn.

The door opens. I drop the silk and spring back like I'm about to get in trouble.

"Oh!" a light voice says. "New friend."

I expect it to be Madam Adelaida or Natasha, but instead, a pale, unfamiliar face hovers in the doorway. Her thin hair is cut razor-straight, a mouse-brown sheet that just brushes her collarbones. I try to place her from the festival, but my eyes must've slid over her without committing her to memory.

She decides I'm not poisonous and whisks across the room on slippered feet. When she smiles, her fair cheeks dimple. She sticks out her hand. "Sofie."

When I shake it, I find my palm grasping a web of sturdy calluses. "Ella."

She's wearing a silver Sacred Breath necklace—two overlapping squares, meant to represent the sails of Kos's ship. The manual Maret gave me was very firm about the no-jewelry-on-the-silks rule.

I wonder if she has to take off her necklace to practice. "Welcome to the flyers," she says. "Natasha's hardly told us anything about you."

"There's not much to know," I say. "I was born on a rugged hillside and raised by ibexes. I can speak seven languages, but tragically, all are derivations of mountain goat."

Sofie claps her hands. "Oh, I like you! I'm not clever enough to think of a colorful backstory on the spot, so maybe by the time you feel like telling me the truth, I'll have come up with an invented history of my own."

"What's your real history?"

"Nothing so fun as ibexes. My father owns a few apartment buildings in Eel Shore. He's an ass. But he did always pay for flying lessons, thank the seas, and I joined the Royal Flyers two years ago."

Two years. I run through the numbers in my head. Cassia died four months ago. I met her three months before that. And how long before that did she flee Kostrov?

This girl might have met Cassia. Might have known her.

"What's the longest a flyer has been here?" I say, trying to sound like I'm not starving for the answer.

"Oh, Natasha has that record. She's been a flyer since she was nine." Sofie pauses. "Though Gretta has been in the palace her whole life, and she's fourteen, so I guess that's longer. And if you count Adelaida, definitely her, because she's been in the palace forever. But don't tell her I said that, because she'll think I'm calling her old."

My heart pounds in my throat. So many people who could've known Cassia. Did Cassia ever mention any of these names to me? I wish I would've listened better. I wish I would've written down everything she ever said.

The door opens again. This time, it's Natasha, and I feel my heart hit the inside of my ribs.

She almost certainly knew Cassia. Cassia definitely saw her perform.

She's dressed in a tight black full-suit and a lumpy maroon sweater that swallows her hands to the knuckles. Her hair is ponytailed and pulled over her shoulder.

Did she and Cassia ever speak? How could they have ignored each other? They're probably the two most unreasonably lovely people I've ever met.

Natasha's eyes run down my body and up again. "You'll need to change. I'll get you a spare full-suit from the closet. The one you're wearing looks liable to fall apart. We'll do a proper fitting this weekend." Natasha walks back out the door. It's not until Sofie gives me a reassuring smile that I realize I'm meant to follow.

I adjust my bag over my shoulder. It's heavy from the weight of the barometer. Other than that, I only brought a few spare pairs of stockings and the dress I wore on the voyage from Terrazza. I wish I had something of Cassia's.

In the hallway, I see six doorways, including the studio door we just came from. Natasha waves her hand indiscriminately. "My bedroom, flyer bedroom, Adelaida's bedroom, washroom." She stops in front of one of the doors and opens it. "Closet."

"I didn't get any of that."

"You'll learn."

The closet is heaped with silks and costumes. Natasha grabs a bundle of black fabric and tosses it at my stomach.

I catch it and try not to be too surreptitious about checking for long sleeves. I exhale with relief when I see them. "Where am I meant to change?"

Natasha shrugs. "I don't care. The flyer bedroom?" Her eyes flick to my wrist. It's so quick I'm sure I've imagined it. I'm just looking for her to be suspicious, that's all. "That's the washroom, if you're more comfortable." This time, she points to the door slowly enough that I can actually tell which one she means.

"Do they let you eat here?" I ask.

"Breakfast is at nine, after we've warmed up. Meals are in the kitchen with the servants."

"Servants?" I say. "So I won't get the chance to steal any solid gold flatware?"

"If you're asking whether we ever dine with the royals," Natasha says, "we do. But only on special occasions. Which today is not. I hope you like porridge."

"I adore porridge," I say.

She pauses. "I can't tell if you're kidding."

"I would never kid about porridge."

Natasha leans against the wall, crossing her arms. The way she moves her body is languid, serpent smooth. "So," she says, "your name's Ella Neves and you have strong feelings about porridge. Anything else we get to know about you?"

"I prefer to cultivate an air of mystery."

She stares at me. I stare back. "Why are you here?" she says.

"In the grand scheme? That's a very philosophical question before I've eaten my porridge."

"I mean," she says loudly, starting to sound exasperated, "why did you want to join the Royal Flyers? Did you hear it would get you a spot on the fleet? Or are you just here for the sheer passion of flying?"

"What can I say? I'm a girl who pursues my passions." Like murder! Best not mention that part.

Natasha tugs her ponytail. It's so tight already, I'm surprised she doesn't rip any hair out. "We're not going to practice any less just because the Flood is coming. So I hope you're serious."

"Oh," I say, "deadly."

I drape the full-suit over my shoulder and slip inside the washroom. I flick the latch on the door.

The washroom is cold and tiled. A pair of basins sit on opposite walls. And on one counter, a comically lovely Roenese sauce boat. *Comically,* because it's meant for urine, and it feels silly to pee in floral porcelain. It really does look a bit like something you'd see on a dinner table holding a fancy salad dressing. I grew up using outdoor privies, but Kostrovians seem to fancy themselves too good for the smell of month-old sewage. Shame. It's very character building.

I change out of the full-suit Edvin got for me, happy to put it and its too-short sleeves out of sight. The new one is too big, but the material is sturdy and soft.

I hate looking at my siren. I hate it when she's out, exposed. I hate when I look down at my arm and catch her staring back at me. When I pull my sleeve over my wrist, I imagine that I'm suffocating her.

When I enter the studio again, everyone has arrived. All eyes cling to me as I step inside. It's as quiet as only an abrupt quiet can be.

Madam Adelaida has a gray cloud of fur on her shoulder. At first, I think it's some sort of shawl, but when she turns, golden eyes stare back at me. It's a cat. It's a cat that looks like it has just gone to war and is still reeling from the experience.

Natasha tilts her head to the side, watching me but speaking to the others. "This," she says, "is Ella Neves. Ella, these are the flyers."

"Say your hellos," Madam Adelaida says. The cat clutches her shoulders. "Then start stretching."

They each say hello in turn. I feel like the Ella I've been is drifting out behind me. As I become a flyer, I stop being who I was before. A farmer's daughter; a big sister; a Terrazzan. All that is left of my identity are the vengeful parts. The Ella who saw Cassia die. The parts that would do anything to make all that pain worth something.

"Welcome to the Royal Flyers," one of the girls says. She gives me a big, neat smile.

My mouth is too dry to say anything back.

Hello, Ella, they say, one after another after another.

Goodbye, Ella, I say, and I shove her back outside so she doesn't see who I've become.

17

NATASHA

I lead the girls through stretches.

I'm uneasy about our trip to the harbor last night, uneasy about telling the girls we're not on the fleet, so having a new flyer here is a welcome distraction.

Ness talks to Ella nonstop. "Dark, isn't it? I always thought it was too dreary in here, but no one listens. And compared to outside, it's just—oh!"

Kaspar leaps from Adelaida's shoulders, knocking the papers from her hands. His claws scrabble across the floor until he comes to rest at Ella's feet, with a quick detour to bump headlong into Ness's shin. He twines himself around Ella's ankles, pawing at the baggy fabric of her uniform.

Adelaida looks up, her mouth folding sourly. "Kaspar isn't friendly," she says, almost like a threat.

"Well, he's got no reason to like me." Ella shakes her foot. "You'll find no friendship here, cat."

Kaspar gazes up at her with unbridled adoration.

Kaspar has never once nuzzled my ankles. More proof that he's a stupid cat with stupid taste.

"I'll lead your stretches," Adelaida says. "Show Ella her basic climbs. Kaspar, come here."

As the other girls sink into deep toe touches, Ella pads over to me. Kaspar looks torn between his old master and his new friend. I do hope the panic doesn't set fire to his little brain.

Ella stops a foot in front of me. I inch backward. Kostrovians, by nature, require a bubble of personal space big enough to swing one's hands without colliding. In a perfect world, we'd all just stand so far apart, we'd never see anyone else.

Ella inches forward. The corner of her lips fights a smile. In such close quarters, she's as pretty as she is in the silks. She's shorter than me, muscular, with prominent cheekbones that I only now, standing so near, recognize.

"I saw you at the festival," I say. I remember catching a glimpse of her—the dark curls, the olive-toned skin, the curious look in her eye—but she disappeared too quickly.

"Did you?" she says. "Hmm. I don't remember that."

I feel a pang of annoyance at her dismissal. I search her expression —is she lying?—but I can't read it. "Adelaida and I think you were relying on your arms too much in your audition. I want to see your climbs again."

Ella follows me to the back of the studio. I stop at the lengths of fabric that used to be Pippa's.

"I know this is just a fundamental," I say, "but if you don't get the fundamentals right, you won't get anything right, and we're going to move quickly. So listen. Unless you're planning to fall and break all your bones today."

"Oh," she says. "I was actually scheduled to break all my bones on Thursday."

I narrow my eyes. Ella looks back at me impassively, blinking her dark lashes. Her hair is tied up in a massive ponytail, but one of the curls keeps springing in front of her ear.

"Do you not understand—" I stop, take a breath, and start again. "This is important. Right now. It's important that the Royal Flyers—and that includes you—are perfect."

"Because if we're perfect, we'll convince the ocean not to kill us?"

"Do you think you're being funny?" I say.

"Well, yes," Ella says. "I've done a survey of the group, and it looks like Ness is already the wide-eyed idealist and Sofie's already the lovable confidante, so all that's left for me is the comic relief. Unless that's you."

"I'm not funny," I say.

"Then what are you?" She has a quiet way of speaking. The kind of voice that forces you to lean forward for fear of missing something.

And I fall for it. I lean closer to her as I say, "What am I?"

"The spoiled heiress? The girl who doesn't realize how pretty she is until a man tells her so?"

"I know I'm pretty," I say.

This, finally, tugs her lips into something almost like a smile. It's as slippery and slow as the rest of her movements, the corner of her mouth coming to a curl. "Then I suppose I'll have to figure it out for myself."

"Well," I say, "I do like to cultivate an air of mystery."

She pauses, tilting her head to the side. That curl swings forward, casting a corkscrew shadow across her jaw. "Well, aren't we just two peas in a pod?"

I point to the silk. "Climb."

Ella wraps the silk around one leg with the other and starts to climb. I take a step back to watch her.

"You look like you're in pain," I say.

"I'm not in pain."

"Well, your face is all scrunched up."

She releases her grip, dropping to the ground in a way that rattles my teeth.

"Don't do that," I say. "It's bad for your knees."

"Oh, bother," she says. A heavy, drawn-out sigh. "I need my knees to stay intact until Thursday."

"Thursday," I say. "When you're scheduled to break all your bones."

She leans forward, smiling. Like a cat playing with prey. "Exactly."

I snatch the silks out from in front of her. "You're still relying on your arms too much. The silk should be cinched between your feet." I thread the silk between my feet and lift myself up a step. My wrist gives a little burn—a friendly reminder, in case I'd forgotten about my fall—but I ignore it.

"Okay," she says.

"Okay?" I slide hand over hand back to the floor. "No questions?"

"Not really, no."

I hand her the silks. "Fine. Go."

The correction is subtle, but it's perfect. I should be pleased. I'm just annoyed. The only thing that's off is her full-suit. It's too big around the wrists and ankles, and the excess fabric keeps snagging.

"You can come back down now," I say.

She does another heavy drop, landing on her feet. She looks up at me. "Oh," she says. "Sorry. I forgot about the knee-breaking."

I'm caught in her voice. It's throaty and warm, honey-smooth words relaxing into each other. It's not quite like the angular, Kostrovian way of speaking.

"Your grip was off," I say. "I think it's the full-suit getting in the way." I reach for her hand, where the fabric of her sleeve is bunched up to her knuckles. She flinches. Not quickly enough.

I catch my mistake a moment after I've made it.

She didn't realize I'd already seen the tattoo on her wrist. She thought she was hiding it.

I feel suddenly, accidentally, invasive. My fingers on the smooth plane of her wrist, pushing back fabric. I see black lines, an inked siren face. My hands are an attack.

I recoil. Ella pulls her arm back toward her chest like I burned her. Her eyes shift—panic, betrayal, and then a cool nothingness.

"It . . . It doesn't matter here," I say. The words are sticky in my throat. And after I've said it, I regret it, because it seems to minimize something that surely matters to her, here and everywhere.

She pulls her sleeve back down to the heel of her hand and clamps the fabric inside her fist. But even with her wrist covered, my eyes keep drifting back to it.

I've heard of siren tattoos before, but I've never seen one so close. Certainly never touched one.

I don't pretend to have done a careful study of *Captain's Log,* but I know there's a passage on sirens. Strange fish-women Kos claims he saw on his voyage. Beautiful enough to be tempting, but not quite *right*. Not human. I don't know whether Kos actually saw—or thought he saw—them or if they're a metaphor.

Nowadays, when someone says *siren,* they don't mean a

fish-woman living in the sea. They mean a woman who'd rather lie with another woman than with a man. People don't tend to use the word kindly.

"What's next, then?" Ella says.

I shake my head, feeling heat rise in my cheeks. "Right. Let's check your arabesque." I hold out the silks for her to take.

She's careful to position her hands around mine, never brushing my skin.

My body is tingly and uncertain. I can't stop looking at her sleeves. She won't look at me at all.

I have too many questions. They feel too rude, too personal, too thorny.

Who put that tattoo on Ella's wrist? What man was so offended by her existence?

When she rises, she commands the silks, flowing through them as easily as though they're water.

"Is that right?" she says.

So many questions. I swallow all of them. "That's perfect."

18

ELLA

There's warm bread at dinner, and no one gets upset with me when I eat seven rolls. We're in a kitchen with stone walls and a suffocating cloud of sulfuric peat smoke.

I haven't been able to look straight at Natasha since she saw my siren. She and Katla spend the meal whispering. I keep inventing scenarios in my head: What if she and Cassia were once friends, or more? What if Natasha knew Cassia went to Terrazza when she fled Kostrov? What if Natasha figures out what Cassia was to me and why I'm here?

Fortunately, it's hard to spend too much time worrying about this, because Ness talks so profusely that I can't hear myself think.

"I promised Twain we'd meet him and some of the other guards at the hot pools tonight." She tears off a dainty corner of bread. "We should all go."

Gretta's bottom lip pulls back. "I would literally rather swim in the Grand Canal than watch you and Twain eat each other's faces."

Sofie tilts her head toward me. "Twain is Gretta's older brother. He and Ness are seeing each other. There's no actual face-eating involved."

"Sad. Palace life would be so much more interesting with a dash of cannibalism."

"I bet Andrei enjoys some light cannibalism on the weekends," Sofie says. To me, she adds, "He's our least favorite guard."

"I'd rather you not suggest my father hires cannibals," Gretta says.

Katla gasps. "Your father is Captain of the Guard? I can't believe you never mentioned that!"

"Hey!" Gretta says. "I don't—"

"So," Ness says loudly, "you'll come to the hot pools, yes? The guards are lovely. And there's always a chance Nikolai will join."

My lungs constrict.

Natasha raises her head. "What? The hot pools tonight?"

I can't help but feel like she lifted from a trance at the sound of Nikolai's name. *Why so interested, Natasha?* My palms itch.

"We'll all go," Ness says.

"Except me," Gretta says, "who will be avoiding the face-eating."

Katla waves a hand. "I have an important date with my bed."

So an hour later, I follow Ness, Natasha, and Sofie into the heart of the palace.

When Natasha pushes open a door to an interior courtyard, the wind breathes cold and wet on my face. I haven't felt fresh air since my arrival at the palace this morning.

"The Stone Garden," Sofie says, opening an arm to the cobbled path. "Just in case your idea of beauty starts and ends with rocks."

We twist through a maze of fountains and sculptures, then a massive glass structure looms into view.

A redheaded guard pokes his head out of a clouded glass door, releasing a burst of warm steam. "Good evening, flyers."

I bunch the fabric of my sleeves in my fists, just to be safe.

"Gregor," Natasha says. "Don't you have a pregnant loved one to care for?"

"I'm on duty," he says.

"Yes, you look like you're working terribly hard."

He looks genuinely hurt. "You know I'd be with her if I could."

I frown between the guard—Gregor—and Natasha as they disappear into the glass building.

"Are they related?" I say. They have the same slender, freckle-dappled noses; the same knobby knuckles and over-long limbs.

Sofie laughs. "No, but they should start telling everyone they're cousins. They could pull it off. Come on. Let's go inside."

When I blink to clear the fog from my eyes, I see plants. More than I can count. They line every wall. Hang from every lattice. Although only a few steps ahead of us, Ness and Natasha and Gregor have disappeared in the tartan of overlapping branches.

The flowers stretch the limits of my vocabulary. A violet bloom too thickly petaled to be a violet; a scaly tangerine tower; blossoms beaked like birds.

"You'll get used to this sort of thing." Sofie nods to a potted tree beside us, its roots slithering in and out of its dirt like a sea serpent in waves. The tree is a skein of branches and a spray of leaves. A horde of ants marches up the trunk, unbound by gravity. "The royals have . . . expensive taste."

Half a dozen young men in guard livery cluster around a sunken pool at the middle of the conservatory. A few have their pants rolled up to their knees, feet dangling in the water. Ness is already kissing one of them passionately.

"Well, that's more than I wanted to see," Sofie says.

"They, um, look very happy together."

Sofie snorts, then gestures to the pool. "Shall we?"

I worry for a moment we're meant to take off our full-suits, but Sofie only rolls up the legs and sits on the edge of the pool like the guards. A more elegant woman, like Maret, would probably take issue with exposed ankles, but as far as joints I'd like to hide go, my ankles rank relatively low.

I take off my slippers and pull up the fabric of the full-suit to my knees. The ground beside Sofie is damp, but when I slide my feet into the water, I sigh.

"Good, right?" she says.

The water burns. My feet prickle with cold, then hot. All the legs swinging around the edges of the pool invent a current, sending miniature waves lapping against the rocky lip. Natasha and Gregor sit across the water from us.

Sofie swirls her hands in the pool. "If the ocean felt this good, I might not mind the Flood."

"How do they heat it?"

"They don't. It comes from some underground hot spring, or something."

I hear Nikolai's name before I notice him. It's—*Nick*—and then—*King*—and then—*shit, stand up*—whispered among the guards. Hasty bows. Then a figure in the steam.

On our voyage from Terrazza to Kostrov, our ship passed a pod of killer whales. One of the sailors pulled me aside and pointed at the ocean.

"See that shadow?" he said.

"No," I said, but then I did, an elongated balloon of darkness just under the surface. It slid airward, a hooked fin, an oblong back, a sleek black head.

This is how Nikolai emerges from the fog. Blurred, then sharp all at once, muffling the greenhouse of its happy chatter at the emergence of his sleek black hair on his narrow white face.

His mouth curls into a smile without teeth. Gray eyes flit from one face to another, and when they land on me, they catch, unrecognizing.

I can't breathe.

The eyes stay fixed a moment too long.

He looks at me, and I look back at him, and I wonder if he feels it the way I feel it. That there is something monumental about the other person.

He'll be the first person I ever kill, and my eyes will be the last thing he ever sees.

Then the moment breaks. Gregor gets to his feet, offers a hand to help Nikolai. Natasha says something I can't hear—because they're too far away or because my ears are full of cotton? Nikolai joins them at the edge of the water.

He rests his hand on Natasha's wrist, the bandage wrapped there. She waves him away—*It's fine, it's fine*. A lazy smirk tugs his mouth.

I hate him. I hate his lazy smirk. I hate the way he's looking at Natasha.

"Are they friends?" I ask.

"Natasha and Nikolai?" Sofie says.

He looks so comfortable. Not like the leader of a small nation. Just a seventeen-year-old boy with a girl too pretty for him at his side. The guards around him, taking Gregor's cue, ease back into their own conversations. A few fiddle with their holsters, guns, but no one looks on edge. This is normal, I realize. Nikolai has no enemies in the palace; certainly none among this young cadre of guards.

Natasha smiles. It might be coy. It's definitely nauseating.

"Yeah," I say. "Do they know each other well?"

Sofie shrugs. "Two beautiful people living under the same roof? Yeah. They gravitate toward each other."

I must look at her sharply, because she shakes her head.

"Not like that," she says. "Nothing romantic or anything. I mean, up until now, he's been engaged." She pauses. "You were at the festival, right?"

I nod.

"So you heard about the marriage thing? That he's going to marry another Kostrovian?"

"It's a lie," I say, almost definitely too loudly. I glance around. None of the guards are looking at us. "I understand why it's not worth his time to marry the princess from Illaset, but why would he marry some random Kostrovian girl? He'd be better off waiting until the New World settles and marrying the daughter of whoever claims the most territory."

"Maybe he needs an heir on the way sooner than that," Sofie says.

I blink. She's right. What better way to cement his rule than to have an heir?

"I could maybe see Nikolai marrying a girl without a title, though," Sofie says. "He's not as pretentious as you'd think." She glances at the nearest pair of guards, then lowers her head to mine.

"Okay, he is. But I feel bad for him. Even though my father is an ass, at least he's family. Nikolai has no one."

"Oh?"

"Parents dead of cholera," she says, nodding at Nikolai, "sister exiled."

"Sister," I say.

"There's a wild story for you," Sofie says.

"Tell it, please." Or I will burst into flames.

"Well," Sofie says conspiratorially, "the Kostrovian throne always goes to the eldest son, so Cassia wouldn't have ever ruled while Nikolai was alive. That's his sister's name, by the way. Cassia."

My heart presses at my ribs. The sound of her name wakes it in my chest, like a tree held in shade that's just remembered the taste of sun.

"Right," I say softly. "Princess Cassia. Everyone knows that." My throat hurts.

"Anyway," Sofie says, "four or five years back, their parents died, and Nikolai didn't know how to rule a country. Gospodin had helped the old king plenty, so he stepped in, and he's been helping ever since. Apparently, Cassia was a total nightmare to Gospodin. Screaming, throwing things, you know. Obviously, I never saw any of that, but Natasha told me about it. I don't know if she saw, or if Nikolai told her."

For a moment, the idea stuns me. But then I consider that this information came straight from Nikolai.

There's a reason I can't picture Cassia, my Cassia, throwing a temper tantrum: Because she never would've done it.

"Okay," I say, "so what happened?"

"She tried to convince Nikolai to help her oust Gospodin, but Nikolai wouldn't budge. He knew how much Gospodin meant to Kostrov. So he exiled his own sister. She's living in Cordova or something now."

My breath catches.

Living in Cordova?

They don't know. Even within the palace, people don't know that Cassia's dead. Maret warned me this might happen—that Nikolai might've kept Cassia's assassination a secret. But there's something uniquely tragic about hearing Sofie say it out loud. My world shattered the day Cassia died; shouldn't the palace have at least trembled?

"Did . . ." I'm scared to ask it; I'm scared not to. "Did Natasha know Cassia, then?"

"I guess she must've." Sofie smiles. "I was actually made a flyer about a week before she got exiled. I never met her, but I ran into her and this brigade of advisors in the hallway. The guards got mad at me for being so lost."

I think if I open my mouth, my heart will leap out of it.

"She didn't notice me or anything," Sofie says, "but seas, she's gorgeous."

All I can do is nod.

Across the pool, Nikolai looks up at us. He tilts his head, curious. Then he smiles at me.

This is why I'm here.

I smile back.

19

NATASHA

The king of Kostrov is sitting next to me. Our legs are touching. He sat beside me and put his feet in the water, opening his knees wide so that one brushed my thigh. I had a choice: Stay and be brushed or shift out of the way and risk offending him.

I stayed. Of course I stayed. He's the king of Kostrov.

"I wasn't sure you'd join us," Gregor says.

"Nor was I," Nikolai responds. He reaches to touch the water with his hand, then pulls back. He slides three gold rings off his long fingers. Sets them on the towel beside him.

"To what do we owe the pleasure?" I say. "Surely you have someone better to spend time with than Gregor."

"Oh, I'd never willingly spend time with Gregor," Nikolai says. "But I heard you were going to be here, so I thought I'd make an exception."

"If you weren't my king," Gregor says, "I would be very offended."

Nikolai laughs. His eyes land on mine again. They're more gray than blue, like a rocky seafloor through ten feet of ocean. He wears a golden crown and a golden necklace—the Sacred Breath sails, about the size and position of his heart. His lids are heavy, sleepy, almost, like he's been afforded such security throughout his life that he's lost the ability to keep watch of his surroundings.

I'm surprised by how casual he is beside me. When I was young and new to the palace, I often dreamed we would be friends: me and the royal siblings, clever Cassia and quiet Nikolai. But Cassia was exiled years ago and Nikolai has always been an elusive king.

To Gregor, Nikolai says, "Actually, I'm only here tonight because Gospodin is in Grunholt. Some meeting of Righteous Mariners. And so the ox is freed from his yoke."

I laugh. Nikolai looks at me strangely, and I shut my mouth, realizing too late that it wasn't a joke. I didn't realize a royal could work hard enough to consider himself an ox.

I scramble for something to say, and the first thing I land on is: "Your speech at the festival was lovely."

"Lovely?" he says.

My mouth feels dry. "Very articulate."

He laughs lightly but his shoulders relax, and only then do I relax too. "Gospodin's ridiculous plan."

I'm thinking of Adelaida's voice. *I want you to marry Nikolai.*

I press my hands against my thighs. "Was Princess Colette mad?"

Nikolai shrugs. "I only met her twice," he says. "She seemed to be under the impression Illasetish wine was better than Kostrovian gin."

Gregor puts a hand to his chest. "Profanity!"

Dryly, Nikolai says, "I do imagine it would've made for a difficult marriage."

"Well," I say, "I'm sure the announcement thrilled plenty of other Kostrovian girls."

He raises his dark eyebrows.

My cheeks warm. I feel suddenly embarrassed, childish, as though I've thrown myself at Nikolai without meaning to. As though I've implied I am one of the many Kostrovian girls.

"I saw one girl faint dead away," Gregor says. "Your admirers are many, Your Royal Highness."

Nikolai laughs again in that light, single-syllable way. "Yes, well. I'm sure Gospodin will have a long line of beautiful, sea-fearing idiots for me."

My body jolts. I hope Nikolai didn't feel it. It's just—his anger. He's never even met these girls. Maybe he's just struggling under the pressure. I can understand that. I wouldn't like to have my whole life orchestrated by councilors either.

"You think Gospodin will choose someone for you, then?" I ask, trying to keep my voice light, trying to ask like I have no personal stake in the answer.

"Let's talk about something else," Nikolai says, turning his gaze away from me.

And just like that, Gregor is asking about the new shipment of Roenese liqueurs the Keeper of the Purse—one of the wealthiest officials in Kostrov, in charge of government finances—had imported, and if Nikolai had the chance to try any of them.

Nikolai only stays another few minutes. Another guard arrives to tell him he's needed in a meeting. What kind of meeting might happen so far past sundown, I don't know. Maybe one of the stodgier councilors heard Nikolai was fraternizing and decided to put a stop to it.

Either way, Nikolai stands, scooping up his rings, and Gregor stands with him.

"Have a good evening, Miss Koskinen," Nikolai says.

"Oh." I blink. His crown catches the candlelight. "Natasha. Please."

"Then you should call me Nikolai."

Heat spreads through my stomach. "Okay. Many breaths, Nikolai."

They're halfway to the door when I realize one of Nikolai's rings is still sitting on the towel next to me. It's small—a golden band with tiny black stones. "Wait," I say. "You forgot this."

He glances back over his shoulder. Half of his mouth slides up in a lazy smile.

I feel everyone's eyes on me. Us.

"Keep it," Nikolai says.

Then they're gone.

I close my fist around the ring.

The pool has gone silent.

One of the guards, Zakarias, whistles. "Tasha wants to be queen," he singsongs.

"*You'd* want to be queen too, if you stood a chance," Ness, arm hooked around Twain's waist, shoots back.

"Oh, come off it," one of the other guards, Sebastian, says. "We all know he'll end up married to some Heather Hill girl Gospodin picks out."

Even though I said almost as much to Adelaida, it hurts to hear it from someone else. Even if that someone else is a nineteen-year-old guard with wine staining the front of his shirt. "Are you kidding?" I say. "Gospodin and I are famous friends."

Titters. When you've been in the palace as long as I have, your whole history becomes common knowledge. Like the fact that your mother, in her last year as a flyer, called *Captain's Log* an illustrious paperweight. Like the fact that you haven't exactly gone to enough Sacred Breath services to make amends.

"Oh, go back to drinking your pilfered liquor," Sofie says. Across the water, she shoots me a sympathetic smile.

Next to her, Ella's face is frozen. Her lips are a line.

I frown. She doesn't even seem to see me.

Slowly, people do as Sofie says and start talking again.

I look down at the ring in my palm. The fine metalwork. The shine of the stones. I don't care what the guards think. I don't care that Katla thinks it's impossible.

I'm going to do this.

I'm going to be queen.

20

ELLA

"Gregor, Zakarias, Mattias, Twain," Sofie tells me over breakfast, pointing around the kitchen at the guards. "Those are the good ones. If you ever need anything, ask one of them."

Gretta sits down across from us with a bowl of porridge. "What are we talking about?"

"I'm teaching Ella who to look out for."

Gretta rolls her eyes. "You don't have to *look out for* anyone. Kostrovian guards are the best in the world."

"The best at what?" I say. "Cornhole? I play a mean game of cornhole."

Ness sits next. "Ooh, are we playing lawn games? I love lawn games."

"Of course you do," Gretta says, not unkindly.

I glance back at the stove. Katla's and Natasha's heads are bent by the porridge pot. I can't see Natasha's face; Katla looks serious.

"What's up with them?" I ask.

Sofie hesitates. "Natasha mentioned she wanted to talk to all of us about something this morning."

We don't have to wait much longer to find out what. When Natasha and Katla sit, neither of them have bowls. I guess whatever they want to tell us was too important to remember porridge.

Natasha puts her palms on the table and leans in. Lets out a breath. Quietly, she says, "I have news. Adelaida doesn't want me to tell you, but"—she glances at Sofie—"I found out we're not going on the royal fleet."

Silence.

Then Ness says, "I don't understand."

If I'd had any plans of surviving to the Flood, I imagine this news would be quite distressing. I try to look troubled.

"I guess they're being really careful about the rosters for the ships," Natasha says. "They're only letting important, powerful people on."

"But we're the flyers!" Ness says. "We *are* important!"

Natasha lifts her hands. "Look, Adelaida didn't want me to tell you because she didn't want you all to worry. We're working on a plan."

"What plan?" Sofie says, her eyebrows wrinkling.

A pause.

That's when I notice the thin chain around Natasha's neck. At the end of it, half-hidden behind her hair—a golden ring, hanging like a pendant.

Oh. So that's how it is.

I fold my arms over my chest and lean back.

"Adelaida thinks I have a shot at being queen," Natasha says.

Ness lets out a happy breath and clasps her hands together.

Gretta looks skeptical. "Even if he *did* pick you, you think you'd be able to bring a bunch of guests?"

"Yes," Natasha says curtly. "Besides, why do you care? You're on the fleet either way."

"Well, I think it's a wonderful idea," Ness says. "Just like a fairy tale."

"Yeah," I say, not disguising my bitterness well enough. "Doesn't every little girl dream of falling in love with royalty?"

Natasha looks up. She frowns, like she can't quite make sense of me.

I wish Cassia were here with me. If she were, she'd roll her eyes at the way Ness is giggling, the way Natasha says, "When I'm queen, we'll all be safe. Nikolai will keep all of us safe."

It's sad. That Natasha thinks Nikolai can do anything for her. That she thinks he is capable of care. That she thinks he is her best chance of surviving the Flood.

I almost feel bad. But when I see the way she tugs on her necklace—slides the ring back and forth across it—my heart hardens. She wants to trust Nikolai? Fine. She'll see how far that gets her.

Cassia trusted Nikolai, once. By now, everyone should know better.

21

NATASHA

Adelaida's furious at me for telling the other flyers that we won't be on the fleet. She pulls me into the hallway while the girls are working on their elements.

"You're not usually this much of a fool," she says.

"I'm not a fool," I say. "Look, they didn't run for the hills, did they? I wasn't about to lie to them until the Flood hit."

She pauses. Narrows her eyes. "Why didn't they?"

"Sorry?"

"Run," she says. "I know Katla. I was sure she'd be livid."

"I calmed her down."

Adelaida runs a hand down her round chin, thinking. "They all seemed a little too chipper this morning, given the circumstances, didn't they?"

"Why shouldn't they be chipper?" I cross my arms. "I told them I'd be queen and get them spots on the fleet. I've never let them down before."

Adelaida's eyebrows meet above her nose. "You told them that?"

"Yes."

"Good."

I'm suddenly uneasy. Why does Adelaida sound conspiratorial?

"If I'm queen," I say slowly, "I will be allowed to bring them all, won't I?"

Adelaida gives me a hard look. "The rosters are finalized. It's not exactly an empty sign-up sheet. And there's a waiting list, assuming the ships from Grunholt ever get here, and that's finalized too."

I shake my head. "You know what? I don't want to hear it. If I'm queen, I'll *make* them make space for the flyers. I don't care what it takes."

"It's not about making space for a few more people," Adelaida says. "It's about making space for all the food they need."

"Do you believe in me or not?" I say.

Adelaida lifts her hands in mock defeat. "No. You're right. Get the crown, and the rest will follow."

I can't tell if she means it. I have to believe she does.

I turn to go back into the studio, but she grabs my wrist.

"No jewelry during practice," she says. "You know that." Her eyes are fixed on the ring around my neck. "Where did you get that?"

I lift the necklace. It catches a flash of light. And I smile at her.

"Well," she says. "That's a step."

The week goes by fast. Getting Ella up to speed eats up most of my own practice time, which I'm fine with, given how much my wrist still hurts when I put weight on it. I don't see Nikolai again.

On Friday night, I tell Adelaida I'll be joining the other flyers—except for Katla, who never goes—at the Sacred Breath service the next morning. I'm terrible about attending, but I know I'll need to get better at it if I want Gospodin and the other councilors to take me seriously. On Saturday morning, though, I'm so exhausted that I don't hear the other girls heading out the door. When I finally wake up, hair sticking to my saliva-crusty face, I'm beyond late.

I pull on a dress and boots in a hurry. Charge out the door without brushing my hair. It's freezing. There's an old expression in Kostrov—*a liar sun*—and that's what the weather is today. Clear and achingly cold.

I forgot a jacket.

When I get to Our Lady of Tidal Sorrows, people are already streaming out. So I'm cold and disheveled for no reason.

I sigh.

I'm about to give up and head straight back to bed when I notice that the crowd is transfixed by the notice board in the window.

A large sign has been posted there. I can't make out what it says from here, but I don't have to. All those who can't read have shuffled out of the way to make room for those who can, and those who can are reciting it loudly.

"Three weeks' time," a nasal woman says. "The royal ball will be three weeks from today, and any girl in Kostrov can go."

Two boys with patches on their coats scuffle for a better view. "No fair," one of the boys says. "I want to go."

"It's just like the Whale King fable," the other one says.

"'Behind seven mountains, beyond seven seas—'"

The nasal woman shoos them. "Don't go speaking Tamm's nonsense in front of Our Lady." She catches me staring and her face transforms into a crooked smile. "Is that my favorite flyer? Will you be performing at the ball?"

I say that I don't yet know and give her a polite smile, setting off again before anyone can ask me more questions. I pull my arms around my torso and wish for a new cloak. The wind is crinkly cold. On the way back to the palace, I pass a single thin-armed maple tree, a valiant burst of nature amid the city, its leaves just beginning to blush.

In my head, as I walk, I see how much of the story I know by heart; as it turns out, I know all of it.

Behind seven mountains and beyond seven seas, there was a whale king who needed a queen . . .

22

ELLA

"**B**ut Ella isn't ready for a performance," Natasha says.

"She'll be fine," Sofie says.

"She'll be a mess," Madam Adelaida says, "but we have no choice."

"This may come as a surprise," I say, "but I have both ears and feelings."

It's my second week as a Royal Flyer, and any confidence I accrued from getting selected has shriveled and died. Each morning, we wake up and stretch, and Adelaida reminds me I'm not flexible enough. The studio is so cold at dawn that my feet go numb if I'm not wearing slippers. Then we have our breakfast of rye porridge and cloudberries. We practice our elements until lunch. Once we've eaten, we practice more. We practice individually and in synchronization, fundamentals and complicated elements. When it's finally time for dinner, my stomach is roaring. We eat bread—good!—and muskrat—very bad. Sometimes we have seal, which tastes fine but makes me sad because, obviously, seals are adorable. After dinner, we have, in theory, free time until nine o'clock curfew. When Sofie first explained this schedule, I thought it sounded manageable. But that was over a week ago, when I was young and foolish. Now, old and wizened, I know better.

I don't have free time after dinner. I don't have free Saturdays and

Sundays. While the other girls filter away to read or sleep or giggle with the guards, I practice. Adelaida tells me I'm about as graceful as a porpoise, and just in case such glowing praise might get to my head, she adds, "On land."

Maret and I did plenty of planning. She asked: What will you do if the guards find you snooping? I asked: What will I do if the assassins Nikolai sent for Cassia are somewhere in the palace? She asked: What if Adelaida sees your tattoo and tries to dismiss you?

Neither of us ever asked what would happen if I simply did not have the chance to leave the flyer studio. Other than the first night, when we went to the Stone Garden, I haven't explored an inch of the palace. I haven't even gone outside. Nor met with Maret. We agreed to meet at the apartment every Saturday, but I had to stand her up last weekend as Adelaida put me through more drills than should exist. I hope she doesn't think I've run away and pledged allegiance to Nikolai. I don't dare send her a letter, so she'll just have to wait.

At the announcement of Nikolai's fairy-tale ball—*a chance to dance with the king, goodness me*—Adelaida told us we'd be performing for the partygoers. Everyone is stressed, but Adelaida and Natasha seem particularly manic about it. I try not to let my disdain drip over when Natasha starts talking about Nikolai and her stupid plan, but I'm not sure I do a very good job.

And now, here they are, arguing about how terrible my planche is. A planche is a move that requires a flyer to hold her body perfectly perpendicular to the silks with just her arms and the strength in her abdominals, and they can argue as long as they'd like, because I'm simply never going to be able to do it.

"If we put Ella in the middle," Natasha says, "and Ness and Gretta on the outsides, it can still be symmetrical."

"Except that Ness can't do half of these elements either," Adelaida says. She glances around. "Speaking of which, why isn't Ness here?"

"Because she's already practiced ten hours today?" Natasha says.

"That," Adelaida says, "is not the attitude of a principal flyer."

"Well, good thing we'll be dead before Ness can audition for principal," Natasha says.

A stillness descends over the room. Natasha and Adelaida watch each other, bristling.

Sofie clears her throat. "Here, Ella, I'll support your feet if you try again."

When Adelaida finally waves us away to sleep, Natasha disappears into her own bedroom while I follow Sofie into ours.

"You're doing really great," Sofie says. "Don't listen to Adelaida. She's just like that."

I give Sofie what I hope is a grateful smile. I think it's more of a wince. I've never been so sore in my life. "She and Natasha fight a lot?"

"You have no idea."

Every night, when I finally collapse into bed, sleep clubs me over the head. I fall asleep quickly and easily, my arms deadened, my shoulders aching. But every morning, long before I'm rested, twisty dreams chase me awake. Drowning dreams; flooding dreams; *bang bang* Cassia shot in the head dreams.

When I wake the next morning, I lie in my small cot and stare at the ceiling with no way to know how many hours of sleeplessness I'll have to endure until the other girls finally rise. I can feel the lump of the barometer. It faces knife-side down beneath my pillow. In case I ever forget why I'm here.

The darkness flattens the shapes and shadows of the room.

Sometimes, I consider getting up. I could start practicing early; could make a fire in the studio; could sneak my way into the heart of the palace. But there's something about these post-nightmare hours that locks me to my bed. If I move an inch, my arms touch freezing sheets. When I breathe, the sound is scratchy and bare. I feel like a tree has grown up through the middle of me and taken my lungs with it, pinning them to the ceiling and me to the bed.

Get up, I tell myself. *Stop lying here.*

I can't leave, I say back. *This tree is in the way.*

Or maybe the nights just last so long because they're the only time I let myself really, truly think of Cassia. It's the only time I can't help myself.

The first time Cassia kissed me, just a few days after we met, we were drunk on cider in the Terrazzan foothills. Maret was asleep in a rented room at an inn. We were supposed to be asleep too, but Cassia coaxed me outside. She pressed her back to the inn's wall. Her curls—springy, blond—framed her face. When she smiled, I could see the sharp points of her canines.

"If you were a noble's daughter at the palace," she said, the words slow between long drinks from her golden glass, "I would've hated you. Here, try this." And then she was tipping a sip of her cider into my mouth, cold and crisp and dizzying, and she kept her eyes fixed on me the whole time.

I swallowed. Licked my lips. "Hated me?"

"Hated you! You're beautiful, so I would've been snarky, but you probably would've been even snarkier back. So I would've told the servants to spill wine on you every time we had a party."

Had anyone ever called me beautiful before? "Maybe I would've started a new trend. Wine bathing."

"Then I would've spread a rumor that you kill baby bunnies for fun," she said.

"I'd tell everyone the bunnies were plotting against the throne."

Cassia took another sip. "Then maybe I'd have to tell everyone you were a siren."

My heart jolted. Did I look afraid? How much could she see written on my face?

"You're right," she said. She pointed to me. Touched her finger to my collar. Then hooked the fabric of my shirt, pulled me a little closer. Her stomach, her chest against mine. I could feel the shape of the royal brooch she always wore, hidden behind the fabric of her coat. "Who would ever believe that?"

When I lie in bed, I can still taste the sour cider from her mouth. I can still feel the point of her canine tugging my lip.

I've started to worship the sun. Dawn spreads the curtains from the window with rosy fingers. The tree melts. I melt. The other girls snuffle and wake. I pretend to do the same.

I think I've done a fine job pretending until the end of my second week, when Natasha pulls me from the stretching circle. She has a mug of nettle tea in each hand. She offers me one.

I take it.

"You're not sleeping," she says.

"What?"

"I can tell," she says. "Drink it. It's good."

I take a sip. It's hot, but it's not good. "It tastes like grass."

"Why aren't you sleeping?" she says, ignoring me.

Her expression isn't cold, exactly, but it's intense. She seems to wear that expression when it comes to anything to do with the fly-ers, whether it's an element Ness isn't getting right or an old injury in Sofie's knee or Gretta waving away food, insisting she's not hun-gry, even when she's hardly eaten all day. On my family's farm, we had a herding dog to help with our sheep. When I first met Natasha, I thought she looked like a fox, but the longer I spend with her, the more she reminds me of that herding dog.

"It's . . ." I fumble for an answer. "Stress?"

"About your flying? About the storms?"

Seas, she doesn't rest. "A little of everything, I guess."

Her eyes search mine. Her mouth is tight.

"Can I go back to stretching?"

She waits a beat. Then she nods. "Drink your tea."

When dawn stirs the next day, Saturday, I expect I'll spend all of it practicing again. But when I wander into the studio, Natasha waves me out.

"Go," she says. "Take a day off. Your body will thank you."

"Are you sure?" I say.

"Go back to sleep," she says, and a smile tugs at her lips.

I don't go back to sleep, but I do go back to the flyer bedroom, where the other girls are getting up and changing.

"We're going to see Pippa today," Sofie says. "Do you want to come with us?"

"Oh, you should come," Ness says. "Pippa's so lovely."

Katla snorts. "Sure, that'll be fun. Here, Pippa, meet your replace-ment."

"Don't listen to her," Sofie says. "Pippa will love you."

"Oh," I say. "Um. Natasha thought I could use some more sleep. So. I'll just stay here."

My heart is buzzing. The other flyers are leaving. I won't be trapped in practice. Yes, I should go see Maret, but—this is a chance to explore. To finally start gathering information about Nikolai, about Cassia.

I'm going to see the palace.

I'm finally going to find something to report back to Maret.

23

NATASHA

I wait for the other flyers just outside the blue door. I was waiting in the studio, but Adelaida started bustling around making pointed comments about Nikolai and what sort of wedding gown his bride will wear. It made me feel nauseated. Nervous. So here I am, shivering in the wind. When the door opens and only three girls appear, I frown. "Ella's not coming?" I ask.

"Nor Gretta," Sofie says. "Come on, let's go."

"Gretta's still upset we didn't invite her last time," Ness says.

"Let's walk, then," I say. "We'll turn into icicles if we don't get moving."

As we set off into New Sundstad, I try not to notice the Ella-shaped space. It's not unusual for Gretta to hang back, but I half expected Ella to forgo a nap and come meet Pippa instead.

Actually, I'm not sure what I expected. She's too slippery for my expectations to stick. Now that she's been flying with us for two weeks, I feel like we know each other. But when I think about what I actually know of her—questions I'm sure I must have answers to—I realize I am blank. Does she have family in Kostrov? She has a faint accent, but she's never mentioned her home, her parents. Anytime any of us asks a personal question, she gives us an answer silly and distracting enough that we forget we've never heard the truth.

"What of your family, Ella?" Ness asked once over dinner.

"Funny you should ask," Ella said. "I'm actually Gabriel Gospodin's illegitimate daughter. Don't tell anyone."

I laughed. Ness looked affronted.

And what about the tattoo? I'm not sure whether any of the other girls have noticed.

Clouds have subdued last weekend's sunshine. The blustery air is salty with sea and the promise of not so distant snow. A gondolier shouts to a fishmonger; a butcher yells at a pigeon for pecking at the strips of seal meat hanging out his window.

Before Storm Five, I never realized New Sundstad was so full of birds. Flocks of pigeons on every street corner. Rafts of ducks in the canals. The occasional hawk, austere from the eaves of a tall building. When the butcher yells at the pigeon, I ask the girls, "Did all its friends fly off without it?"

"That's kind of tragic," Sofie says. "You wake up from your nap and realize ninety percent of your species left you."

It takes us an hour to walk as far as Southtown. With each passing bridge, the grime on the buildings grows a little thicker; the water in the canals a little grayer. My mother and I lived all over New Sundstad, but we always seemed to end up back in Southtown. When everything starts to smell like dead fish, Ness puts her sleeve over her nose and says, "Oh, foul."

I can't call it foul. This is where I was born. I am of dead fish.

"Did Iskra let Pippa into the house without a fight?" I ask.

"As if Pippa would tell us otherwise," Sofie says.

"Iskra has taken to calling it *The Clipped*," Katla says. "As in, the place flyers go when they get their wings clipped."

Shivers runs down my shoulder blades, where wings would grow if I had them. "Cute."

"There's just three of them there now," Sofie says. "Iskra, Pippa, and Rasa."

"What happened to Josephine?"

"She went back to Roen," Katla says. "To find her family."

"I can't believe she never wanted to meet me," Ness says. "It could've been such a lovely rite of passage."

Katla catches my gaze and rolls her eyes. Between the two of us, we've seen our share of flyers come and go. On the whole, they don't tend to be eager to wave goodbye to the palace. Josephine left right after the storms started. Her family was an ocean away and she was convinced they would die in the storms. There's no right way to handle the end of the known world, but there are certainly a few wrong ways. Throwing away a position as a Royal Flyer is a wrong way.

My footsteps stiffen as we near a familiar stone bridge. I'm tempted to call out to Sofie, who leads the pack, that wouldn't it be faster to take a different route? But Sofie charges ahead, and Ness chatters on about ex-flyers, and even Katla doesn't realize what this street means to me. I lock my teeth and walk on.

A little farther down, there's a ruined apothecary with a smashed front window and a heap of shattered jars across the floor. On the left, a butcher's shop, a stuffed goat head watching us from the glass display with wide, rectangular eyes. That butcher's shop closed years ago.

Above the butcher's shop, there is a window. The curtains are closed. A trickle of light fractures the edges.

This is the last place my mother and I lived before she died. A dusty apartment, too hot in seal season and too cold in bear season, above a butcher's shop.

I wonder if they still have the sofa my mother lounged on, feline, absorbing scraps of sun. Where she read me fables from Tamm while I sat on the floor, dragging my fingers through the dust in tidal swirls.

How badly I wished those stories were true. That I could be a brave princess with eleven clever sisters and a true love. That I could find a castle made of ice or make friends with a bird or row down a river to a different world. That I could go somewhere, be someone, else. This was before I discovered that Tamm's stories are just like Kos's stories. Just meant to keep us calm. Just meant to give us false hope.

There is no river to a different world. My mother taught me that.

I'm still staring at the window of the butcher's shop when Katla clears her throat.

"Tasha?" Katla says. "I hate to break it to you, but if you're trying to befriend that goat, he's dead."

"Right. Sorry."

I hurry to catch the other flyers. A few subdued minutes later, we stop at our destination.

It's a blue door—I think it might be an homage to the door in the flyer hall in the palace. The buildings on this street creep in on each other, shoving their neighbors like oversized teeth in an undersized mouth.

My heart pounds steadily faster. The shadows of the bowed buildings want to swallow me. They recognize me and want me back, and I don't want to go. I pull at my collar.

Sofie pounds on the door with her fist. "Pippa! Iskra!"

The door opens a crack. Big eyes gaze up at us from knee-level. I recognize him, but only vaguely. Children's faces never make an impression on me. The boy turns back, calls into the house.

"Mama?" he says.

My whole body revolts at the word. Sweat leaks down my neck. If I'm ever to have some sort of maternal instinct, it has yet to develop, because when this small, helpless animal stares up at me, all I can think is: *I can't save both of us.*

Maybe that's what my mother thought too. She couldn't save both of us. She chose to save me.

I hear a shuffle from behind the boy. The door opens all the way, revealing a woman a few years my senior, shark-like, with a flat white face and wide-set eyes.

"Iskra," I say.

"Flyers," she says. Then she breaks into a pointed-tooth smile and says, "Pippa will be glad to see you."

I let out a breath. I'm never quite sure which version of Iskra to expect. She's as likely to smile as she is to tell you to take a swim in a canal. Once, in one of her smiling moods, she told me she couldn't afford to be predictable, because nothing about life outside the palace is.

We shuffle single file into the narrow home. It's as dark and leaky as the tunnels beneath the Stone Garden.

Iskra's little boy stares at me through eyes that I'm quite sure are too big to be human. He clutches Iskra's arm. "She fall."

I try to scoot farther away from him, but in the cramped corridor, there's nowhere to scoot.

"She did," Iskra says. "It was very embarrassing."

"And how's the bad leg doing?" I say.

Sofie bats me with the back of her hand. "Tasha," she says. "Don't."

"I'm just being friendly," I say. "Showing collegial concern."

Iskra holds her son tightly to her chest. Her eyes narrow. "Pippa is upstairs. I'd hurry up there, if I were you, before I change my mind about letting you in."

As we climb the narrow stairs, Sofie whispers, "Don't goad Iskra."

"It's the kid's fault," I say, probably louder than I need to. "At least I didn't shatter any bones when I fell."

Sofie grabs my arm and drags me the final few steps to Pippa's door.

"Oh!" Pippa says when Katla knocks. Her smile is the brightest thing in this house.

During those sticky tavern table conversations about which of us is prettiest, people—mostly men—seem to run in circles until they decide the answer is probably Pippa. I'm too tall; Katla too small; Sofie too plain; Ness too made-up; Gretta too sour. And then there's Pippa, of short but not too short stature, thin but not too thin build, skilled at making cosmetics look natural, and naturally beautiful underneath it, with bronze-colored skin and perfect teeth. Pippa is palatable to everyone.

I know this because people—mostly men—feel compelled to tell me the conclusions of these conversations when they see me on the streets. And how do they expect me to respond? *Thank you—I'll strive to hunch so that I cut a less intimidating figure.*

Pippa ushers us inside a room too small for five. The room is dominated by a cot. An atlas rests against the pillows.

"Did you steal that from the palace?" I ask.

"No," Pippa says.

Sofie tugs at one of Pippa's long braids. "But?"

Pippa smiles. "But Gregor might have."

Sofie is bursting with questions and Pippa answers them all cheerily, but my eyes keep going back to that atlas. What was Pippa doing before we showed up? Flipping the pages, wondering if she'd survive on Illaset, or Cordova, or Skarat? It reminds me of my mother with *Tamm's Fables*. Dreaming of a world behind seven mountains and beyond seven seas.

I press my palms to my thighs to dry the sweat.

This isn't your bedroom. This isn't your life.

"Have you managed to find a job yet?" Sofie asks.

Pippa smiles too brightly. "I have some leads."

"Won't one of the youth flyer studios hire you?" Ness says.

"They've been struggling to get enough girls to pay for lessons what with everything going on," Pippa says, "so they're not really hiring new instructors." A pause. "But I'd be nervous to take a fall with the baby, anyway, so it's just as well." Her hand lights on the gentle curve of her stomach. It's just barely visible underneath her gray tunic.

How long has she been pregnant? How long did she hide it from us?

My stomach clenches, shunning the notion that life could grow inside me. Ever since my body decided I was an adult—a cold morning at age fourteen when I woke up with blood on my sheets—I've had a recurring nightmare in which I look down to discover my stomach is inflated like a balloon. Everyone around me is full of congratulations. They coo and touch my belly. And for the life of me, I can't remember how my body got this way.

While the other flyers share birth control herbs, tell each other of the pillowed words whispered by lovers, and grow into women in ways still foreign to me, I remain. When my stomach cramps and I feel blood in my underthings, relief washes over me. But I have no reason to be so afraid. I've never slept with a man. I've never even kissed one.

Ness has Twain; Pippa has Gregor. Even Katla had a brief romance, with a noble boy from Roen who swept into Kostrov, took her heart, and swept out again. Gretta, I think, is too young and too famous as the Captain of the Guard's daughter to have any romantic conquests. I'm not sure about Sofie, but I've never seen her stare at a man as lovingly as she stares at Pippa.

Ness sets a hand on Pippa's stomach. I flinch, but Pippa doesn't seem to mind.

"Oh, you're going to be such a good mother," Ness says. With fervor, she adds, "I can't wait."

"I can!" Katla says. "No offense, Pip."

Pippa smiles. "None taken. "

"I just think there's something really lovely about it," Ness says. "The idea of bringing a child into the New World. It's like Kos says—'a mother is a vessel for the tender cargo of humanity.' I think that's beautiful."

"Thanks, Ness," Pippa says.

"I think I'd like to have kids," Sofie says. "Especially in the New World. They'd be part of a blank slate, you know? It's a chance to make the world better than you found it."

"Exactly," Ness says. "And Pippa, you'll come with us, won't you? On the fleet?" Ness looks at me. "You can bring Pippa, right?"

I feel nauseated. "I hope so."

"Why is Natasha bringing me on the fleet?" Pippa says.

"She's going to be queen," Ness says, so matter-of-fact. "And she'll protect all of us."

"That's lovely," Pippa says, her voice light and level. When she looks at me, I know she doesn't buy it. Pippa knows well enough—maybe better than any of us still sheltered by the palace—that anything that sounds too good to be true probably is.

Sofie gathers Pippa's hands up in her own. "How is Gregor?" she asks. "He's been to see you?"

"Nearly every day," Pippa says.

"And has he proposed?" Ness says.

Pippa laughs. "Nearly every day."

Ness squeals. Katla winces.

"You should say yes," Sofie says. She's looking at Pippa seriously, her brows drawn, her jaw tight like she's trying to keep herself steady. "He wants to put a roof over your head and food in your stomach. Say yes."

"It's not that simple," Pippa says. "Gregor is one of Nikolai's favorite guards."

There's a long silence. I'm the first to realize what she means.

"Ah," I say. "The fleet."

Pippa nods.

Ness frowns. "What about the fleet?"

"With hundreds of guards to choose from for the royal fleet," Pippa says, "why would Nikolai choose a guard who needed to bring a wife and child with him?" A pause. "Just in case Natasha can't add me to the roster," she adds.

Outside, water *drip, drip, drips* off the corner of the roof.

"You know," Sofie says, "it's pretty shitty of you to be that self-sacrificing."

Pippa smiles tightly. "I love him too much."

Drip, drip, drip.

There's a buzzing in my head. Filling my ears. I press my back against Pippa's creaky wall.

A child to care for. A suitor to worry about.

Pippa doesn't stand a chance.

I press a hand to my stomach. Empty, empty, empty. Black spots dance in my vision; I don't know when I started holding my breath.

Why would you choose to love someone when this is what it does to you?

24

ELLA

I wait in the flyer bedroom until all the other girls have gone to visit Pippa. I've never been alone in this room before, and now that I am, every nightstand brims with possibility.

I glance at the door and swallow the bubble of guilt. I rifle carefully and quickly. I'm not sure what I'm looking to find, so I don't spend longer than a few moments in each girl's belongings. Sofie: a few books; a hidden stash of hazelnuts. Gretta: a silky baby blanket, folded into a small square and tucked out of sight. Ness: a well-annotated copy of *Captain's Log*. Katla: a bundle of incense and a leather-bound book, singed around the edges, like someone considered burning it. When I open its brittle spine, I frown at the jumbled letters inside. I can read Kostrovian nearly as well as I can read Terrazzan, but this looks like Kostrovian untidily mixed with something else. There are letters whose sounds I don't know and words I can't translate.

"Kostrov was one of the longest holdouts against the Sacred Breath," Cassia once told me. "Before they came, our land was called Maapinn. Then the crusaders from Grunholt showed up and bastardized our language, our culture, our beliefs. If I sound bitter, it's because I am."

"Oh, hush," Maret had told her. "Without the Sacred Breath, you wouldn't be a royal."

"Except that our however-many-greats-grandfather was the leader of a powerful clan," Cassia answered. "So we would've been basically royals."

"You expect me to believe," Maret said, "that you would have settled for *basically* royal?"

My fingers skim the words of Katla's book. Is this Maapinnen? A prayer book, maybe?

I flip the page. A clump of folded letters falls out and lands at my feet. I peek at them just long enough to see that they're from someone named Henri and all dated from two years ago.

I shove them back into the book. Maret won't care about any of this.

Adelaida's room might have something useful, but when I put my ear to her door, I hear her humming softly to herself.

I hurry into the heart of the palace.

The first person I see is a maid with a pile of tablecloths so tall, she balances them under her chin. I step to the side to make myself unobtrusive, but she does the same. She attempts a curtsy, and when she doesn't drop a single cloth, I consider applauding.

"After you, Miss Neves. Many breaths."

I don't know what part of this interaction to be most confounded by. For starters, I have never in my life been curtsied at. More horrifying, this is a maid I've never even noticed who knows my name. And while I don't particularly care if the maids gossip about me, what if the guards do the same? I haven't seen any sign of the men Nikolai sent to assassinate Cassia, but that doesn't mean they're not somewhere in the palace.

I walk a little faster. Soon, I find myself passing an elegantly carved wooden door, and I press my ear to it. No sound filters out.

I open it. The room is some sort of salon, with a wall filled with several life-size portraits. My eyes flit past one, two, three, and the fourth buckles my knees.

Princess Cassia Aleksandra, the nameplate reads. Seas, why didn't Nikolai take down her portrait?

She smirks at me from her frame. Did I really doubt she was as beautiful as I remembered? She was more.

"Ella, right?" I feel the roughness of hands on my shoulder, turning me. I blink at a face full of freckles, crooked nose, thinnest stubble. It's jarring after so much Cassia, like the sudden dark after blowing out a candle. Gregor. I recognize him from the hot pools.

"Look, you shouldn't be in here." He glances around. "What are you doing?"

I didn't hear his footsteps. Cassia's portrait plugged my ears with wax.

Another voice, male, sounds around the corridor's corner.

"Yeah, one second," Gregor calls back. He pulls me into the hall and shuts the door behind me. Softly, he says, "Are you lost or something? The flyer hall is in the east wing."

I force myself to swallow. "I . . . Yes. Sorry."

"It's fine. Just—"

Another guard appears around the corner. I think I saw him at the hot pools too. He gives us a funny look, and I step away from Gregor.

"Thanks for the directions," I say. "Many breaths."

I hurry away before they can ask me anything else.

I'm still halfway in a daze when I pass a set of windowed double doors. I loop back and open them.

Shelves of books and books and books line the room in long rows. Through the windows, the Stone Garden stands stoic under a gray sky.

When Cassia told me about the library, I imagined thirty, forty books. That was as many as I could hold in my head at once. But there are thousands. One shelf is just copy after copy of *Captain's Log*, each one a different edition, a new translation, a glossier binding.

After a sweep of all the aisles, I conclude there's next to no fiction among all these books. It's a scandal.

I wish I could talk to Maret. What does she hope I'll find? Nikolai's personal diary?

At the far edge of the library, a haphazard assortment of texts sits on the shelves facing the fireplace. These shelves aren't as dusty as the others.

I glance at the hearth. The chairs. Perhaps these are the relevant books. The recently read.

My hands fly over their spines, fueled by the fear of Maret's disappointment. *Two weeks in the palace, and you haven't discovered anything? No new information about the state of things? Nothing to help you kill Nikolai?*

But what I find is, distressingly, exactly what one might imagine finding on a royal library's shelves. Books proclaiming the nation's naval might. A botanical encyclopedia with a green cover of native Kostrovian plants. In a history of the Royal Flyers, I read:

Maapinn was ruled by warring clans before the Sacred Breath's intervention. Scouts—usually agile young women—would climb to the highest branches of the bog oak trees to see over the thick mist that shrouded the island. *Visitors often exclaimed, upon seeing the girls in their swaying branches, that it looked like they were flying. When members of the Sacred Breath from Grunholt converted Maapinn and established a clan leader as king of Kostrov, they generously agreed that girls of such beauty and grace deserved a place in the new regime. In the early years of the Royal Flyers, the group performed dances in a ring of oaks in the gardens of the palace. As the group evolved, the trees were replaced by wooden beams and fabric silks. The emblematic oak trees have since died, but the tradition of flyers lives on.*

"What are you doing?"

I slam the book shut.

Gretta stands in the doorway. She tilts her head to the side. Her eyes are narrowed.

I shove the book back on the shelf. "Reading about the flyers."

"We're not supposed to be in here without special permission," she says.

"But you're in here."

She points at her feet. "I'm in the doorway. It doesn't count. Besides, my father is Captain of the Guard." She waves her hand like she's scooping air toward her in the universal gesture of *get over here*.

"I thought all the other flyers were off seeing Pippa," I say.

"Why should it matter whether or not all of us left the palace?"

When I stop opposite Gretta, I realize for the first time that she's well taller than me. She's terribly lean, save a youthful roundness to her face that the other flyers have already lost.

"I didn't realize we weren't meant to be in here," I say. "That's all."

"Don't think I haven't noticed the way you deflect questions about yourself," she says. "You're obviously hiding things."

My wrist burns. "Hiding things? What would I be hiding?"

"For starters, you're not Kostrovian," Gretta says. "You have an accent."

"My parents were Terrazzan," I say. "I moved here as a little kid. I don't see what difference it makes."

Gretta crosses her arms. Her eyes hold mine, searching. If there's youth in the rounds of her face, the sharpness of her gaze more than makes up for it. "I was raised among palace guards," she says. "I have very good instincts for when I'm being lied to."

My heart beats higher and higher in my chest until I can feel it thudding against my throat. "Well, my congratulations to you and your keen investigatory eye. If you'll excuse me, I've just been informed I'm trespassing." I turn myself sideways to slide past her.

I feel her eyes following me as I hurry down the hall.

Well. I finally have news for Maret:

I'm being watched.

25

NATASHA

We're a more subdued party than we were on the way out. Somehow, I end up in the front of the group, and I take us the long way, past the rye fields and the distant boglands. Grass of amber and emerald, carved out by pools that reflect the low sky. The trees are spindly, fewer and farther between with each passing year.

Where else on this world can you stand on the edge of a stone street, city-loud with voices and industry, while staring across a canal and onto a land that looks so viciously wild? New Sundstad must be one of the most beautiful places person and ocean ever co-conspired to create. I wish the sea wouldn't take it back again.

When I stop, the flyers stop with me.

"Have you ever seen a peat harvester wander off the path like that?" I say. Someone lopes across the boglands, forgoing the elevated wooden paths. The shape resolves itself into a man, hooded, with friends behind him. I count six in all.

Everyone looks at Katla for the definitive verdict.

"Never," she says.

"Look at the two in the back," Sofie says. "They're carrying something."

I squint and realize she's right. The two hooded figures trailing the small pack have a long rectangle of shadow—a crate, I think—hoisted between them.

Katla frowns. "Smugglers, maybe? Packing out food and supplies before the royal fleet can take them?"

Ness looks aghast. "That's illegal."

"Illegal?" Katla says. "In that case, it must be something else. Maybe they're going to a birthday party."

"It looks like they're headed north too," I say. "We'll see them when we get to the Wharf District."

But by the time we've reached the end of the Division Canal and ocean opens in front of us, the men are gone. It's starting to mist and the sun is fading to a memory, so we hurry the rest of the way to the Gray Palace, the men and their crate forgotten.

When the palace rises into view, it seems only fitting that the surrounding sky has gone to black. The windows burn gold, rejecting the night. The palace is a beacon in the darkness.

Since I was nine, this is always what it has been. Kostrov: dark, wild, dangerous. The Gray Palace: life.

Inside, the other girls drift back to their room. I knock on Adelaida's door.

"Come in," she says.

She's at her desk flipping through letters. A lantern burns beside her, casting her in an uneven glow. I shut the door behind me.

"I know you said there wasn't room for the other flyers and provisions on the fleet," I say.

She looks up.

"But if I'm queen," I say, "there must be a chance I can change the councilors' minds. Even if it's just a tiny chance. There must at least be a *tiny* chance, right?"

Adelaida surveys me. "You don't really want to know the answer to that."

I let out a breath, slowly. No. I don't. I want to keep believing I can fix this for them. For all of us.

And a terrible part of me wonders—even if only one of us will survive, isn't that better than no one?

"But if Nikolai really cared for me," I say, "and I told him how important it was to me—"

"You're right," she says, placating. "I can't be sure Nikolai will pick you. I can't be sure you'll be able to call me your personal advisor and get me a spot on the fleet. I can't be sure about the girls. But Natasha—you're my best shot."

My throat is dry.

"The ball is in two weeks," Adelaida says. "All the girls who think they have a chance will show up. You'll perform, and Nikolai will want to talk to you, and you'll flirt, and you'll make sure he knows that you are a better match for him than the shiniest heiress in all of Heather Hill. I asked Gospodin about you, by the way. If he could imagine that Nikolai marrying a flyer would create the kind of compelling narrative they're after."

"And?" I say.

"He hoped I was talking about Ness," she says.

"Ness loves Twain."

"I know. But Ness also loves the Sacred Breath. And Gospodin. So take a hint." She pulls open the top drawer of her desk and produces a leather-bound book.

"What's that?"

"You really are your mother's daughter, aren't you? Take it."

It's heavier than it looks. The pages are thin and many. When I flip open the cover, I see: *On the day the Flood pulled the last land asunder, I took to my ship with a crew of fifteen men.*

"You're giving me *Captain's Log*?" I say.

"Skim it," Adelaida says. "At least pretend that you're a good daughter of the Sacred Breath. If you want to be queen, you'll need to have an intelligent conversation about these things with Gospodin."

I tuck the book under my arm. "Okay."

"Oh," she says, "and give me my cloak back. Entitled little thief."

In my room, I lay *Captain's Log* open on my quilt. Up to this point, I've carefully kept my attitude about the Sacred Breath noncommittal. When we're made to go to holiday services at Our Lady of Tidal Sorrows, I pretend to listen while mapping out choreography in my head.

I smooth the pages and begin to read. I'm surprised to find that questions of belief soon go from my head. Kos's voice is brash and bold. He never once seems to consider that he's anything less than divinely chosen to survive the Floods, and I begin to understand the magnetism of his certainty. He writes of whales with flippers longer than a man is tall. There are wonders: the night sea shimmering white and palest blue, like someone spilled milk in the waves. There are horrors: the shape of a ship on the horizon, clarifying through the fog to reveal the only crew: a man swinging from a noose on the mast.

The tales are marvelous and grotesque in equal measure, and

they make me feel a curious sense of the fantastical that I've only before ever felt when reading *Tamm's Fables*. Is it a crime to compare the two? Does the comparing make *Captain's Log* more fictional or *Tamm's Fables* more real?

I read until my room gets cold and I have to bury myself under blankets, only my hands and eyes peeking out, to stay warm. I'm about to tuck the book away for the night when I catch a word halfway down the next page.

Sirens.

I hold a breath in my cheeks and read on.

After I tended my sails and my journal, I took a gaze through my telescope. Lo! A kelp raft, and on it, a naked woman. A stranded soul? As I neared, I saw this was no ordinary woman. She was a face of extraordinary beauty, but with a tail made for a fish. My men rushed to join me. All exclaimed of her comeliness. Swept up in a current of curiosity and infatuation, I trimmed my sails to reach her.

She spotted me when I was but a hundred yards away. From her mouth came a song as sensual as I have ever heard. It rang like freshwater on a salt-parched sea. On her call arose two other women. Their heads broke the surface of the water. They looked at me inquisitively, then joined their sister's magnetic song.

I found myself leaning so far over the rails of my ship that I thought I might fall into the sea. When my men joined in, we threatened to capsize the ship. The fish-women laughed coyly, and I thought them as infatuated with me as I with them.

But as I neared, I noticed a blackness in their eyes. Where there should have been white was an abyss of dark. Their irises were not round, but long and slitted like seeds. I heard a voice, masculine in tone and as if from outside of me, thunder: Antinous! Do not allow sirens to tempt you. Your wife awaits in the first dry year.

This voice broke the spell of their song. I recoiled violently from these siren women. At my disgust, they bared ugly, needled teeth.

I adjusted my sails at once. My men protested, but I called directions over the sirens' angry songs. By the time I left the women on their raft, I no longer saw the beauty with which they had tricked me. They were no more beautiful than a storm-tossed sea.

Not for the first time on my voyage, the voice—which I had come to think of as a voice of all humanity, a collective of human experience with more wisdom than any one man could amass during his life—had saved me. I now saw the sirens for what they were: temptresses. What would they have done had I not come to my senses? Stripped my skin with their sharp teeth and worn my bones for crowns? The sea maidens delighted in beguiling. I swore to never trust such a woman.

We sailed on.

Slowly, I close the book and set it upon my nightstand. I knew that the passage on sirens had something of this shape. But I didn't expect it to settle into my stomach the way it has, with a chill my blankets can't fend off.

Nowadays, when the Sacred Breath accuses someone of being a siren, they don't mean to call her a fish-woman with seedy eyes and needle teeth, but they mean to call her a monster just the same. *Temptresses,* Kos wrote, for singing and looking beautiful and having no interest in men. They are given the burden for tempting; Kos takes no blame for being tempted.

I think of Ella, with her quick mind and sharp tongue and reluctant smile. With her eyes as dark and prettily lashed as a deer's. With the line of her shoulders, her arms, strong and steady as she pulls herself into the silks.

If Kos's sirens were real, and not just some sea-induced halluci-nation, I should like to think they didn't even notice him sailing by. Perhaps they were just singing to each other. Perhaps they were just living their lives.

Twelve hundred years have passed since Kos wrote these lines, and yet, so little has changed. Perhaps powerful men will always want to own women. Perhaps powerful men will always want women to be beauty, meant for their own consumption.

As I lie in bed, waiting for sleep, I raise a hand to my lips. With the tip of my finger, I skim the surface of my teeth, imagining they are needles.

26

ELLA

As the royal ball barrels toward us, I begin to panic. Madam Adelaida, the dear, reminds me each day that my flying is very bad indeed, and however nervous I am, it's probably not nervous enough. A week passes after Gretta corners me in the library. I'm hoping Natasha will feel generous again and give me a day off, but I'm out of luck. Maret's going to be furious. It's coming up on a month since Storm Five struck; some of the servants are whispering predictions about the onset of Storm Four. Storm Four's meant to be the "Panic of the Livestock," and though I don't know exactly what it's going to entail, I have a feeling my parents, if they were still tending our farm, wouldn't be looking forward to it.

Three nights before the ball, Natasha stands up from her place at the long kitchen table and says, "Ella? We've more work to do."

"But René hasn't brought out dessert yet," I say. The kitchen already smells of sweet cardamom bread soup.

"And yet, the world continues to spin," Natasha says. "Come on."

As we leave, Sofie calls after us, "I'll save you some, if there's any left."

The studio is hushed. The kitchen is too far away to hear even muffled voices. The loudest thing is Natasha's gentle breathing.

I stop at the silks that have become my own. She takes the ones beside me.

When we climb, I watch her, copying her movements, imagining our limbs are connected by a puppeteer's long strings. She moves; I move. She hooks her leg in the silks, and I do the same. When she hangs her head back, her ponytail dangles, a flame erupted from the tip of a match. The way she moves is stunning. To acknowledge this, I have to call it envy. If I call it anything else, it makes me feel like I'm betraying Cassia.

There's one move that I hate with a special passion, and not because it's more difficult than the others. Natasha keeps her legs pressed tightly together as she spins herself in the fabric. Soon, the silks are wound around her ankles, knees, hips, like a glossy tail.

The siren lift, they call it.

Natasha watches me as I fuse my legs into a tail of my own.

There's a siren lift in our upcoming performance, so I don't think Natasha is doing this just to torment me. But still, when we hold the position, her eyes meet mine, and a flush creeps up her neck and into her cheeks.

"Good," she says. "That's enough for tonight."

Natasha unravels quickly back to the floor. I stay in the air. The long strings between us snap one by one.

"I'll practice a little longer," I say.

She crosses her arms. She looks like that determined herding dog again. "You should sleep."

"I'm fine." I don't want the other girls to be awake when I go back to the bedroom.

I wait for her to leave, but she doesn't. She stands at the base of my silk, neck craned, watching me tangle and untangle myself.

"You're doing really well," she says. "I know Adelaida can be harsh."

"She's not so bad," I say.

"You're unyielding," she says. "It's impressive."

If I'm unyielding, it's only because I have no other options. If I lose my stubbornness, I might not be able to kill Nikolai, and without revenge, what's left of me?

"I'm not, really," I say.

"Then what are you?" she asks.

I look down at her. "Sorry?"

Natasha's hands press against her thighs. Her eyes are streaked orange by the flickering lamplight. "You don't talk to any of us. When we try to get to know you better, you just—quip. Evade. I don't know anything about you."

"Does it matter?" I say.

"It matters to me," she says. There's a pause. "Just tell me something. Anything."

I think of the flush on her freckled cheeks in that siren lift. Does she want to know the story of my tattoo? Or the part that came before? How it felt to weave my hands in Cassia's hair under a beech as old as the land itself? Her lips, soft, hummingbird-light, grazing mine for the first, second, third time? The shiver of the wind, of the beech, of me?

I'm silent for so long, I'm surprised Natasha doesn't leave.

I keep my voice soft so it's less likely to break. "The last time I saw my brothers, they'd forgotten my birthday." I don't know why that's what comes out. I don't know why I'm telling her anything.

Natasha lifts her chin. Ten feet apart, our eyes meet.

"They were twins," I say, tightening my grip on the silks, "so their birthday was a double celebration and easier to remember. But they were four years younger and we were playing a game and . . . and they forgot."

I've relived the game so many times now that I can't remember if we invented it that day or played it all our lives. The game went like this: I was a big, scary badger who ate identical little boys for breakfast. Filip would say, *No, you're supposed to be a friendly badger,* and Milo would whack my arm with a stick and say, *Take that, badger,* and then my mother would come laughing outside and say, *Ella! I've run out of apples, and how am I to make your birthday pie? Off into town, quick as you can. Boys, go with her.* But they couldn't go with me because they were aghast at having forgotten. Filip said, *But I meant to come up with a song for you,* and Milo said, *And I meant to kill a mouse for you, like the cats do,* and so while I set off for town, and apples, they set off to make my birthday trove.

"Were?" Natasha says. "They *were* twins?"

Storm Ten came while I was gone.

"They're dead," I say.

"I'm sorry," Natasha says.

"Don't be," I say. "Everyone has the same story these days. Waters rise; everyone drowns."

Again, even softer: "I'm sorry."

The only other person I've ever told about my brothers, about that birthday, was Cassia. Why did I start telling Natasha? She's not my friend. And she's certainly not Cassia.

"I'd like to practice," I say. "If you don't mind. Alone."

"Of course," she says. She lets herself out.

By the time the door is closing, quietly, gently, in Natasha's long-fingered hands, a tear has made its way to the tip of my nose. I lift a hand from the silks to dash it, furious, but I'm too late.

It falls fifteen feet. I don't see where it lands.

27

NATASHA

I close the studio door and press my back to it. Why is it that I'm so desperate to ask her more? *Your brothers—what were their names? How did they die? Did they have your eyes, gold in the middle and brown around the edges?*

Ella doesn't want me to check on her. She doesn't want me to know who she is.

I stand by the door for a long time anyway, hoping she comes out. She doesn't.

The next day, I wait for Ella to say something about that moment—that *whatever*—in the studio. Nothing. When another day passes without so much as a lingering glance, I get mad at myself for hoping. I should be focusing on the upcoming flight. Not Ella.

I finally manage to make it to a Sacred Breath service. I flip through *Captain's Log* every night before bed. I join the guards every time they gather for a mind-numbing card game. None of it makes a difference; I can't seem to run into Nikolai again.

The day of the ball arrives with the first frost. My window is bordered by the faintest white fur. Real snow won't be far behind.

I try to dress without ever leaving the safety of my quilt. On top of my rehearsal full-suit, I add my lumpy maroon sweater, two pairs of woolen socks, and mittens for good measure. I know I'll have to take them off before I get on the silks, but they're staying put until the last possible moment.

When I tromp into the studio, Adelaida and Gretta are already there. Gretta stops working on her saltos to giggle at me.

"I was cold," I say.

Adelaida's eyes sweep me up and down. "You look like you're on an expedition to Skarat."

"Or a little Sacred Breath orphan wearing donated clothes," Gretta says.

Adelaida smiles. "Or a farm girl gone to collect the turnips before they freeze."

I press my mittens to my cold, cold face. "Gretta, do fifteen pull-ups."

Gretta's mouth falls into an angry O. "Adelaida started it."

"But I can't punish Adelaida for being a bully," I say.

"Correct," Adelaida says. "Gretta, do your pull-ups."

Gretta grumbles loudly as she descends to the ground and starts in on her punishment. I slide across the wooden floor on my thoroughly socked feet to join Adelaida by the mirrors.

"Are you ready for tonight?" Adelaida asks.

"I'm offended you would ask."

Adelaida considers me. "Fine. Are all your girls ready for tonight?"

"You know," I say, "it doesn't seem fair that whenever they've done something bad, they're mine, and whenever they've done well, they're yours."

"Oh," she says, "you're feeling cheeky today. I'm sure that will go over swimmingly with the esteemed members of the court."

I ignore her and take the choreography notes out of her hands. One of the court sculptors was commissioned to build a long pool across the first floor of the Iron Hall for tonight. We'll perform over the water. Partygoers can watch from below or on the balconies that run the hall's second-story perimeter. It was Gospodin's idea. According to Adelaida, he said he wanted to remind everyone about the beauty of water, that the ocean isn't here to destroy but to purify and re-create. I imagine it's easier to appreciate the beauty of water when you're not counting down the days until it kills you.

Nikolai's birthday is racing toward us. Everyone at that ball will be thinking about how soon he'll have to choose the next queen.

We spend the morning reviewing final choreography. We've never performed over water before, but there's no arguing it'll be striking if it goes to plan. Adelaida created this routine just for the ball. When I first looked over the moves, I asked her, "So your plan to help me win over Nikolai is to give me a thousand solos?"

"If my director gave me this many solos when *I* was principal," Adelaida said, "I'd be queen right now."

Just hours before the ball begins, three palace seamstresses rush into the studio with folds of fabric heaped in their arms. Normally, we would've been practicing in our performance full-suits for days, but since Gospodin only unveiled his plan for this ode-to-the-ocean performance a few weeks ago, we've cut it as close as we could have.

"Finally," Adelaida says. "Try them on, quickly, so we have time to make adjustments."

I pull mine on in the shelter of my bedroom. It's tight and cool against my skin. The fabric is a dazzling and dark ultramarine, with an airy skirt that breezes over the backs of my legs and hangs open in the front. My legs are enclosed in fabric but my arms are free. The neck has a high collar and a risqué cutout from the base of my throat to my breastbone.

I stare at my reflection for a long moment. It's the most daring full-suit—the most daring thing—I've ever worn. I inspect it for a moment longer, following the curve of the fabric up my hips, my shoulders, down to the seamless lines of my arms—

My reflection's eyes go wide, realizing.

Sleeveless full-suits.

I run to the studio.

All the flyers have left the studio to try on their full-suits. Only Adelaida and the seamstresses remain.

"Oh, Miss Koskinen," one of the girls says, her pink cheeks rounding. "You—"

"Do you have spare fabric?" I say. I hold up the trail of my skirt. "More of this?"

She ducks her head to her bag of scraps. "This?"

I gather all the gauzy fabric in my arms, start for the door, and loop back for a pair of scissors.

"In something of a frenzy, are we?" Adelaida says.

"Thanks," I say to the seamstresses, and hurry out again.

I push open the door to the flyer bedroom. Gretta, half-naked, jumps and presses her full-suit to her chest. "Seas, Natasha."

Ness bounces over to greet me. "Oh, Tasha, so pretty. Your hair with that blue."

It doesn't take long to count; four girls here. Ella is missing.

Katla and Sofie, as wings, are pulling on full-suits of vivid blue. Gretta and Ness wear a dusty, pastel shade. All lined up together, we're a gradient, swatches of the ocean as the sun arcs overhead.

Katla tugs her braid free of the full-suit's collar. "What are you carrying?"

I begin cutting long strips of the gauzy fabric. "Wrist scarves. Like all the fashionable Roenese ladies wear."

"Won't that make it harder to perform?" Gretta says.

"No. Give me your hand."

Gretta looks at the other girls, like someone might jump in to save her from my sudden, aggressive interest in fashion. When no one does, she extends her hand toward me. I wrap a length of fabric around each forearm and tie tidy knots.

"Wow," Katla says, "you got much better at that after bandaging your wrist twelve million times."

"Thanks," I say. "You're next."

When they're all satisfactorily scarfed, I gather my fabric and knock on the door of the washroom.

"Um," Ella says. "Just a second."

"It's me," I say. "Natasha." No response. "Can I come in?"

My heart is starting to hurry from one beat to the next. What if I've overstepped some sort of boundary? What if this is just like when I pushed up Ella's sleeve and exposed her siren? Invasive, aggressive—

The door opens.

Ella's full-suit is palest blue. The strap across her neck trembles as she takes a breath. Her hair is in a loose bun on top of her head. Across her stomach, her arms are crossed.

Adelaida said she wanted Nikolai to spend half the night staring at me. Why would anyone waste their time with that, once they've seen Ella?

I swallow. I hold up the fabric. "I . . . We've decided to wear scarves. On our wrists."

Ella tips her head just barely to the side.

"You don't have to," I say. The words are clumsy in my mouth. "I just thought, if you didn't want everyone to . . . you know, know. All the other girls are already wearing them."

Ella watches me for a long moment. Then she extends her wrist.

"Thank you," she says.

My fingers twitch against the smooth skin of her forearm. I bite my tongue against my lip to focus as I wrap, twist, tie. I can feel her pulse against mine.

"Your turn?"

She takes a length of fabric and encircles my wrist. Her eyelashes make long shadows across her cheeks. Her fingers are warm and careful. When she's done, her thumb lingers against the base of my palm. She doesn't look at me, just at her hand, my hand, our hands. I'm not breathing.

She steps back. My hand drops, burning.

"How do I look?" she says. "Sufficiently like a raindrop?"

My cheeks are hot. "You look like a character from *Tamm's Fables.*"

Her lips curl at the corner. Seas. *I* did that. I made her smile. "Should we finish rehearsing?" she says.

I nod.

She leads the way back into the studio. My throat is dry. The seamstresses exclaim over our dashing new scarves and Adelaida meets my gaze with an expression that says *I see what you just did.*

We're still practicing a few final elements when voices begin clattering through the window.

"That'll be guests arriving," Adelaida says, striding back into the studio. "Natasha, walk with me. The rest of you, go on ahead."

Adelaida's changed into her party dress—a shade of blue darker still than mine with a provocative neckline. On top, she wears a capelet with feathers, dyed cobalt and gold to match the rest of her ensemble.

"The seamstresses are really leaning into the feather look for you," I say. "We'll know they've taken the flyer thing too literally when they give you a beak."

"Natasha," she says, warning.

"You look lovely."

She huffs out a breath. "Thank you."

I glance over her shoulder as the last of the girls—Ella, her curls pinned back carefully—disappears out the door. A pang.

I look back to Adelaida. "Everything okay?"

She gestures with her head to the door. We walk slowly, out of earshot of the other flyers as they laugh, joke. "I overheard a few of the councilors talking when I went to check that our silks were set up right. It sounds like they've already decided they want Sylvia Kanerva as the next queen."

I frown. "Kanerva? Like the Keeper of the Purse?"

"His daughter," Adelaida says. "Keep an eye out."

I've spent most of my life as part of a troupe with other girls, all competing to be the best, but supporting each other for the collective good. Adelaida's warning sits uneasily with me. I don't want to go to war with a girl I've never met.

"I'm not sure about that," I say.

Adelaida stops. Gives me a hard look. "Nikolai's birthday is in two months," she says. "*Get* sure."

28

ELLA

When I step into the Iron Hall, shame washes over me. It's a riot of opulence—of waste—and a reminder of why Nikolai shouldn't be on the throne. We're a matter of months from the Flood, and the palace is wasting food on party appetizers?

I've let myself get distracted. By flying. By Natasha.

I amend the thought. By all the flyers. Not just Natasha. I need to focus.

I've never seen so many people packed into one room. A chandelier glitters from the ceiling. A quartet of musicians plays in the corner, and their music washes through the hall.

The most elegant women sweep through the room in little bubbles; their skirts are so vast that no one can get closer than arm's length of them. There are plenty of more shabbily dressed women too, though, in clean but exhausted frocks.

The men wear suits. I can't tell which are elegant and which are shabby, because all suits look the same to me.

Eyes begin to investigate my body. I glance around for the other flyers. Gretta has vanished among a circle of older guards, all of whom share her sharp nose and light brown skin. Katla is just ahead. I glance over my shoulder, hoping for Sofie or Natasha, but I've lost both of them. I consider hanging back by the door until they show up, but the memory of that night, practicing—of gazing down at Natasha's upturned face, of letting myself cry—rears up. I hurry into the ballroom after the other flyers.

When I reach Katla's side, she glances at me. "You look absolutely terrified."

"Oh, I am," I say.

Katla's lips twist. "I'd be disappointed if you weren't."

"You've been to a lot of these parties?"

"The palace hosts a few every year," Katla says. "Though usually more . . ." I watch her eyes scan the room as she waits for the right word to come. She purses her lips at a huddle of young women in simple dresses of identical mauve fabric, like they all stitched the gowns from the same bolt for the occasion.

"Aristocratic?" I say.

Katla snorts.

Though I'm a month into my time among the Royal Flyers, I still don't feel like I know Katla well. I don't blame her for keeping her distance this close to the Flood. The more people you care about, the more people you have to lose. This is the longest conversation we've ever had.

"I take it you aren't of an aristocratic bloodline?" I say.

"Not unless you consider peat harvesting an aristocratic profession," she says. "Most people don't." She turns her skeptical eyes on me. They're outlined in black and drawn to feline points at the outside corners. "You're not, are you?"

"Farmers," I say.

"Thank the seas. I don't think I could've stood it with another . . ."

She tilts her head pointedly at Ness, who's waving enthusiastically to a girl on the other side of the room.

The girl beams, excuses herself from a conversation with a man twice her age, and glides toward us. Of all the massive skirts in attendance, hers might be the biggest.

"Ness comes from money, then?" I ask.

She nods. A waiter drifts past with a tray of wine flutes. Katla grabs two and hands one to me. "You might need this."

Ness throws her arms around the girl. "Oh, I've missed you! And this dress!"

When they detach, Ness gestures at us. "This is Katla and Ella. And this is Sylvia. She's my dearest friend from Heather Hill."

"It's a pleasure," Sylvia says. Her smile is slight, like she's saving bigger smiles for more important introductions.

Sylvia and Ness have the same posture—a steady sort of confidence that says they both know they're meant to be here. Sylvia's long hair—dark black—is coiled around her head. One silky strand hangs loose by her temple. Her skin is beige, poreless. I wonder if Cassia ever told the servants to pour wine on her.

Ness grasps Sylvia's hand in hers. "Love, I have so much to tell you. I want you to meet Twain. Oh, and your father! Is he here?" To us, Ness adds, "Sylvia's father is the Keeper of the Purse. He's an absolute dear. A true follower of the Sacred Breath."

"As opposed to a fake follower of the Sacred Breath," Katla says.

Sylvia's eyes dart toward Katla, the space between her brows wrinkling for just a moment. But Ness keeps talking and Sylvia quickly smooths out her expression.

"How are you?" Ness says. "Tell me about your dress. Oh! And tell me what I've missed in Heather Hill. I heard Meri had the loveliest birthday party. Did her father really import a tiger?"

I can't resist. "What a gaffe," I say. "It sounds as if Meri copied my birthday party completely."

Katla chokes on her wine.

Sylvia turns back to Ness. "I should tell you, Meri and some of the other girls won't be here tonight."

Ness's lower lip falls. "But I was so excited for everyone to see the performance."

"I'm sorry," Sylvia says. "They thought tonight's festivities were beneath them." Sylvia's eyes drift to the girls in mauve dresses. Two of them have seized a tray of appetizers from one of the waiters. The third is staring at the floor with a face redder than the sugared cranberries.

"Well," Ness says, holding her chin aloft, "Nikolai has invited girls of all stripes to be here tonight, and if Meri and the others think they're too good for that, then that's their loss."

"Of course," Sylvia says, looking at the girls in mauve again. "There's no reason to judge a girl by the fabric of her dress, as I always say."

"Exactly," I say. "That's why all my dresses are made of stitched potato skins. Might as well get the snobs out of the way early, right?"

Sylvia looks affronted.

Ness glances between us. "Sylvia, you wanted to meet Twain, remember? I just spotted him." Ness puts her hands on her friend's shoulders and begins to steer her away.

"Many breaths," Katla says to Sylvia's back. She crosses her arms and turns to me. "Well, this ball is exactly what I expected so far."

I'm about to agree with her when I see something—someone—out of the corner of my eye.

A group of guards stands near the wall. I know some of their faces from meals in the kitchen. Gretta's brother, Twain. Gregor, the guard who looks so much like Natasha. But there's another face among them that I know, and not from my month in the palace. His hair, slicked back, buttermilk blond. His eyes, pale. His skin, paler. His gaze tracks Ness and Sylvia across the room; his tongue slicks a slow sweep across his lower lip.

I know him.

He was there when Cassia died.

Distantly, through water, I hear Katla saying, "Ella?"

I can't say anything. I can't even open my mouth.

He was there. I know him. *I know him.*

Then another voice. Natasha, from nowhere. "Hey. What's going on?"

"Ella," Katla says. "You okay?"

Finally, I force out: "Who is that?"

"Which one?" Natasha asks, following my gaze.

"Blond," I say. "Looking at all the women who walk by like he'd like to cook and eat them."

I watch Natasha and Katla share a glance in my peripheral vision. "That's Andrei," Natasha says.

"We hate him," Katla says. "Remember what an ass he was to Josephine?"

"I thought he was in Mau La," Natasha says. "I hoped he'd just stay there."

"Mau La?" I finally break my gaze away from Andrei so I can frown at Natasha. "Why? When?"

She shifts her weight, looking uncomfortable. "I don't know. I think he was guarding an envoy or something. They're always sending out diplomats to make last-minute trade deals and alliances for the New World."

"How long was he gone?" I ask.

Natasha glances at Katla. "Six months?"

"Not long enough," Katla says.

"Why?" Natasha says. "Do you know him?"

"No." I sound bitter as root. "Of course not."

When I close my eyes, I remember darkness. A canopy of trees to block the spitting rain. The crackle of a campfire and an ember that landed on my leg, hissing.

I remember four men. The clink of their bottles. The fullness of their laughter. The way their conversation whirlpooled around: *Nikolai'll put us on the royal fleet for this*, and *I can't wait to get out of this shit country*, and *What about the girl?*

I remember a face. Skeletal cheekbones and long forehead. Colorless eyes. Andrei crouched in front of me. "I always knew Cassia was a siren bitch. But what about you? Maybe you just haven't met the right man yet."

When I spat, it hit the bridge of his nose. He blinked and leaned back as the other men laughed.

"Fucking siren," he said.

One of them stumbled into the nearby town for ink and needles and more liquor. They gave me my siren, taking turns when someone got too bleary to hold the needles. They drank themselves unconscious.

When I spat in Andrei's face, I hoped he would kill me for it. By the time he was lying facedown in the dirt, cradling a bottle of whiskey, I was glad he hadn't.

Because I would kill him instead.

My hands were bound, so I used the tree trunk to help myself stand up. I stepped over their bodies. I walked into the town and found Maret, told her what had happened while she was away. She cried with me, then she screamed with me, then she planned with me. I'd always thought that Maret loved only one thing: the crown. When Cassia died, I realized Maret had loved two things.

Maret and I talked about going back to that thicket. Killing those men. But we would get to them later. We would let them live, for the time being, because they were under a worse monster's employ. I would tear Nikolai out at the roots. Then all his friends could wither and die with him.

When Adelaida gathers us for our performance, I'm too busy drowning in memories to realize what's going on. To remember that I have to climb those silks with every eye in the palace on me.

If I recognize Andrei, he could recognize me. Did he drink so much that the night vanished from his memory?

I press my wrists to my stomach, crumpling the elegant fabric tied there. If Natasha hadn't thought to give us our scarves, I'm certain Andrei would have known who I was when he saw his handiwork.

We go to our places at the edge of the long pool. When the music starts, we'll swing out above the water and climb to the tops of the silks.

There's no hiding from Andrei. From anyone.

I tighten my grip around my silk.

Sofie puts a light hand on my shoulder. "Are you okay? You look like you're going to vomit."

Cold sweat trickles down the ridge of my spine. "Just nerves."

"You'll do great," Sofie says. "Copy Ness and Gretta if you forget anything."

The Iron Hall is starting to quiet. So many eyes. I feel them scrubbing every inch of me.

A flurry of whispers, a fanfare as Nikolai finally enters the hall. I watch him step to the balcony's edge above us. I try to use my reliable hatred to center me, but I can't shake the feeling of Andrei's eyes.

A screech of violins, preparing.

Sofie is right. I'm going to vomit.

Then, all at once, Natasha is on the other side of my silk. Her face is all I see, cut in two by shimmering blue fabric. Her cheekbones glisten silver. She puts her hands between mine on my silk, our fists in a stack. When she tilts her forehead to mine, her voice makes everything else hushed.

"Watch the water," she says. "Don't look at the crowd. Don't even think about the crowd. Just keep watching the water."

"The water," I say. I feel slow, like I'm stuck in a fog bank.

"That's what I do when I'm nervous," she says. "At the festivals. I watch the canal water."

I didn't know Natasha could get nervous.

Before I can thank her for the advice, she's gone again, back at her own silk, and the violins begin to weep.

As I climb, I stare at the water below, just like Natasha told me to. When I spin and thread and loop myself through the silks, my gaze returns to the water. I try to focus on a spot between the surface and the bottom.

When I finally look up, not at Andrei, not at the crowd, but at the shimmer of fabric and flyers around me, I feel like I'm made of water. We are rain-dropping, cascading, sea-spraying, up and down above our pool.

Is this what Nikolai and Gospodin wanted? Does this make the watching partygoers less afraid of death-by-ocean?

We think we've outsmarted water, with our ships and roofs and barometers. We collect it in basins and sieve it through wool and charcoal so we can drink it. We give it to our cattle and we give it to our grains. Nikolai has installed a pool in the middle of the Iron Hall just for tonight, just for this performance, so that everyone might gather around and marvel at how we have tamed water, when really, it has tamed us.

I'm glad for the nonstop rehearsals now that we're in the middle of the flight. My mind can be elsewhere and let my body do the rest. When I've finished executing my trickiest sequence, I hang still on the silks. Only Natasha keeps moving.

She is water. Flowing and seamless and liquid, her face calm, her hands steady. The whole room is transfixed. I only manage to drag my eyes away from her for a moment. I look to the balcony, near level with us, and I see Nikolai, his fingers curling over the railing's edge, his jaw set, his eyes pinned to Natasha with such intensity, I think I could light myself on fire before he looked away.

The final sequence: wheeldowns, fast as can be, all of us together. We hurtle toward the water. Someone gasps.

I catch myself on the silk inches from the surface. We hang for a breath, the violins humming their final notes.

Then we slide into the water.

When I come up again, the applause shakes the chandelier overhead. Someone's hand touches my shoulder; someone calls congratulations. A towel is draped over me.

I tilt my chin, water running down my nose, and look up at Nikolai.

He still hasn't looked away from Natasha.

A coldness settles in my stomach. I can't put a name to it, but it leaves me feeling unmoored. The hairs on my arms stand on end.

I track his gaze across the Iron Hall, back to Natasha, with her streaming hair, her dripping full-suit, the faint shake in her legs from the exertion of the performance.

She's staring back at Nikolai, and her lips are curling to a smile.

29

NATASHA

Nikolai's eyes are steady as they meet mine. He looks kingly, imperious, adult.

Adelaida wraps a towel around my shoulders. I startle; when I look back to Nikolai, he's walking away from the balcony.

"You look like a drowned rat." Adelaida runs her thumb along the underside of my eye. It comes away smudged with makeup.

"And you look like a giant blue jay," I say.

I'm buzzing too much from the performance to absorb Adelaida's barbs. Every moment on the silks, I felt power refilling my veins, a confidence I've missed since the crane season festival. I feel brilliant and reckless and alive.

"You should go change," Adelaida says.

"I'll dry off as I dance." I hand her back the towel. I'm vaguely conscious of the other flyers gathered behind me, and I know that I ought to debrief with them, but there is Nikolai, striding down the stairs, guards fanning out behind him.

So I walk away from the other flyers.

The crowd moves in eddies. Everyone wants to step out of Nikolai's way, for politeness' sake, but stay close enough to watch him, for gossip's sake. And as I walk through the crowd, people jump, afraid I'll dampen their finery. Then the crowd has parted between us, and Nikolai and I stop, and he tilts his head at me, and I drop into a low, slow curtsy as the musicians start in on a waltz.

"Miss Koskinen," he says, my name made a formal, royal thing on his tongue, "would you have this dance?"

I step forward so we're toe to toe. I'm surprised to find that we're the same height.

"I'm afraid I'm a bit sodden," I say.

"Indeed." Nikolai is smiling. At me. "You're also not wearing shoes." He extends his hand.

I take it.

I have spent most of my life thinking of Nikolai as less of a person and more of a title. With his face so close to mine, our palms pressed, it's harder to forget the young man underneath the crown.

"I haven't seen you since the hot pools," he says.

"Adelaida keeps us rehearsing," I say.

If he minds that my hand is wet on his shoulder, he doesn't show it. Around us, men and women pair off. We begin to dance.

"I like your necklace," he says.

I glance down at it. The ring hanging over my heart. "We're not supposed to wear jewelry to perform, but I convinced Adelaida to make an exception."

"Well, I'm flattered."

"You should be," I say. "She never lets me wear the jewelry the prince of Cordova gave me."

His eyebrows lift.

"I'm joking," I say.

"Thank goodness. I would so hate to fight the prince of Cordova. I'm told he's a biter."

A surprised laugh comes out of me. He's joking too, I know—but does it mean something that he would joke about fighting for me? "Are you enjoying your party?"

He gives one of his single-breath laughs. "It's hardly mine."

He's a good dancer, sure-footed and rhythmic. His grip on my hand is barely too tight.

"But you're the king," I say. "Everything is yours."

I'm pleased to see the way he smiles. I feel as though I've begun to unlock a secret.

"Your performance," he says, "was astonishing."

"Astonishing enough that you might put the flyers on the royal fleet?" I say.

As soon as I say it, I know I've made a mistake. His eyes narrow. His shoulders stiffen. I let the heady feeling of a successful performance intoxicate me. I was too bold. A curtain drops between us.

"You've heard, then?" he says.

I'm grateful he doesn't try to reassure me with a lie.

"I've heard," I say.

"And now you're here," he says, nodding at our joined hands as we twirl across the floor, "because you're trying to get on the royal fleet a different way. You play Gospodin's game well."

"Gospodin's game?" I say.

"It was his idea," Nikolai says. "That I marry a Kostrovian girl."

"Whatever game Gospodin plays," I say, "you're the most powerful man in Kostrov. That's why I'm not dancing with Gospodin. I'm dancing with you."

Nikolai's smile is a serpentine thing, sly and curling. The lift of his lip reveals teeth as white as young pearls. "You pander to my ego."

"And you to mine. I imagine I'm the envy of every girl here, being your first dance."

"You're the prettiest," he says, almost off-handedly, and I can't tell whether it's meant to be a compliment or whether he really believes it. "And none of the merchants' daughters can fly." That's also not precisely true—half the girls in Kostrov have taken a flying lesson at one point—but I'm smart enough not to speak my mind this time.

Instead, I say, "Did Gospodin ever ask you whom you wanted to marry?"

Nikolai frowns. "No."

I tilt my head nearer to Nikolai's, the better to keep my dangerous words private. "Has anyone ever asked you?"

"No," he says.

"Well, maybe they should." I know I'm walking on a knife's edge. Nikolai trusts his councilors. Gospodin more than any of them. But I can also hear the tinge of bitterness in his voice when he says Gospodin's name. "Like I said. You're the most powerful man in Kostrov. I don't see why you shouldn't get to choose for yourself."

We step one-two-three-four beats to the music. He lets go of one of my hands, so I spin away from him, then he pulls me back. "You're bold."

"Too bold?"

The music ends, and he raises my hand to his lips. "Just bold enough." He presses a kiss to my knuckles. Softly, he adds, "Natasha."

This is the first moment I believe I could truly be queen.

The song has scarcely faded from the air when a man I recognize vaguely, his cheeks alcohol-flushed, arrives with a young woman on his arm.

"Your Royal Highness," he says, dropping low. "My daughter, Sylvia."

Sylvia and her father both ignore me as I'm exchanged out. A new song begins. I catch Nikolai's gaze one last time over Sylvia's shoulder. Then the crowd pushes me, and he's gone.

Before I can pick my way to where the flyers are clustered, Gospodin appears in front of me in a white suit. He holds a flute of fizzing wine by the stem and greets me with a smile.

"Mariner Gospodin," I say.

"Miss Koskinen. A lovely performance."

"I've been meaning to talk to you since the festival. I was horrified. About the mud."

"Why?" he says.

I wasn't expecting that. "Because—because those people disrespected the crown and the Sacred Breath."

"And that horrified you? Those people were expressing frustration because they fear they won't be allowed on the royal fleet. You have no empathy for them?"

"I . . . Of course I have empathy for them. We all want a spot on the fleet."

He looks at me, head tilted slightly. Calculating. "You overheard Adelaida and me talking that day in the Stone Garden, didn't you? I should've known as much."

I stand up a little straighter. "With all due respect, Mariner Gospodin, I think you're making a mistake. The Royal Flyers are an important part of Kostrovian history. I don't think any fleet would be complete without—"

He holds up a hand. "Every Kostrovian life is an important part of Kostrovian history."

I shut my mouth.

"You're a determined girl, Miss Koskinen, I'll give you that. I can tell from the way you perform. You don't accept anything less than the best. We have that in common. I will do whatever it takes to save as many lives as I can save. I will do whatever it takes to bring Kostrov and the Sacred Breath into the New World. So if you think I've miscalculated, you should consider the possibility that I'm simply operating with more information than you have access to."

I see the flyers on the other side of the room. I want to get to them. I want to get out of this conversation, where I feel myself losing ground with every word. "Um," I say. I start to inch away.

"I love history," Gospodin says, "so if you'll indulge me, I'd like to share a story. I remember the first royal festivities I attended. When I was no older than you and just a good friend of Nikolai's father. You know, I remember meeting your mother at some of those parties."

"Oh?" I can hardly get the sound to leave my lips.

"Oh, yes. She was a beauty, to be sure, and she knew it, sauntering around the room in her costume. I thought she'd try to steal the king out from under the queen, truth be told, until I saw her kiss that guard father of yours right on the mouth, in front of everyone."

My heart pounds.

"You know," he says, "I find that *Captain's Log* has some excellent wisdom about productive unions."

Productive unions. It takes me a moment to understand what he means, and even then, I'm not sure I've gotten it right. Happy marriages? Sacred Breath–approved sexual encounters?

"I do hope you'll share," I say.

He accepts my sarcasm generously. "Every Flood thrusts the world closer to a destined, golden era. Each one of us, in turn, can see ourselves as steps on this long staircase. Our children must be better than us; their children, better than them. A woman must be well in her place at a loving man's side if she hopes to rear children better than herself."

"Is that so?" I say. I hear the tightness in my own voice.

"Your mother didn't heed that wisdom," he says. "And look at you. You're her twin."

I fight to steady my breathing. "Mariner Gospodin," I say, "should I assume your advice is a way of telling me you don't want me to dance with Nikolai again?"

"Perhaps you're smarter than your mother after all." His eyes sweep to Nikolai and Sylvia, dancing still though two songs have passed. "Sylvia Kanerva would make an elegant queen, don't you think?"

"She's lovely," I say. "But like you said, I'm determined. You need a determined queen in the New World, don't you? Someone who would do anything for Kostrov?"

"Are you suggesting we could be allies?"

I search his expression for approval and find none. "You don't trust me," I say.

"No, Miss Koskinen. I do not."

"Well, then," I say. "I'll have to prove you wrong."

His eyes run the ridges of my face, counting up the pieces as he might sum numbers in a math problem. "I look forward to it."

30

ELLA

I can't tear my eyes from Natasha. She meets Nikolai in the middle of the ballroom. She smiles. Flirts. He smiles back, and for a minute, something in that smile—the round curve of his lips or the gleam of teeth beneath them—reminds me of Cassia.

The room spins.

Katla, Sofie, Ness, Gretta, and I stand by our forgotten silks as we watch Natasha dance. With Nikolai. Midway through the song, Ness's friend Sylvia swishes past us in her glamorous gown.

"Have you seen my father?" she asks Ness. She doesn't look at us. Her eyes are glued to Natasha and Nikolai too. Without waiting for an answer, Sylvia says, "Handsome pair they make? Very . . ." Her lips tug as she searches for something suitably complimentary. "Tall."

"Wow," Gretta says, grinning at the crowd. "I've never seen so many people looking furious at the same time."

It's true. The crowd, as a whole, doesn't look thrilled to see Nikolai and Natasha dancing. I suppose everyone wants to dance with Nikolai tonight. I hope they all treat themselves to a nice, long shower to scrub away the smell of him. I don't understand how Natasha can't feel it. How cold he must be. How calculating.

"Well," Sylvia says, voice straining, "perhaps Natasha will be kind enough to give the rest of us a turn at some point."

Ness turns to Sylvia. Frowns. "Are you angling for queen? What about Johan?"

"A few of my father's friends from the Sacred Breath thought I should consider the possibility. It's over with Johan," Sylvia says.

Ness's eyes are wide. "Oh, but I so hoped Natasha and Nikolai would be together. But I—I can support both of you, of course. I mean . . ." She glances at the rest of us. Poor Ness. She really is too kind for her own good.

"Wait," Katla says, turning on Sylvia. "Your father is a high government official. Surely you're on the royal fleet whether or not Nikolai knows your name."

Sylvia's smile grows stonier. "I'm not sure I see your point."

"Are you sure?" I say. "Because you kind of look like you do."

"I'm sorry," Ness says, taking Sylvia's hand. "We don't mean to be rude. We're just—don't tell anyone, but there's news that the flyers won't all be on the fleet, and we've been hoping that if Natasha is queen, she could get us all on board."

"Don't be silly, Ness," Sylvia says. "Surely your family has a spot confirmed."

Just how rich is Ness?

"That's not really the point," Ness says.

Sylvia glances at the rest of us. "And as for rest of you, you may as well go dance with Nikolai yourself tonight. The roster is finished. My father showed it to me. They can't just add half a dozen people wherever they feel like it. Don't let Natasha fool you into thinking she'll whisk you along into the New World. She'd know as much. Oh—there's my father. Lovely talking."

And then she's gone.

"Well," Katla says. "Shit."

We're all quiet as we watch Natasha break away from Nikolai, her dance ending. She stops to talk to Gospodin. He lays a fatherly hand on her shoulder. They smile.

She'd know as much.

It's not that I feel like I, personally, have lost a place on the fleet. But I can't help but feel a little betrayed anyway. I misread Natasha. She's not out there fighting for the flyers; she's fighting for herself.

And I told her about my brothers. I let myself feel—I don't know what. Softer. Like the person I used to be. But Natasha isn't my friend. She isn't my anything. She's part of the palace. Part of the court I'm going to destroy.

I feel sick.

When she rejoins us by the silks, her cheeks are dancing-pink.

Katla crosses her arms. "We just had an illuminating conversation with Sylvia Kanerva."

Natasha blinks. "What?"

"Sylvia said there was no way you'd be able to bring us on the fleet, whether or not you were queen. Know anything about that?"

I wait for her to refute it.

She doesn't.

"You've got to be kidding me," Katla says.

Ness rocks back and forth on her toes, scanning the hall, face flushing. A few partygoers turned to watch us at the sound of Katla's voice. "Maybe we should go somewhere else."

"Look," Natasha says, "yes, okay, Adelaida mentioned that she wasn't entirely certain how flexible the roster for the royal fleet was, but I *know* I could make it work if I was queen. I didn't think it was worth worrying you all for no reason."

"No reason!" Katla says. "What about planning for our death? That's a good reason."

"Hey," Natasha says, "I don't see *you* doing anything to save all of us."

"We're not saying you're not trying hard enough," Sofie says. "We're just saying that you have to be honest with us."

"You promised me," Katla says, voice low and cold. "You promised."

As Natasha struggles to come up with some excuse, I wish more than anything that I could leave this room, with the smell of spilled alcohol and overripe perfume, with Andrei and Nikolai and Natasha.

Then I realize that I can.

I turn my back and I walk away.

A pair of older guards push open the doors for me without question.

In the sudden stillness of the hallway, my ears ring. Soon, footsteps echo behind me. I turn to see Sofie and Katla.

"You know what really gets me?" Katla says. "It's not the first time she lied about this. She hid the truth from us so we would perform better during the crane season festival, and she swore she wouldn't do it again."

In the distance, the music of another song begins. I wonder if the other girls are dancing to it. I wonder if Nikolai's hand is on Natasha's hip. I glance over my shoulder without meaning to. Katla watches me do it.

"If you're waiting for the others to follow us," she says, "they won't."

"I wasn't," I say.

Unconvinced, Katla continues. "Gretta doesn't care, of course. Her father is the Captain of the Guard—in case you forgot since she last mentioned it—so she'll be on the fleet no matter what happens with the flyers. And Ness, you know she'll be blindly optimistic about things turning out well. Her family has money, and she's devout besides. No one who loves the Sacred Breath as much as she does could really believe the Flood will kill her. And then there's Natasha, off flirting with Nikolai, off trying to be the queen, which just leaves the three of us." She frowns at me. "Unless you're secretly engaged to a noble."

I force a laugh. "No engagements."

Katla nods with grim satisfaction.

"Look," Sofie says, "I'm mad at her too. But she is trying."

"I'm tired of being lied to," Katla says.

"She's your friend," Sofie says. "Let her explain."

Katla ignores this. Instead of responding to Sofie, she turns to me. "We *never*," she says, bitter-vicious, "betray another flyer."

I'm about to agree, to let the fury of her voice leak into my own. But then I remember that I'm not a real flyer. I'm an assassin, and my betrayal will rock the Gray Palace more than Natasha ever could. So instead, I say, "People do strange things to survive."

It's not as though I have just lost a place on the royal fleet. I was always going to be dead by then anyway.

When we get back to the flyer wing of the palace, Katla and Sofie go to our bedroom. I make an excuse about not being tired, even though I'm tired to my bones. I go to the studio and stare at the silks. I can't find the energy to climb.

I lie down beneath them, the way I did in Maret's apartment at the end of a day of practice that beat me to dust. When I breathe, the silks swirl; if they're the surface of the sea, I'm the undercurrent.

I imagine Cassia beside me. I imagine her thumb running down the length of my jaw. Her hands never trembled against my skin; like everything else she did, she touched me with confidence.

"You wouldn't have done it," I ask in Terrazzan, "would you? Lied about who was going on the fleet?" The sound of my own voice in my own language is supple, a blanket wrapped around me by a mother's hands.

Her thumb stops at my chin. "I would have ruled this country as Nikolai never could," she says, her Terrazzan halting and accented. "I would have ripped out the corruption by the roots."

I squeeze my eyes shut, trying to seal the tears at the corners.

Even in my imagination, I can't quite believe her. She never would've answered me in Terrazzan. She would never choose to stumble over her words when, in another tongue, she could speak like a royal.

The rain falls lightly on the roof. The music from the hall is distant but audible, even from here. Outside, I can make out the voices of fashionably late partygoers. And then, footsteps, quick and scratchy, too soft to be human feet.

A paw bats my cheek.

I open one eye.

Kaspar, Adelaida's monstrously fluffy cat, leans over me. He gives my face another pat, as if to make sure I'm not dead. I'm not fooled into assigning empathy to the creature. He probably just wants to know whether or not he can eat me.

"Go away, cat," I say, again in Terrazzan, because it's all the same to him.

He blinks his big golden eyes.

"Why have you decided I would make a good friend? I'm very mean. Really."

I don't mind Kaspar's favoritism quite so much when the other flyers are around. I think it makes me seem more trustworthy. But there's no one here, no one to watch Kaspar pestering me.

I sit up.

There's no one to watch me. There's no place I'm meant to be right now.

Ten minutes later, I'm wrapped in a long cloak, hurrying through the night-washed streets to Eel Shore. When I reach Maret's, I'm shivering. My full-suit never dried after our performance and my cloak is soaked through with drizzle.

Maret opens the door. Her hair is piled on top of her head in a messy bun. Her eyes are small with sleep for only a moment. When she sees it's me, she inhales sharply.

"Well, it took you long enough!" she says, and she tugs me into the apartment.

Tears sting my eyes for the second time in too few hours.

I think I started to believe the flyers were something like family, and I was a fool. I let myself get caught up in the rehearsals and the dinners at the long kitchen table and the talking of the future, as if it existed.

"Come here, darling girl." Maret holds my hands and sits me on the sofa beside her. "I had begun to think you were dead in a dungeon."

"I'm sorry." My throat is scraped raw. "They've kept me busy."

"Tell me everything."

Her smile is so bright. So terribly Cassia.

I tell Maret everything about the last month. About the meeting with Nikolai and the guards in the hot pools. About the way Nikolai stared from his balcony, haughty, and about spotting Andrei. The revelation about the flyers and the fleet. If my voice catches on the name *Natasha,* Maret doesn't seem to notice.

"Interesting," Maret says. "Do you think the flyers will be disbanded and dismissed from the palace?"

"I'm not sure," I say.

Maret smooths my hair. A flyaway strand clings to my sticky eyelashes. "You're upset, aren't you?"

"No."

"Ella."

"I'm fine," I say. "It's just, seeing the palace like that. Wasting food and time. All these old men scheming and faking politeness." I look at my lap. "I imagined killing him tonight. When he was dancing with the principal flyer. I had a clear view of his back. And I imagined where I would put the knife."

But that's not the end of what I imagined. I also imagined what would happen after. I've never thought much about the after. I kill Nikolai; nameless guards kill me. But they're not nameless anymore. Now it's more like: I kill Nikolai. Ness screams. Gregor rushes forward. Katla shouts. Twain raises a gun. Natasha looks at me, horrified, lips parted—

You wanted to know me, I'd say. *Well, now you do.*

Maret laughs. "Now, that sounds like the Ella I know." A pause.

"So the principal flyer wants to be queen . . . Interesting. On the one hand, it could draw undue attention to you. On the other hand, it could give you a better chance to get close to Nikolai yourself." Maret drums her fingers on the arm of the sofa. "What do you think of her? This Natasha girl?"

I try to swallow the knot in my throat. "I hardly know her at all."

31

NATASHA

A kind director would let us rest the day after the ball. But we have Adelaida instead, so this morning, we gather in the studio at sunrise.

I look around at the flyers. They all look as bleary as I feel. Katla still won't meet my gaze. Any triumph from my conversation with Nikolai last night is snuffed by her anger.

"You can all stop looking so sour," Adelaida says. "Your flight went well. No need to let little squabbles ruin that."

"I don't see why we should keep rehearsing," Katla says. "It sounds like there's no hope we end up on the fleet. Zero. As far as I'm concerned, the palace doesn't care what happens to us."

I'm surprised when Ella speaks. "We should keep rehearsing," she says, her voice soft and level, "because there's always a chance. Right? Who knows what the final roster for the fleet will look like? Maybe, by the time the Flood comes, it won't just be up to Nikolai."

I'm not sure what she could mean by this—if she truly believes that the queen would have such power—but it has Sofie nodding, at least.

"It's a fair point," Sofie says. "We're not guaranteed spots on the fleet if we stay, but we're definitely not going on the fleet if we leave."

Ness presses her fingers to her lips. "Why does it seem like you've all resigned yourself to die?"

"Because we *are* going to die," Katla says. "How do you know you're not? There are plenty of Heather Hill girls out there with rich fathers and only so many spots. Only so much food."

I feel a flash of hot anger. Usually, I'm on the same side of Katla's moods. But at the look on Ness's face—like a dog just kicked—I feel the last of my patience dissolve.

"Stop it." I step between the two of them. Katla's eyes are fierce. "Your fight is with me and Adelaida. Would you leave Ness out of it, just this once?"

After a long moment, Katla leans around me. "I'm sorry, Ness. We'll all be very happy for you when you sail off into the sunset." To me, voice low, she says, "But *you* should've known better."

My throat is tight. Katla's never looked at me so scathingly before.

"I should go back to my family today," Katla says. "And I should stay there."

"You could," says Ella, her eyes trained on Katla. "But that would only spite us. And it wouldn't help your family at all."

Katla's jaw is fixed, proud.

"Go be with your family today, then," Adelaida says. "Come back tomorrow when you're ready to fly."

Katla gathers her cloak and disappears out the door.

After the ball, I don't see Nikolai again for a week.

The days following the ball are my loneliest since I came to the palace. When I walk into the kitchen for dinner and find the other girls already there, they don't shift their seats to make room for me. When I arrive mid-conversation, no one bothers to catch me up on what's been said. When someone is struggling with a tricky element, they always seem to ask someone else for help before they ask me.

This is what I asked for, isn't it? I thought I could cloak myself in selfishness and—what? Everyone would understand?

So after dinner each night, instead of lingering in the kitchen or the studio, I head for the library. If the guards find me here, I could get in trouble, but I'm willing to risk it. In my bedroom, I get distracted by every set of footsteps passing my door. In the quiet of the library, I can't fool myself into thinking someone is coming to forgive me.

I light a fire in the hearth. It bathes the austere room in a warm, trembling glow.

I curl in the armchair in front of the fire and find where I left off in *Captain's Log*. The more of it I read, the more I regret not reading it sooner; it feels like being taught a language I've heard all my life but never understood.

The door opens behind me. I look up.

"Oh," Nikolai says. "No, no, don't stand up. It's fine."

He's dressed all in black save the gold of his crown. When he crosses the library toward me, a pair of guards stay by the doors.

"Sorry for interrupting you," he says. "I couldn't sleep."

"No," I say. "No, please. Sit. If you want."

He stops by my chair. "What are you reading?"

I hold up *Captain's Log*, feeling sheepish. "I've never actually read it before."

He frowns at my page. "Oh, the fertile vessels. Good."

Kos calls women *vessels*. That's what women are in the New World. He always adorns the word: *lustrous vessel* or *fertile vessel* or *precious vessel*, but there's no adjective complimentary enough to make me wish a man would compare me to a boat.

"Do you think he called women *fertile vessels* to their faces?"

Nikolai laughs lightly. "So you're at the part where Kos finds Grunholt?"

I nod. The first third of *Captain's Log* is about the storms during the Harbinger Year. The next third is about the year of the Flood, sailing with his men and drawing ships into his fleet as they run across other survivors on the open ocean. The last section follows Kos as he makes landfall on the island that became Grunholt.

"They're building Sundstad now," I say.

"I like that part," Nikolai says. He sinks into the chair across from mine. "It seems fulfilling. Building a city from the ground up. He talks about being so exhausted all the time, but—falling into bed, tired from a hard day's work? That sounds nice."

Nikolai does look tired. His eyes are underlined in purple.

"The women don't seem to do much city-building," I say. "Mostly child-building."

Nikolai's lips turn up at the corners. "Ah. Right. The *fertile vessels* have to stay home to protect their child-bearing abilities."

"'She who protects her body protects humanity,'" I say, running my finger across the sentence. I curl into a tighter ball in the chair, my stomach pressed to my thighs. I'm too conscious of my hips watching me, my abdomen staring back at me, this body I inhabit. If I make it to the New World, is that what they'll expect of me? My heart flutters. I shift under the weight of Nikolai's gaze.

"You know what I wonder?" Nikolai says.

"What?"

"How does Kos know how many Floods there were before his?"

I frown. In *Captain's Log,* Kos says his Flood is the fifth one the world has ever faced. But Kos never explains how he knows this. Like so much else in *Captain's Log,* it's so ingrained in our culture that we accept it.

I wish I could see the history of the world written out on a long scroll. I wish I could hear tales of every great ruler and every long-dead beast. But that's one of the great cruelties of the Floods. We don't only lose land and lives. We lose records, wisdom, stories, the history of our kind.

And how we cling to *Captain's Log.* It's our lifeboat in the fog of unknown past.

"I don't know," I say. "Maybe you should ask Gospodin."

Nikolai purses his lips. "Maybe *you* should ask him."

"I—what?"

"Right," Nikolai says. "Well, I better leave you to your reading."

"No, wait!"

He pauses halfway out of his chair and raises his eyebrows at me. I clear my throat. "I, um . . . Do you come to the library often?"

Nikolai stands up all the way. "Not really. This was always Cassia's domain." His eyes flit across the shelves.

"Do you hear from her?" I'm not sure what the protocol is on writing letters from exile.

Nikolai doesn't meet my gaze. "No."

He turns swiftly to the door.

I flail for something useful to say. All I come up with is: "So, I'll see you around the palace?"

He glances back over his shoulder. My cheeks are hot. "I'll send for you. Maybe we can chat when it's not so late."

Then he's gone.

My heart keeps hammering for a long time. It's not a pleasant sort of heartbeat. It's panic. Desperation.

I smooth the pages of *Captain's Log* again. Maybe, if I stay a few more minutes, Nikolai will come back and I can make slightly less a fool of myself.

He doesn't come back. I finish the book. I tuck it under my arm and head back through the palace. My feet, despite better judgment, stop in front of the flyers' door. I give it a long stare.

Then I keep walking.

I lie in bed for a long time, straining for the sounds on the other side of my wall. Sofie snoring. Ness singing. Ella laughing, sharp, like she's surprised to have made the noise. I hear nothing. The only thing to keep me company is the sound of my own breathing.

I am so, so alone.

32

ELLA

After the ball, the flyers separate into camps. In the first, Natasha, Ness, and Gretta, who all have an edge to survive the Flood. In the second, Katla and Sofie, whose prospects are markedly bleaker.

I don't realize that I've been invited to join the latter camp until, on a particularly cold morning a few days after the ball, Katla and Sofie come into the studio and head straight for me. Sofie sips a cup of tea. Katla holds two more. I'm confused, at first, when they sit down on the floor beside me. Katla extends one of her cups.

I stop stretching to look at her.

"Nasty cold out," she says. "This helps."

It tastes like cinnamon and burns the back of my throat. When Natasha comes in, wearing her big sweater and a knit hat, she glances at the three cups. Her eyes slide over them quickly. She goes to her silks without a word.

I start to spend nearly all my time with Sofie and Katla. When I eat, they sit beside me. When I practice a new element, they offer to help.

I enjoyed fashioning myself as a detached, indomitable outsider. I'm disappointed by how much I appreciate their company. As it turns out, you can call yourself an assassin and still want friends.

I can't remember the last time I had friends. Cassia was always more than that. Before her, I had my brothers and a few acquaintances near my age, but even our closest neighbors were a generous walk from our farm. There was the flower girl in town I always held a candle for, but I hardly knew more than her name.

But the more I see of Sofie and Katla, the less I see of Natasha. She misses meals. She practices hard and leaves quickly. I feel a pinch in my stomach whenever I think of the way she danced with Nikolai, but still, it's hard not to worry.

As the weeks pass, no one shows any sign of budging. The sun is sleepy and more reluctant to rise each morning as we tumble toward bear season. We've all been counting the days since Storm Five. Two months? Already? Our luck can't last forever. The feeling of Storm Four, overdue, hangs in every heavy cloud. I'm antsy for its arrival. Unlike everyone else, I'm not counting to Storm One—I'm counting to Storm Two, when I get to kill Nikolai and finally be free of the suffocating weight of vengeance. And also be dead. I've been hung up on that whole "dead" part lately.

On the coldest morning I've faced yet, a Friday, I'm stretching on the floor of the studio. Trying to remember if I have anything planned for the weekend ahead. I have no excuse not to go visit Maret, except for the fact that I don't want to. She'll want to talk about murder and Cassia and Nikolai, and—I just want to think about something else. For once. Just for a few days.

Katla sits down next to me. "It's my sister's birthday," she says. "Sofie and I are going to visit her. You should come." When I pause, Katla adds, "I can promise cake much better than René's."

But ten hours later, after practice is over, I don't just find Sofie and Katla by the door.

"My sister said I had to invite Natasha," Katla says, rolling her eyes. *"Please, Katla, Natasha's so nice. Please, her flying tips are so much better than yours. She's so good at sucking up to royalty, blah, blah, blah."*

"Wow," Natasha says, straightening her knit hat. "That felt really good. Like a big hug to the soul."

"Let's just go, okay?"

The four of us hurry through New Sundstad by the dying light of the sun, carrying unlit lanterns for the way back. Katla has a rucksack with presents—a set of playing cards and a burnished brass compass. We have to trek along a muddy road, past the fields of harvested rye, before the path becomes an elevated wooden platform beneath us. We cross a stretch of upturned mud, and Katla tells me it's where they've lifted bricks of peat out of the earth. After all that mud, when we've gone so far the lights of New Sundstad are barely a twinkle behind us, our surroundings turn wild. The fog is a soup; the trees are few, scraggly, and determined. Katla's bright red home perches on the edge of a pool of dark water, hemmed by golden grass.

"That pool wasn't there when my parents built the house," Katla says, frowning. "I think it gets closer to the door every time I come back."

I've seen enough maps of Kostrov to know that this is its skinny neck. New Sundstad is nearly a country unto itself, edged on all sides by ocean and bog. All the other little Kostrovian towns sit in and beyond the boglands. I once asked Maret if she'd ever visited the rural towns, and she just waved a hand. "Growing rye and complaining," she said. "That's what they're good for."

Katla pushes open the front door without knocking. We're quickly engulfed in a flurry of small bodies. Two of them leap on

Natasha so enthusiastically, I'm surprised she doesn't topple over. Katla has three sisters and four brothers, all younger, and they manage to all shout their names at the same time.

"Don't worry." Sofie puts a hand on my shoulder. "I've been here twice before and still don't know anyone's name."

Katla's mother is taller than she is by a head and her father wears a beard. Half the siblings have Katla's dark hair, and the other half have waves of potato-blond. Every nose is identical.

It's impossible not to notice that Katla is the only sibling who doesn't look dangerously underfed.

I glance around the cramped room. I spot Katla surreptitiously sliding a little bear, carved from wood, behind a picture frame on the mantel. Maret told me that a lot of the people who live in the boglands—Brightwallers, she called them—refuse to believe in the Sacred Breath's teachings, no matter how much trouble it gets them into. Maret said Brightwallers believe in nature spirits—the things people believed in when this country was called Maapinn.

Quietly, Sofie says, "You don't have to do that on my behalf."

"My parents should know better," Katla says.

"No," Sofie says firmly. "I couldn't care less."

I don't think I'm supposed to overhear any of it, but we're squished too tightly together to help it.

I learn that the birthday girl is the oldest sister after Katla. In my head, I take to calling her Sister One. She's one of the potato-blond siblings, and she wears a gray frock with a blue ribbon around the middle. She's more subdued than the rest, and she watches us with a discomfiting intensity.

The youngest brothers, by my guess nine and seven, fawn over

Natasha. Apparently, they remember her from when she last visited, and they are determined to show her their pet lizard. Brother Three promises Natasha he'll be right back and runs into the bedroom.

"We named him Fredrik," Brother Four says, "but that might've been a bad name, because Fredrik had baby lizards."

Brother Three returns, holding aloft a scaly horror. It looks like it couldn't decide between being a snake and being a lizard, so it resigned itself to doing both poorly. Its long tail snaps and curls around Brother Three's wrist.

Natasha squats to look it in the eye. "Hello, Fredrik."

"You probably don't want to stand so close," Brother Three says. "He's bitey."

I stare at the creature. Its hands are like bird talons, fingers tapering to points, and its scales are tiny and rounded. Each gleams a different shade of gold, amber, and onyx, enough to make a jeweler jealous, rippling as it moves, like a pebbled riverbed through the water.

"What did you do with the eggs?" Natasha says.

"Eggs?" Brother Four says.

"You said he had baby lizards."

"He didn't lay eggs," Brother Four says. "The baby lizards popped straight out of him, all slimy and alive."

"Lizards can't do that," Natasha says patiently.

"Fredrik did," Brother Three says.

Brother Four nods emphatically. "It was gross."

Fredrik squirms, trying to wriggle out of Brother Three's hands.

"He keeps trying to get away," Brother Three explains. "Ever since Storm Five."

"But Storm Five is for birds," I say. "Not weird lizard things. No offense, Fredrik."

"I know!" Brother Three says. "Cool, right?"

I lean against the wall and take a breath. The backs of my eyes burn. I don't want anyone to see me upset, but seas, the boys remind me so much of my brothers. When the twins were seven or eight, Milo caught a water vole. It looked like a rat, but fatter and more courteous. Filip named it Paulina and made it a bed out of duck down he pulled from one of our mother's good pillows.

I shut my eyes, just for a second. But when I open them again, Natasha's looking at me. I push off the wall. Drop her gaze.

Katla's mother sets a hand on each brothers' back. "Boys, put your lizard away. We have to sing to your sister."

"Fredrik can help sing."

Katla's mother stares at her sons in a way that leaves no doubt that Fredrik is not invited to the singing.

The cake is a twist of soft dough, decorated with honey and dried cranberries. It's good enough that I'd ask for more if it weren't already too small a cake for a party of thirteen. We eat with our fingers off wooden plates. It's so crowded that I end up sitting on the front step outside, braving the night to escape the intense heat of all those bodies pressed together.

I lick the last bubble of honey off my finger and stare into the fog. Water laps against shore. It's a different flavor of wild than the forests of Terrazza, but I find I like it anyway, despite the sulfuric bog smell and the sharp cold in the air.

Brother Three finds me outside. "Oh," he says. "I was hoping you didn't like your cake."

I look at my empty plate. "Sorry."

He shrugs. "Hey, want to see something cool?"

I'm skeptical. "Is it another lizard?"

Brother Three drops to his knees and begins picking through the dirt in front of the house. His face glows white like a second moon. A moment later, he sits up again, a shiny beetle pinched between his thumb and forefinger.

"No offense," I say, "but I liked the lizard better."

"You have to watch," Brother Three says. With his non-bug-laden hand, he gestures for me to crouch at the corner of the house with him. He squats in front of a plant, bright green stalks with feathery pink whiskers at the ends. If it's a flower, it's like no flower I've ever seen. "This isn't the biggest one, but all the others bloomed in Storm Eight and never opened up again." When I don't rush to join him and his bug beside the plant, he gestures wildly at me again. "Well, come on. I can't hold this thing forever."

I squat next to him. Brother Three extends the beetle toward the pink whiskers of the plant, each of which is beaded with a delicate dewdrop. The plant moves so quickly I think at first that it must have been the wind. But no—the beetle struggles valiantly against the whiskers as the plant draws it into a mouth I can't see. Just as quickly as it started, it's done. The plant is still and plantlike again.

"What is that?"

"Isn't it fun?" Brother Three says.

Brother Three and I have different definitions of *fun*. "Did it eat that beetle?" I ask.

He nods. "Some of the really big ones can eat other stuff too, but like I said, they're all asleep or dead or something now."

"Could it eat a person?"

Brother Three giggles. "That's silly. People are too big to fit inside plants."

I stand up again and brush the dirt from my knees. "You know an awful lot about plants and animals, don't you?"

He shrugs again, but I can tell he's proud. "I don't see why you wouldn't, when they're around you all the time. You just have to pay attention."

His father calls for him and he heads back inside, but I stand by the strange, hungry plant for a minute longer. I feel like he's struck an edge of something important, but I can't yet put words to it. What sorts of things does a child learn, living with pink-whiskered plants and lizards that don't lay eggs and leaves that rustle like the first notes of a song? Different lessons than you find jammed between stone buildings.

When I go back into the house, Sister Three, in her nightgown, tugs on Natasha's arm.

"When are you going to come back and finish reading to me about the twelve princesses?"

"I can read to you," Katla says.

Sister Three lets out a soft whine. "You don't do any of the voices."

"Very soon," Natasha says. "I promise."

Over the top of Sister Three's head, Katla narrows her eyes.

Katla's father sweeps the girl up in his arms, promising lots of voices tomorrow. Soon, all the young siblings have been spirited off to bed. In the end, it's just the flyers, Katla's parents, and the birthday girl: Sister One, who turned sixteen today. We gather around the wooden table. Katla's mother sets a pot of tea on a cloth napkin in the middle.

Without the children, the evening takes a hasty somber turn. Katla sets her rucksack on her lap and begins removing jars: flour, salt, lard. I realize she must've stolen them from the palace kitchen. She pushes them across the table with her mouth set in a stubborn line.

"Make sure Sander is eating," is all she says. "He looks like a ghost."

Then she pulls a book from her bag. I recognize it. That was the book I found snooping through her room. The one I couldn't read.

"Can you take this? It's making me nervous, having it in the palace."

Katla's father takes the book, frowning. "Maapinnen's not a crime, last I checked."

"Yeah," Katla says, "but sometimes it feels like it's about to become one."

Sister One sits quietly, but it's impossible to ignore the way she watches us. I wonder how often she gets to see people outside of her family—if she's anything like I was on the farm, the isolation gets to her.

As Katla's father puts the jars into their cupboards, her mother begins pouring tea. "There was an arrest not far from here," she says, handing Katla the first cup. "Just today."

"An arrest?" Katla says. "Seas, did someone try to stockpile Flood supplies again?" She glances over at me and adds, "Our neighbors keep trying to evade the tithes. It never works. They always get caught and someone gets arrested."

"They weren't even Kostrovian." Katla's mother hands me a cup of tea. "Skaratan."

Katla frowns. "Why would anyone come all the way from Skarat this close to Storm One?"

"Scholars," her mother says, as if this explains it.

"I used to see the Skaratan scholars wandering around Eel Shore," Sofie says. She tilts her head toward me. "That's where my father lives, near the university."

I'm about to say that I know as much—Maret's apartment isn't far from the university walls—but I catch myself just in time. Instead, I say, "What law did the Skaratans break?"

Katla's father rejoins us at the table. He takes the teakettle and pours his wife the final cup. I like the way they sit together, Katla's parents. They don't share any coy smiles or pointed glances, and yet, their shoulders are glued firmly together in some gentle reminder of the other's presence. They're a steady, earthen pair; watching them makes my heart ache for what I will never again have.

"They were digging for fossils," Katla's father says.

I blink. "Fossils?"

"What's illegal about fossils?" Natasha says.

"And why would anyone want them?" I ask.

Sofie smiles around the edge of her cup. "I think it's the Skaratan mandate to pursue science until the end of days."

Katla wrinkles her nose. "It must be a stodgy place, Skarat."

"But why fossils?" I say.

Katla's father studies me, as if wondering how freely he can speak in the presence of a stranger. In the end, he must decide to trust his daughter's judgment of character. "I met one of them out in the boglands while I was looking for a new harvest site. He was nervous of me at first, but I gave him the lay of the land, speaking slow and easy so he could translate. He took a liking to me, so I offered him a drink. Ten minutes later, he tells me he's looking for polar bear fossils."

I glance at the others. "This is a joke, right? There aren't polar bears on Kostrov."

"Definitely no polar bears on Kostrov," Natasha says. "Skarat, maybe. Not Kostrov."

Katla's father affords us a smile. "I laughed too. But that's what he said he was looking for."

There's a joke that Skaratans think they're smart enough to solve anything—give them a heart and they'll try to make it beat again. In Terrazza, I occasionally heard mutters that some miracle of science would burst from Skarat to cure us of the Flood. My hopes were never particularly high, but still, I'm disappointed to learn that what their brightest minds have been working on isn't a glass bubble to encase the world, but the search for polar bear bones in a country without polar bears.

"I don't profess to know a great deal about the scientific method," I say, "but that sounds like a really stupid way to spend your time."

"Ah." Katla's father nods. "I said the very same. And he told me: 'No polar bears in Kostrov now, yes. But what of the land that was here before?' Then I suppose he figured he'd said too much, because he hurried off without finishing his drink. No surprise they got caught, I figure, with lips as loose as those."

I'm still confused, but the same sensation I felt looking at the pink-whiskered plant grips me again, like I'm on the brink of something.

"Land that was here before?" I say. "Like, before the last Flood?"

"There was land before," Sister One says. Her voice is quiet, and though today's meant to be her party, it's the first I've heard her speak. She reaches for the napkin underneath the teakettle. "It was just underwater for a while." She pulls the edges of the napkin so the cloth lies flat against the table, then scrunches the corners together.

The fabric in the middle rises in a bend. I picture land sinking into the earth. Rising up again in bends and valleys and ridges.

"So that man," I say, finally feeling the first dawn warmth of understanding, "the Skaratan scholar. He thinks that polar bears lived on Kostrov—or whatever this land used to be—before the last Flood?"

"He does seem to think that," Katla's father says.

And finally, I understand.

According to *Captain's Log*, the Floods wipe out all life, except for humans and their ships and whatever else is on board. New animals are born at the depths of the ocean, appearing as the waters recede.

The scholar wants to prove that polar bears aren't a Post-Kos's Flood creation. The scholar wants to prove polar bears—and who knows how many other animals—lived, swam, moved, *survived*, all without us knowing it.

"And they arrested him?" Natasha says.

"For trying to disprove *Captain's Log*," Katla's father says.

To say there are old polar bear fossils in the bogs is to seek an untruth in *Captain's Log*. Hence the heresy. Hence the arrests.

We pull on our cloaks and light our lanterns. We've only made it three steps out the door when Sister One hurries after us.

"Da wouldn't say anything, but his back's going bad again."

"You've tried the willow bark?" Katla says.

"Not working," Sister One says.

Katla nods. "I'll try to get medicine."

A pause. "Thank you for the cards," Sister One says. "And the compass."

"Happy birthday," Katla says.

"And thanks for the dress, Natasha."

Katla looks over at Natasha sharply. Natasha doesn't meet her gaze. "Don't mention it."

"Lovely to see you again," Sofie says.

Sister One's teeth catch her lip. She leans forward on her toes like she has something more to say after all this time of not saying much. In the end, she just watches us go.

Once we're out of earshot, ensconced in a bubble of lantern light, Katla says, "You gave Sini a dress?"

"I outgrew it," Natasha says.

"Uh-huh."

"Has she started taking flying lessons again?" Sofie asks.

"No," Katla says. She shoots Natasha a dark look. "I told her not to go back once we found out we were off the fleet." To me, Katla says, "She was really good. She would've auditioned for your spot, but she had a nasty fall a few weeks before it. She missed a leg wrap and tumbled through the middle of her silks. Not that it makes any difference now."

Softly, Natasha says, "I'm sorry, Katla. How many times do I have to say I'm sorry?"

"A few more."

We walk in silence for a moment.

I try to decide if I'm brave enough to ask the question on my tongue. Finally, I say, "What's your family's plan?"

"For the Flood?" Katla says.

I nod.

"Well," Katla says, "there's Plan A, where we find some aban-doned ship and pile on board with moments to spare, but seeing as they hardly have enough food to last a week, let alone a year, and a person can't survive on just fish for that long, my hopes aren't high. Plan B: The government gets their act together and expands their fleet to save every last Kostrovian." She pauses. "Okay, that was a joke, but I'll keep going. Plan C: Storm One never comes, the ocean doesn't swallow everything. It feels about as likely as anything else."

I think of Sini rising on her toes, the better to watch us leave. I think of what it must have felt like to see me, the girl who took a spot in the palace that could have been hers, sitting at her kitchen table.

"Sometimes," Katla says, her voice as dark as the fog-drenched sky, "I wonder why we don't all just jump in the ocean now and save it the trouble of killing us later."

Sofie loops an arm through Katla's. "Because of Plans A through C." She loops her other arm through mine. "Now, at the risk of sounding like Ness, stop acting so terribly bleak."

Natasha's gaze meets mine.

I swallow. Then I extend my arm to Natasha.

She hooks her elbow around mine. Her breath mists the air in front of her lips. Our hips bump.

The four of us walk in a tight line along the wooden platform above the boggy earth. Our footsteps echo on the wood. I keep expecting to see a carnivorous plant or a serpentine lizard or a polar bear skeleton. But no: just the slender shadows of tree branches and the faint glimmer of lantern light reflected between blooms of algae.

Plants closing up after Storm Eight. Birds and lizards disappearing after Storm Five. The boglands are doing something. Preparing for the Flood. I don't know how. But something is happening.

When I feel a drop of water land on my nose, ice cold, my heart falters in its beating. I've spent so long counting down to Storm Two. Looking forward to it. Seeing nothing at the end of it. But that one lonely raindrop is enough to scare me.

Since when have I been afraid of the storms?

What does it mean, that I might be afraid to die?

33

NATASHA

The morning after I visit Katla's family, the sun shines too brightly through my window. When I throw open my curtain, I see why. The first snow of the year covers New Sundstad.

I meet Ness, Gretta, and Sofie in the kitchen. Although I don't think Gospodin has noticed me yet, I'm staying committed to my promise of attending services at Our Lady. I make a promise to myself that he will today. I'll go talk to him afterward, even though I'm still shaken from how badly our conversation at the ball went.

When we step up to the stove, René gives us each an extra-big helping of porridge.

He shakes his wooden spoon at me. "The storms finally scared some sense into you, eh? Extra porridge every time you go to Our Lady, lazy girl."

I'm left unsettled at this moralistic bribery, but at least I'm unsettled with extra porridge.

Ella walks into the kitchen, then, glancing around like she's not quite sure she's in the right place, or maybe like she's looking for someone.

It's hard to believe she's the same girl who auditioned those months ago. Any semblance of baby fat has hardened to muscle.

Her skin glows with new, well-fed health. Even her smiles are a little more believable than they used to be. Today, her curls are loose around her face.

"You're up early," I say.

She shrugs. Her eyes are pinned to mine. I wonder if she's thinking about the walk back from Katla's last night, her arm linked in mine. "Couldn't sleep. Kept having dreams of plants trying to eat me."

"Spooky," I say.

I smile when Ella sits down next to me. Last night, at Katla's house, I wasn't stupid enough to think that Katla and Sofie wanted me there. But Ella was no more distant than usual. And the thought that they might not hate me forever—seas, I've been lonely.

"Ella!" Ness says. "Finally. You haven't been to a single service with us yet."

"I, uh . . ." She glances around. "Usually go on Sunday nights instead?"

"Oh, that makes sense," Ness says.

Gretta narrows her eyes suspiciously.

"You're coming with us today, though, right?" Sofie says.

"Yeah," I say. "Come with us."

She glances over her shoulder, as though Katla might stomp in at any moment to heap judgment upon her. Then: "Okay. Sure."

"Oh, lovely!" Ness says. "Let's all put on our mittens and hurry over so we can get seats."

Outside, the air is thin and crisp. The sky is lavender-gray, and when I inhale, the insides of my nose tickle with frost. Snow, a full foot of it, has settled into the cracks of the city, bringing everything into sharp contrast. All the little details, usually lost in a blur of stone and soot, are sharp with icing white. Ness leads us through it, her hair bouncing merrily as she walks.

I've traded my slippers for a pair of fur-lined boots. When they break the crust of frost lining the streets, it crackles like a bear season bonfire.

I don't realize Ella is watching me over her shoulder until she says, "You look like you've never seen snow before."

I grin, trapping my lip under my teeth. I take aim at a chunk of ice and kick it down the path to Ella.

She catches it with the side of her own boot—borrowed from Katla, I think—and kicks it back.

"Natasha loves snow," Gretta says, "because it makes her hair stand out even more."

I smile. I do love snow; my hair isn't the reason.

In snow, New Sundstad starts to resemble the cities from *Tamm's Fables*. It feels less a sinking rock and more an enchanted kingdom of the kind my mother dreamed. It's not easy to believe in fairy tales in a city of ash and Flood. But in the snow, it's different.

Ella turns her chin up to the sky. A stray flake spins toward her. She sticks out her tongue and twists in circles underneath it, tracking its spiral, until lands in her mouth. She frowns. "I thought that was going to be more satisfying than it was."

"Now *you* look like you've never seen snow before," I say.

"When I was little, I took a trip to the mountains with my family," she says.

"Which mountains?"

"In Terrazza." She says it fast, then even she looks surprised at her answer. And then, quickly: "But I moved to Kostrov years ago. So I've dealt with the snow here before."

Terrazza. I feel like I've asked so many questions so many times, and she's masterfully evaded all of them. I've asked this very question before. The last time, she told me she was a reanimated corpse from the boglands. But now I have this tiny mote of truth.

I sift through my memory, trying to find anything useful about Terrazza. I know it was hit particularly hard by Storms Ten and Nine. I know it's famous for fertile farmlands and a few snaggle-toothed mountains. It's farther south than Kostrov or Grunholt or even Roen, distant enough that the palace isn't as full of visitors from Terrazza as it is from nearer nations.

Then I remember all at once. The butcher's shop underneath my mother's apartment. A Terrazzan couple owned it.

I remember the butcher's wife laughing, teaching me how to say *Hello*, and *Thank you*, and *I would like an apple, please*. I part my lips, straining to remember the feel of the word on my tongue.

Finally, I find it, and in Terrazzan, I say, "Hello."

Ella's face blooms with a smile, too startled to wear her usual mask. "Your accent is terrible," she says.

"Hello," I say, again in Terrazzan, because I've forgotten how to say *Thank you*.

I carry a warmth in my stomach for the rest of our walk, and it keeps out the chill better than my new cloak. Adelaida gave it to me as a gift after I danced with Nikolai at the ball. As if I needed to be bribed. By the time we reach Our Lady of Tidal Sorrows, I've almost forgotten why we've come. When I see the imposing shell-and-sea-glass building, the warmth snuffs out.

I'm not here to talk to Ella and revel in the snow. I'm here to show Gospodin I can be a good, sea-fearing queen.

The square in front of Our Lady is packed with people. The closer we get to Storm One, the bigger these crowds seem to get.

"Will all these people really fit inside?" Ella says.

"Services have been filling up lately," Ness says. "That's why Mariner Gospodin had those word trumpets installed." She points to a copper horn fixed to the side of the building. Underneath is a podium, and as I watch, a man climbs the stairs and lifts the horn off the wall. The horn seems to be connected to some sort of long tube, coiling inside the building and out of sight.

Ella points to the man. "Who is he?"

"That's the echoman," Ness says. "He listens to what Gospodin says through that tube, then he repeats it to all the people who don't get seats and have to stand out here. Doesn't that sound like a fun job?"

"No," I say. "It's freezing. Let's be the people who do get seats."

Ness gets on her tiptoes to see above the crowd. "Drat. This is why I wanted to get here early. Come on, let's keep pushing."

Finally, we clear the threshold. I glance around.

The ceiling is vaulted, wooden beams meeting in a triangular peak. It feels like being inside a ship. Long blue curtains run from the ceiling to the floor of every wall. All the jostling bodies raise the temperature thirty degrees. I pull at the neck of my new wool cloak.

"Do you come here often?" Ella asks.

"Recently? Yes. Before that . . . ?"

I could go months without going. On the anniversary of Kos's landfall—the biggest holiday in Kostrov—it's all but mandated that you celebrate. I sat in the last row and played lexicant with Katla on the back of a song sheet.

That's one of the things I remember being most surprised about in Our Lady: the paper. Song sheets. Pamphlets. Copies upon copies of *Captain's Log*. I've heard of newspapers closing down and publishers forced to let books fall out of print, saving trees to build ships instead, but Our Lady exists in a world above such scarcities.

Ness forces her way through the crowd. She smiles prettily at an already crowded pew until the people sitting there sigh and squeeze closer together. Gretta eyes the crowded bench and breaks off to meet up with her family. I end up wedged between Ness and Ella on the wooden bench, with Sofie on Ella's other side. We're pressed together from shoulders to hips to knees.

"Cozy," Ella says. "I feel spiritually warmed already."

I laugh and look at her, but I turn away again just as quickly. We're in such close quarters that if I don't face forward, our noses will brush.

When Gospodin walks through a door by the dais, the voices hush.

Ella points at the door. "What's that?"

"Gospodin's apartment."

"His apartment is connected to Our Lady?" Ella says. "That sounds awkward. I wouldn't like to think Kos was looking over my shoulder every time I bathed."

"Shh!" Ness says. "It's starting!"

I try to settle into my seat and behave, but I'm tense and fidgety. Gospodin wears a pristine white cloak. His hair is somehow roguish and intentional at the same time. I wonder if he'd have half his following if he weren't so handsome and self-assured. I don't remember who was Righteous Mariner before him. Maybe it's a rule that they're always dashing.

He stops at the dais. The building is open on that end, I realize, though the breeze doesn't reach us this far back. The dais sits on a balcony overlooking the ocean. Around Gospodin's shoulders, the pewter sea tumbles over itself.

Gospodin lifts a copper funnel from the dais and holds it near his mouth. That must be the other end of the word trumpet Ness told us about.

"Today," he says, "New Sundstad was cleansed."

The hushed whispers evaporate. Ness leans forward, elbows dropping to her knees.

"Just as the snow paints the city anew, alive with fresh possibilities, the next Flood will cleanse this world. It will cleanse our very souls."

Ella leans toward me, her breath stirring the loose hair at my ear. "What's that supposed to mean?"

I dip my head to hers. In the quietest whisper I can manage, I say, "It means that the ocean will do a nice culling of anyone who doesn't donate enough."

"I didn't know the ocean was such a miserly ass," Ella says.

I can't hold in a snort. Ness shushes me.

My eyes snag on Ella's knee, twitching against mine. Her whole body is taut. I can feel the tension running down the length of her leg. She has her wrist laid across her knee. She runs her opposite thumb across the edge of her palm. I catch a glimpse of the siren from underneath the hem of her sleeve.

I know I'm supposed to pay attention to Gospodin, but I feel myself sliding back into old habits. His words begin to fade behind the distant washing of the waves. I'm distracted by a bead of sweat rolling down the back of my neck. Whenever Ella moves, shifting against my leg, it's all I notice. My stomach is hot.

Then, quite suddenly, everyone around me is clapping as Gospodin says, "Let no one take your hope away from you!" Then he's waving and stepping off the dais.

I blink and shake myself out of my trance.

"My butt hurts," Sofie says. "Can we get tea on the way back?"

"Is that going to help with your butt?" Ella says.

"No, they're unrelated."

"Great," I say. "We'll go get tea, right after I say hello to Mariner Gospodin."

"You don't just *go say hello* to the Righteous Mariner," Ness says.

"Sure you do." I get to my feet. My sleeves stick to my arms with sweat.

"Tasha," Ness says.

"I want to meet him too," Ella says.

I blink. Ella has already slid into the crowd of people and begun making her way toward the front of Our Lady. I have to hurry to follow her. Ness lets out a loud sigh behind me, but when I glance over my shoulder, I see she's pushing after us.

It's colder at the front of the room, closer to the open balcony. When we make it all the way forward, Gospodin has his back to us. I hear a snippet of his booming, earnest voice, and as I step closer, I see to whom he's speaking: a narrow young woman with a sage-green frock and the perfect posture of someone used to being watched. Sylvia, the Keeper of the Purse's daughter. I haven't seen her since the ball. I study her as she nods at something Gospodin says. Sylvia is pretty and expertly made-up in the sort of way that flattens her age: She could be fifteen as soon as she could be thirty. When she spots me, she smiles.

"If you'll excuse me, Mariner Gospodin," she says. "I see an old friend."

Gospodin turns. When he sees me, his smile goes flat.

I'm relieved not to have Ness and Sylvia peeking over my shoulder—they've embraced and started a lively conversation, pulling Sofie in too—but Ella isn't so forgiving. She hangs just behind me, her arms crossed. Her mouth is sealed tight. All the better to watch me play Gospodin's games.

She said she wanted to meet him, but all she does is stare.

"Mariner Gospodin," I say, hoping to affect the same elegant, polite voice as Sylvia.

"Miss Koskinen," he says. He sounds bored with me already.

"I wanted to let you know that I read *Captain's Log* start to finish. I found it illuminating."

He raises his eyebrows. "And now you seek reward?"

"I . . . The reading was reward itself," I say.

I hear Ella exhale loudly, almost a laugh, behind me. I clench my fists.

"Is this your first service here?" Gospodin says. His eyes keep flicking into the crowd, like he's eager to find someone better to talk to.

"Of course not," I say. "The flyers all attend every Saturday."

His eyes sweep the room. "Your friend. The brunette. I can't remember ever seeing her."

I tense. "She—I'm—"

His eyes roll toward me. His smile is patronizing. Setting a hand on my shoulder, he says, "I'm glad you found Kos illuminating, but a devout follower might have read *Captain's Log* ten times by your age." My cheeks are beginning to burn as he says, "It's good of you to try. But you aren't trying hard enough." Then he strides back into the crowd, greeted by waves and adoring smiles, leaving me to stand by the dais, my face hot.

"That was painful to watch," Ella says.

"Thanks."

"Like, really, physically painful."

I dig my nails into my palms. "Anything more useful to add?"

"Not really," Ella says. "I'm just trying to figure out why you care whether or not he likes you."

I almost laugh.

"What?" Ella says. "He has Nikolai's ear, but he's not a royal. Right?"

I shake my head. "You don't understand at all."

"Obviously," she says. "That's why I came here today."

I feel sharp and bitter. "Well, I hope it was useful to you, then. That would make one of us."

Not trying hard enough, Gospodin says.

Fine. Then I will try harder.

34

ELLA

The service at Our Lady of Tidal Sorrows leaves me unsettled. Kos, apparently, was fond of his death-by-ocean imagery. I have to figure that the only reason people like it is because they're convinced they won't be among those who drown. Always the survivors, never the cleansed.

When we get back, Katla gives me her best derisive look. I don't know what she's angrier at: that I spent the morning with Natasha or that I went to a Sacred Breath service. I just shrug and say, "I was curious."

She hmmphs.

As far as I know, she hasn't seen the siren on my wrist. I wonder if it would change what she thinks of my attendance.

Later that day, I pick my way through the snow to Maret's apartment. After the hugs and the offers of tea, I tell her that I spent my morning in the pews of Our Lady.

She laughs, high and bright. "Why?"

"I wanted to learn more about Gospodin," I say.

She frowns.

"Obviously, Cassia was worried about how much control Gospodin had over Nikolai," I say. That's why she was exiled. "It seems like he's more involved with the crown now than ever."

"Yes. *Involved* with the crown," she says. "But he doesn't wear it. Without Nikolai, Gospodin will have no choice but to work with me. The Sacred Breath means nothing without the crown behind it."

"If you're sure . . ."

"Ella." Maret takes my hands in hers. In comparison, mine are small and inelegant. "I know you come from a . . . humble background, so try not to take this the wrong way."

A useful warning. Now I surely won't take it the wrong way.

"Those people," Maret says, "listening to Gospodin. Make no mistake—I value them tremendously. They're an important piece of the machine that is this city. But most of them will drown in Storm One. It doesn't matter if they adore Gospodin, because soon, they won't be around to say so."

"What about when you take the throne?" I say.

The corner of her lip twists so quickly, I think it might be automatic. "What about it?"

"What will you do with Gospodin?"

Maret shrugs. "He'll be a thorn, of course, but I'm not particularly worried. The Sacred Breath is a tool, wielded by the crown, to keep the rest of the country on their best behavior. If the nobles cave to him now, it's only because Nikolai is too weak or too stupid to take seriously." She pats my hands. "Don't worry. Gospodin won't get in our way."

That service, though—all those people leaning toward him like plants to the sun. Maret is underestimating him.

"Now," she says, "on to things that matter. Have you seen any more of Nikolai?"

"No. I think he's hiding in his personal chambers."

This isn't exactly true. I haven't seen him, but I also haven't been looking very hard. I hate him, I want him dead—that hasn't changed. But I'm also more nervous than I used to be.

"And what of his search for a queen?"

I shake my head. "No news."

"Not surprising. He needs to draw out the farce right up until Storm One if he wants to use the hope of queen-dom to keep people distracted. Have you considered using this to get close to him?"

"What?"

"You know." Maret waves a hand. "Dance with him at the next ball. Flirt with him when you pass each other in the halls. You might learn something."

"I'm not going to dance with Nikolai," I say.

Maret blinks, surprised. This might be the first time I've ever refused one of her suggestions. But she must know that I can't betray Cassia that way. To let Nikolai put his hands on me—I can't even think about it.

Also.

I don't want to be ostracized like Natasha. I like being around the other flyers. I like their laughter, their fierce loyalty, their quiet dedication. I know it's not permanent. I know I'm going to die soon enough.

But until then . . .

"Fine," Maret says.

She doesn't fool me. She's starting to doubt if her dear little assassin is up to the task.

She's not the only one.

~~~

The snow doesn't melt. Instead, it changes into a grainy slush, heavy with soot. I miss Katla's boglands, with their strange plants and algae-ripened waters.

I think I'll get a chance to stand among the mist-draped trees again when the next weekend arrives, but Adelaida instead announces that we'll be holding a workshop for a group of seven- and eight-year-old junior flyers.

"What's the point?" Katla says, incredulous. "It's not like they'll become Royal Flyers someday."

"Perhaps they enjoy flying just for the art of it." Gretta sniffs. "Unlike *some* people."

"Eat your silk," Katla says.

I'm not sure who to agree with. Was survival, security, always what drew girls to learn to fly? Katla has been a flyer since long before Storm Ten; even without the promise of the royal fleet, the palace meant food, clothing, friendship, warmth. But when being a Royal Flyer isn't enough to keep you safe, what else is a girl to do? New Sundstad isn't rife with opportunities for enterprising young women. Our odds aren't great, but they're better than most.

I shake myself. *Our odds.* I'm not part of this *our.* My odds have nothing to do with this. I have no odds.

"As far as New Sundstad knows, you're all still on the royal fleet," Adelaida says. "Keep it that way."

"Why should we?" Katla says.

Adelaida lets out a heavy breath. "Will it kill you to let a few little girls have some hope?"

To this, Katla says nothing. None of us do.

In the end, guards lead fifteen junior flyers into the studio. It's a snow-flurried Saturday morning, the second to last of crane season. Adelaida tells us the girls are from two different studios—two of the only studios still open. Sofie whispers that other studios have shuttered for a dozen reasons—storm damage, lack of funds, directors who died under collapsed roofs. Of the two studios that send us their junior flyers, one caters to elite clientele, the other does not. It's not hard to guess who's who. Only half the uniforms have holes.

I pick out our own personalities in the girls: The one with her hair in a terrifyingly tight bun, her face constantly screwed up in concentration, is a perfect Gretta. The girl who laughs so hard, she falls off her silks reminds me of Sofie. And the girl who is better than all the others by a mile is, of course, Natasha.

I gravitate to a silent, dogged girl on a corner silk. She attempts the same hip key over and over again, never asking for help, never so much as opening her mouth to speak.

"Hi," I say.

She blinks back at me.

"I'm Ella," I say.

After a moment, she says, "Kirsi."

"Want to practice your hip key with a knot? I can tie one if you'd like to sit on that for support."

She looks at me very seriously. "I don't want a knot."

I lean toward her and lower my voice. "I don't like using knots either. I always liked the challenge." I take a step back and hold up my hand. "Try to kick my palm when you do it. I think you just need to lift your legs a little higher."

She does it again, and she kicks my palm, and when she cinches the fabric between her legs, she grins.

"That was better," I say.

She drops to the ground. "I'm going to do it again."

And so she does. It's not unlike how I first learned my hip keys—not very elegantly, but with great determination. Maybe Kirsi is the girl most like me.

Natasha is so light on her feet that I don't realize she's behind me until she says, "You're good at this."

I start. I turn to look at her, and I'm overwhelmed by how near she is, by how fully her face fills my view: her flushed cheeks, her freckle-dappled nose, a strand of hair that's come loose from her ponytail and curls with sweat. When I first got here, she never would've stood so close to me.

I swallow, but I don't move away.

"Good at what?" I say.

She nods at Kirsi. "The kids. Teaching."

"Oh." I try to find something clever and self-deprecating to say. It's what I would normally do. Her eyes are such a complicated shade of hazel. "Thank you."

One of the loudest girls calls for her then, insisting she come see the arabesque she's done, and Natasha trots away from me, exclaiming what a lovely arabesque it is. When she's gone, the air isn't so thin; I breathe like I've just descended some great height.

Natasha isn't harsh and critical with the young girls like she often is with us. She teases out what each girl is best at and gives special attention to everyone in turn.

When Kirsi asks me a question, she has to repeat it. My eyes sting.

It's like being around Katla's siblings all over again. I wish my brothers were here. They'd love the silks.

We're counting our final minutes of the workshop when someone knocks on the studio door. I'm the nearest, so I answer it.

It opens onto the vestibule between the studio and the blue door to the street. The blue door is open. Behind it, rain falls in ropes.

Gregor's hair clings to his skull. Water drips down the end of his nose.

"The rain," he says.

I step forward.

The palace sits at the edge of New Sundstad. All that separates this door from the ocean is a stretch of stone street, ten feet wide.

Ten feet has never felt so insignificant.

The ocean is livid.

Rain pummels and pockmarks the snow. Whole drifts wash over the edge of the street and fall to the ocean below. The waves twist and froth. I can't hear them. The rain is too loud.

The rain, Gregor said, like to call it by another name would make something worse than just rain come to pass. But Gregor knows the truth, and so do I.

This isn't just a drizzle over New Sundstad. I can feel it in my stomach. An ache.

I turn. I jump.

Natasha, on her silent feet, at my side.

I say what Gregor wouldn't. "Storm Four."

35

NATASHA

Adelaida, Katla, Gretta, and I stand in a huddle at the corner of the room. The other flyers keep the young girls entertained.

"They can't walk home in this," I say.

"Obviously not," Adelaida says.

"So, what?" Gretta says. "We keep them here?"

"Of course we keep them here," Katla says. "Sofie can go ask René to make them some food. She's his favorite."

When I rejoin the girls, Ness is leading a few of them in a song. Sofie is asking a few more riddles. "What's the difference between a killer whale and a rye biscuit?" Ella is sitting with the smallest of the girls, the serious one she helped on the silks. Though the girl's eyes never leave the rain-splattered window, Ella manages to coax a smile from her.

The rain falls steady and long.

I lose track of the time. The clouds are so dense that it could be noon as easily as midnight. I think it's probably dinnertime.

Serving women bring blankets and pillows into the studio for the kids, and Adelaida lights a fire in the hearth. Sofie convinces René to bring us a pot of stew and a few loaves of bread.

In the face of the storm, Katla's fury ebbs. She catches me by the arm at one point and says, soft enough that no one else can hear, "I'm worried about the little blond one. Sofie can't get her to stop crying."

I nod. But by the time I sweep through the room and find the teary junior flyer in question, Ella already crouches beside the girl. And held tightly in Ella's arms—Kaspar. Kaspar, who always hides in the darkest reaches of Adelaida's bed when so much as a loud wind rustles outside. Ella has melted him completely, and the love-struck cat, in turn, has roused the girl from her tears. She holds out her hand for Kaspar to sniff. Kaspar stares at the hand in the utmost confusion.

Ella looks up. Her eyes meet mine, like she knew I was there, like she knew I'd be looking. I feel a shiver on the backs of my arms when she smiles, and I don't know what to do with it.

I think of Ella as cynical and sharp, but today, she's not. That version of Ella is eclipsed by a new incarnation, one who holds a befuddled cat so frightened, little girls can pet him.

She's from Terrazza. She has a way with children and cats alike. Her wrist is inked with a siren.

Is that really all I know? I want so much more than that.

I sit down next to them. "How are you?" I ask the girl.

She shrugs, keeping her gaze on Kaspar so she doesn't have to look at me.

"I was just telling her," Ella says, "that you know lots of fables. Do you want to tell us one?"

I blink at her. Have I discussed Tamm with Ella before? Mentioned my mother and her stories? How does she know so much about me when I know nothing about her?

"I'd have to go get my book," I say. I don't want to leave. It's warm, and Ella's expression is gentle. My fingers are tracking spirals across the floor, just like they did when my mother read me stories. "Or I could tell it from memory. But I might get a few details wrong."

"Let's hear it," Ella says. Her eyes are amber with firelight.

The little girl is still for a minute. Then she nods.

I take a breath. What's the story my mother would tell me right now?

"Behind seven mountains and beyond seven seas," I say, "there was an island called Turelo. It rose from a turquoise sea, and the people who lived there built houses high in the treetops. Turelo was full of brilliant thinkers, and it was rumored that if you wanted to play the best instruments, paint with the finest oils, or learn from the wisest scholars, you had to sail to Turelo."

The girl is curling against the wall, pulling a blanket to her chin. Ella is watching me. I shift closer under the skin-prickling weight of her gaze.

"When ships arrived from faraway lands, Nadia, the princess, watched them from her treetop palace. Like all Turelans, Nadia wanted to learn. Nadia wanted to sail away with the strangers and learn everything the world could tell her—more even than she could learn from all the books in Turelo's many libraries. On a warm summer day when one such ship arrived, Nadia decided she would go meet the sailors. Her parents told her she mustn't.

"'These strangers are not like the others,' the king told her. 'I don't trust them. They told us of a dangerous prophecy, and I do not believe it to be true.'

"But Nadia, like all Turelans, was curious. So she snuck out of the trees and down to the shore, where she found the strangers making camp on the beach. She tried to eavesdrop, but she was caught by one of the strangers—a girl who looked not so different from herself. The girl introduced herself as Atalanta. Nadia tried to heed her father's warning and be suspicious of Atalanta, but she could not bring herself to do it.

"'What brings you to our island, Atalanta?' Nadia asked.

"'Our wisest prophet warned of a storm to end all storms,' Atalanta said. 'The sea will encase the world, and no one will survive.'

"At first, Nadia didn't believe Atalanta. But when they went to the library—for Nadia spent many hours in the library—Nadia realized that long ago, wise Turelan scholars too had predicted a storm to end all storms.

"'It's hopeless,' Atalanta said.

"Nadia thought for a long time before she spoke. Finally, she walked to a window and pointed outside. 'But look at your ship. It won't sink if the ocean rises.'

"'Then we will starve,' Atalanta said.

"'Not if all of Turelo is our ship,' Nadia said.

"The girls marched to the ocean. They were both strong swimmers, but it still took them all day and all night to enact Nadia's plan. They held their breath and dove underwater, cutting away Turelo's roots with the edges of jagged shells.

"At first, the king and queen were angry at Nadia. They told her she'd been foolish, violating the island they loved so dearly. They told Atalanta's ship that they had to leave Turelo forever first thing in the morning. But during the night, the storm to end all storms fell upon Turelo.

"No longer connected to the ocean floor, the island bobbed to the top of the sea, free to float on the ocean's surface until the waters rose all they could.

"All these years later, sailors still say they glimpse Turelo on the horizon once in a while. It's floating somewhere, always slipping out from under the cartographer's pen. But rumor is, if you manage to land on its shores, you'll be greeted by the queens of Turelo, and they will ask you what knowledge you've brought to add to their library."

The girl's eyes have closed. She's breathing softly. Ella tilts her head. I'm almost afraid to meet her gaze. It was just a story. But I feel like I cut my chest open in front of her.

"Thank you," she whispers.

"I should—I should go help Adelaida," I say. "With the fire."

"Right," Ella says.

I stand up and walk away like I'm coming out of a dream.

Hours pass.

Every time I think the storm has to end soon, fierce wind rattles the doors and windows. The dark descends in earnest. It's so heavy, I can't believe I thought it was dark as midnight before. This darkness swallows us like we'll never see sun again.

Adelaida adds more peat to the fire, then vanishes to get some sleep in her own bed. Gretta leaves to find her parents. Katla stokes the hearth. Ness and Sofie fall asleep among the kids.

I think Ella is asleep too until I see her get to her feet. Kaspar leaps to the ground and scrabbles away. Ella tiptoes among the sleeping bodies. She reaches the door. It opens, the softest creak.

I look around the room. Only Kaspar watches me.

I follow Ella. Ease the door shut behind me. She turns. A few stray strands of hair drift back and forth around her temples, caught in drafts like the lantern she holds is exhaling beneath her.

"Hi," she says.

"I—" I don't know why I followed her. I don't know what I meant to ask her. Nothing. Everything.

"Nice story," Ella says. "The queens, huh? Plural?"

My voice soft, I say, "Tamm doesn't exactly explain the nature of their friendship in the footnotes."

She doesn't ask what I mean. Doesn't ask why I chose that story. I'm trying not to ask myself.

Instead, I ask her, "What do you think will happen in the Panic of the Livestock?"

"I don't know," Ella says. "You're the one who read *Captain's Log*."

I swallow. "Kos is never specific about anything useful."

She laughs lightly. "Right."

The rain beats overhead. I sift through useless words, searching for something to say before she can walk away.

"Do you really want to marry Nikolai?" Ella asks.

I blink. I open my mouth, but before I can speak, Ella says, "It's just, I was thinking about the storms. And the Flood, and the fleet, and I was just wondering if—" She falters. "Do you love him, or something?"

If she didn't look so sincere, I'd laugh. Nikolai is clever and handsome and intriguing. I can imagine kissing him, maybe on the prow of a ship. It would be exciting enough. I once kissed Gregor on the cheek after he sprinted halfway to Southtown to catch a runaway Kaspar, and that's the extent of my kissing experience.

But love?

"I hardly know him." And then, because I realize I still haven't answered the question, I add, "Of course not."

Ella's shoulders relax like they've been coiled. The lantern light bobs.

"I just want to survive." My voice is low; I can't hide the plea in it. *Don't hate me.*

A foot of space separates us. If she closed it, I would let her.

"What are you going to do? In Storm One?" I ask.

She holds my gaze for such a long time, I think she must've forgotten the question. But finally: "I don't know."

I hold my breath. She leans toward me.

"I'm scared," she whispers.

She's so close that I can feel the words against my skin.

"Of what?" I say. "The storm?"

"I—"

The hallway door flies open.

Ella leaps back so fast, her lantern goes out. I press a hand to my cheek, stinging with a blush, as three guards stampede into the hall. Gregor leads Twain—Gretta's brother—and Sebastian, another of Nikolai's favorite guards. Their bodies are too big, voices too loud, for this private little space. Somehow, the whole trio gets wedged between Ella and me. I try and fail to catch her gaze around Gregor's shoulder.

"We just wanted to come check on you," Gregor says.

"We're fine." I realize I'm still pressing my hand to my cheek. I let it fall.

"Ness in there?" Twain asks.

"Seas' sake," Sebastian says, "we're on duty." He's nearly as tall as Gregor but twice as loud. The scruff on his white-pink chin makes him look older, but I know he's the same age as me. "You doing okay, Tasha?"

I shift under the weight of the nickname. I didn't know Sebastian and I were such good friends. "Yeah. We're fine."

I just want them all to leave. I want Ella to finish saying whatever she was saying. Or doing.

Instead, she backs toward the flyer bedroom door. It creaks behind her.

"Are you going?" I say.

"I, um . . ." Ella glances at the guards. "Yeah."

"Need anything?" Gregor asks.

Ella disappears without answering.

"Okay, be honest," Gregor says. "She hates us."

"No, she just . . . We were just in the middle of talking about something."

"Nah," Sebastian says. "She hates us. I've seen her leave the kitchens mid-meal when a big enough group of guards arrives."

I'd argue with him, but I've seen Ella do it too.

"Besides," Sebastian adds, "she always has that weird, blank stare."

Cold pools in my stomach.

Sebastian grins at Twain. Is this a joke to them? "I can't tell if she's wrong in the head . . ."

"Sebastian," Gregor says, warning.

Sebastian puts his hands in the air. ". . . or just a bitch."

I punch him in the mouth.

He lurches back. His hands fly to his face. "Shit, Natasha!"

My knuckles sting. The inside of my head pounds. Gregor grabs me by the shoulders and propels me away from Sebastian and Twain.

I look back over my shoulder. "Don't talk about my girls."

Sebastian groans. Twain squints at his mouth.

Gregor guides me out the door, back into the dim studio. Katla looks up from the fire, frowning.

Gregor bends his forehead to mine. "What was that about?" he whispers.

"Nothing." I stare at the back of my hand. Blood wells from the tips of my knuckles where they hit Sebastian's teeth.

"Nothing?" Gregor says.

"You know I'm protective of the flyers."

"Protective?" he says.

"Are you just going to repeat everything I say?"

Gregor gives me a long look. "You know," he says, "punching guards to defend the honor of a flyer isn't really what a queen would do."

"Yeah," I say. "And?"

"Is Ella—"

I set my jaw.

"You know what?" he says. "Never mind." He nods at my hand. "Put some ice on that."

But as soon as Gregor leaves, I forget his ice suggestion. I go to the flyer bedroom. But when I open the door, I find Ella lying in bed, pretending to be asleep. Pretending?

"Ella," I whisper.

She doesn't respond.

What was she going to tell me?

Outside, Storm Four howls.

36

ELLA

I don't sleep the night of Storm Four.

I spend hours with my face pressed to my pillow, clutching Maret's barometer, furious with myself. What was I thinking? Talking to Natasha that way? Leaning so close to her, as if I wanted to—

I'm glad the guards showed up when they did.

My stomach winds itself into a knot so tight, I think I might vomit. In the morning, the nausea hits me even harder. I can barely stand.

I wobble into the studio. The rain outside has eased to a heavy drizzle. Most of the young girls are still asleep, but all the Royal Flyers, plus Adelaida, cluster near the fireplace. Sofie clutches a squirming Kaspar to her chest.

Using the wall to keep me upright, I make my way toward them.

Katla lies on the floor, pressing a hand to her forehead. When she sees me, she says, "Oh, thank the seas. At least someone else looks as bad as I feel."

Natasha is on her feet in an instant. She sets a hand on my shoulder. I want to shake her off—last night's near mistake is still too fresh—but I can't find the energy to do it.

Adelaida squints at me. "How do you feel?"

"Like a shark got halfway through digesting me, then spat me back out," I say.

"Mmm," Adelaida says. "Did you—oh, not again."

Kaspar, who has managed to squirm free of Sofie, leaps to the floor. He throws himself against the far door—the one leading to the vestibule that opens onto the street. When it doesn't collapse beneath his ferocious attack, he paws at the wood dejectedly.

"He's been doing that all morning," Sofie says.

When the parents arrive to scoop up their junior flyers, Adelaida has to lock Kaspar in the storage closet so he doesn't make a break for it. I'm sitting with Katla by the empty hearth when a damp breeze skates into the studio. My skin prickles.

"Maybe we should go outside," Katla says. "Get some fresh air."

"I was just thinking that."

As soon as I take my first step onto the wet cobblestones, some of the tension in my stomach loosens. For the first time in hours, when I breathe, I can fill my lungs all the way.

Katla and I cross the width of the stone street. On the far side, a metal railing keeps us from falling into the ocean. I press myself against the rail and shut my eyes, listening to the sound of waves. All that's left of the rain now is a gentle mist. It must be just north of freezing, but I hardly feel the cold.

"Look at that," Katla says.

I open my eyes. She's pointing to a place two wave crests out, where a sleek, dark form bobs against the current. Its ears rise in pointed tufts. It's swimming.

"Is that a seal?" I ask.

"At the risk of sounding like I hit my head," Katla says, "I think it's a lynx."

"A lynx. In the ocean."

"I know," Katla says, "but you see it too, don't you?"

I do. I stare at the swimming creature until it bobs out of sight. "Kos called Storm Four the Panic of the Livestock, right? Not the Panic of the Cats?"

Katla is quiet for a long moment. We're both thinking. The nausea has faded nearly to nothing by the time Natasha joins us outside. She's bundled in a cloak, hat, and mittens, and when she sees us, she shivers.

"First of all, brr."

"It's not that bad," Katla says.

"Also," I say, "I'm half snowman on my father's side, so this is whatever."

Natasha snorts. "Gretta just came back from talking to her father about the storm. Guards have been all over the city surveying the damage. Lots of bridges down and canals flooding, like usual. And a ton of livestock is missing. All those goat farms near the boglands? Empty. The goats either jumped into the river, ran into the forest, or threw themselves against the walls of their enclosures so hard, they died."

"Ella," Katla says slowly, like she's still thinking something through. "You said you grew up on a farm, right?"

"What are you getting at?"

She frowns at the ocean. "I just . . . Look, it's clearly not *just* livestock. Kaspar started acting weird during the storm too. And we both started feeling sick."

"Oh, right," I say. "I forgot to mention that I'm half snowman on my father's side, but half goat on my mother's side."

"I just wonder," Katla says, "if maybe there's something about growing up around animals and, I don't know, nature, or whatever, that makes Storm Four worse on some people than others."

"Well, I feel left out," Natasha says.

"Yeah, because you grew up in the middle of the city."

"I don't know about this," Natasha says.

I think of Fredrik, the lizard Katla's brother showed me. *He keeps trying to get away. Ever since Storm Five.* If Storm Five was misnamed—Exodus of the Birds instead of Exodus of the Birds, Lizards, etcetera—then couldn't Storm Four have been misnamed too? Panic of the Mammals? Panic of the Domesticated Animals and People Who Grew Up Outside?

"Even if you're right," I say, "what are we supposed to do about it?"

"I just feel this thing in my stomach," Katla says. "Like I'm supposed to be doing something."

"I know," I say.

"Can you be more specific?" Natasha says.

"No," Katla says.

"Me neither," I say.

The feeling—it's like when you know you've forgotten something. I know that it's there, but it keeps dancing just out of reach. The harder I fight to grab it, the less convinced I am that it was ever there in the first place.

"There's a thing my family says." Katla's eyes are fixed on the water. *"Sing as the sea."*

"Sing as the sea," I repeat.

"Right," Katla says. "Get it?"

And actually, I think I do. Something about listening to the water. Something about being more like the ocean, or maybe being more with the ocean. It's like the feeling in my stomach. The more I try to put words to it, the farther away it goes.

When I go back inside, my stomach starts to knot again.

In the studio, a few older, unfamiliar guards repeat some of what Natasha already told us: Bridges are down, streets are blocked, canals are flooding. The guards say we'd best stay put in the palace. We promise them mightily that we'll do just that. As soon as they walk out the door, everyone readies to leave.

Katla and Ness plan to visit their families; Sofie plans to visit Pippa. Gretta asks me where I'm going, but I evade the question by saying "Out and about!" and fleeing through the door.

I wrap my arms around my torso and head to Maret's apartment. Being on the streets between tall buildings, out of sight of the ocean, is nearly as bad as being inside the studio. The walk takes me twice as long as usual. I have to wind this way and that around all the impassable streets.

Buildings have collapsed and vomited their contents into the canals. People huddle on the streets. The city is quiet with panic.

Six months ago, I would never have imagined I would be panicking with them. But that feeling in my stomach—like there's something I need to remember, something I need to do.

Kill Nikolai.

That's what I have to do. All I have to do. Soon, I can kill Nikolai. I can give Maret the throne. After Cassia died, this was exactly where I wanted to be: in the palace, ingratiated, poised to avenge her murder.

But six months ago, I would never have imagined what it would mean to be a flyer. To have friends. To know Sofie, and Katla, and— and Natasha.

I know it's not nothing, the way my pulse gallops when Natasha walks into a room. I know it because I've felt it before. I felt it when I first met Cassia.

I didn't think I could ever love someone again. I didn't think I wanted to.

Last night, in a fit of almost-sleep, I caught myself imagining Natasha's hands in my hair. Of her lips forming my name. Of my stomach to her stomach, our bodies pressed, my chin tilting up—

But Natasha isn't part of our plan. And Cassia would never forgive me. She wasn't the forgiving type.

I keep reliving the moment in the hallway with Natasha. The way the lantern glowed on her skin. The way she leaned toward me like she had more to say than she would let herself. Most of all, the way she made me realize something I didn't know was true:

I don't want to die.

37

NATASHA

When the door slams behind Ella, the other girls are busy buttoning their coats to leave, off to visit family and friends. I am fixed, staring at that door. "What does she mean, *out and about?*" I say.

"I've been saying all along that she's hiding something," Gretta says.

"What? No you haven't."

Gretta lets out a breath in a huff. "You all think I'm mean, so you never listen to me when I'm making a good point."

"We don't think you're mean, Gretta," Ness says.

"Sure we do," Katla says.

I take Gretta's arm to draw her attention back to me. "Why do you think Ella is hiding something?"

"Well, for starters, sometimes when she walks into the kitchen, she turns straight around again."

I'm reminded of what Sebastian said last night.

"Second," Gretta says, "I caught her snooping around the library."

I draw my brows together. "When?"

"You were all off with Pippa."

"Maybe she likes to read," Katla interrupts. "Truly, the highest of crimes. Sofie, come on, let's go."

Katla walks out the door. Sofie pauses a minute. She looks at me. "I'd let it go, Tasha. The storms make everyone a little strange from time to time." And then she follows Katla.

Tasha. She called me Tasha, like we're friends again.

After the door closes behind them, Gretta says, "Well, I still think Ella is suspicious."

"Hmm," I say. Maybe I should stop asking her questions and seek answers myself.

"Where are you going?" Gretta says.

I open the door. "Out and about."

38

ELLA

When Maret opens her door, she's bleary-eyed. Her breath bears the faint sweetness of old wine.

"Come in," she says. There's no *love*, no *hello, darling!* I'm nervous before I've even begun.

I sit stiffly on the pink couch beside her. A bruise has appeared on the ceiling, drip, drip, dripping water into a bucket below. Out the window, the street is a stream.

"How are you feeling?" I ask.

"Tired," she says. "But happy we're done with Storm Four."

"You're not feeling strange?"

"Strange?" Maret says.

"Like you promised someone you'd meet them somewhere, but you've forgotten when and where."

She presses her fingers to her temples. "Did I promise I'd meet someone somewhere?"

I shake my head. "Never mind."

"You're acting odd today."

I settle my hands on my lap and take a breath. "What if I didn't want to die?"

Maret's face is impassive. "Pardon?"

"I know why I'm such a valuable assassin. Because it's a lot easier to send someone into the palace to kill Nikolai if they don't care whether or not they get away with it."

She leans back in the sofa. Her lips are thin as she lets silence settle over the room. "Well, you always said *I'll die for Cassia, I'll do anything to kill Nikolai.*"

I listen to the drip, drip, dripping.

"Right," I say. "But what if I wanted to survive?"

A scraping at the window. I look up and give the glass a frown. Then I look back to Maret and find her staring stonily at me.

"Explain," she says. "Everything."

39

NATASHA

I manage to catch sight of Ella just before she disappears into the maze of New Sundstad. I follow her from a distance, always keeping a street behind as she zigzags through the city. The whole way, I fight with myself. This is an invasion of privacy. But also, where could she possibly be going? She claims to be an orphan with no connections, no friends outside the palace.

So who is she going to see?

She stops at a creaky-looking building in Eel Shore a few blocks south of the university and disappears inside.

There are no windows on the first floor, but I catch a glimmer of light from the second. And something red, waving. Silks?

I don't dare follow Ella into that building, but the adjacent building has a board nailed across the doorframe. Abandoned.

I look up at the window with the silks, then I stride purposefully toward the boarded-up door. The wood is only nailed to the frame, so when I turn the handle, the door opens. With a glance over my shoulder, I duck inside.

It's dark and the stairs squelch and bow under my feet. The floorboards on the second story look ready to cave in, but I'm not interested in the room. I'm interested in the window. I step lightly across the perimeter and open the window, wincing when the frame shrieks.

When no one comes thumping up the stairs after me, I lean on the moldering frame.

Ella's window is just below, and I see her sitting on a tattered pink sofa, crossing her arms and pursing her lips. On the other side of the sofa sits a woman, old enough to be Ella's—or my—mother. Her face is in profile to me. She looks . . . familiar? I scan her bony face. She's wearing a thin headband around her forehead, the kind I've seen stylish noblewomen wear.

The windowsill digs into my ribs as I lean a bit farther.

Ella's mouth moves. I can't hear what she says. I lean farther out the sill.

If either of them looks up, they'll see me.

40

ELLA

"Maybe I'm reconsidering this suicide mission," I say.

Maret stills. "You don't want to kill Nikolai for what he did?"

"No! I do. I still want—he deserves to be dead. He does. I just . . . I don't want to die."

Maret makes her hand into a fist and tilts her head to rest on it. Her mouth curls.

Finally, I say, "Is it so bad? To want to live?"

"No," she says. "I'm just curious what caused your change of heart. I mean, it's wonderful. I'm happy for you. When we made this plan, you were a bottomless abyss of a girl."

"I'm still prepared to kill Nikolai. That hasn't changed."

Maret considers me. Her faint smile never wavers. "It's not as if I wanted you in unnecessary danger. I'd rather you didn't die too."

"So we'll change our plan?"

"What did you have in mind?"

All the words come out in a rush. "Well, I just have to figure out a way to catch him when no one else is around. So instead of waiting for one of the guard parties—instead of trying to do it in front of all those people—I'll just have to sneak into his bedroom while he's sleeping, or something."

"You know there's a reason that wasn't the plan all along, don't you?" Maret asks. "Because when Nikolai is asleep, he's surrounded by guards. He doesn't just wander the palace unattended."

"But—" I can't keep the hurt out of my voice. "You should want this. You should want me to survive."

"I do!" She takes my shoulders. "I do want you to survive. Very much. But if you try and fail to kill Nikolai, all this will have been for nothing. Cassia's killer sails away into the New World. Hundreds of thousands of Kostrovians—Kostrovians who could've been helped, saved, by a better ruler—will drown. You are incredibly dear to me, Ella. But the crown means more than either of us."

"What if I can come up with a plan? Something you approve of. A way to kill Nikolai and get away with it."

Maret is quiet for a long moment. Finally: "If you're serious about this, we need time to plan for every detail. Can you come up with something by the bear season festival?"

I count the days in my head. "That's only two weeks away."

"Then you'd better hurry."

I nod.

"Come back after the festival," Maret says. "Everyone will be distracted, so it will give you a chance to slip away. You can tell me your new plan then."

"I will."

"The crown is everything," she says. "Don't forget that." She lifts her chin toward the door.

I let out a mouthful of air. I head for the door before she can change her mind.

"Oh, and Ella?"

I turn back to Maret. She's outlined by hazy light, her hair a golden crown. In the window behind her, a flash of something, a movement.

"You will tell no one who you are," she says.

"Of course not," I say.

"No one," she repeats. "I don't care if you think you've made friends or allies in the palace. I am your friend. I am your ally."

I nod again.

She dismisses me with a wave.

41

NATASHA

Much as I strain, I can't hear what they're saying. I almost think Ella sees me at one point, but I duck out of the way before her eyes can focus on me.

When I peek through the window again, Ella is gone. The older woman lifts a sheet of paper from a side table and frowns. I squint at the paper, straining to decipher any of the cramped letters.

"Natasha?"

My breath catches dry in my throat.

I turn slowly. Ella is coated in shadows.

"I thought I saw you," she says.

My heart pounds.

"What are you doing here?" I point to the window. "Who is that?"

"You don't have the right to ask me that," Ella says. Her voice is edged. Gone is the soft, breathless girl from the lantern-lit hallway last night. She frowns at the window, like the woman on the other side might be able to hear us. If I felt like being useful, I could tell her that room is soundproof, but I'm not feeling so inclined.

"Come on," she says, taking my wrist.

I jolt at her touch, the roughness of her grip. She pulls me down the stairs and out the door, under the board. We both spare a glance back at the pink building. Then Ella drags me away, far and fast, into the depths of the city.

When we reach an empty street, quiet save the movements of water left behind from the storm, I say, "Why do you seem so scared?"

"I don't seem scared," Ella says. She sloshes through a puddle.

"But who was that woman?"

Ella looks over her shoulder at me. Her eyes are narrowed and sharp. "Why did you follow me?"

"Because you were acting suspicious," I say. "I wanted to know where you were going." Stubbornly, I add, "I'm the principal flyer. I'm allowed to do that."

"You're allowed to follow me?" she says. "Well, good for you. Did you find it illuminating?"

"Just tell me who that woman was."

"A family friend," she says. "She's a family friend, and my parents knew her from Terrazza, and I would've mentioned her before, but I didn't know it was so important that I told you every facet of my life. All right?"

I feel heat beginning to flush my cheeks. "Why are you so evasive all the time?"

She stops walking. She looks at me.

For a long moment, she says nothing. Her mouth opens. No words. And then, finally, soft, cold: "I am not your puzzle to be solved."

She turns on her heel and walks away.

I don't follow.

ELLA

Walk.

Don't look back.

Just keep going.

To admire Natasha's cleverness but never suspect that it would turn against me? Naïve.

Seas. I've been a fool.

She's Nikolai's friend. She wants to marry him. If she can talk to Nikolai and not feel the deepest, darkest repulsion, then she's clearly a fool too.

This isn't about Natasha. This isn't even about me. This is about Cassia, and it always has been.

There is no Natasha and me. We're not friends, or allies, or anything else. We stand on opposite sides of Nikolai. She wants to be his queen. I want to kill him. Only one of us will get what we want.

It will be me.

NATASHA

I force myself to think of anything but Ella on the walk back to the palace. Nikolai. The queen's crown. The Flood. Not Ella. Not Ella.

It doesn't work.

When I reach the palace, I head straight for Adelaida's room. Inside, I shut the door behind me and cross my arms.

"I don't trust Ella," I say.

"And I don't trust Gretta," Adelaida says. "She always looks like she's watching all of us to compile a report for her father, doesn't she?"

"This isn't a joke," I say. "I followed Ella today. She went to visit this woman, and she said it was a family friend, but she was acting suspicious."

Adelaida, sitting in her desk chair, leans back. The hem of her cloak dusts the floor. "Now you sound like Gretta."

"I'm serious," I say. "I followed her all the way to Eel Shore, and—"

Adelaida holds up a hand. "She's a seventeen-year-old girl. Forgive me if I'm not overwhelmingly nervous about her suspicious doings."

"I'm a seventeen-year-old girl," I say.

"Yes," she says, honey-sweet, "and you're very capable of all sorts of nefarious deeds. Now." She turns to a stack of papers at her desk.

I'm prepared to protest more, but I stop when she fishes out a folded sheet of paper and hands it to me. "I think you'll find this more important than whatever the other flyers were up to this morning."

I take it. It's a letter. The paper is creamy, the golden seal already broken.

"What's this?"

"From Nikolai," Adelaida says. "It's addressed to you, but as your future advisor, I took the liberty of reading it first."

Natasha—

I kept hoping I'd run into you in the library again, but Adelaida must be keeping you too busy. Meet me there at four? I have something for you.

—Nikolai

When I lower the note, Adelaida grins.

"You failed to mention you and Nikolai 'ran into' each other in the library," she says.

"Did I?"

She shoos me. "Go. It's almost four. And for seas' sake, brush your hair first."

Though I make it to the library right at four, Nikolai isn't there yet. It's empty. I light a fire in the hearth and glance at the grandfather clock in the corner.

I drop into a velvet armchair. A lynx and crane board covers the table in front of me. I pick up one of the white crane pegs and roll it between my thumb and forefinger. When I was little, I spied on Nikolai and Cassia as they sat here, playing this game. Cassia always won.

The door opens.

Nikolai strides in, flanked by guards. His hair is windswept. Pink blotches brighten his usually pale cheeks.

I leap to my feet. "Your Royal Highness."

"Sorry I'm late. Everything is madness after the storm."

I wait until he sits to lower myself onto my armchair again. He glances at the board. "Do you play?" he says.

"I can play," I say. I *can* play, yes, but do I want to play? No, I want you to give me whatever it is you have for me, and then I want you to propose, and then with my newfound queenly power, I'll send a platoon of guards to figure out who Ella Neves really is.

"Oh, good," Nikolai says. "You be the cranes."

I bite the inside of my cheek and start slotting the crane pegs in the board.

He takes off his rings and sets them on the table, just like he did at the hot pools. What an odd habit, to be so bothered by your own rings, you have to take them off every time you want to use your hands for anything.

"So," he says, adding his lynx to the board, "you want to be queen."

It's so abrupt, the way you'd say: *So, you want porridge for breakfast?*

I move my first crane slowly, trying to give myself time to come up with a good answer. "Doesn't everyone?"

He moves his piece quickly, then waves a hand to erase my question from the air. "That's not an answer." He stares at me for a minute. "It's your move, by the way."

I move another crane. Swallow. "I mean, if you handed me a crown . . ."

"My council made a list for me." He shifts his lynx one spot closer to my crane. "Of people they want me to marry."

"Let me guess. I'm not on it."

"No," he says. "But I asked Gospodin to add you."

I feel a surge of hope. "Really?" I sound too eager. Like a child.

He meets my gaze over the top of the board. "I can't do anything unilaterally," Nikolai says. "You get that, right?"

"So what should I do? How can I convince your councilors?"

"Make friends with Gospodin," he says. "Convince him you'd be the best queen. Not just for me, but for the Sacred Breath. For the whole country."

My jaw twitches. Each turn, I march my cranes forward one by one, encroaching on Nikolai's lynx in a neat line.

He frowns down at the board. "You're good."

A memory tickles the back of my head. Nikolai and Cassia, playing this game as I spied from the tunnels. Cassia teasing him when she won, time after time. *What if you take the first three moves? What if I played with my eyes closed?* Sometimes, after she'd flounce out, undefeated, I would watch young Nikolai kick the table dully. "Cheater," he'd say, like even he didn't quite believe it.

We make the next few moves in silence. Nikolai slips free of my knot of cranes and manages to gobble up half of them before either of us speaks again. I watch his face as my cranes move. When he takes one of them, he smiles.

He thinks he can play better than me, but we're playing different games.

He moves his lynx across another of my cranes. "I win."

"Ah," I say. "Looks like it."

He reaches into his pocket. "Gospodin asked me to give you this." He hands me a letter. A ship embosses the blue wax seal.

I open it and scan Gospodin's slanted, scribbling scrawl. It's the

handwriting of someone who doesn't care how long it takes for anyone else to untangle it. "His penmanship is really something."

Nikolai laughs. "Squint and try your best."

> Dear Miss Koskinen,
>
> I hope you find yourself well in the aftermath of Storm Four.
> The energy in the city is palpable as we await the arrival of the
> New World.
>
> Perhaps I was too short with you when I saw you at Our
> Lady of Tidal Sorrows. Over the past few days, the king has
> been emphatic about including you in our search for his new
> queen. If you will forgive my honesty, I admit that this is against
> my counsel. Nevertheless, the king's powers are given by the sea,
> and I respect his authority.
>
> Perhaps the two of us should get to know each other better.
> I'm planning a tour of the city. I'd like you to join me. Should
> you agree, our first day will be next Sunday, eight o'clock in
> the morning. Meet me in front of Our Lady. Consider giving
> Captain's Log another perusal. I recommend Book 3, Lines
> 121–144.
>
> My very best,
> Righteous Mariner Gabriel Gospodin

I refold the letter along the seams. "A tour of the city?" I say. "Any
idea what he means by that?"

Nikolai coughs. "You know. Just spreading the teachings of the
good brothers of the Sacred Breath. Telling people to stay calm.
Smiling."

So, what? A propaganda tour?

"There has to be a copy of *Captain's Log* in here, right?" I ask.

"A dozen editions in a dozen languages."

I scan the shelves until I find a copy in Kostrovian. Nikolai stands over my shoulder as I hunch with the book. I leaf through the pages until I find Book 3 and drag my fingers down the numbered lines.

When it came time for our second harvest in the New World, we found our crops had spoiled. It was the work of a small insect, red-bodied and black-footed, that I named the crop louse. They bred prodigiously and flattened our fields. One farmer came to me and admitted he had seen such an insect moons ago, but did not squash it, so entranced was he by the vivid color of the creature's shell. I told him that one toxic bug can spoil the whole crop. Soon, I realized my words had greater wisdom than even I first knew.

One of our fellow survivors had begun speaking nonsense that it was only luck, rather than the sea's fated intervention, that we should have survived the Flood. His dissent caused rumblings throughout the whole village. I had no choice but to act decisively.

Much as one insect can spoil the whole crop, one dissenter can spoil the peace. We must root out dangerous individuals, whether they be insect or man, and see them to their deaths before they can contaminate others.

"Gospodin told you to read that?" Nikolai asks.

I scan the passage again. "Is he suggesting I'm a dissenter? Or a nonbeliever? Or a crop louse?"

Nikolai frowns. "You've heard of what's happening with the boglands, right?" he says. "There've been a lot of, well, stirrings. Uprisings. Among the Brightwallers. So maybe Gospodin is just making sure you know how important it is that we're all on the same side heading into the Flood." Nikolai smiles at me. "But that's no problem, right?"

I force myself to smile back.

So Gospodin wants me to prove myself. To prove how thoroughly I'm committed to the Sacred Breath.

To root out dangerous individuals—*to see them to their deaths*—before they can contaminate others.

Dangerous individuals like Katla and her family?

"Right," I say. "No problem at all."

44

ELLA

In the week that follows Storm Four, I hurry out of the studio every evening the moment rehearsal ends. I feel Gretta's suspicious eyes and Natasha's angry ones. Once, when I'm leaving practice, Sofie takes my elbow and says, "Don't you want to come to dinner with us? I feel like we've hardly talked lately."

"I haven't been very hungry," I say.

And I slip away. I can tell she's hurt by my rejection, and I tell myself that I don't care.

Maret wants me to come up with a plan, and so I will. I'll figure out a way to kill Nikolai and get away with it. And then, once Maret is queen, I can tell her that Sofie deserves a place on the royal fleet, and all will be forgiven.

I return to the library, careful this time about being followed. I study maps of the palace, then trace my fingers along walls that don't seem to meet the way they should and staircases that go nowhere. Hidden passageways?

I still have the knife from the barometer, but I don't know how to catch Nikolai alone so I can use it.

The best weapon I can think of so far is poison, but I've spent enough time in the kitchen to know that René personally handles all of Nikolai's food. According to a demoralizing text I found on failed assassinations, every king in the history of Kostrov has had a food-taster.

There's no obvious solution. It's infuriating.

The shelf by the fireplace is stacked with those same books that look recently read. I wonder who sits here, leafing through these pages.

I open the green botanical book that I noticed last time I was here, thinking of the carnivorous plant Katla's brother showed me. I don't see it, but there are plenty of other strange plants. On a dog-eared page, I inspect a mushroom with lavender gills. *Smells of honey,* the note says, then, inexplicably, *Otto von Kleb?*

I put the book back where I found it. Someone other than Nikolai must be sitting here, reading these books and scrawling notes in the margins. I can't imagine him marveling at plants. I certainly can't imagine him leaving the palace to explore the boglands.

The doorknob rattles.

I freeze. Just as the door begins to open, I regain my senses and dart behind the nearest shelf. Footsteps echo down the long aisle at the library's middle. I hold my breath. Another set of footsteps.

"And the others?"

"All in Skarat."

Lowered voices. I peek out from the edge of the shelf. Two men. The backs of their heads. One blond, one dark-haired.

Nikolai and Andrei.

My breath catches. I'm positive it's audible. *Don't move. Don't breathe.*

"Fine," Nikolai says. "Now, where is that stupid ring?"

He's still walking. Footsteps getting perilously close. I press myself into the shelf and try to disappear.

He stops at the chairs by the fireplace. Shuffles around until he finds—something. I squint over the tops of book spines. He's holding a ring up to the light.

"How'd you lose that?" Andrei says.

"I was here with Natasha Koskinen."

I immediately jump to the worst-case scenario. They were tucked away together like to-be-married lovebirds. So naked Nikolai had to take off all his silly-looking jewelry. Gross, gross, gross.

Apparently, Andrei's mind goes the same place as mine, because he starts to laugh.

"Playing lynx and crane," Nikolai adds, sounding annoyed. "Thank you very much."

"Sure," Andrei says. "Hey, I told you Captain Waska wanted to meet with you about security for the bear season festival, right? For your receiving line."

"Great," Nikolai says. "Do feel free to murder me before then."

They start walking again. Back toward the door. I crouch low, but just as I do—

I only see it for a second. But it's enough.

Pinned to Nikolai's chest, right over his heart, I see a flash of pearls. A strange little brooch shaped like a beetle.

Cassia's ladybug. The one she wore on the inside of her jacket every day.

I'm sick.

Once they're gone, I stay in the library for a few long moments. I rest my pounding head in my hands.

It's only after they're gone that I realize I should've had a weapon on me. Nikolai and Andrei were both here, *right here,* and—

I didn't feel like a killer. All I felt was terrified.

The bear season festival—my deadline for Maret—is one week away. A week after that, Nikolai will announce who he's going to marry.

I need to kill him. Even if he's going to pick Natasha. Even if by killing Nikolai, I end up killing her too.

I don't have a choice.

45

NATASHA

When the day of my meeting with Gospodin arrives, my arms ache from all the extra flying practice we've been doing. With the festival just a week away, I've hardly spent a waking hour off the silks. Plus. I've needed something to distract me from Ella.

I beat Gospodin to the square in front of Our Lady. All the rain that can drain away from Storm Four already has. More snow fell last night, coating the parts of the city that were not already water-filled in a freshness of white. A skin of ice tops the less trafficked canals. I bury my face in the coils of my scarf and stomp my feet against the frosty stones to keep warm. The big hand on the clock-tower ticks five, ten, fifteen minutes past eight, and there's still no sign of Gospodin.

When he finally arrives, striding out of the apartment attached to Our Lady with his shoulders back and his hands in the pockets of a long coat, he's a half an hour late and I'm grumpy.

I plaster on a smile. "Many breaths."

"Almost believable," he says. "Let's walk."

Gospodin and I walk to Southtown in what I hope is companionable silence. We stop at a square at the farthest southern reach of the city.

While the Grand Harbor is full of international bustle, as bright a place as any in New Sundstad, this wharf is industrial and gritty. The ships that dock here come from the rivers of the boglands or the fields on the other side of Kostrov.

I follow Gospodin to a row of tables set up by the water. Two men in the white cloaks of the Sacred Breath and a few women in modest dresses stand behind it. One of the tables is stacked with pamphlets. The rest are covered in cloth-draped baskets. Savory smells emanate from them. My stomach gurgles.

Everyone *many breaths* each other. I take one of the pamphlets. The paper is thick and pulpy, the texture of plentiful recyclings. Printed across the front: *There is still time to find hope!*

"It helps if you don't frown at our literature," Gospodin says.

I affix a smile to my face.

The crowd flocks to us. In all, there are six tables with two volunteers manning each. Whenever a basket dips low, another one appears in its place.

"How did you get so much food?" I ask Gospodin. We're stationed at the same table, and every time someone points at me, whispers something excited about the Royal Flyers, he smiles.

"Nikolai and I did it together," he says. "We convinced the nobles to donate some of their usual rations for the greater good. He'd be here too, but we thought it might make everything too chaotic."

"Oh." I find that I like imagining it: Nikolai, purposeful, directing people and resources. I feel a little guilty, even. I know I carry my mother's resentment of the Sacred Breath. Maybe I shouldn't.

I pull a white cloth away from a new basket. This one is laden with loaves of rosemary rye bread and glistening little tarts. I hold one of the tarts up to the light. The pastry is a perfect gold. The filling, bright cranberries and bits of brown mushroom. I think the glisten comes from honey. A dab of it leaks onto my finger, dyed red from the berries.

"Save the food for the less fortunate, Miss Koskinen," Gospodin says.

"I know, I know." I hand the tart to the next person in line with a smile. He's a light-skinned, well-whiskered man, and he wishes me many breaths before he goes.

I'm about to lick the honey off my finger, but the next woman in line steps forward. She eyes me skeptically. I wipe my finger on the table. "Would you like the bread or a tart?"

The first woman to look more intrigued by our literature than our food wears her gray hair long and loose. She takes a pamphlet, holding it a full arm's length from her face in case it turns out to have teeth.

Gospodin sets down a loaf of rosemary bread and goes to greet her. I hesitate, then follow.

"Can you read, miss?" Gospodin says, showing off his bright teeth.

The woman raises her chin. "My grandson can." Then she notices me standing behind Gospodin and says, "You're a flyer."

"Yes?"

"Are the flyers part of the Sacred Breath now too? Instead of *Inna and the Bear*, will you be performing the story of Kos at the next festival?"

Gospodin laughs. "That's very funny."

The woman blinks as if Gospodin is speaking a dialect she doesn't quite understand. "Wasn't meant to be." She looks at me again, still waiting for an answer.

"The flyers all appreciate the Sacred Breath's guidance." I glance at Gospodin. "The royals and the Sacred Breath are closely entwined, and as Royal Flyers, we're willing to support the Righteous Mariner however we can."

"Well," the woman says, setting the pamphlet back on the table. "I should've expected as much."

She leaves in a hurry. I frown. One of the Sacred Breath brothers slips out from behind the table. He vanishes into the crowd, as if to follow the gray-haired woman.

"Where's he going?" I ask.

Gospodin doesn't answer. He's already back by our table of bread and tarts.

I watch the alley where the gray-haired woman and the Sacred Breath brother disappeared for a long moment, but there's no sign of either of them. I go back to my table.

Being in Southtown makes me feel eight years old again, at the mercy of my mother's desperate sadnesses and sudden determinations to move us elsewhere: to a new apartment; to the converted closet of a seamstress's shop; to the cabin of a ship captained by a man with a fishhook smile.

I'm left with the disturbing sense that Gospodin can peek into my brain when he says, "You were born in Southtown, yes?"

"Yes," I say. I keep my eyes on the edge of the square, watching the people in their long coats go about their Sunday morning business.

"So was I."

"Really?"

A crooked smile.

"How did you make it to the palace?" I say.

"Same as you. Hard work. Being the best at what I did. As a boy, I worked in a lawyer's office, cleaning his floor and sewing the buttons back on his coat. He took a shine to me and helped me learn to read. Really, I think he just wanted someone to file his papers for him, but I learned my letters anyway. By the time I was your age, I was studying law at the university. Nikolai's father, Orest—this would've been right before he became king—sometimes deigned to show up to classes too. I made a point to become his friend, and he decided he liked me."

"You were a lawyer?" I wouldn't like to battle Gospodin in a courthouse.

"Not for long," he says. "It was tedious and bureaucratic. What I liked was persuading people." He nods at the pamphlets. "That's mostly what I do nowadays. Persuade. But now I do it for a better cause."

"So you didn't grow up following the Sacred Breath?"

"I came to it later in life," he says, "which is why I know the importance of being here today."

I think of the brother leaving our table and slipping down the street. I think of Book 3 of *Captain's Log*: *One dissenter can spoil the peace.*

"You don't expect these pamphlets to convince many nonbelievers to leap headfirst into the Sacred Breath, do you?" I say.

He tilts his head, considering, smiling slightly as though he's pleased I've gotten it. He doesn't answer for a moment, not until no one is standing in line. Then, "No, Miss Koskinen. I do not."

"You don't care who wants to talk to us," I say. "You want to see who's angry."

"Like I said. I grew up in Southtown among nonbelievers. I know what my father would've done, had he seen us standing here. He would've spat at our feet and gone straight home, to an altar to a bear spirit he thought lived in the boglands. If you camped out there for a night, you would've seen two dozen other men knock on his door, gather around his hearth, and tell blasphemous stories to undermine everything Kos wrote."

I'm almost too stunned to respond. "Does the Sacred Breath know that?"

He lifts a shoulder. The curve of his smile steepens. He's pleased at my shock. "How do you think I found my footing among them so quickly?"

"You turned in your father?"

"For the good of New Sundstad," he says. "Always for the good of New Sundstad."

My mouth is dry. Is his father imprisoned? Dead?

The cloaked brother who followed the gray-haired woman rejoins us. He gives Gospodin a short shake of his head.

Thankfully, most people don't stop when they see us. A few show genuine curiosity. Just when I have convinced myself that Gospodin was exaggerating when he said his father would have spat at our feet, a man does just that. He's large in every dimension, with cheeks as round and ruddy as apples. "The Maapinnen survived just fine without Kos and his fanatics," he says. Then he spits. It arcs through the air and lands with a resounding splatter on Gospodin's chest.

Gospodin laughs. He pulls a handkerchief from his pocket and dabs away the man's offering.

The man, who looks unsettled by the laughter, hastens across the square, glancing over his shoulder as he goes. Gospodin, still smiling, nods to one of the cloaked brothers. Only now do I realize how disconcertingly well-muscled the two brothers are.

The people in the square do an excellent job of pretending they don't see the spit, or the spitter, or the brother following him. And yet, suddenly, the square is empty. Everyone seems to remember something urgent they must do in the opposite direction.

I shift my weight.

"How do you think the Maapinnen people survived after the Flood?" Gospodin says in the calm that follows. His voice is level. Chipper, even.

"Pardon?" I say, more to stall than because I didn't understand him.

When the Sacred Breath arrived to conquer Maapinn, the country was full of people who'd never heard of Antinous Kos. They had their own Flood legends, but no one ever wrote them down. Not like *Captain's Log*, written and rewritten and translated so many times that the whole world knows it. So when you're looking for a template for how to survive a Flood, it's a lot easier to look at Kos than at the Maapinnen.

"The Maapinnen." Gospodin turns his gaze to me. I've never noticed how pretty his eyes are: brightly irised, blue, with long black lashes. "How do you think they survived the last Flood?"

"Isn't it a mystery?" I say.

"Venture a guess."

I try to invent the answer Gospodin most wants to hear. "I guess they were good people? They adhered to the same virtues as Kos, even though they'd never read *Captain's Log*?"

He hmms. "Not a bad theory. Kos was the one who told us

patience, hope, and resilience are the core virtues; doesn't mean other people didn't have them, though."

"'In times of strife and storm,'" I quote, "'we wait with fortitude.'"

Gospodin's eyebrows raise. "You really did read *Captain's Log*, didn't you?"

"I told you I did."

"So now," he says, "do you understand why it's important to spread Kos's message?"

Captain's Log was abundantly clear about it. "The more people who know Kos's virtues—who know why the sea saved him—the more people who have a chance at surviving."

"Correct," Gospodin says. "To teach a man about Kos is to save his life."

I nod, but my skin prickles under the heavy folds of my wool cloak. I wish that I believed Gospodin. Everything would be worlds easier if I could just convince myself that his logic is sound: The sea saves people who are patient, hopeful, resilient, *good*, and kills all the rest. If I believed it, I could relax. Just decide to be good. But from our pamphlet-laden table, I have a wide view of sea. It looks to me vast, gnarled, churning, a thing more ancient than words and more beautiful than song and more formidable than any beast I've ever seen.

But does it watch us? Judge us?

It's already so much. It's already so glorious and terrible without all the rest. I would worship it for what I know it is sooner than for the powers I'm told it has.

My stomach is tight, so for a moment, I shut my eyes and listen to the sound of the waves.

"You feel it too?" Gospodin says.

I open my eyes. "What?"

He nods at the waves. "The call. It hit me during Storm Four."

Is that was I was feeling? The same thing Katla and Ella told me about?

"It's the sea's way of talking to you," Gospodin says. "That's another thing I'd wager the Maapinnen people did. Listened to the ocean. Worshipped the sea. Worshipped it differently than Kos but worshipped it all the same."

I press a hand to my stomach. "Really?"

"*Sing as the sea,*" Gospodin says. "Interesting rallying cry, no?"

"I'm not sure what you mean."

"It's part of an old Maapinnen song. Brightwallers say it because they're trying to claim that they understand the ocean better than we do. Like the sea sings in a language only they can understand. But it's an interesting rallying cry, because if they'd ever read *Captain's Log,* they'd know Kos said something similar."

I try to remember everything I read. "He did?"

"'I will sing to the sea, and the sea will sing to me, for as long as I am good to it, it will show me its brilliance.' Book Two." Gospodin frowns. "Shame that Brightwallers these days seem more interested in vandalizing Our Lady and the royal fleet than worshipping the sea quietly, like the Maapinnen would've."

"Oh," I say. "Right."

A girl, maybe seven years old, approaches our table. She wears a hat with flaps over her ears. If she has parents, they're not here. She ignores the food and comes straight for me, pointing at my chest with a mittened hand.

"You're Natasha," she says. "You're my favorite."

I can feel Gospodin watching me. I come out from behind the table and crouch in front of the girl. Her eyebrows are so pale, I'm not convinced she has them. "I am. What's your name?"

"Livli," she says.

I rest my forearms on my knees so that I'm eye level with Livli. "Do you like flying?"

"I never tried it," she says. "I like watching it."

"Perhaps you can learn to fly in the New World," Gospodin says.

Livli gives me a skeptical look, awaiting my confirmation. She's young; she isn't stupid.

I'm cold from the inside out. There's a long silence, and I know what I'm meant to say: *Yes, Livli, the ocean will save you. Yes, Livli, if you believe in the Sacred Breath, you will make it to the New World. Yes, Livli, if you're patient, resilient, and hopeful, the ocean will protect you.*

The words are tar in my throat.

"Miss Koskinen?" Gospodin says.

"I very much hope the sea will save you," I say.

I have never loathed myself quite so acutely.

"The sea's going to save you?" Livli says.

I turn my gaze to Gospodin, and with it, my loathing. "Only if I'm very good," I say. "And do all the things the Sacred Breath tells us to do."

Gospodin smiles.

When the sun starts to droop behind the horizon, Gospodin says, "We'll take it from here, Miss Koskinen. You've done well."

Have I? I feel grimy.

"Thank you," I say.

"I'll see you at the bear season festival," Gospodin says. "Nikolai's announcement won't be far behind."

I try not to shiver.

"And best of luck on your performance," he says, smiling. "I know the city could use the cheer."

I turn his words over in my head as I walk away from the tables. Every time I start to think I have Gospodin figured, he twists to show me a new side. A man who was willing to expose his own father to the Sacred Breath is also a man concerned with how to make New Sundstad more cheerful.

No sooner have I stepped onto the path home than I see two familiar heads bobbing down the street in front of me.

"Ness!" I jog to catch up. "Sofie!"

They turn in unison, their coats swishing the snow. Their lips are stained in identical cranberry smiles.

I cross my arms. "You two went to the food drive?"

"Don't be annoyed," Ness says.

"We were visiting Pippa," Sofie says. "We didn't realize the food was for the hungry."

"I was hungry," Ness says.

"Remember how we talked about times to think before you speak?" Sofie says.

I shake my head and fight a laugh. They look so pleased with themselves that I struggle to hold my annoyance.

"Fine, little thieves," I say. "Walk home with me?"

We fall into step together.

"What were you doing there?" Sofie asks.

"Gospodin invited me to volunteer," I say.

"Really?" Ness says. "Mariner Gospodin himself?"

Sofie whistles. "It sounds like you've made some progress, suitress." I don't hear any accusation in her tone.

"Well," I say. "We'll see."

"Hey," Ness says, "do you think René will make us spiced wine if I ask him nicely?"

Sofie laughs. "Definitely not."

"What if you asked him?"

Sofie considers. "Maybe."

"Why does he like you so much?" Ness asks.

"Because I eat everything he cooks," Sofie says. "Even when it's fish stew."

For the first time in months, I feel the sense of togetherness that was once my favorite part of being a flyer. Ness links one of her arms through mine and the other through Sofie's.

I forgot how much I missed it.

46

ELLA

A week before the bear season festival, I wake up to find half the flyers gone.

"They really never invite me anywhere," Gretta grumbles.

They don't get back until dusk—Sofie and Ness covered in berry juice, Natasha looking distracted. Her eyes meet mine once, but she looks away again quickly. Natasha disappears without saying anything.

One more week. One more week, and I have to have a plan to kill Nikolai.

Two more weeks, and she could be engaged to him.

We're about to head to dinner when one of the guards—I think his name is Zakarias—shows up with a letter. We huddle around it. Sofie lifts it to the lamplight to try to read through the envelope, but the paper is too thick. All we know is what it says on the envelope: *To Miss Natasha Koskinen*. On the back, Nikolai's seal is embossed in golden wax.

"Can anyone see anything?" Sofie says, squinting.

"Are you sure that's Nikolai's seal?" Ness asks.

"It says *Seal of the King*," Sofie says. "I'm pretty sure it's his seal."

"I think we should just open it," Katla says.

"Yeah," I say, "that sounds more fun."

Ness snatches it from Sofie and holds it high above our heads. "No one opens this until Natasha gets back."

"Where is she, anyway?" Gretta says. "She's getting as elusive as Ella."

"No fair," I say. "Elusive is *my* epithet."

"See?" Gretta says. She waves at the other flyers. "Does no one else care that she talks like a noble and she's not even from Kostrov? Does no one else think that's odd?"

"Not really," Sofie says. "Here, give me the letter back."

A scuffle ensues, and in the end, Sofie reclaims the envelope. More important, she reclaims the attention of the room. I'd like to be mad at Gretta for being so annoying, but my indignation is somewhat inhibited by the fact that she's completely correct.

Sofie holds the envelope so close to the flame of the oil lamp on the wall that I think it's going to catch fire. Before it can, the door opens.

"What are you doing?" Natasha says. Her cheeks are pink; her freckles are conspicuous. "You all look furtive."

"Where were you?" Gretta asks.

"On a walk. Clearing my head." Natasha frowns at Sofie. "What are you holding?"

Sofie tucks the letter behind her back. "We're planning you a surprise birthday party."

"My birthday's in deer season," Natasha says.

"Nikolai sent you a letter," Ness says. "Sofie's hiding it."

Sofie sighs and produces the envelope.

Natasha takes it. She takes one look at the seal and shoves the thing in her pocket.

"You're not going to open it here?" Ness says.

"I'm sure you've all already read it, so what's the point?"

There's great protest about how we couldn't actually read it, despite our best efforts, but Natasha slips inside the privacy of her room and shuts the door behind her. The other flyers dissipate, muttering. I stand in the hallway a moment longer. I have to read that letter. I need to know what Nikolai is up to.

I sit just inside the flyer bedroom, listening for the sound of Natasha's door. I expect her to leave to come dinner, at least, but all is quiet. Sofie tries to convince me to come to the kitchen, but I shake my head and tell her I'm feeling sick.

When the other girls have been at dinner for nearly a half an hour, I hear a creak. Soft footsteps. Another door opens and shuts farther down the hall.

I force myself to stay still for another long moment, just in case she comes back. Then I dart into the hallway. When I push open Natasha's door, I feel a twinge of guilt. But if she can follow me, then I can snoop on her. We'll be even now.

I've never been in her room before. It's a smaller version of the one I share with the other flyers. A narrow bed is pushed to one side. Above it, a pane of warped glass shows the night-dull sky. The room is hardly big enough for the bed, but a desk is squeezed against the opposite wall, leaving only a strip of floor so narrow, I have to turn sideways to walk through it.

On her desk, a small wooden clock ticks steadily. Beside it, a copy of *Captain's Log* sits on top of a copy of *Tamm's Fables*. I'm tempted to flip through both, but I keep searching. I open the top desk drawer. In it, I find a stack of flyer choreography, the handwriting varied. I recognize both Adelaida's and Natasha's from the flights for the ball and the upcoming bear season festival.

Finally, in the next drawer, I find the letter with the golden seal.

Natasha—
  How was your day with our mutual friend? I'd love to hear
how it went.
  Meet at the conservatory? Seven o'clock.
  Best,
  N

It's so familiar. The way he signs it, *N*, as though they're already more than just acquaintances. Natasha told me she didn't love Nikolai. She told me they hardly knew each other. Maybe she was lying.

My face goes hot. It doesn't matter what Natasha told me. There's no reason Natasha should be honest with me. There's no reason she'd think of me as anything other than the newest flyer.

When I replace Nikolai's letter in the desk drawer, I frown at another one I hadn't seen tucked beneath it. This one has a blue wax seal instead of a gold one, and the handwriting is so swoopy that it takes me a long five minutes to read.

It's from Gospodin.

So that's what Nikolai meant by *our mutual friend*. Natasha spent the day helping Gospodin.

I think again of the way Maret laughed away my concerns about Gospodin. My arms prickle with goose bumps.

I close the desk drawer. The wooden clock tells me it's ten past seven.

If I leave now, I'll have just enough time to figure out what Nikolai and Natasha are up to.

47

NATASHA

When I arrive at the Stone Garden, the sky has breathed new snow across the ground. It gleams ghost pale with reflected light from the palace windows. Overhead, there's no moon.

My slippers crunch against the frost. The conservatory looms above me, a wall of glass panes steamed through from the inside.

Gregor waits at the door. His coat is pulled tight against the cold. When he sees me, he presses his lips together. I get the feeling he's trying his best not to laugh. "Evening," he says.

"Don't say it like that."

"Like what?"

I struggle for the word. "Suggestively."

"Sorry, Tasha." He steps out of the way. "What's a fellow to think when he's instructed to stand guard *outside* the conservatory?"

The path to the door is clear, but I'm frozen in place. Nikolai, alone. I didn't know that was what tonight would be. I imagined it would be like the last time I saw him here, surrounded by guards and other flyers.

But of course there won't be more flyers here tonight. I made sure none of them knew where I was going.

Gregor opens the door. There's nothing to do but step through it. The room is dizzyingly hot and thick with steam. Waxy green leaves droop over each other. Little fires flicker from the sconces on the glass walls, streaking the ground with ghoulish shadows. I push an overgrown branch out of my way.

Nikolai sits half-submerged in the stone-tiled pool at the end of the conservatory. To his left, a vase of water lavish with mint leaves and cloudberries, the glass sweating furiously. To his right, a plate of pale bread. Around him, plumes of steam.

He's not wearing a shirt.

I consider turning back. But this is just Nikolai. He's never seemed dangerous or frightening before, and that doesn't need to change just because we're alone. Or because he's shirtless.

I'm going to be queen.

I cross the conservatory.

"You're dressed for the cold," he says in greeting, propping his elbows on the ledge behind him.

"Well, it's practically bear season outside." I take off my cloak and fold it carefully on the stone path. Next, my slippers. I hesitate on the hem of my sweater, but I take that off too. Underneath, I wear a plain black full-suit. I put it on before meeting Gospodin this morning in pursuit of dressing myself in as many warm layers as possible. I didn't imagine I'd be going for a swim.

"Aren't you going to get in?" he says. "It's hot." His crown rests on the edge of the stone by his elbow. His dark hair is spiked from the humidity, lifted off his forehead in horns.

I dip one foot in the water, and then I slide the rest of the way into the pool.

It does feel good. Hot, urgently so, shocking the breath out of me.

Nikolai smiles at me, his lips lazy and slow. I can see where the water hasn't reached yet—a glistening band across his collarbone where the skin turns matte.

My heart beats high in my throat. I can't put a name to what I'm feeling. Fear? Excitement? Attraction?

For a moment, I'm tugged back to Storm Four when Ella's lips and eyes gleamed in the lantern light and I wished she'd come closer. If this is nerves and excitement and attraction, then what was that?

I extinguish the thought as quickly as it appears. There's no point in thinking of Ella unless it's about all the reasons I can't trust her. I'm here with Nikolai. I need to convince him I would make a good queen.

"So," he says, "you spent the day with Gospodin."

I'm relieved at the distance between us: Nikolai on his end of the pool, me on mine. He doesn't try to come closer. "I did."

"And did you talk about me?"

"Maybe a little. I think he's starting to trust me."

"Should that make me nervous?" Nikolai says. "Did you promise to be his spy?"

"I'm on your side," I say. "Not his."

He laughs, short, light. "You're on your own side, Natasha."

I blink.

"I'm not a fool," he says. "You want to survive. I understand that. I want to survive too. That's why I want a queen I can trust."

When I look at him, I see a version of him I've never seen before. Not brooding, not compensating, not nervous. What I see now is a young man, just a few months my senior, who has spent his life surrounded by those who would use him for his power. He's self-absorbed, but so am I. He was never going to be as charming as

Gospodin; never going to be as powerful as his father. Even when I was a child, when people spoke of the *clever little royal*, I knew they meant his sister, Cassia.

He's tragically normal. Had he been born something other than an heir, maybe he would have made a happy life for himself.

"Do you know whom you're going to pick?" I ask.

He shakes his head. "My birthday can't come soon enough. I want this game to end."

"And then you'll pick . . . ?" I say.

He shrugs.

"How do I prove that you can trust me?" I ask.

"Can I trust anyone?" he says. "All anyone ever tells me is what I want to hear." He purses his lips. "Maybe you'd be better served figuring out how to earn Gospodin's trust."

"I'm trying to convince him," I say. "But I've lived in this palace half my life. My mother lived in this palace. I've always believed in the crown more than *Captain's Log.*"

Nikolai's eyes search me. I can tell he's thinking.

I feel impossibly close.

I stand. Water streams off my shoulders. It laps against my stomach as I walk one, two, three steps across the pool. I stop at Nikolai's side.

He's not so bad. Not so scary, not so exciting. Just a boy with a crown.

And he's considering me.

I reach, not for but around him. I lock my fingers around his golden crown resting on the lip of the pool. The jagged edges press into my skin.

We watch each other.

I move slowly, to see if he stops me. He doesn't, so I put the crown on my head.

The metal is damp. It sends beads of water down my scalp, down to where the wet ends of my hair cling to my arms and chest and back. And seas, I have never felt more powerful in my life.

Nikolai's tongue sweeps his lip.

"We're going to walk onto the royal fleet," I say. "Both of us."

He swallows, and I watch him do it, watch the knot on his neck bob. I know he can see it: me, in a crown of my own. The queen. Surviving. Ruling.

"I—" he starts.

The conservatory door opens with a clang of glass.

"Your Royal Highness," Gregor says. "I'm so sorry—"

Nikolai curses and snatches the crown from my head. His cheeks are flushed red, and I feel my own face heating. I sink under the lapping surface of the water until my shoulders are submerged.

At the door, Sebastian stands beside Gregor. Their faces are red too.

"It's urgent," Sebastian says. "The Righteous Mariner just sent word. He wanted to meet with you about—something about the festival."

Nikolai curses again and hauls himself from the pool. Water streams from his black trousers.

"Bye, then." I sound like a child, and I hate it. All that power I just felt surging through me, gone.

Nikolai, either too embarrassed or too distracted to pay me any more attention, doesn't respond. He slings a towel over his shoulder and turns to the guards. "How long ago? Did he say what was wrong?"

And then he's gone. The door slams shut behind them.

The festival. What, Gospodin urgently had to talk to Nikolai about his receiving line?

I want to scream. Then I do scream, because there's no one left to hear me.

For a moment, it feels good. Once the noise gets bored of echoing around the glass walls, the conservatory feels even quieter than it did before.

I hear the door open again. I lift my head, wondering if Nikolai has decided to come back for something.

"You're not drowning in here, are you?"

Ella leans against a snarl of vines. Her arms fold across her chest.

If my face wasn't already red, it is now.

On all sides, semi-tamed plants surround her. The petals of a fury-red flower stretch to touch her.

"What are you doing, Natasha?" she says. Her voice has no irony and no artifice. Any chance I had of playing confident goes to dust.

I sink into the water until it touches my chin. "Taking a pleasant soak. Why are you here?" I ask.

She tilts her head. The red flower folds against her temple. "I happen to enjoy the occasional pleasant soak." She pushes off the wall of vines. Her steps are soft against the wet stone.

My mouth is too dry for the humidity of this room. "Is that so?" I say.

She peels up her sleeve and shows me her wrist. "Of course. Siren. Half fish, and all." She tilts her head at me. "What about you?"

My breathing—shallow. "I don't trust you."

She takes one slipper off, then the other. She drops them on the stone. Her legs slip into the pool. "That wasn't an answer."

"You've been lying to me about—about something."

Ella slides fully into the water. "We all lie."

The curling ends of her hair flatten against the pool's surface.

"I don't trust you," I say, forgetting I've said it before.

When she moves, the warm water laps at my stomach, tugs at the fabric of my sleeves.

"We have that in common," Ella says. "Among other things."

I'm standing on an edge. Everything about this moment feels like a before, in the tips of my waterlogged fingers and the trembling of each breath. It stretches, elastic, Ella staring at me and I at her, this sweet, reluctant delay.

Her smile curls at the edges. "You don't love Nikolai."

We stand so close that if I reached my hand through the water and she reached hers, they would meet. I keep my hands pressed to my thighs. "I already told you," I say, my voice softer than I mean it to be, "that I don't."

She takes a step closer. Now only one of us need raise a hand to touch the other. "He's not a good person," she says. "Surviving isn't worth marrying him. You have to see that."

"I didn't know you'd ever spoken to him."

"I don't need to," Ella says. A half-step closer. I can see the humid gleam of sweat across her steep cheekbones. "You can't possibly like him."

I imagine telling her that I don't. I will take the last half-step. I will touch the underside of her chin with two fingers to raise her face to mine.

But I'm standing in water, and the water doesn't let me forget its own importance that easily.

Seas rise. Everyone drowns.

"I want to be queen," I whisper.

Ella's face hardens. "You're a fool," she says. She hoists herself out of the water and tosses her wet hair over a shoulder.

"And you're a liar," I say.

"I'm not a liar just because I don't tell you everything there is to know about me," she says. "You're the one who isn't honest."

"About what?" I say.

She lets out a short sound, breathy and through her nostrils. When she throws open the door to leave, a burst of frozen wind stings my cheeks. The door slams shut again.

I count the moments that pass, waiting for her to come back.

She doesn't.

48

ELLA

After the incident at the hot pools, I start performing an experiment on myself. I'm trying to see how little sleep I can get without dying. Sleeping is bad. Sleeping means dreaming, and dreaming means imagining myself with Natasha, and I'm not allowed to do that. The dreams aren't always lascivious. Yes, there are the dreams where she doesn't push me away in the hot pools, but there are also dreams where we sit under a tree eating porridge together and she tells jokes in fluent Terrazzan. Both sorts of dreams are equally bad.

Maret's deadline approaches like a stampede of cattle. I know I only have until the first day of bear season to come up with a new plan—a plan that allows me to assassinate Nikolai without dying in the process—and instead of concocting something brilliant, I spend all my time in endless flyer rehearsals trying not to think about Natasha.

So the day of the bear season festival arrives, and I haven't come up with anything.

Natasha walks into the kitchen while the rest of us are eating breakfast, her hair in a loose bun, her eyes finding anyone but me. "Adelaida wants everyone in the studio for festival makeup."

Everyone stands. I squint at Sofie.

"Come on," she says. "On your feet."

"I'm tired," I say. "I'm just going to prepare myself for a few more minutes."

She grabs my arm and hauls me out of my chair.

"Ow," I say. "Bully."

"Seas, Ella, you look half-dead."

"That's rude," I say.

She shakes her head. "Stay here."

The other flyers follow Natasha out the door. Sofie walks to the stove, where the chef, René, is working. I stay at the table and sway. A moment later, Sofie pushes a mug of something hot and black into my hands. I take a sip.

"Ew. This tastes like . . ." I take another sip. "Burnt toast."

"It's coffee," Sofie says. "René brews it for himself and only gives it to people he likes. It has to get shipped from across the world."

"Does he know it tastes like burnt toast?"

"Drink," she says. I think she's trying not to laugh. "Or else you'll fall off your silks."

The flavor never gets less awful, but I finish the cup anyway, and when I do, I feel a bit of life trickling back to my limbs. I manage to keep my eyes open as Ness does my makeup and Adelaida talks us through final performance notes.

The bases—me, Ness, and Gretta—are all dressed as snowflakes, which feels not quite as silly as it sounds. Our full-suits are white with glimmering skirts. I expect the makeup to turn us ghostly, but Ness has a good eye for it, and in the end, our faces shine with silver frost.

Inna and the Bear, the flight we'll be performing at the festival, is based on an old Maapinnen legend, which in turn became one of Tamm's fables, and is as old as the Royal Flyers themselves.

When Katla first walked me through the story of *Inna,* I was sure she was joking. "A Maapinnen legend? I thought the Sacred Breath was against Maapinnen things," I said.

"They are," Katla said.

Natasha shook her head. "I have a copy of *Tamm.* It's not like they're burning them."

"Gospodin doesn't like it," Katla amended. "But I suppose he's okay with it as long as everyone knows that his story is fact and all the other stories are fiction."

And thus, I was introduced to *Inna and the Bear.* As the legend goes, Inna was a Maapinnen girl whose clan was attacked by invaders from another island. These invaders, we are made to note, were not the kind Grunholters who renamed the country Kostrov and converted everyone to the Sacred Breath. Those were good invaders, obviously. These intruders insisted Inna would marry their king. Inna, determined not to marry, fled into the boglands in the midst of a snowstorm. Everyone thought she was going to die in the snow, but instead, she stumbled across a bear whose hibernation was interrupted by the invaders' arrival. Inna befriended the bear, and together, they marched back to her clan. The bear ripped open the intruding king's throat and Inna drank his blood.

I, for one, think it's a fabulous story.

Sofie is playing the conquering king, and when she emerges in her costume—a green full-suit and a costume crown braided into her hair—she lifts her chin and lowers her eyelids in a perfect imitation of Nikolai, haughty and bored. Katla and I are the only ones to laugh.

Katla is playing the bear. Her hair is spun up into two dark buns to be her bear ears. Ness delights in smudging a big dollop of black on the tip of Katla's nose.

Natasha is Inna, because of course she's Inna. When I first heard the story, I had hoped that some of Inna's regicidal desires would rub off on Natasha.

No luck as of yet.

Too bad. Maret's deadline is tonight. And I have nothing.

49

NATASHA

"Does Ella seem off to you?" Sofie asks. She catches me by the elbow at the edge of the festival stage moments before we're supposed to perform.

I'm annoyed. I spent my entire warm-up driving Ella from my brain. "How do you expect me to know?"

"Dunno," Sofie says. "I just thought maybe you'd be concerned."

"Well, I'm not," I say. I scan the crowd in front of the stage. I spot Nikolai and Gospodin under their awning, but their heads are bent low with a few other official-looking men.

"Maybe I should be asking if something is off with you," Sofie says.

"I'm fine," I say. "And Ella is fine too. She's just . . ." Infuriating? "Enigmatic."

"Maybe she's a ghost," a voice says, directly in my ear.

I whirl. My arms fly across my chest instinctively.

Ella tilts her head at me, her expression unfazed as ever. "Adelaida sent me over. She said, and I quote, 'Tell them to get their asses on the silks.'"

She hasn't stood so close to me since the hot pools. I think she must realize it at the same time I do, because she takes a quick step back.

"Right," I say. I inhale. Crisp air. Peat smoke. Distant ocean. "Let's go."

I hold my hands under my armpits to keep them warm right up until the violinists begin to play.

Then I start to climb.

My muscles remember the motions even when my brain doesn't. At every cue, my legs swing where they're meant to go. Every wrap, twist, spin clears the clutter from my head until all that's left is me, and the air, and my silks.

I'm distantly aware that the crowd is a good one. Though they've probably all seen this flight more than once, they lean forward, riveted. They gasp as bear-Katla lowers herself upside down, snarling and showing off her teeth. When Sofie finally tumbles, hanging by an ankle, and I throw back my shoulders in triumph, the crowd roars like they truly just saw an enemy king vanquished.

At the end, I bow. Nikolai claps. His eyes never leave mine.

"Well," Adelaida says after gathering us at the back of the stage, "don't let it go to your head, but that wasn't bad." She turns to go.

"Is that all?" I call after her.

"Go enjoy the festival," she says.

The other girls start chattering, but I'm distracted by a fragment of something I hear from the crowd.

"There's to be a receiving line," a voice says. "We haven't seen one of those since King Nikolai was crowned."

Two women stand at the front of the stage. They're probably as old as my mother would be by now. One wears an orange scarf and the other wears red.

"And your Ester is going, yes?" Orange Scarf says.

"She's already waiting," Red Scarf says. "They danced at the ball. Did you know? She was one of the only Southtowners to get a dance, but you know what a pretty face she has."

"Mmm," Orange Scarf says.

I sense a stillness beside me. I look up, and there's Ella, quiet, listening. I turn away.

"Sofie," Ness says, "you promised me a baked apple if I got my double-back dive perfect today."

"Oh," Sofie says. "I don't remember promising that."

Ness crosses her arms. "Liar. We're going to get baked apples. Ella, come with us. They're the best thing you've ever tasted."

"I don't like apples," Ella says.

"That's silly," Ness says. "Everyone likes apples."

Ness leads an enthusiastic charge through the festival. The first flutters of a new snowfall dust my skin. I shiver and bury my hands in my pockets.

Carts and booths sell necessities—fish, bolts of cloth, peat briquettes—and bear season treats—honey-rye biscuits, blackened eel, steaming cranberry wine. Children dart and slide across an especially icy patch of street. The air is woven with smoke and a bonfire roars on every corner.

Ness grabs Sofie's arm and yanks her forcefully to the apple cart. The other girls keep drifting forward through the crowd. I spot a cluster of guards on the other side of the street. I rise on my toes. A flash of black hair. Nikolai?

I squeeze through the crush of festivalgoers.

A line of young women stretches from the front of Our Lady through the square and around the corner. It looks like half of New Sundstad showed up for his receiving line.

I spot Adelaida on the fringes. She smiles broadly at an older man I think I recognize as one of Nikolai's councilors. His own mouth is flat. When I walk toward them, he excuses himself quickly and her smile falls away.

"Remind me not to play nice with the councilors," she says. "They're all ancient and stodgy."

"Will do. What's this line? This is so Nikolai can shake hands, fall in love, and find his queen?"

"Apparently," Adelaida says. "And it's their last chance to meet him before he makes his choice."

Nikolai's birthday is one week away. One week until he picks the queen.

I eye the line. How long will it take to get through? An hour? Two? "Will you wait with me?"

Adelaida snorts. "You're not waiting in that line."

"What?"

"You see the girls in that line?" she says. "Do you see the Sylvia Kanervas of the city standing there?"

I look again. The line is a wash of outdated dresses, buzzing with the Southtown accent I worked so hard to rid myself of once I got to the palace and realized I sounded different from the other flyers.

"I don't see a lot of Heather Hill gowns, if that's what you're asking."

"A king doesn't find his queen in a receiving line," Adelaida says. "Go. Explore the festival. Eat a honey-rye biscuit."

Guilt washes over me. "If the line is pointless, shouldn't someone tell all those girls not to bother?"

"I didn't say it was pointless," Adelaida says. "Hope is one of the most useful things humans ever invented. But pointless for you? Yes. Nikolai already knows you."

So I leave her. And the line. But I feel unsettled the whole time.

I skirt the edge of the festival, searching for the Royal Flyers. I follow the smell of baked apples, pushing through the lines that snake from each booth. I have to dodge the barrage of limbs and woven shopping baskets.

A hand brushes my shoulder. I turn quickly.

Sylvia Kanerva stares back at me.

She wears a fine lilac coat and pale pink lipstick. An older man—one of the councilors, I think—stands behind her. "Can I interest you in a walk, Miss Koskinen?"

I don't have a good feeling about this. "Sure. That's, um, a lovely coat."

"Thank you," she says. "It was a gift from Mariner Gospodin."

"Ah," I say.

"Ah," she agrees.

The councilor clears his throat. "Miss Kanerva, should I assume we'll continue our conversation later?"

"Oh," Sylvia says, looking up at him through her eyelashes. "Would you mind? I would so love to take this chance to talk to my good friend Natasha." She smooths the edges of her voice until it's tame and soft for him. She gives him a palatable smile.

I'm struck by a memory of another girl pulling a similar trick. Nikolai's sister, Cassia, had the royal advisors wound around her finger like old string; I saw it more than once. I can't say that it surprised me when she was exiled for trying to seize Nikolai's throne. Like Sylvia, she had that airy laugh frosted over a blade-sharp canniness. Perhaps it's something about being a daughter of wealth and power. You might never rule, but you can learn to wield the men who do.

"I . . . Of course," the councilor says. "A pleasure, as always." He gives me a quick nod, then turns to go.

When he's gone, there's no one to protect me from Sylvia's icy smile. She turns it on me in full force.

"Miss Koskinen," she says. "I've been looking forward to speaking with you ever since the ball."

"Oh?"

"Without any councilors or kings getting in the way," she amends. "I think it will be easier to talk if we're not busy pretending our aching hearts are smitten." Her lips are set in a cool, disinterested smile. I get the sense she's already played out this conversation in her head and I've arrived underprepared.

"I'm not sure what you mean," I say.

"Please stop," she says. "This conversation will be leagues more efficient if you don't act like you're really in love with Nikolai. And I know you're not. It's something we have in common."

I'm slow to meet her gaze.

"Do you think it's ever crossed his mind?" Sylvia says. "That none of us—me, you, the line of Southtown girls over there—really love him?"

I think about what he said in the hot pools about trusting me. "I think he knows well enough."

"Hmm." It's a prim sound, prettier than a *hmm* has any right to be. "I disagree. I think Nikolai believes we both adore him. I've spent a lot of time around men like him. It's a terribly princely thing, I've seen, to assume women ought to fall in love with you." She smooths a pull in her elegant coat. "So, let me guess. You think I'm a selfish person because I want to be his queen, even though my father is wealthy and powerful already. Am I right?"

I blink. "Well. Maybe. You've always known you'd be on the royal fleet, with your father as the Keeper of the Purse. I'm the one whose life hangs on Nikolai's decision. You'll survive either way."

She raises her chin. "I may wear finer gowns than you, but we're the same, you and me. My life depends on Nikolai's proposal just as surely as yours does. You're right that I'll be on that fleet, but if I don't marry him, whom do you expect I'll marry instead? Most of the advisors and nobles who've weaseled their ways onto the fleet are older than my father. What do you think I was discussing with that old councilor? Tariff arrangements?" She sniffs. "And there's no scenario in which I don't marry and have to bear children. You know that, now that you're a scholar of *Captain's Log*. To marry Nikolai is the best thing I can do for my family and the best thing I can do for myself. We can play this little game, pretending that we have some power over Nikolai, but we both know the truth. This world doesn't bestow power upon women. He may want us, but we need him. There's no power in scrounging for scraps at a man's feet."

"It's a shame you weren't born five centuries ago," I say. "You would've made a remarkable Inna."

"And you as well. You make a terribly convincing bog princess." She straightens her gloves. "If I'm simpering the next time you see me, rest assured it's a charade. Stay away from my king, Miss Koskinen."

Her heels click across the path, steady over ice and snow. She never once slips.

When Adelaida first pointed Sylvia out to me, back at the ball, I thought how little I wanted to go to war with a girl I'd never met. Maybe I shouldn't have worried. There's no war. I don't stand a chance.

50

ELLA

Once we finish performing, I wait for the other flyers to get distracted by the baked apples and fireworks. Then I slip away. From the edge of the festival, I see Natasha find Adelaida. Together, they watch the receiving line. All those girls, looking for a crown. Looking for safety. Looking for things they'll never find with Nikolai.

I stare at the back of Natasha's head for a moment. Her wild Inna hair. Her glimmering full-suit.

I have to go tell Maret that I don't have a plan. No idea how to kill Nikolai without getting myself killed in the process. Cassia would've figured it out by now. She always was the clever one. And I've let her down. I have to tell Maret what I came up with: nothing.

The streets are busy, even as I leave the festival behind. So many people are coming, going. I keep my head ducked, but I catch a few whispers, lingering glances. In my full-suit and festival makeup, I'm conspicuous. I don't like it. I pull my cloak up higher and hurry to Eel Shore. In the distance, I can hear festival fireworks going off.

When I'm a few streets away, my stomach starts to twist. I'm feeling nervous. Cagey. I try to tell myself it's just because I'm worried about letting Maret down, but I know there's something else.

I turn the corner to Maret's street.

A swarm of guards.

I lurch back. Duck behind the alley wall, press myself to the brick. Holding my breath, I peek back around the corner.

Probably six men. They're wearing dark blue palace guard uniforms. Guns at their hips.

That's when I realize. The feeling in my stomach. That something was off. It was the sound echoing through the air. Not fireworks—gunshots.

"Looks like she's been here for months," one of the guards is saying. I recognize that guard—with his light brown skin and long limbs, he looks just like Gretta. It's her father. The Captain of the Guard.

"How did you know it was her?" a younger guard says.

"Spotted her coming back from the university. You don't forget a face like that."

The other guard grunts his agreement.

Where's Maret? Did they arrest her? Shoot her? Are they coming for me next? I think of everything I left behind in her apartment. One of Cassia's old dresses? That can't incriminate me. The silks? Edvin?

A moment later, two of the guards step through the front door. And slung between them—Maret. Her blond curls are matted with blood.

I duck back around the corner. Press my palm to my mouth.

"For seas' sake," Captain Waska says. "Zakarias, go inside and get a bedsheet. You can't take her through the city that way."

Maret's dead. She's dead.

I push myself to my feet and walk back down the alley as fast as I dare. They found Maret. They killed Maret.

I'm breathing too hard. Too much air, not enough of it reaching my lungs. I don't know which way I'm walking. Now, when people spot me, point at the costumed Royal Flyer, I'm too foggy to duck my head.

I have to get out of here.

Where am I supposed to go? If they know about Maret, they could know about me too. They could be waiting for me. On the other hand, if they don't know yet, they'll surely figure it out if I disappear today. And where would I disappear to? Katla's family? I can't put them in that kind of danger. They hardly know me. I could try to get on a ship out of Kostrov, but I don't have the money.

And I can't walk away now. Maret's dead. Now I'm not just getting revenge for Cassia's sake. It's for Maret's sake too.

I have to go back to the palace.

Captain Waska said he spotted Maret outside. He didn't say that Edvin betrayed us. Or that Andrei figured us out. He didn't mention anything about a rogue flyer.

No one suspects me. They can't.

The moment I step back inside the flyer studio, I know I've made a mistake. Instead of our usual one guard, three of them have their heads bent to Adelaida's by the knotted silks.

I start to backpedal.

Adelaida claps a hand on my shoulder. "Ella," she says. "Glad I found you."

My heart is ready to burst out of my chest. Adelaida's nails pinch through my cloak. The guards turn to me, eyes raking me up and down.

"I'll take her back," Adelaida says.

Adelaida steers me through the studio. She says nothing. Her grip tightens.

I'm too afraid to speak. If I do, I'm sure she'll hear the guilt and fear in my voice.

"You're to stay in your room with the other flyers, understand?"

In the studio mirror, I see the hard set of her crimson mouth. Her back is fiercely straight. I look tiny and cowed in comparison.

"Anyone knocks on the door," she says, "don't open it. Anyone but me shows up with food, or letters, or asking to see any of you, tell them to find me."

When I still don't answer, she shakes me. "Do you understand?"

I force my mouth open. "Yes."

She exhales. "Walk."

Sofie and Gretta are the only girls in the bedroom when Adelaida shoves me inside. Sofie lies in her bed. Gretta paces. The door shuts behind me.

"Let me see my family!" Gretta calls after her.

Through the door, Adelaida's only answer is the click of her shoes.

There's just one window in the flyer bedroom. It's narrow and it only opens about two inches, and if I try to climb through it, Gretta will surely tackle me for acting shifty.

I glance at the door again. It doesn't lock from the outside, so Adelaida can't trap us in here unless she shoves something in front of it. So I'll give Adelaida a few moments to leave, then I'll run. Maybe I can make it back through the outside door if I catch the guards by surprise.

"Did she tell you what was going on?" Gretta says.

It takes me a moment to realize she's talking to me. I turn slowly to face her suspicious eyes. "No. She just told me not to let anyone but her into the room."

Gretta nods.

"Mrrph," Sofie says into her pillow.

"Sofie?" I say. "You okay?"

She curls into the cocoon of her blankets and makes another unintelligible noise.

The door opens again. Adelaida and Natasha stand on the other side. Adelaida pushes Natasha through the door with her standard disregard for gentleness.

"Hey!" Natasha says.

"How about now?" Gretta says. "Can I see my family now?"

Adelaida points a finger at her. "Stay."

The door slams shut again.

"Anyone want to explain what's going on?" Natasha says.

"Adelaida is being ridiculous," Gretta says. "Obviously."

"I have no idea," I say, glancing again at the door.

"Ungh," Sofie says.

Natasha crosses the room to sit on the edge of Sofie's bed. She pulls the quilt away from Sofie's face. "Dear, what are you doing?"

Sofie blinks with sleepy eyes. "Having conniptions."

"And why are you having conniptions?"

Sofie pulls the blanket back over her head. Through it, her voice is muffled. "I'm sick."

"Well, maybe when Adelaida stops being a terror, I can get you some tea."

A new unease finds footing inside me. None of the girls suspect me of anything—at least, not more than they normally do—and for the first time, it occurs to me that this could be about something other than Maret. And if it's something else, should I risk running into a danger about which I know nothing?

Ten minutes later, Adelaida opens the door again.

"Where are Ness and Katla?"

"Ness is with my brother," Gretta says, making an exaggerated retching noise.

"Where?" Adelaida says.

Gretta shrugs. "That's not the kind of information I want to know."

"And Katla?"

No one says anything.

"Sofie?" Adelaida says. "Where's Katla?"

"Sofie is asleep," Natasha says.

Adelaida growls. Her cloak flaps up around her as she goes.

No one but Sofie sleeps. Gretta keeps pacing. Natasha flips through one of Ness's poetry books. I watch the window.

Outside, the sky turns from purple to black. A new dusting of snow cleans the street. The lamps spill circles of gold against the white like a row of freshly cracked eggs. Adelaida doesn't return to shove Katla or Ness through the door.

Sofie lurches upright. She claps a hand to her mouth.

Natasha drops the poetry book on Ness's bed. She's at Sofie's side in a second. Sofie hardly seems to notice. She kicks the tangle of blankets off her feet and stumbles to the door.

All three of us run after her. She falls to her knees in the washroom and leans over one of the basins.

I wince. A moment later, I hear the splatter of vomit on porcelain.

Natasha crouches at Sofie's side. "Are those the conniptions coming out?"

Sofie starts to laugh, but she's interrupted by another surge of vomit.

Gretta backs away. "I hope you feel okay, Sofie, but this is gross and I'm leaving."

Sofie waves us away. "Go, go. You too, Tasha. I don't want . . . Oh, seas." She leans over the basin again.

"Is it a storm thing?" I say.

Natasha glances at the ceiling like rain might suddenly pour through it. "I think the next one is frogs."

I put a hand on my stomach. I don't feel any worse than I have since Storm Four. And whatever caught Katla and me then didn't seem to faze Sofie.

Natasha sets a hand on Sofie's back, but Sofie shakes her head. "Really. I'm just a little nauseated. None of you should have to watch this."

From the hallway, Gretta says, "You're not pregnant too, are you?"

"Yes," Sofie says. "I've borrowed Gregor from Pippa and we're going to raise our children together."

"You still have your humor," I say. "You can't be that sick."

"I'll take my humor to my deathbed," Sofie says.

Back in the flyer bedroom, Gretta's antsy energy is rubbing off on Natasha. Now both of them are pacing. I resume my post at the window, pressing my shoulder to the icy glass and staring outside.

"You know," Gretta says, "I half expected a man with a gun to be running around outside our door if we went as far as the washroom."

"You really have no idea why Adelaida was so adamant we stay here?" Natasha says.

"None," Gretta says.

Natasha looks at me expectantly. I swallow and shake my head.

"This is ludicrous," Gretta says. "I'm going to go ask my parents about this." She strides to the door, but before she can open it, it flies open.

Katla bursts in. Wisps of hair cling to her face. She drops an empty rucksack on the ground and scans the room. "Where are Sofie and Ness?"

"Ness is with Twain," Natasha says. "Sofie's in the washroom."

Katla collapses on the end of her bed and lets out a big breath. "Good."

The uneasiness inside me tightens its hold. "Where were you?" I ask.

"After the festival, I went to visit my family," she says. "I only just found out, coming back through the city."

"Found out what?" Gretta says.

Katla looks from one face to the next. Her brows furrow. "You don't know? Seas. It's everywhere. There's some sort of illness. People are calling it a plague. All across the city, I heard people shouting about it, not to mention everyone I saw stumbling around sick. I thought . . . Why are all of you looking at me like that?"

51

NATASHA

They're calling it the bog plague.

I hear it muttered on the mouths of guards who leap to the side of the hallway as Katla and I drag Sofie to the infirmary. We each hold one of her pale arms around our shoulders. Sofie keeps trying to make us laugh, insisting that she feels fine, and why do we look so afraid of an upset stomach? Ella and Gretta trail behind us.

The infirmary is long and stark, a colorless room not meant for living. Each side is lined with pallet beds. Sleeping bodies curl in a few of them. A nurse bustles toward us and tries to take Sofie out of our arms. I have an urge to pull Sofie closer to me and away from the woman's clutches.

A white mask covers her face, arching out from her nose in a long, pointed beak. It's tied around her head with string. Each eye is visible through a thin slit. Her hair, a cloud of frizzy blond, bursts from the edges of the mask. She looks like she's wearing a giant bird skull.

"No one in here but the sick." Her voice echoes around the insides of the mask. "Give her to me, quickly now."

Sofie takes a step away from the nurse. Katla and I hold her up. "I'm not sick," Sofie says. "Really, I'm not."

The nurse holds out her hand, opening and closing pinchy fingers. "You're pale."

"I'm always pale," Sofie says.

I hold her arm tightly. "It's okay. We just want to make sure you're fine." I try to keep my voice steady, for her sake, but I don't want to give her to the bird-masked woman.

Sofie lurches forward, bending at her waist. The nurse has a bucket underneath her within five seconds. It's just enough time to catch the next wave of vomit.

"For seas' sake," the nurse says, "lie down."

When Sofie finally concedes to the pallet bed, I examine the heavy shadows swelling underneath her eyes. The nurse is right: Sofie is even paler than usual.

"I'm fine," she says again. But when she glances around the infirmary at the other beds, the sleeping forms, she bites her lip.

As the nurse turns to us, the beak of her mask cuts a deep shadow down her front all the way to her belly. "Anyone who isn't sick leaves."

I start shaking my head before she finishes her sentence. "I'm staying."

"Are you mad? You can't be around this."

"We've been around her all night," I say. "We're still walking, aren't we?"

The slitted eyes stare back at me. "There's a miasma in here. Bad air. You breathe it in, you could be the next one turning your guts inside out."

"You're here, aren't you?" I say.

"This is my job," she says.

"Well, they're my job," I say. They are. These girls. Their lives.

The nurse considers. "You're the principal flyer, aren't you?"

"I'm not leaving," I say.

"Fine," she says. "But the rest of your girls have to go."

I turn to Katla before she can start hurling insults. "You have to go find Ness. Make sure she's okay."

"But Sofie—"

"Please," I say. "Please."

I don't realize I'm gripping her hands until she squeezes back. I can't find the words to describe the fear coming alive within me.

Did I ever really think I could stand at Nikolai's side on the royal fleet while the other flyers sank with Kostrov? I will not see them hurt. I can't.

"Okay," Katla says. "But I'm coming back once we find Ness."

I nod.

Gretta is the first one out the door. She buries her face in the collar of her sweater, a weak mask.

Ella lingers by Sofie's bed.

"Help find Ness," I say.

Her face is tight like she's gritting her teeth.

"Go," I say.

When my girls have gone, the nurse hands me a mask.

I swallow my discomfort and take it. The face is rough canvas, the beak cold metal. When I raise it, the metal clatters. It smells like René's herb collection—some clean and earthy mixture of thyme and rosemary.

"Aromatics," the nurse says, nodding her own beak. "Fights the miasma."

My vision reduces to what I can see through the mask's slitted eyes.

"You look terrifying," Sofie says.

The mask is a relief. Through it, Sofie can't see the fear written plainly across my face. "Maybe we should wear these in a flight. Very crane season."

"More like dead crane—"

She doesn't finish her sentence. I hand her the bucket.

I lose my sense of time in the amber light of the infirmary. Whenever the door opens, I look up, my mask bobbling. I watch as guards and servants stumble in alone or are lugged by friends. The other flyers don't come back.

Sofie and I talk of little nothings. Pippa's pregnancy, and whether or not she should name the child Baby Gregor. Katla's siblings. If the deer season flight is better than the seal season one. We don't talk about storms or Floods or plagues.

She falls asleep when the infirmary beds are half-filled.

The door opens again.

"Seas," the nurse says. "Not another one."

At first, I don't see Ness. I just see Twain, his round belly, his boyish brown face, his deep blue guard uniform. Ness is so small beside him. She clings to his side. Tears stain her face; splotches of brown, her front.

"There you are, up you go." The nurse maneuvers Ness out of Twain's arms and into the bed beside Sofie. Ness lets out a series of watery coughs.

When I stand up, she recoils from me. I put a hand to the edge of my mask. "Ness, it's me."

"Tasha?" she says.

I sit down on her bed. "I'm right here."

"I'm scared," she says. "I don't feel good."

I try to swallow. I try to speak. In the end, all I can do is squeeze her hand.

Adelaida arrives as the sunrise soothes the grisly night shadows. She opens the door and waves me over but doesn't pass the threshold.

It takes me a long moment to rise from the chair I situated between Ness's and Sofie's beds. My neck aches from the weight of the mask.

In the hallway, I take off the mask. Morning air chills my sweat-licked face. I raise a hand to my cheek and find a divot in my skin from the pressure of the mask's frame.

"What do you think you're doing?"

I blink at the sharpness. "Sitting with Ness and Sofie."

"You've been there all night?" she says.

"They've been sleeping," I say.

"I didn't ask about them," she says. "I asked about you."

"But I'm not sick," I say.

"Keep breathing the air in there and you will be soon."

I sat silently with my fear for so many long hours. I welcome its flow into anger. "They're sick. Don't you care?"

"Of course I care. Why do you think I spent all night trying to find the six of you? Why do you think I forbade the others from coming back here once they told me about Sofie? Sofie and Ness are already sick. The best I can do is keep the rest of you from catching it."

I tighten my hands into fists. "Sofie and Ness are your girls too. Not just mine."

"I've seen dozens of girls come into this palace and go out again. I wouldn't be surprised to see the backs of more before the Flood."

"That's all we are to you?" I say. "Names in an endless list?"

"No," she says, vicious. "There are names on an endless list, and then there is you."

For a moment, I'm almost fooled into believing she cares for me the way a mother would.

Then she says, "If you die, who do you think will bring me on the royal fleet? Gretta?"

We stand in silence for a long moment. I realize I'm mirroring her. Our hands are fisted. Our chins are held high. We both lean forward, ready to fight.

But I won't be like her in this way.

"Let the other girls come back if they want to," I say. "If you're so determined to see me safe, you'll have to come in there yourself and drag me out."

I tie my mask around my face as I step back inside the infirmary.

"Natasha," Adelaida says. But she doesn't follow me.

It's only a few hours before Katla and Ella appear to ask the nurse for masks of their own. She tries to shoo them, but they stand fast.

"We already breathed plenty of Sofie's miasma," Katla says. "Besides, what do you care? I'm bound to be another Storm One victim anyway. Let me stay with my friends."

The nurse gives them masks, but she doesn't do it happily.

When Sofie and Ness wake, they're in good spirits. They smile and joke and reassure us that they feel much better.

"Really," Ness says. "I think the worst is over." She glances around. "Is Twain here?"

"He wanted to be," I say. "He had a shift."

She looks down at her hands.

"As for Gretta," Katla says, "she's just being selfish, but we already knew that about her."

"She was crying," Ella says softly. "She's just scared."

We all quiet for a moment.

"Well," Sofie says brightly, "nothing to be scared of. I feel good."

By the next day, I don't believe her.

Day three sees Ness and Sofie fluttering in and out of sleep, and day four sees them drifting still further away from us. Katla, Ella, and I leave only when we can't keep our eyes open any longer. We bring them porridge and toast. They vomit it back up. Sofie shivers; Ness cries. The Captain of the Guard made a rule that no guard is to enter the infirmary, but Twain defies it. He sits with Ness whenever he's off duty, and when she wakes, her smile shines for him.

Ness's parents arrive at the palace by special escort. They ask to take her back to their home. The nurse won't allow her to be moved. Pippa, through Gregor, begs to be allowed in to see Sofie. In a spurt of fierce coherence, Sofie makes me swear I won't let Pippa inside. For both Pippa's and the baby's sake.

By day four, all the beds are full. By day five, some have emptied again. It's not because anyone has gotten better.

That morning, I wake after four hours of nightmares. I'm sore but not sick. I haven't been able to make myself eat more than a few bites each day. I'm too afraid of vomiting it up again.

I can't remember the last time I went a week without flying. Not since I was seven or eight.

Ella is already at their bedsides when I arrive. Her mask lies lopsided on her face. "I don't think they're awake," she says. "What's that?" She nods at the book in my hands.

"*Tamm's Fables*," I say. "Can you help me? I couldn't tie my mask with the book."

Ella smooths my hair over my shoulder. Her hands are careful and steady and soft against my head. When they drop, I take a shaky breath.

It didn't occur to me until the third day to be surprised that Ella joined my vigil. But it's no trivial thing, not just to risk the miasma, but to bear the fear so intimately. I wouldn't blame her if she kept her distance; I don't blame Gretta. But I've never been able to predict what Ella will do. She's only known Sofie and Ness for a few months, and yet, here she stays.

"You can have the chair, if you want," she says.

"Or we could share?"

She nods. Her mask bobs.

The chair is big enough for both of us, but it's close. When I open the book—large, water-stained, dog-eared—its spine settles between our legs.

I look at Sofie, her hair stuck to her forehead in sweaty clumps and her thin lips pursed. I look at Ness, her curls deflated, her head sunken into the pillows like they might consume her.

The knot in my throat isn't an easy thing to clear.

I've considered throwing this book into a canal every day since my mother died. It's my most precious and most painful reminder of her. And it's the only thing I can think to offer Sofie and Ness.

It's what my mother offered me, after all, whenever I felt small and powerless and alone.

I offer them a fairy tale. A story. Hope.

Behind seven mountains and beyond seven seas, there was a king with twelve daughters. Each daughter was clever and each daughter was beautiful, but Talia—the seventh daughter—was the most adventurous. While the fifth princess read and the ninth princess sang and the third princess stitched and the eleventh princess danced, Talia took her father's smallest sailboat onto the sea. The sea in her father's kingdom was cold, and so Talia wore her warmest furs and her softest gloves as she steered her boat around big floes of ice. The ice held many secrets.

A small black bird landed on her bow.

"Hello there, friend," Talia said, extending a hand.

The bird hopped to Talia's finger. He was a dovekie, she decided. She recognized the white belly and webbed feet from illustrations in books in her father's library.

With one flap of his wings, the dovekie landed on the boat's tiller.

"No, friend," Talia said. "That is my tiller, and I need that to steer."

The dovekie let out a long, desperate cry.

Talia felt overcome by something deep inside her she could put no name to. She reached for the tiller and gave it a sharp turn. The sailboat responded in kind. Not a moment had passed before a black whale thrust its head from the water beside Talia's boat. The whale's big shiny eye met Talia's, and then the beast slowly sank back under the sea.

Talia let out a breath of wonder. If the dovekie had not warned her, her sailboat would have overturned.

"Thank you," Talia said, and the dovekie fluffed his feathers and took skyward.

From then on, every day that Talia spent on the water was a day spent with her dovekie friend. The dovekie guided her, and when she followed his instructions, she found herself sailing into seascapes more beautiful than she had ever known. She grew to trust the dovekie, and it was to him she turned for counsel when the storms began to come.

These were no normal storms, the king told his daughters. These were storms destined to change the shape of their world. There would be ten, as old legend dictated, and after the tenth, all the world would flood for twelve long moons. The king told each of his daughters to think as hard as they could of a way to save themselves and their kingdom, for if they didn't, all would drown.

Talia spent many moons musing with her sisters, but by the time half of the storms had come and gone, she began to fear for her dovekie friend. Birds across the kingdom vanished, and she was sure she wouldn't see him again. Another storm came and went, and Talia could no longer bear the castle walls. Only the sea air could calm her anxious heart.

While all the daughters were troubled by the thought of losing their family, each daughter carried an extra trouble on her shoulders. The fifth princess wondered, "What will the world be without any books?" The ninth princess asked, "And what of a world with no music?"

As Talia sailed through the choppy waters, she said aloud, "What of the boreal pines, the long-eared hares, the indigo wildflowers that rise through the snowmelt each deer season?"

The dovekie landed on her bow. For a moment, Talia was overjoyed. Then she thought of the storms and the terrible fate that awaited them. "Ah, friend," she said. "What of you?"

When the dovekie guided Talia's ship that day, he took her to a place they'd never gone. She sailed and she sailed until she reached a mountain of dark stone rising from the sea. Smoke curled from its crown.

"A volcano?" Talia asked.

The dovekie flew to the shore and looked expectantly at Talia. Talia, never daunted by danger and trusting the dovekie, moored her sailboat and climbed ashore.

It was a long trek to the top of the mountain. As Talia climbed, big clouds began rumbling on the horizon. She was coming to recognize such clouds. Another storm was approaching. Talia climbed faster. The dovekie flying beside her was tireless.

By the time she reached the top, rain was falling. Talia looked over the edge of the volcano. It was a pit of liquid fire, and her whole body burned from being so close.

The dovekie tilted his head at her. Talia felt a tug in her stomach, just as when the dovekie guided her hand to avoid the black whale. She felt as though she could hear a voice in her head, like that of the dovekie, or the volcano, or those who died in the last Flood.

Talia leaped into the volcano.

At her sacrifice, the volcano grumbled. The fire roared. As the storm began to rage overhead, the volcano raged back. The dovekie let out an anguished cry and took flight. The volcano erupted behind him, throwing rock and smoke and fire into the air.

That night, when the storm had gone, the eldest princess frowned. "Talia still has not returned," she said. She went to the balcony of the castle and looked out. She did not see the silhouette of Talia's sailboat traveling back to her through the rain. Instead, she saw a plume of smoke, silver in the night sky.

A drift of white volcanic rocks floated along the horizon, so vast they could have been an island unto themselves. A dovekie flew toward the raft of floating stone, clutching the green bough of a boreal pine in his talons. He landed on the rocks and dropped his branch carefully. From the bough, a pinecone, scales still tightly pinched, protecting its seeds—stoically, patiently—from the world.

The dovekie took flight again, in search of an indigo wildflower.

52

ELLA

I didn't think my heart had enough left in it to break.

It breaks when I watch Natasha read to Sofie and Ness. It breaks when she tugs Ness's blanket over her shoulders and dabs the sweat from Sofie's brow. It breaks when I see a tear drip from underneath the mask and splatter on *Tamm's* yellowing pages.

After Princess Talia, Natasha doesn't stop reading. She reads about a princess who marries a whale king and births a people who can out-swim a Flood. She reads about another princess who is more tempting than the moon and convinces the waves to leave her be. When she reads, I can shut my eyes and almost forget where I am.

No one has come looking for me since the guards killed Maret. If they haven't by now, it's because they don't know. And now, more than ever, I can't leave. Not just because there's no one else left to kill Nikolai. But because I can't imagine leaving the flyers behind.

Inside the infirmary, there's no room to feel anything but sadness and fear. But when I'm outside the infirmary, something else starts tugging at me. It's elusive, like zigzags of light on closed eyelids, and when I try to look it square in the face, it skitters away.

Call it an instinct. Something feels wrong.

On the sixth morning after Ness and Sofie fall ill, as I walk the hallway to the infirmary, I tally the oddities.

One: Bog plague began all at once. I've heard of diseases spreading quickly, but it seems to me that nearly everyone who fell ill did it within the span of a few days. After the initial outbreak, few new patients have entered the infirmary.

Two: Why have Natasha, Katla, and I not felt even a flutter of sickness? Are some people immune?

Three: Twain. Twain is the sticking point for me. If anyone should've inhaled the miasma around Ness, it's Twain. He admitted they kissed not ten minutes before she first vomited. What's most curious to me, though, is that Twain is allowed to see Ness at all. When I first heard that the Captain of the Guard had granted Twain the ability to visit the infirmary, I thought it was just a father showing care for his lovestruck son. But the more I consider it, the more I'm confused. The Captain is one of the most powerful figures within the palace—as his child, Twain is practically guaranteed a place on the royal fleet. Why would the Captain risk his son's life now? Unless, of course, the Captain knows something I don't. If Natasha, Katla, and I are immune, maybe Twain is too.

I've almost made it all the way to the infirmary when I turn around again. I walk the winding halls back to our bedroom. It's been mostly empty since bog plague struck. Gretta's been staying with her parents. Even Adelaida's been largely absent, as though the rest of us might bring the miasma back when we stumble here to sleep.

It's empty when I arrive. I gaze around the room. It looks the same as it did that first night when Sofie lay in bed.

I lift her quilt. It smells like sweat. Her nightstand is full of pleasant clutter: her stash of hazelnuts, a tarot deck, a few beads from our bear season festival full-suits. I stoop to the rucksack tucked halfway beneath her bed. Inside, I find a pair of mittens and a bundle of cloth. I open the cloth: a hunk of bread and half a berry tart, stale but not yet molding. I rewrap the parcel and put it back where I found it.

Before I can search further, the door swings open. I jump, but it's only Natasha, and she looks too tired to care that I was sifting through Sofie's things.

"I was going to sleep in here," she says. "In Gretta's bed."

I nod. I don't blame her for avoiding her lonely bedroom.

Her eyes are veined pink. Her hair is loose around her shoulders and as tangled as I've ever seen it. I thought I did a good job of avoiding sleep leading up to the festival, but Natasha might have me beat.

"How are they doing?" I ask.

"The same," she says. "I read them a few more stories."

"Are all of the fables like the ones I heard?"

"What do you mean?" she says.

I struggle for the words. "My parents told me stories when I was little. I don't know if they were Terrazzan, or just stories they made up. But they always had happy endings. Everything turned out all right in the end."

Natasha sits on the edge of Gretta's bed. "Tamm liked bittersweet endings. I think they make the stories feel more real. And of course, some of the fables start from a kernel of truth, like with Inna, and true stories don't often have happy endings."

I blink. "Are you trying to tell me there really was a girl named Inna who befriended a bear?"

She exhales through her nose. It's the tiredest laugh. "No. But there's some scrap of Maapinnen history—I don't know all the details—about invaders coming here and a young girl killing their king. Hans von Kleb, or something. I don't remember. That's the sort of thing my mother would know. She always told me these stories from the—"

"Hans?" There's little that could make me interrupt Natasha in the middle of telling me about her past. But I have to ask. "Are you sure it's not Otto? Otto von Kleb?"

Her weary brows scrunch together. "I guess? Sure. That sounds right."

"And he was mauled by a bear?" I say.

"I don't know. Probably not. I mean, some girl killed him, but she probably didn't sic a bear on him. That's just the way the fable goes. I don't know what actually happened."

In my mind, I see everything like the pieces of a jigsaw puzzle: not yet assembled, but there, ready to snap into place.

"How do you think Inna killed him, then?" I say.

Natasha watches me skeptically. "I just told you, I don't know." A pause. "Though if you think about a young girl killing a king, there's really only one clear way she could've done it."

I've spent long enough wondering the same thing that I have the answer ready. "Poison."

"How on earth do you know Otto von Kleb's name, anyway?" Natasha says.

The last piece snaps into place.

"Seas," I whisper.

The book. The botanical book in the library. I remember the page in my mind now: a watercolor mushroom, fairy-tale charming, with a rounded top and feathery gills. The kind of mushroom you'd choose to live underneath if you were a caterpillar. The notes written by hand beside the illustration: *Smells of honey. Otto von Kleb?*

It's poison. Sofie and Ness were poisoned. But—it's not possible. We eat all the same food, always, and the chef adores Sofie. Did someone slip something onto their dinner plates while they weren't looking? And why the two of them? Why the two most harmless flyers?

Then I look down at my fingers. A golden crumb, the tiniest stain of red berry juice on my thumbnail. And I remember them coming back to the palace, tarts in hand, faces stained with berries.

I have to get to Ness and Sofie.

They're not dying of a plague. They're dying of a poison.

"Ella?" Natasha says. "What is it?"

I run.

53

NATASHA

I tear after Ella down the hall to the infirmary. What's she thinking? What's going on?

My slippers skid along the marble floor. I slam into a guard and don't bother to apologize as I right myself and keep running. When Ella and I barrel through the infirmary door, I'm gasping and sweaty.

The nurse stands between Ness's and Sofie's beds. When she sees me, she looks up sharply. "Mask," she says.

I don't put it on. I can't. Not when I see Ness's and Sofie's faces.

I run to their beds, then I collapse to my knees. I sense, distantly, Ella's presence beside me.

Ness's skin is colorless and stretched like wax.

"I'm sorry," the nurse says.

My mind refuses to process what she's sorry for. I crawl to Sofie's bed and grip her hand as tightly as I can. After a moment, I feel the faintest squeeze in return.

"Sofie?"

Her eyes open halfway. She parts her mouth to speak, and I lean forward to listen. "Many breaths," she whispers.

I smooth her hair. My eyes burn. I want to memorize her

precious, hopeful face. The words are slow to come. "Many breaths."

I say it a moment too late. There are no more breaths to stir the air between her lips.

54

ELLA

The thing about awfulness is this: Everyone wants it in small doses.

The storms are an adventure if you have a home at the end of them. If you can watch them from the dry side of a window. Light a few lamps. Drink a bottle of cider with your loved ones. You say you're scared, but it's an exciting little façade. A fervor in being The Toughest People Who Ever Lived in the Grimmest Time That Ever Was. You drift through the fog of awfulness like a tourist. It's a miasma, the awfulness. You'll be fine if you wear a mask. Stay long enough to breathe it into your lungs, and you can't ever leave.

Natasha curls on the floor between the beds, pressed in on herself like a wounded animal.

I cover her body with mine. I wrap myself around her and I press my face to her hair as she shakes.

"Shh," I whisper, over and over again. "Shh."

Her heart beats against mine. I don't think she even registers I'm here.

Why would anyone poison all these people? Half of Kostrov? The only one who has motive is—is Nikolai. Fighting Gospodin to keep his tenuous grasp on power. Battling the straining population.

There aren't enough supplies for the royal fleet, everyone says that. So Nikolai figured out a solution: Kill the people who were going to get left behind in Storm One. Then, when he gets to save everyone else, save whoever's left, he's a *hero*.

I bury my face in Natasha's shoulder.

Sofie and Ness and Maret and Cassia.

"I can't," Natasha says, choked. "I can't. I can't."

I know what she means well enough. She can't bear the loss of Sofie and Ness. She can't fight back against this world, this sick city, this vile palace.

But I can.

55

NATASHA

I spend the day after they die wandering the halls, caught in a trance. A silky curtain in front of a window reminds me how long it's been since I flew. I find I don't care.

I only go to their bedroom once. Katla's incense clouds the air. I stare at Sofie's bed. The sheets are still messy from when she kicked them off to vomit the first time. Ness's bed is strewn with hair ribbons. Those beds will probably never be filled again.

The flyers are over.

Maybe the ocean should eat all of us. Not just all the people excluded from the fleet, but the palace and the Sacred Breath and everyone else.

The incense makes my head fuzzy, but I have nowhere to go, so when I leave the bedroom, I just keep pacing the palace halls. The snow outside thaws in a riotous, unfair barrage of sunlight. I walk and I walk and I walk until the sun sinks beneath the ocean and the clouds squeeze out the moon.

I need to talk to Nikolai. Surely, he can do something. To protect the rest of my girls. To stop this plague before Gretta and Katla and Ella die too. He has to know something. He has to *do* something.

Distantly, I remember that his birthday is soon. Maybe it's already passed. He hasn't chosen a queen yet.

My heart is hollow. After all this—I still want the crown. I still want to survive. Want my girls to survive. When I picture Katla's face, Gretta's face—Ella's face.

A shiver runs through me.

I can't lose her. Them. Any of them.

Back in my room, I sit down at my desk and begin to write. I only have three sheets of paper to my name, so I choose each word with care.

Your Royal Highness,

As you may have heard, two flyers died yesterday. My grief is difficult to describe. I hope you haven't lost anyone. I wouldn't wish this on you.

If you can, I'd like the two of us to talk. I'll be at the conservatory at midnight.

Best,

Natasha Koskinen

I melt a blob of sticky wax and seal the letter shut. I find a familiar guard: Zakarias, one of Nikolai's favorites. I give him the letter and tell him it's important.

I lean against the wall and shut my eyes. I hold my breath, like the Flood came early and the ocean found me. *One, two, three . . .*

I'm already drowning.

56

ELLA

If I'd killed him sooner, Sofie and Ness might still be alive.

I know from the floor plans I found in the library that I'm in the right area. I've never dared walk the heavily guarded part of the palace where Nikolai lives. If there's a silver lining to the bog plague panic, it's that everyone is too distraught to notice a wandering flyer.

When I near the door I think is Nikolai's, I double back around the corner. Two men stand in front of it. I peer around the corner again. It's Gregor and Andrei.

"Why does he want to go to the conservatory?" Andrei asks.

Gregor shakes his head. "I don't know. Just go with him and don't talk too much. He's not in the mood for a chat."

"Well, tell Sebastian to check the conservatory if I'm not here when his shift starts."

I duck out of sight. Stepping as quietly as I can, I hurry back the way I came. *He* can only be Nikolai. And Nikolai in the conservatory is easier to reach than Nikolai in his bedroom.

I grip the straps of Sofie's rucksack. When I think I'm out of earshot of the guards, I run. In my haste to get through the Stone Garden unseen, I cut too fast a corner around a statue of a soldier with a pike. The pointed tip of his weapon slices open the sleeve of my full-suit. Blood wells along the siren's tail. I slap a hand to the stinging skin and keep moving.

The conservatory is empty when I arrive. The air smells like muggy earth. I'd hoped that the hot pools would be set up as they were last time, and when I push aside the dangling ferns, I see I've gotten lucky. A servant must've just swept through. Sitting by the pool's edge is a platter of bread. Beside it, a vase of water. Mint leaves float on the surface. Cloudberries settle at the bottom. A set of empty glasses sit beside it.

I pour one half-full. My hands shake as I open Sofie's rucksack. My fingers, bloodstained from my arm, smear red across the buckles. I remove the bundle of cloth and unwrap it carefully. I'm afraid to touch the contents, but I make myself do it anyway. The inside of the tart is sticky and wet. I scoop the contents into the water glass. The cranberries tinge it pink. The bits of chopped mushroom settle at the bottom with the cloudberries.

By the time I put the leftover tart back in the rucksack, my whole body is trembling. I swing the rucksack over my shoulder. The steam from the pool is hot, but I can't stop shivering.

I need to get out of here. Not just the conservatory but out of the palace.

I rise on unsteady feet.

Through the ferns, a door opens.

I freeze. A boot crunches snow.

I lunge for the tangle of plants on the far side of the pool. The net of branches pushes back against me. The flapping fabric of my sleeve catches a thorn and tears another few inches. The leaf at my hand smears red, whether from my blood or the cranberries' innards, I don't know. The plants close tightly around me. I crouch in the shelter of their arms. Through the crosshatch, I see Nikolai.

He approaches the pool. Inhales the thermal steam. Takes off his boots, rolls up his pants, and dangles his feet in the water.

He picks up the glass of water. Around me, the leaves still. He doesn't drink. He swirls the glass and moves his legs in lazy circles in the pool.

No. I bury my hand in the rucksack again, searching, but—I didn't bring Maret's barometer. It's still under my pillow. I don't have my knife.

I stare at the glass, willing him to drink it. He raises it to his lips.

I don't know which is more fitting: That he should die by poison or that he should die by water.

Then the creaking of wind against glass. The door opens again. He sets down the glass.

I wait for Andrei to walk in. Let him drink too. I'll gladly see them both dead. But it's not Andrei who next pushes through the ferns.

Not Natasha. It can't be.

She sits down beside Nikolai, and the leaves shiver against my skin.

"I'm sorry about your flyers," Nikolai says.

A long silence. Natasha's eyes are red.

"I'm sorry, Natasha." He sounds genuine. It's almost convincing enough that I could believe it. Please don't let Natasha be fooled.

Nikolai lifts a hand like he means to take Natasha's. When she doesn't move, he pulls back. "I had something I wanted to ask you, actually, but I don't know if now is the right time."

That's when I realize. The start of bear season came and went. In the chaos of bog plague, Nikolai never announced his queen.

"Every day that passes, the more I realize how right you were. That I need a queen I can trust. But you told me I could trust you, and so you should trust me too."

No. She can't. She can't trust him.

She stays very still as she considers. Their silhouettes match: two tall, slender figures, smooth-haired, sharp-jawed. The queen and king. It's too easy to imagine.

"If anyone else dies . . ." Natasha says. "I don't think I could . . ." Her voice is hoarse.

Nikolai puts a hesitating hand on her shoulder.

"I—" She purses her mouth, words failing. She shakes her head.

"Here," Nikolai says. And he hands her the glass of water.

She raises it to her lips.

57

NATASHA

Nikolai's eyes are gray and serious. My throat is tight. We watch each other over the glass as I tip it to meet my mouth.

"Stop!"

The glass slips and shatters on the stone. Ella bursts from the snarl of plants not three feet from me. Nikolai and I lurch backward and leap to our feet.

"You didn't drink?" Ella says. She doesn't look at Nikolai. She doesn't even seem to see him. "Tell me you didn't drink."

Her sleeve is torn to her elbow, her siren exposed. Blood beads her skin. Her nails are stained pink.

"Ella," I say, "what's going on?"

"Tell me you didn't drink!"

Why is she yelling? I can feel my heart beating in my throat. Nothing makes sense.

"Natasha!" she says.

Dazed, I shake my head. No, I didn't drink.

The conservatory door slams open. Andrei thunders in. He turns wildly from us to the glass to Nikolai's stricken expression.

When I look at Nikolai, he stares at the shattered glass on the ground. The soggy mint leaves and crushed fruit.

"I heard something smash," Andrei says. "What's going on?"

But Ella's still looking at me, pleading, almost, and I don't *get it*. Nothing has made sense since Sofie and Ness died.

"How did you get in here?" Nikolai says. His voice is sharp, accusatory—scared. It makes me flinch. Ella doesn't even look in his direction. She's still staring at me.

Andrei takes a step toward Ella, but something he sees makes him reel back like he's been punched. "You." He's staring at her wrist, bloodstained and ink-marked. "It's you."

Her eyes are wide. Then they find mine. She whispers one word, the way you would speak a prayer to the sea.

"Help."

What is going on?

I've spent my whole life fleeing danger, running toward the place most secure. Guarding my heart, my body, my safety, my survival.

Blood rushes in my ears. I don't know why Ella is here. I don't know what Andrei means when he says *It's you*. But I know the way he's looking at her, reaching for her. Like he's going to hurt her.

I grab Ella's hand and we move.

Andrei is fast but we're faster. We scramble past him and through the conservatory door. My heart leaps in my throat when Nikolai yells my name.

We tear through the snowy garden. Ella tries to tug me in the direction of the door, but I pull her the other way. I drop to my knees in the frost where a long, rectangular fountain spills over into a grate along the edge of the path. I lace my fingers through it and tug until the grate comes free. The opening is almost too narrow. Too narrow for Andrei, at least.

I slide through the gap and splash into the tunnel beneath. The water laps my knees.

A moment later, Ella lands beside me, spraying me with water, mud, and snow. When she looks at me, her eyes are wild, gleaming in the darkness.

Who are you?

Am I making a terrible mistake?

My hand swallows hers.

We run.

58

ELLA

I follow Natasha blindly through the black passageways. My breathing is shallow and sharp. I get the sense that we're running downhill, deeper underground. Soon, the water laps my waist. It struggles against every step I take.

The sound of rushing water and sea grows louder. The passage ends at a grate overlooking a canal. Water spills out at our ankles.

Natasha squeezes through the bars of the grate. I turn myself sideways and slip out after her. Natasha's hand appears above me. I take it. She hauls me onto the edge of a street. I recognize it. We're a few blocks south of the palace.

Rain falls. It's only a drizzle, but the melting snow has the canals teeming. Overhead, clouds disguise the stars. I shiver. My feet are well past numb.

Now that we've stopped, Natasha drops my hand. "Want to explain what happened in there?" she hisses.

I wince. Before I can say anything, I hear a clatter, like a cart tipping over a few streets away.

"Come on," Natasha says. "We need to keep moving."

Maybe we'll keeping moving forever. Then I won't have to explain what I just tried to do.

She sloshes through the puddled street, keeping a step ahead of me. The rain darkens her hair to rusted bronze, painting strands of it against the back of her neck. What's going on inside her head? Does she realize I was trying to poison Nikolai? I don't think she'd be helping me if she knew.

I don't ask questions as we wind through the streets. I know we're heading south, but once we pass Eel Shore, I don't recognize anything. The buildings cram together. A few shadowy figures slog through the water with hunched shoulders.

Natasha leads me down a dark, slanting street, penned on either side by crooked buildings. The alley ends on a canal that's trying its best to make this stretch of street its own. The water rises to my knees. I'm too numb to care.

She grabs me by the shoulder as though I might run—and really, I might—and says, "Here. Talk."

"Do you know this place?"

"No," Natasha says. "This is a shitty street. One of many in Southtown. This is where we stay until you tell me—" She pauses. There are too many things to tell. "Until you tell me who you are."

I tug at my hair, heavy with water.

I'm so aware of her hand on my shoulder. I take a half-step forward, and when she doesn't retreat, I move closer.

"You know me," I say softly. I want it to be true. So badly. I don't want to explain everything to her. I just want her to know. Who I am. What I did.

Natasha's back hits the wall of the alley. She sinks to the ground and curls her legs to her stomach. She's trembling, afraid. It's my fault. Seas. I'd do anything to make her feel safe again.

I drop to the ground in front of her.

Natasha leans her head against her knees and shuts her eyes. My hand hovers above her arm for a long moment before I'm brave enough to touch her.

"Just tell me this, then," she says. "Were you trying to hurt Nikolai?"

I don't say anything.

She lets out a long, thin breath. "And I helped you."

Her words go through me like a knife in my ribs. Twisting. "I can explain," I say.

"And now," she says, "there are probably palace guards chasing after both of us. All because I just *had* to help you. I'm so stupid."

"Natasha—"

"I was going to survive," she says.

"I'm sorry," I whisper. My eyes burn.

I'm strong. I'm vengeful and awful and *strong,* and my whole reason for being is supposed to revolve around Cassia, around killing Nikolai, and now—

"I had everything under control," Natasha says. "I was going to marry Nikolai and sail away on the royal fleet and tell this island and everyone on it goodbye, because that's the kind of selfish person I am." I can't tell whether the water beading on her lashes is rain or tears. "I was going to survive. Until you arrived." She looks at me like I can't possibly understand. But I do understand. I understand waking and wanting. Falling asleep and wanting. The way, if you find something good enough to want, it eats up all the empty space. It fills you.

I understand.

Surviving is her purpose like revenge was mine.

Between us, there could only ever be one happy ending.

"You still could," I say. My voice is scraped hollow. "I didn't kill him, did I? I failed. I failed because I couldn't let you die. But you can still go back. Marry Nikolai. Survive, Natasha. You can still survive."

"You don't get it," she says. "You've ruined everything."

"Why?"

She shakes her head. A tendril of hair sticks to her skin, tracing the shape of her jaw and collarbone. Her arms shake. Every muscle in them is long and taut.

"Because I don't just want to survive anymore," she says.

Then she reaches forward. The water surges up around us. Her fingers lace through my hair.

She kisses me like the world is ending.

59

NATASHA

Ella's lips are sticky with salt water and sweat. She swings her legs over mine. I hold her face in my hands, a thumb on each temple. I press my lips to hers and hips to hers and I breathe what she breathes, there in the flooding street, the water and night swirling around us. When she shifts, the current pushes, pulls. She tugs at my hair and draws me closer. Our noses brush.

I run my hands down her arms and find goose bumps there.

When I kiss her, I try to forget that she's not mine and I'm not hers. That we have people to go back to and people following us. This kiss isn't a beginning but an end.

Her lips leave mine. Our foreheads press.

Do I have time to memorize her? The way her nose turns up at the tip, just a little? The way the water gleams on her skin?

"Natasha," she whispers.

"We can't stay here," I say.

She nods her head against mine. Then she closes her eyes. Winces. "I have to tell you something."

"What?"

"The reason I wanted to kill Nikolai," she says.

Kill Nikolai. When she says it, it's real. She wanted to kill Nikolai. My lungs aren't cooperating. I feel dizzy.

"Cassia," she says.

I understand it. All of it. In that word.

Cassia. Beautiful, clever Cassia. The exiled royal princess. Of course I understand. I always envied Cassia. Admired Cassia. Maybe even had an inkling of something more toward her, the same way I always had an inkling of something toward Nikolai, something I never tried to put words to. Cassia.

"We were—" Ella says, but I shake my head against hers.

"You don't have to," I say.

"Maret," Ella says. "Her aunt. She's the woman you saw me talking to. We came here together. Nikolai sent his men to kill Cassia. So I wanted revenge. Maret wanted the throne."

Cassia's dead? And Nikolai killed her? I think about that boy. That boy I've started to know over the past few months. So unsure, so cautious, so aware of how little Gospodin and the rest of the councilors expect of him.

"You really think," I say, "he could've killed his sister?"

"I was there," Ella says. "I saw Andrei kill her."

I feel nauseated. Nikolai? Nikolai, who couldn't even stand up to his sister when she beat him at a board game?

Ella searches my expression. She must see my doubt, because she says, "And bog plague. Nikolai orchestrated the bog plague. It was in the food at the food drive. Poisoned mushrooms, just like Inna used."

My body stills, but my mind is leaping. Grabbing at memories. The food drive. Gospodin wiping his fingers so meticulously on the tablecloth. Sofie and Ness, giggling with their treats in hand.

"Natasha?" Ella says.

"It was Gospodin." I'm shaking my head. I'm shaking all over. "Not Nikolai. It was Gospodin."

He stays in power because he promises to keep people safe from the Flood. And only so many people can fit on the royal fleet. So the fewer people who survive until Storm One, the better his success rate. The better his odds of getting the royal fleet well-stocked for the Flood year.

They would've died anyway, he'd say. *This was a necessary evil. To keep the peace. You understand that, don't you, Miss Koskinen?*

Ella shakes her head. "No, it was Nikolai. That's what Cassia always said. That *Nikolai* was after her. Not Gospodin."

Then she's quiet too, and our foreheads are still pressed together, and the smell of her is drowning my senses, and I just want everything to freeze, no more Gospodin, no more Nikolai, no more Flood, just Ella.

"You're wrong," I say.

We must root out dangerous individuals, whether they be insect or man, and see them to their deaths before they can contaminate others. That's what Gospodin told me to read from *Captain's Log.* That anyone who threatens his power, anyone who threatens his idea of peace, should be snuffed out.

"You weren't there," Ella says sharply. "You didn't see Cassia die."

When she says Cassia's name, my stomach tightens. I'm jealous of a dead girl. "I know you knew Cassia. But I know Nikolai. And I don't think he could do it. Tell someone to kill her."

Ella sits back. "If you're so sure he's innocent, then marry him." She doesn't try to disguise the derision in her voice. "Survive." She stares at the water moving across the ground. I feel the abrupt distance in every part of me. "He wants to marry you. A fool could see it. So be the queen."

If she looked at me, she'd see how badly I want her to tell me to do the opposite. Forget Nikolai. What does it matter, whether Nikolai or Gospodin is the bad guy? Ella and I could find a boat. We could run away. She hid from me for so long, fearing that I would hate her, but now that I see all of her—it's the opposite. If she looked at me, I'd kiss her again and she would know.

She never does.

"No," I say. "Ella, no. I'm . . . I'm not leaving you."

She looks up. Voice soft, she says, "Then where should we go?"

I pause. "Long term? Or right now?"

It's such a painfully big question. I've spent months desperate to secure a future with Nikolai. Imagining myself sailing away on the royal fleet, waving Kostrov goodbye and basking in my luck to survive at least longer than my mother did.

I want to not want that.

But.

This future—this stupid, impossible, tempting future—is all I know how to want. I don't have an answer to anything long term, so I'm relieved when Ella says, "Right now. Just . . . just right now."

"Pippa," I say. "We can go ask Pippa for help."

"Okay," Ella says. "I—okay."

I look in her eyes. She looks in mine.

I forget about breathing.

"Natasha, I don't know what I just did," she says. "I can't believe . . . I'm sorry."

What am I supposed to do? Tell her it's fine? Tell her it doesn't matter that she just tried to kill someone? It's not fine.

But I helped her. And wasn't there a part of me that knew she must, *must* have been up to something terrible the moment she tumbled out of the ferns in the greenhouse? I helped her anyway. Because it's Ella. *It's Ella.*

I just wish I could take this moment, all the good parts, and siphon them into a bottle. I would take that bottle far away from Kostrov, and I would revel in something beautiful and astounding and more than this.

Ella nods. Then she bites her lip, hesitant in a way I'm not used to seeing Ella look. "I just . . . I know that you're probably . . . I—"

I grab her by the shoulders and kiss her again. I hold her to me, I feel her heartbeat. Then I let my hands drop to my sides. "Let's go."

For a moment, she looks shocked. Then she nods.

The city is still dark, but window lights flicker valiantly, casting streaky squares of yellow across the wet street. As I pass through one of these boxes of light, a dark shape trembles in the waves shuddering out from my foot. A rat. Dead. It's curled in on itself like a comma, clutching its tail in death-stiff claws. Ella's calf brushes it. She chokes.

I reach back and grab her hand, just for a moment, and squeeze.

"I've never liked cities," she says.

"Well, I'm not all that fond of New Sundstad right now, either," I say. "What is there to like?"

"I hear the Royal Flyers are pretty spectacular," she says.

I laugh before I can stop myself. But it's gone as quickly as it arrived. Too soon, the enormity of what I've just done starts to sink in.

I ran away from Nikolai. I ran away from the palace. That means I made my choice, doesn't it? I made my stupid, spur-of-the-moment choice to chase the wild feelings in my stomach instead of the logical plan I've been constructing since I was a child. *Stay in the palace. Survive.*

"Where are we?" Ella says.

I feel an uncomfortable jolt in my stomach looking around at all the buildings, like my guts stopped while the rest of my body kept moving. It's familiar in the worst way possible. The butcher's shop. The brown-stained bricks. My old neighborhood. I keep moving.

"Almost there," I say.

We don't stop until we reach the blue door, the crooked house where Pippa and Iskra and Rasa live.

I reach out and take Ella's hand. She laces her fingers through mine. I rub my thumb along the black marks crawling up and down her wrist.

"Come on," I say.

I never liked it here but we have nowhere else to go. I tell myself it is not permanent. It's just a good hiding place. Somewhere Ella and I can sit for a few hours until we have a plan.

A small voice within me asks—*but then what?* Am I supposed to leave Kostrov? Am I supposed to run back to the palace, pray that I'm right about Nikolai, and plead my innocence?

Everything is upended.

There could be guards chasing us now. There probably are.

"Are we going in?" Ella asks quietly.

I take a deep breath. Then I step forward and raise my hand to knock.

60

ELLA

Natasha raises her hand to knock, then lowers it again.

"I . . ." She shakes her head. Never finishes her sentence.

I rise up on my toes and press my lips to hers. I wish it were brighter in this dim street so I could chart each freckle on her nose and commit them to memory.

How can I feel this way? After Cassia, I couldn't imagine myself with anyone else. Even as I felt my attraction to Natasha grow, I never thought it could be like this. Never thought I'd feel this much. And I'm surprised at the realization.

What I feel for Natasha doesn't make what I felt for Cassia less true. It's like when a Flood consumes old land to make way for the new. It doesn't mean the old land never existed. It doesn't mean no one ever danced, sang, raged, loved, on that land. While it stood, mountained and rivered, the land was good.

Now that it's gone, it's not less. Just past.

When our lips come apart, I squeeze Natasha's hand one last time. Then I drop it.

Natasha knocks on the door.

A minute later, it creaks open. A young woman with long braids opens it. Her stomach, under her tunic, curves gently.

"Oh, Tasha!" Pippa says. "And you must be Ella. It's awfully early for a—" And then Pippa's eyes trail across us, our wet clothes and my red-stained hands. Her lips part. "What's going on?"

"Please," Natasha says. "We need your help."

Pippa leads us inside. Through a narrow hall and up the stairs. It's dimly lit. Smells like old flowers. I don't blame Natasha for not liking this place. Pippa takes us to a small bedroom, cramped. Stacks of books and newspapers fill the space under her bed. A colorful atlas lies open on the quilt. Pippa closes the door behind us.

"Well," Pippa says, "I'm not sure where to start."

Natasha glances at me. "Neither am I."

"What happened?" Pippa says. "Why are you here?"

"We had to run," Natasha says. "Ella—Nikolai was—"

She won't say it. It's a kindness I don't deserve.

"I tried to poison Nikolai," I say.

"What?" Pippa says. "Why?"

I close my eyes. Wince. "Cassia," I say.

"The princess?" Pippa says.

So I explain. I tell them about losing my family but finding a new one in Cassia and Maret. I tell them about Andrei and the others arriving in Terrazza, murdering her. I tell them about revenge.

"How can you be sure it was Nikolai?" Pippa says. "Tasha, you know him as well as any of us. Do you really think he could've done something like that?"

"I can believe he was jealous of her," she says. "Jealous of her cleverness. Jealous of her power." A pause. "Do *you* think he could've sent Andrei to kill her?"

Pippa chews on her lip. "I don't know. Gregor would probably say no. But—but things changed after Nikolai exiled Cassia. Everything got . . . tenser."

"I know Nikolai is guilty," I say. Even to my own ears, I sound exhausted. I feel like a one-note song.

Cassia wanted Nikolai dead; Nikolai wanted Cassia dead. Are they so different?

I sink onto the edge of Pippa's bed.

Seas. I was going to murder someone. The enormity of it hits me. If not for Natasha, I would've. I would be a murderer right now. I might never know whether or not Nikolai was guilty—but *I* would be.

A shiver runs through me. I curl in on myself. Wrap my arms around my knees and stare at my wrist. When I rub my thumb across my siren, my skin puckers across the wide plane of her face, and it looks like she winks at me. Can I hate her and love her at the same time? She's seen everything. The truths and the untruths. The heartbreak and the vengeance and the love. She's seen plenty of things I'm ashamed of, plenty of things I regret. But I don't ever want to regret who I am.

"What now?" Pippa says. "Are you going to go back to the palace?"

Natasha tenses. "Ella can't."

I can't go back to the palace, but can she? Would she? Will she?

"Natasha," I say softly. "Can I talk to you in private? For just a minute?"

Pippa nods and steps outside. Seals the door gently behind her.

Natasha hesitates by the bed. I stand up. Take her hands.

I'm so tired of living for someone else's memory.

I'm so tired of pretending I don't love her.

"You saved me," I say.

She shakes her head, and I kiss her.

"You saved me," I say again. I feel pressure building behind my eyes. "And now I want to save you."

"I can't—" she starts, but I kiss her again.

"You have to go back to the palace," I say. Is my voice steady? If it is, it's a lie. My heart is breaking. "Go back to the palace. Marry Nikolai. Save the flyers. Save yourself." I kiss her a third time, desperate, missing her already. Then I whisper, against her lips, "Survive."

"No," Natasha says. "Not without you. I wasn't sure, but I—"

"You have to," I say. It comes out fierce. Angry, almost. But this can't all be for nothing.

"*No,*" she says, and I see tears at the corners of her eyes. But I can't let her do this. Give up everything. For me. She's so close.

"Listen," I say. "The guards will be looking for us. They'll think to come here. You need to leave before they do." She's trying to interrupt, to protest, but I keep going. "Nikolai cares for you. Genuinely, I think. You just . . . You just have to tell him that you were trying to figure out what I was up to."

"I'm not leaving you," Natasha says.

I start talking faster. "Gospodin might be dangerous, but if you get one of the mushrooms he used, you'll have a way to protect yourself. To prove what he did." I explain quickly, where to find the botanical book in the library, the page about the mushroom, and though Natasha doesn't say anything, she never stops shaking her head.

"Ella, no," she says. "What about you?"

"What about me?" I say. "It doesn't matter. I'd rather see you safe. Don't you understand?"

"Don't you understand that I'd rather see *you* safe?" she says.

I feel myself go still. *No,* I want to say, *of course I don't understand.* It never occurred to me that I could love anyone else after Cassia. But even more impossible is the idea that someone else could love me.

I sit back down on the bed. Natasha sits next to me.

"We could go somewhere, right?" Natasha says. "Run?"

She pulls Pippa's atlas closer. Flips through the pages. All the countries the ocean will soon swallow. All the land that won't be there much longer. I watch her flip past illustrations of gleaming lakes and crumbling cliffs and mountains that rise from the tundra to pierce the northern lights.

"We could go anywhere," Natasha says.

I would go anywhere with Natasha. But nowhere we could go will give her as much as Nikolai could give her on the royal fleet.

Am I selfish if I say yes? I want to. So badly.

"Tasha—"

The door opens again.

"You two have to run," Pippa says. "Now."

We get to our feet. "Why?"

I hear a pounding on the door downstairs.

"Guards," Pippa says. "They're here."

My heart is hammering. A door creaks open. Voices from below drift up to us. A man—a guard—saying, "Iskra. Come on. We were friends when you were in the palace."

"Well, we're not friends now."

"We just need to check for the flyers."

Pippa motions us forward. She runs down the hall on silent feet.

I reach back behind me, searching for Natasha, and I find her there. I find her hand, her fingers, lace them through mine.

She squeezes.

We race after Pippa down the hall and through a short door that moans when she pushes against it.

"What was that?" a man's voice says.

"Hurry!" Pippa leads us down the stairs at a run. My heart surges to match the pace. We careen down the stairs, abandoning any pretense of stealth. One flight of stairs, two flights—

We fly to the ground floor and barrel through another door.

I don't let go of Natasha's hand the whole way.

The door opens into a wet, grimy alley.

"Go," Pippa says.

Natasha and I spill out onto the wet street and start to run.

We shoot around a corner. Natasha stops so abruptly I slam into her. She stumbles but keeps her footing, grabbing my shoulders and turning me in the other direction. I catch a glimpse of why.

Four tall men in guard uniforms are running down the alley after us.

We take off the opposite way. Run until we're gasping for breath. Run until my legs and chest ache.

There's nowhere to go. Nowhere.

We hurdle around a corner, and I reach for Natasha's hand. Behind us, footsteps, fast on the wet cobblestone.

This wasn't—this wasn't how any of this was meant to go.

Guards behind us. City disappearing in front of us. And then the edge of New Sundstad, the ocean open in front of us.

When I shouted at Natasha—when I saved her from my own

poison—I ruined any chance I had to kill Nikolai. I didn't have time to think. But I'd do it again.

I couldn't save Cassia. I can save Natasha.

We skid to a stop at the edge of the city. I look over my shoulder in time to see shadows, the guards, surging out of the street we just ran through, cornering us against the sea.

"What are we going to—" Natasha says.

"I trusted you!" I shout. "And you betrayed me!"

The guards are here. Natasha's eyes are wide, confused.

"You and Nikolai deserve each other," I say.

And then I push her into the ocean.

61

NATASHA

I splash into the water. The cold shocks the air out of me. When I surface, I gasp.

Why did Ella do that?

I grab at the seawall, trying to find a way back up. The stone is slick and rises higher than I am tall. I can't stop coughing.

Distantly, I hear a voice. The guards?

I open my mouth to shout. A wave hits me sideways. Fills my lungs with seawater. I start to cough. Slap the side of the wall. But the ocean is big, loud, and I'm tiny.

And then—hands reaching down. Pale and freckled. I grab them, and someone strong lifts me out of the water and into a puddle on the cobblestones. I cough up another mouthful of water.

"Natasha?" Gregor crouches next to me, sets a gentle hand on my shoulder. "You okay?"

I see the boots of a few other guards. All of them hunching down, looking at me with great concern.

So that's what Ella did.

She made it seem like I tricked her. So that I wouldn't get in trouble. So that the guards would set gentle hands on my shoulder and look at me with great concern.

I gaze around the street.

Ella's already gone.

"What happened?" I say. I'm shivering and dizzy.

"You're fine," Gregor says. "Come on. Let's get you home."

Fine? I'm not fine. I've never been further from fine.

"Where's Ella?" I ask.

"Don't worry about it." Gregor's voice is sharp. He gives me a warning look. "That was clever of you. Leading her to a dead end."

I feel slow, heavy. "Right."

Where is she?

When we get back to the palace, Gregor deposits me in the flyer bedroom. Katla's the only one there. She springs to her feet, hurries toward me.

"What's going on?" Katla says.

Gregor nods at me. "Get her warmed up. Captain Waska will want to talk to her. Nikolai too." Then he leaves.

Katla wraps a towel around my shoulders. Frowns at me.

"Ella tried to kill Nikolai," I whisper.

Her face pales. "What?"

I tell her everything. If she's surprised to hear about my feelings, Ella's feelings, the kiss, she doesn't show it. When I ask, she just shrugs. "I noticed Ella's tattoo months ago. I figured she would tell me if she wanted to."

"And me?"

"I am neither surprised nor unsurprised."

"What's that supposed to mean?" I ask.

"You know I've been in the room when you and Ella look at each other, right?"

My cheeks heat.

"You know what does surprise me?" she says, lowering her voice. "The fact that you'd help someone who wanted to *assassinate the king*."

"It was a split-second decision," I say. "Momentary insanity?"

But . . . was it? If I had to do it over, would I still help Ella? Now that I know what I know. That I wasn't misunderstanding. That she wasn't innocent. She wanted to kill Nikolai—simple as that.

Would I help her again?

I start shivering harder.

"Okay," Katla says, exhaling. "Okay, here's what we're going to say. You knew she trusted you, so you decided to help her get out of the palace to figure out who she was working with. Once you knew what her motives were, you led her to a dead end so the guards could catch her. You are loyal to the crown. You want nothing to do with Ella. Got it?"

"Where do you think she is?" I say.

"You're not allowed to ask that. All this is too suspicious as is."

"Please, Katla," I say. "Go talk to the guards. Gretta. Someone has to know something."

She frowns. Inspects me carefully. "Okay. But—be careful, all right? Don't do anything stupid while I'm gone."

When she leaves, the room is too quiet. I can hear my heart beating. I stand very still in the middle of the room.

Was Ella telling the truth? If Nikolai killed Cassia, maybe he orchestrated bog plague too. I want to tell someone, but I'm afraid that if I do, I'll just incriminate myself more.

The door flies open.

Adelaida slams it behind her and raises a finger at me. *"What,"* she says, "is going on?"

I open my mouth. Close it again.

"On the list of worst ways I've ever been woken up, let's put at the top: 'The Captain of the Guard storms into my room to tell me two of my flyers have attempted to assassinate the king and are currently missing.'"

"I . . . I wasn't helping Ella." I try to repeat the excuse Katla fed me. "I was just trying to figure out who she was working with."

"And?" Adelaida says. "Did you?"

"Maret."

Her eyebrows life. "Nikolai's aunt?"

"Ella knew Maret and Cassia," I say. "She was traveling with them. She told me Nikolai had Cassia killed, and then she told me this theory about bog plague, and I think it's actually—"

Adelaida holds up a hand. "I don't want to hear it."

"Sorry?"

"You're in enough trouble," she says. "Don't spout theories about bog plague. Or about the king sending assassins after his sister. You are going to be quiet and cooperative. The pinnacle of loyalty. Understand?"

I nod slowly. "But what about Ella?"

"It's better if you don't ask about Ella."

Dread creeps in.

"Where is she?"

Adelaida's eyes inch across me. Her lips purse. And then she turns away, like she can't bear to look at me. "Captain Waska just told me. Executed."

She might as well be speaking another language. My ears are ringing too much to make sense of anything she says. "There must be some kind of mistake," I say. "No. I—she's going to be executed?"

"No, Natasha," Adelaida says, her voice almost soft, just for a moment. "She's already dead."

62

ELLA

When the guards drag me into the bowels of the Gray Palace, everything goes dark. The stairs are so damp, I feel like I'm being rained on. The farther we go, the colder the air gets.

Andrei's hand is tight around my wrist as he forces me down the stairs. He's enjoying this. He runs his thumb across my tattoo, like I always do when I'm nervous, or sad, or thinking about a girl I love. "Crap tattoo," he says.

"Yeah," I say, and I'm furious to hear my voice hitch with tears. "Shame you didn't brand me with more care."

Andrei snorts. "Shame you couldn't just shut your legs and go marry a nice man."

I bend my knee and lift my foot, slamming it up between his legs. Andrei hisses and stumbles, and the guard in front of me peers back with concern.

"Watch it," Andrei says.

"Shame you couldn't just close your legs and keep me from kicking you," I say.

His grip wrenches my skin, and I have to bite my tongue to keep from yelling in pain.

But Natasha is safe, right? It has to be worth it as long as Natasha is safe.

We reach the bottom of the stairs. One of the guards unlocks a cell and shoves me inside. The rattling of the door, slammed, echoes.

When they leave, I wrap my hands around the bars. Gaze through the darkness.

Silence.

Then, a man's voice, accented: "You okay?"

I peer at the cell across from mine. I see a shadowed, tan face. Younger than I expected. An aquiline nose.

"What are you down here for?" he says.

"Really bad poetry," I say. "You?"

"Really good science."

I suddenly place the accent. "Oh! You're one of the Skaratan scholars. You were hunting for polar bears."

The man winces. Behind him, someone says something in Skaratan. Skaratan was never one of my father's languages of choice—I have no idea what they're saying.

"Polar bear fossils, actually," the man says.

"Did you ever find one?"

He nods. "And more birds than you can count."

I remember what Katla's parents said about the scholars, hunting for fossils that might disprove parts of *Captain's Log*. Fossils to show that animals can survive Floods, that humans aren't all that special. "So?" I say. "Have you successfully disproved Kos yet?"

"Not if we can't date the fossils," he says. "But we found a dovekie I'm almost positive is at least a few thousand years old. And then our best, nearly complete, was a gull, biggest wingspan I've ever seen on a—"

"Dovekie?" I say.

The scholar blinks. "Yes. Well, half of one, at least. Do you know something about dovekies?"

"I just . . . heard a story once."

In the distance, I think I can hear waves lapping against the palace. If I close my eyes, I can imagine Natasha reading to Sofie and Ness. *Behind seven mountains and beyond seven seas . . .*

"So how did they survive the Flood?" I say. "The birds."

"Well, there are lots of theories," the scholar says. He starts ticking off options on his fingers. "Underwater caves, mangrove forests, pumice rafts . . ."

"What's a pumice raft?" I say.

Obligingly, the scholar says, "Pumice is a rock full of air pockets. It's light enough to float. Some scholars—present company sometimes included, depending on the day—think that pumice ejected from volcanic eruptions could have formed massive rafts big and sturdy enough for animals to walk on. Certainly big and sturdy enough for seeds to drift across the globe."

Tamm wrote about a princess who threw herself in a volcano so seeds and dovekies could live. He wrote about islands unmoored from the seafloor. He wrote about a girl who killed an invading king with what she found in the boglands.

If Inna's story is based in something true, why couldn't Princess Talia's be? And Turelo's? Maybe they're true the same way Kos's writings are true: a mix of fable and fact that we've lost the line between.

Tamm's Fables is a book of fantastical ways people survive the Floods. But what if they're not all fantastical? What if *Tamm's Fables* can teach us how to survive the Flood?

I get to my feet. Press myself against the bars.

The only person in the world I want to tell is Natasha.

Those fables, I'd say. *Those fables you love so much. They mean even more than you know.*

I imagine a string, running from me to her, wherever she is. Connecting us. I imagine tugging on it. Can she feel that I'm here? She must.

The bars are cold under my fingers.

She'll find me.

She has to.

63

NATASHA

Something fundamental inside of me breaks. It feels like my heart has been severed from all my arteries, and now it's just free-floating in my chest, useless.

Someone slipped a note under the door an hour ago. I haven't picked it up yet.

I'm curled in Ella's bed, which smells like her still. When I first lay down, I found a barometer under Ella's pillow. Around the outside: *Dry, Fair, Showers, Stormy.* The hand is stuck on *Stormy,* but the sky outside is clear and pale.

Katla finds me staring at all the empty beds. Everyone's things are just where they left them. A moment, frozen in time, that I can't go back to. Ella is dead and Sofie is dead and Ness is dead. Why am I so desperate to survive when being the survivor feels like this?

"Adelaida told me," Katla whispers, sitting beside me and setting the note on the quilt. "I'm sorry."

I don't say anything.

"Look." Katla gathers my hands in hers. Pulls me upright. "They would want you to survive. All of them. I'm sad too. And angry. Seas, I am so angry. But we can't just stop trying."

She hands me the note from under the door.

Official summons. From Nikolai.

"Tomorrow's his birthday," Katla says. "Did you remember?"

I touch a hand to my chest. His ring still hangs there, cold against my unmoored heart.

"Go," Katla says. "This is why Ella saved you, isn't it? So you could survive."

So I could survive.

Slowly, I get to my feet. And I go to meet the king.

Nikolai is waiting in the throne room. He sits on a raised chair under a swoop of velvet. His hair rises in rogue waves around his crown, his tired eyes underscored with purple. His chin rests in his palm. I stand in front of him with my hands clasped.

His eyes sweep over me. Then he says, "Captain Waska told me what happened. What you told Adelaida." He studies me, and I swallow. "She was really working with my aunt?"

Come on, Natasha. Play the game. You know how.

"Yes." My voice creaks. "Yes," I say again. "And Princess Cassia."

He narrows his eyes. Just barely, but it's there. "Is she here? In the city?"

A pause. "Cassia's dead."

"How do you know?" Nikolai says. "Because Ella told you? What makes you think we should trust her?"

"Because Ella loved Cassia. That's why she was here."

"Revenge," Nikolai says. His brows knit. "Ella thought *I* was responsible?"

"She was with Cassia in Terrazza." I swallow. Glance at the

guards lining the walls. Captain Waska. Gregor, Twain, Sebastian. Not Andrei, thank the seas. "You saw, that moment in the conservatory. Andrei recognized her. Ella told me that Andrei was the one who shot Cassia."

Nikolai lifts a hand, and Captain Waska steps forward. "Send word to Terrazza. See what you can find out about my sister." Then he shuts his eyes. Leans back in his chair.

I saw enough of Nikolai and Cassia together to know they weren't close. He exiled her, after all, whether that was his idea or Gospodin's. But close or not, he grips the arms of his chair like the world beneath him is shaking.

"What about Ella?" I ask. I know I shouldn't; I have to.

"You don't have to worry about Ella." His eyes open again. "She's not going to hurt you or trick you again."

I swallow. The lump in my throat doesn't budge. "There's something else."

Nikolai tilts his head.

What if Ella was telling the truth? What if Nikolai is every bit the villain she told me he was?

I have to believe he's not.

"Bog plague," I say. "That's what made Ella act when she did. She thought you were involved in creating it."

"Creating it?" Nikolai says. His attention seems to sharpen. "How do you create a plague?"

I tell him about the food drive and the mushroom and Otto von Kleb. I tell him about handing poisoned tarts to dozens of passersby.

His face goes very still. "Excuse me?" His voice is hoarse, a whisper.

"Ella figured it out," I say. "That's how she poisoned your water."

He stands. "Did you know about this?" He's staring at his guards. "Any of you?"

They're all quiet.

"*Well?*"

I take a breath.

Nikolai trusts Gospodin. Maybe more than he trusts anyone.

But I *know* that Ella was right. Maybe not about Cassia but about this.

"Have you talked to Gospodin?" I ask.

Nikolai looks at me. For a long time. Then he shuts his eyes again. Exhales. I'm so used to seeing his face masked. But it's stripped bare.

I've never seen someone look so exhausted.

"You think it's possible," I say, "don't you?"

His head hangs, the crown sliding. "It doesn't matter whether or not I think it's possible."

"But—"

"Peace in Kostrov is hanging by a thread. We found four Brightwallers murdered on the path to the boglands two days ago. Yesterday, it was two Sacred Breath brothers dead. And do you have any idea how many people have tried to loot our Flood stockpiles this month? How many people have tried to break onto the royal fleet ships? People are terrified. Gospodin giving them hope could be the only thing keeping us from chaos, from turning into Illaset. Do you know what happened to Princess Colette after Storm Four?"

I open my mouth, but it's too dry to speak.

"They put her head on a spike," he says.

"But what if it happens again?" I ask. My voice is so small. So weak. "What if more people die?"

He crosses the room. Meets me at the middle. Taps my chin gently so I'm looking up at him. "There's nothing you can do, Natasha."

So Sofie and Ness and Ella died for nothing? So Katla and Gretta could die next? "What if I got the mushroom?" I'm desperate. "That would be proof, wouldn't it? Maybe one of the doctors could look at it. Inspect it for . . . for . . . I don't know, toxicity. Or we could compare it to those tarts. There have to be some of them left over somewhere. We can find the people Gospodin worked with. He can't have made all of those by himself."

But Nikolai is shaking his head. "No. Don't do anything to threaten him. *I'll* talk to him."

I don't believe him.

"Listen to me." He's looking at me intently. Pleading. "Without Gospodin, I don't have any power."

I erupt. "*With* Gospodin, you don't have any power! Can't you see that?"

He takes both of my hands. His are too big, spindly, swallowing mine. "I know you're upset. I know your friends died because of this plague. But you need to calm down."

I'm shaking.

"Natasha," he's saying, but I'm not hearing him.

I need to do something. To make all this worthwhile.

When I kissed Ella, I told her I didn't just want to survive anymore. I wasn't lying. I need to do something bigger. I need—I don't know. A reason to survive.

Nikolai is staring at me expectantly.

I blink. "What?"

"I said it's obvious you care about the people of Kostrov."

It's a lie. I don't deserve it. I care about my girls and about myself.

That's all I've ever fought for, isn't it? It wasn't until I didn't have a place on the royal fleet that I bothered to realize just how difficult it was for most people to survive.

"That's kind," I say.

"Tomorrow's my birthday," he says.

My throat is hot, itchy like I just inhaled smoke. "I know. I remember."

He nods at my necklace. His ring. "You're still wearing it. May I?"

Ella's gone. Ella is gone.

I nod. He smooths my hair out of the way and unclasps it. Lets the chain pool in his palm as the ring slides off.

"Kostrovians would be lucky," he murmurs, "to call you their queen."

This is what I wanted. This is what I've always wanted.

I'm numb.

I let Nikolai take my hand in his. Carefully, he slides the ring, the ring that has sat against my skin for months, over my finger.

"Natasha?" he says.

My eyes burn. "Yes," I say, the word sticking in my throat. "I'll marry you."

64

ELLA

I have no idea how long I've been trapped below the palace—hours? A day?—when I hear the door to the stairs open. I press closer to the bars, wrapping my hands around the rusty metal. Squinting.

His crown glints in the lantern light.

Nikolai.

"Ella, is it?" Nikolai says.

At first glance, he doesn't look much like Cassia. If she was gold—honey curls and tawny eyes—then he's silver. Even his skin has a cold undertone that makes him look like he's not accustomed to the sun. But the longer I look at him, the more similarities I see. High cheekbones. Long noses. Straight teeth.

"Cassia's brooch looks ridiculous on you," I say.

He glances down at his chest. Then back at me. Softly, he says, "You really did know her, didn't you?"

"I loved her."

"Well," he says, running a hand down one of the bars of my cell, "things never turn out very well for people who love my sister."

I look at him. At his familiar diamond face and the haughty lift of his chin. "You disgust me," I whisper.

"Sometimes," he says, "I disgust even myself."

"You don't deserve to wear that crown."

"And Maret did?" he says. "Cassia did?"

"At least Cassia was brave enough to stand up to Gospodin," I say.

He laughs, humorless. "Brave. You think that would've made any difference? If I hadn't backed out and told Gospodin what we were planning, she would've. It didn't matter which one of us had the crown. Without Gospodin, there would've been a revolution. Cassia knew the score. We could fight, the two of us. But neither of us would ever beat Gospodin. So Cassia and I spent all our time trying to kill each other. And I won. She lost. I'm king. She's dead. Is that what you wanted to hear?"

"You're proud of yourself, aren't you?"

"Proud of myself?" His voice is low, even, empty. "Proud of myself for living at Gospodin's beck and call? For letting him talk me into sending men after Cassia?"

"Stop blaming Gospodin. You know that you're the one—"

"Fine," he says. "You're right. It's *my* fault Cassia is dead. I wanted a crown more than I wanted a sister. I was and remain a noxious, power-starved asshole, and you have the audacity to ask if I'm *proud of myself?*" His eyes skim me up and down. "I doubt you want to hear me wax poetic about the sleepless nights I've had. Or the trying to drown myself in gin. You don't want to hear me tell you how guilty I feel, or that I'm sorry, because that doesn't make any difference. That doesn't bring her back. I can count the number of times in my life I've been *proud of myself.* I was proud of myself when I beat Cassia at a board game. I was proud of myself when I made her laugh or said something smart enough to get her to change her mind. I thought what made me proud was besting Cassia, but I was wrong. The only time I ever felt proud of myself was when Cassia was proud of me. And now she's dead, and it's my fault. Am I proud of myself?" Nikolai stares at me. His cheeks are wet. "I know Cassia was trying to kill me. I know she would've succeeded if I hadn't gotten to her first. But if I could go back, I'd let her do it."

I touch my own cheek. It's wet too. "We'd all be better off. She wouldn't have poisoned half of Kostrov."

"I didn't poison anyone."

I stare at him. Try to find a tell in his angry, tearstained face. "Really?"

"I told you it was my fault that Cassia died," he says. "But this wasn't me."

"Do you think Gospodin—"

"You shouldn't have told Natasha any of this. She's going to get herself hurt."

"She's okay, though?" I say. "Natasha's fine?"

He looks at me, searching for something. "She will be. As long as she doesn't ask too many questions about Gospodin."

"You think he's guilty," I say. "I can tell."

"It doesn't matter what I think. Gospodin is the person who keeps me on the throne."

"You really are a power-starved asshole, aren't you?"

"You don't understand," he says. "I have no family. No one. Nothing except this crown. And yes. I am desperate to keep it."

"Why do you want power so badly if you don't *do* anything with it?" I say.

He's silent for a long moment. Looks at my bars, my cell, not me. Finally: "I guess you let the little evils pass by so you can be the one who's still around to save the day when something really terrible happens."

It's so sudden, the honesty, that I blink. It takes me a moment to find my voice.

"If this isn't something really terrible," I say, "what is?"

He doesn't say anything. Just shakes his head. Then he turns. Heads for the stairs to leave and starts climbing.

"Make sure she's safe," I say, gripping the bars. "Please. Natasha. Make sure she's safe."

Nikolai looks back at me. "I will."

65

NATASHA

On the morning of Nikolai's birthday, Adelaida tells Katla, Gretta, and me that we'll have to perform.

"But there are only three of us," Gretta says. "And no one's been practicing."

"We'll do *Evelina*. We can manage with three."

Evelina was one of the first flights I learned as a junior. It's not in our regular festival rotation, but Adelaida makes us practice it every few months just in case something—like an engagement celebration, I guess—comes along.

My mother loved *Evelina*. It's about a boy who asks a girl to marry him, which is fitting. The boy says he'll give the girl, Evelina, everything. He promises her they'll be rich beyond belief; he promises her they'll grow old and gray together; he promises her they'll dance under clear skies every day. The boy is a liar. He can't give Evelina any of these things. But, as it turns out, Evelina didn't love him for the wealth or the health or the stormless days. She knew he was lying all along. So she marries him anyway.

Adelaida makes us practice all morning, then shoos us away after lunch, which I can't eat any of. "Rest up!" she says, giving my cheek a pinch. "Try to look a little queenlier tonight."

We're going to perform on the Sky Stage, at the top of the palace's southernmost tower. We haven't had the chance to perform up there since before Storm Ten. Normally, I love any excuse to fly so far from the ground. Today, I just feel sick.

The flyers know about Nikolai's proposal, but the rest of Kostrov doesn't. We're meant to perform for the whole city, gathered around the palace, to see. Then Nikolai will appear in one of the tall windows just below the Sky Stage with his bride-to-be. Me.

As soon as Adelaida lets us go, I make a break for my room. My *Evelina* full-suit hangs off the back of my door, but instead of putting it on, I find a cloak, boots. I catch a glimpse of myself in the mirror and pause. I look like a ghost, pale and hollow. I look like my mother.

A knock at my door.

I freeze.

"Tasha?" Katla says. "It's me."

The door opens. She takes in my clothes and frowns. "Going somewhere?"

I hesitate.

"Let me rephrase that," Katla says. "Yes, you're clearly going somewhere, which means that I am too. Let me get my cloak."

Ten minutes later, Katla and I are sneaking away from the palace with our hoods pulled up. Wind shivers over the waves. I hope this only takes a few hours. The flight is at sunset.

Under my arm, I carry the thin botanical book from the library. The green one Ella told me about. Without slowing, I flip through the pages until I find the one Ella described. I show Katla the page. *The tremble cap.*

"It just looks like a mushroom," she says.

"So you don't know where I might find one?"

"No. Somewhere boggy? I know the paths well enough to stop you from getting lost out there, but I'm not a mushroom expert." She frowns at me. "Even if you find one of these things, what are you going to do with it?"

"I haven't exactly worked that part out, okay?" I say. "But maybe if I show Nikolai this, show him that it's real—well, maybe he'll confront Gospodin. I have to try, right?"

"For the record, I think this whole thing is a bad idea."

"Why?" I say. "You hate Gospodin."

"Yes, but you're my favorite non-blood relation," Katla says. "And you're going to get yourself killed."

"So what?"

Katla lets out a sharp sound, not quite a laugh. "Who are you? Where's Natasha?"

When we step onto the raised wooden platform leading into the heart of the boglands, fog settles around us. It muffles the city. I can't see farther than a hand's distance in any direction. Katla is ghostly through the thick air.

Somewhere in the distance, or maybe very nearby, bells tinkle.

"What was that?" My voice echoes back to me.

Katla appears at my shoulder. "The peat harvesters hang bells on trees for days like this. It's how they find the main path."

"But we need to get off the main path, don't we?"

Katla nods. "Assuming Gospodin's people collected hundreds of tremble caps, there probably aren't any left in plain sight."

"So into the boglands?"

She points off the edge of the wooden platform. "Into the bog-lands."

My feet squelch into deep mud. "Oh, that's a pleasant feeling."

Katla leads me across the soggy earth. After a few sodden minutes, the ground shifts from plowed and plucked dirt to slippery gold-and-green growth. Wind-stripped pines dot the drier patches of land. The wetter sections glisten, long reeds swaying with the wind.

Once, when I was eleven, I asked Adelaida if we could visit the depths of the boglands. I hadn't yet met Katla and I didn't know that people not only came but lived here, in these wilds. I'd never been beyond the fringes.

Stay on stone streets, city girl, Adelaida told me. *You have bigger things ahead of you than drowning in mud.*

The wind whistles. Bells ring. I jump and Katla glances back at me.

"Scared?"

"No," I say.

"Don't be," she says. "It's not trying to scare you."

"Because it's an inanimate landscape or because it's trying to do something other than scare me?"

The wind comes again, sliding through bells and branches. When it rushes, it could be saying my name. I start humming to scare away the sounds.

"Natasha," Katla says, "hush."

"It's creepy," I say. I don't just mean that it's spooky. I mean that the surroundings creep, twisting around me, too soft or slow for my city girl eyes to locate but moving all the same.

"Let it creep," she says.

When I stop making my human noises, my words and my hummed songs, when I stop even considering things I might say to Katla, I find the opposite of silence. Not eerie quiet but vivid detail: the creak of a tree, the distant cadence of waves, the draining of rain through already saturated dirt. The smells, I couldn't describe if I had to. I have no original words for smells, just similes. *Like* pine, *like* mud, *like* morning rain in a northern patch of Kostrovian boglands. The harder I try to find the right words, the less I notice the smells themselves.

I'm struck by the overwhelming sense of being touched. Not only my feet pressing on mud, but mud granting my weight above it. Not only my ankle brushing flat-bladed grass but the grass touching me. I see little of the bog; it sees all of me.

Only now that it's gone do I fully realize the *wrongness* that settled inside me after Storm Four. But in the boglands, my body, my head, clears. It feels like . . . remembering.

Katla stops walking. I stop beside her. She stands at the edge of a pond. The water reflects the bone sky. A tuft of grass, eye-shaped and no bigger than a rowboat, waits at the pond's center.

Obviously, that's where I'm meant to go. If I say it out loud, I'm afraid I won't remember why it's so obvious.

"Do you wish," Katla says softly, for softly is the only way to speak in this place, "that the Sacred Breath never came here?"

"I don't know," I say. "It's hard to imagine."

"The other flyers always acted like I was too cynical to believe in anything," Katla says. "But I believe in everything."

Any other day, any other place, I wouldn't have understood. But here, cradled in reciprocity with this land, it's the clearest thing in the world. Not a deity or a spirit in this pond or that tree. The pond itself. The tree itself. The power of sap under fingernails and the feather nestled softly among the grasses.

I think of a question Gospodin once asked me; a question I only answered as he expected me to and never once wondered for myself.

"How do you think they survived the Flood?" I say. "The people who first lived here. In Maapinn. They didn't have ships and agriculture and industrialization."

There's a long not-silence in which neither of us speaks. "I've always thought," Katla finally says, "that's the whole reason they survived."

My mother didn't believe in Kos, but she believed unfailingly in old legends and river rapids and trees and me. I have long tallied the things I inherited from my mother; I never before counted the feeling of detachment she felt—from family, from the Sacred Breath, from the boglands our ancestors called home. I'm not sure I ever realized it was part of my inheritance.

"I'm going to pick the tremble cap," I say.

"Can you see it?" Katla says.

"No." I don't bother to explain it. She too stopped at this pond, after all.

I slosh on bare feet until the water reaches my waist. The mud rises through my toes. I stop, hands light on the surface, and I stand until my soul goes numb.

The lapping water whispers the same thing again and again. I don't know its tongue well enough to translate.

The water streams off me as I reach the island. I pull the

mushroom from the grass. It smells like clover honey. Its feathered gills are lavender as dawn. I wrap it in the corner of my cloak.

When I reach Katla's shore, she says, "Back to the palace?"

My voice is soft and childish. "I don't want to leave."

Katla takes my hand. "I know."

When we reach the edge of the boglands, the Storm Four feeling settles through me again. My stomach clenches. My lungs tighten. Grass clings to my calves like little hands pulling me back. It feels like they're saying, *You're leaving? So soon?*

I'm sorry. I glance back at the mist-swimming trees. *I'll be back. I just have to do something first.*

66

ELLA

I wonder if I'll still be in here when the Flood comes. I imagine the way the water would fill this place—first the cracks in the stone. Then a layer of cold across my feet. Up to my knees. Buoying me to the ceiling. A crush of pressure. Darkness.

That anxious, nauseated Storm Four feeling has been worse than ever since they put me down here. I've never wanted to see the sky so badly.

I hear footsteps. Guards have brought me water a few times. No food. I wait for the telltale clink of a metal cup against stone.

Instead, I hear, "Ella?"

Slowly, I turn. Squint.

Red hair. Stick-out ears. His eyes are huge.

"I thought they'd executed you."

"Gregor?" I say. I crawl to the bars. "Where's Natasha? Is she okay?"

"She's . . . she's fine. Seas, I really thought you were dead." Gregor keeps glancing over his shoulder, back at the stairs. "I shouldn't be talking to you. Look, Pippa told me everything. She seemed to think there was some sort of—"

A screech of metal. The door at the stairs opens, and Gregor jumps back. Another guard calls out, and Gregor glances over at me.

For a moment, I'm almost hoping—

But then he heads back up the stairs without another word.

I swallow.

Natasha is fine. That's what matters. Gregor said she was fine, and he has no reason to lie to me.

I try not to count the minutes ticking by. I curl against the wall, wishing I could sleep, wishing I could do something.

When the door opens again however many hours later, I'm seized by this sudden, cruel hope that I'm going to see Natasha on the stairs. I know it's stupid. It's probably Gregor, or worse, Andrei. But when I look up—

Two figures, not one. Yes, Gregor. But also, someone smaller. Not clomping down the stairs in heavy boots, but whispering on slippered feet.

I sit up. And their faces come into view in front of the bars.

67

NATASHA

The crowd surrounding the palace is loud and celebratory tonight. I suppose everyone is hungry for good news. Something to break the dark cycle of sickness and storms.

"What's Katla playing at?" Adelaida says. "How can she be late? Today, of all days?"

I shake my head. After we got back from the boglands, we split up to gather our full-suits and makeup. That was the last I saw of her.

Adelaida, Gretta, and I are waiting in the high tower room where Nikolai will present me as the future queen after our performance ends.

Gretta sighs. "I'll go look for her."

In the corner of the room, tucked under my folded cloak, I have my evidence. The green book. A poisonous mushroom hidden inside a velvet bag.

I let out a shaky breath and smooth my full-suit. It's white. Tulle.

I'm suddenly reminded of my mother on one of her good days, dancing across the floor of our apartment in her stockings. I can hear her singing, *Evelina, love, I should have known; your love was never stormswept or windblown.*

My mother is grabbing my hands. Spinning me. *Evelina, love, you are my earth; you are my breath, my song, and all I'm worth.*

I press a hand to my lips.

If I could see my mother right now, I'd say to her, *All those fairy tales you loved so much? I'm in one. Just look at me.*

But when she dreamed of fairy tales—she was never dreaming about crowns or royal weddings, was she?

The door opens and Gospodin comes in. I scrub my eyes and try to look excited.

"Miss Koskinen," Gospodin says.

"Mariner Gospodin."

"Congratulations," he says. "I look forward to working with you as queen."

I want to lunge at him. I force myself to breathe, steady myself.

"Mariner Gospodin," Adelaida says, touching his elbow lightly. "If I may, I'd like to discuss Natasha's accommodations on the fleet. I think, you see, she'll need an advisor . . ."

The door flies open.

Katla.

Her full-suit is bunched in her arms. Her hair is a mess. Adelaida shoots her a lethal glare, but she's too occupied with Gospodin to say anything.

Katla collides with me. Her voice low, she says, "Ella's alive."

My mouth parts. "What?"

"Gregor told me," she whispers. "He and Pippa want to break her out."

I'm slow to process what she's saying. Break her out? Of where? Why would Adelaida tell me Ella was dead? "I—I have to go see her."

"No." Katla grabs my hands. Glances back at Gospodin. "It's the crowd around the palace, don't you see? That's how they're going to get Ella out. Everything will be loud and chaotic, and everyone will be distracted by the performance."

She's alive.

I let out a slow, steadying breath. "Then we better make it a good one."

68

ELLA

"Look lively," Pippa says.

"Not too loud," Gregor says.

I blink. "What?" Shake my head. "I don't—"

Gregor pulls something from his belt. "Here's the thing you need to know about Pippa," he says. "She's an excellent judge of character." The lock thunks. The door squeaks open. "And incredibly persuasive."

Pippa shoves a bundle of clothes into my arms. In the dim light, I recognize the navy-blue dress the palace maids wear, and a dark, hooded cloak. "And what you should know about Gregor," she says, "is that he's a very kind person. But maybe not, you know, the *best* guard."

"Hey," Gregor says.

"Put those on," Pippa says. "Come on. Don't just stand there."

I take one unsteady step, then another.

"What about us?" the Skaratan scholar asks.

Pippa gives him an apologetic look. "We're going for stealth today, actually, but I'll put in a good word."

"We're not making this a regular thing," Gregor says.

I suppose I'm still not moving fast enough, because Pippa starts yanking my mud-stained dress over my head and the new one on in its place. I don't even have the time to be embarrassed.

"Does Natasha . . . Is she . . . ?"

"The flyers are performing on the Sky Stage in about . . ." Gregor looks at his watch. "Three minutes. We need to get you out while they're performing. All the guards will be at the front of the palace corralling the crowd. No one will pay any attention to a guard and a couple of maids slipping out the back."

When we get upstairs, I see Gregor was right. The inside of the palace is deserted.

"Dear," Pippa says, "running might be a little suspicious."

Gregor barely slows. He keeps glancing over his shoulder.

"Where are we going?" I ask.

"Back to the dungeons, probably," Gregor mutters.

We turn a corner, and suddenly, I know where we are. The flyer hall. It's empty. Gregor jogs through the studio. Pushes open the blue door.

And then we step outside.

The air is salty and cold. I can hear the music streaming from the roof of the palace. The violinists playing something slow, soft, sweet.

"Oh, I love *Evelina*," Pippa says, humming a few bars.

"Come on," Gregor says.

We walk fast from the palace.

I try so hard not to look back. But then I do. Back to the tallest palace tower. Back to where three white silks dangle from impossibly high wooden beams. Three girls spinning themselves in silk.

And Natasha.

I can see her hair, bright against the white of the silk.

My heart hurts.

"It's Nikolai's birthday," I say, "isn't it?"

Pippa takes my hand and gives it a tug. "Yes."

"And Natasha . . . ?"

"Once the performance is over, they'll announce it."

"Oh." I swallow the lump in my throat. "That's wonderful."

Gregor, a few feet in front of us, turns back to wave us forward. "I'm begging you to hurry."

Natasha's going to be the queen. That's good. Great. She deserves to survive.

The music fades behind us. I don't look back again.

"Can you tell me where we're going now?" I ask.

"The harbor," Pippa says. "There's a boat waiting for you. It's tiny, and there's not exactly a crew for you—"

"That's fine," I say. I learned how to sail well enough on my trip from Terrazza. "How did you get a boat?"

"Sofie left me some money," Pippa says. "She was always careful. She saved a bit while she was in the palace, and she had an inheritance."

I start shaking my head. "I can't possibly—"

"Don't," Pippa says firmly. "Sofie would want this."

I swallow. "Thank you."

Ahead of us, Gregor curses.

"What?"

"Something's going on," he says. "I see smoke."

The closer we get to the harbor, the more I smell it—burning. When we turn the last corner, I'm half expecting to see the royal fleet on fire. Instead, it's a squat, nondescript building tucked between a few boarded-up shops. The street below is littered with glass. Sooty plumes blacken the sky.

Gregor makes a disbelieving sound.

"What is that place?" I ask.

"Storage," Gregor says. "For the fleet. No one's supposed to know about it."

"Food and water?" I say.

If I'm not mistaken, Gregor is fighting a smile. "Mostly antique furniture, actually."

"Isn't space kind of an important constraint on these ships?" I ask. "They'd really waste it on antique furniture?"

"Well, they wouldn't anymore," Pippa points out.

The harbor is chaos. People are dragging buckets from the sea to the burning building. Gregor, Pippa, and I shove through the crowd. I finally see where we're headed—a tiny boat, its sails furled, bobbing against a dock.

"Are you sure?" I ask.

"Positive," Pippa says. She's practically shoving me on board. "I really would love to have a drawn-out goodbye, but—"

"—about a hundred guards are about to show up to try to catch anyone involved in that," Gregor finishes, pointing at the blaze.

"Okay." I glance one more time in the direction of the palace, but I can't see it from here. Not even the tallest tower. Not even the white silks above it.

"Any idea where you're going?" Pippa says.

Seas. Where am I going?

I speak before I've even finished having the thought: "Turelo."

Gregor gives Pippa a sideways look. "You know that's not a real place, right?"

"Yes?" I say.

"Well, glad that's cleared up."

In the distance, shouts. I see a flash of uniforms—guards turning into the harbor.

"Okay, definitely time to go," Pippa says.

I nod. "Thank you."

Pippa grabs my boat with both hands and shoves.

And then I'm leaving Kostrov behind.

69

NATASHA

It's breezy on the Sky Stage. Up here, in velvet chairs—Nikolai, Gospodin, the council. Far below, all of Kostrov. Somewhere in the palace, Ella. Trying to escape.

We take our positions, and the musicians start to play.

I hold the edges of the silks in each hand. Flap them like wings.

Evelina, love . . .

I wrap my foot in my silk and spin skyward.

It feels so good. The tightness of the fabric holding me in place. All the aches and burns of so many years of practice have turned to this—familiar, secure.

I look at Nikolai. He's frowning slightly, like he's as far from this place as I am.

Then I twist myself higher, higher. Hook myself in place and spin. The world flashes around me. Katla, Gretta, open sky, fluttering silk—

Three silhouettes hurrying along the cobblestones, moving fast from the palace.

And I know.

I don't want to be queen.

Run, Ella. They're distracted. Run.

At the top of my silks, I flip upside down. Hook my knees

through the fabric and wrap my torso, my arms. Part my legs like a star.

It always makes the crowd gasp when we drop.

As one, Katla, Gretta, and I are caught in the twisty fabric knots we've wound, springing on our taut silks.

Just a little bit longer. Just a few more minutes, and Ella will be safe, free, gone—

The next time I climb to the top of my silks, I see smoke rising from the harbor.

No. Ella. *No.*

Captain Waska is rising from his seat beside Nikolai. The crowd is murmuring below.

Katla, Gretta, and I glance at one another. We stay frozen in position for one, two, three beats.

Captain Waska is calling instructions to the guards. Gospodin is gesturing for Nikolai to go inside the tower. He's waving at the crowd, trying to calm them. Adelaida is gesturing wildly at the violinists, trying to get them to start playing again.

And I know what I want to do.

I climb down my silk. Katla and Gretta follow my lead. Adelaida yells at us to get back on the silks, but I ignore her.

I grab Katla's hands. "I have to find her."

Katla's lips twist. "I know."

"What are you talking about?" Gretta says.

I'm already walking backward. "I love you both."

"Love you too," Katla says.

"What's going on?" Gretta says.

I hurdle down the stairs and slam into Nikolai at the door to the tower room.

"Natasha," he says. "I was just—"

I take his hand and pull him inside. If he's surprised at my sudden ferocity, he doesn't let on. I grab my cloak, then the book and the velvet bag.

It's not that I never had feelings for Nikolai. I did. At some point. If I were his queen, we would've kissed. Slept together. Had children. And—and I think I could've. Think I could've grown to love him.

But Ella.

If there was any conceivable way I could choose *not* to want Ella—this chaotic, vengeful, dangerous person—I would've chosen it a long time ago.

There was no choosing.

I hand Nikolai the green book. The velvet bag. And then I slide his ring off my finger and press it into his palm.

"I'm sorry," I say. "I can't."

He's shaking his head. Lifts the bag and looks inside. His face pales. "What am I supposed to do with this?"

"Be the king Kostrov needs," I say.

He exhales. Looks at me, then back at his hands, the bag, his chance to be more.

"I have to go," I say. "I'm sorry. I have to go."

And then I run.

70

ELLA

I may have oversold my ability to captain a boat.

Pippa and Gregor are still watching me from the dock, looking nervous, as I fumble with the lines. The harbor is slowly but surely filling up with guards, and the longer I struggle ten feet offshore, the more likely someone is to notice me and raise the alarm.

And then I see her.

Natasha hurtles through the harbor, crashing into Gregor and Pippa, saying something the wind tugs out of earshot. She's wearing a full-suit, swan white, her hair braided into a crown.

Pippa points. And Natasha turns to look at me.

Our eyes meet across the water.

I turn the boat around.

Gregor presses his palms to his face and sighs.

The dying light plays off Natasha's hair, the little copper filament strands that curl out from her braid.

She steps onto the dock. "Pippa tells me you're sailing to an imaginary island from *Tamm's Fables*?"

"When you say it that way, it sounds silly."

In a small voice, an entirely un-Natasha voice, she says, "Without me?"

I look at her, at her pointed nose and hunched shoulders and her eyes, her hopeful but nervous hazel eyes. And I hold out my hand.

She takes it, lacing her fingers through mine. When she does, she pulls the boat closer. It bumps against the dock.

"What about Nikolai?" I say.

Natasha steps closer. Our arms fold between us, and quite suddenly, she's everywhere, in my air and my head and my heart. "What about you?" she says.

71

NATASHA

Ella's breath is warm and she smells like mint and pine trees. Her skin is cool but it makes mine feel alive.

So I lean forward all the way, and I kiss her.

When I was eight, I spent a year wondering if I would starve to death. When I first came to the palace, I feasted, eating until my stomach ached and my head pounded. And eventually, I learned how magical a meal is when you know it won't be your last.

That is this kiss with Ella.

I don't kiss her like I did in the alley, in the rain, hungry and desperate. I kiss her in a way that says: *Yes. But just think of the next kiss.*

She pulls her lips away from mine by half a breath, her nose still brushing mine. "Are you sure?" she says.

"I choose you."

I choose the sound of waves and the bristle of wind. I choose not ten years from now but today. I choose the horizon I don't know.

"Natasha—"

I press my forehead against Ella's. "I choose you." She opens her mouth, like she's going to ask why. So before she can, I answer. "I don't care what happens tomorrow. I don't care what happens when the next storm hits. I care that today I'm with you."

She laughs, lighter than breath.

~~~

Nine years ago, a woman who shouldn't have drowned did. Before she went, she told me fairy tales until I breathed them. She told me stories of girls who knew how to fly and girls who trusted each other and girls who trusted themselves.

My mother told me stories about love.

As it turns out, I know them all by heart.

I take Ella's hand in mine.

The storms can do what they want to me. Tear me apart. Drown me. But I'll ask the sea to save her.

72

ELLA

The wind beats the sails and the sails beat back.

Natasha and I are not, as it turns out, world-class sailors. For starters, we're somewhat lacking in the way of nautical knowledge, reading maps, adjusting sails, and fixing literally anything that goes wrong. To make matters worse, whenever we're in the middle of executing some daring maneuver, like tacking against a mighty wave, one of us will unfailingly say something stupid and make the other one laugh so hard that the wave ends up soaking us and we have to spend the next ten minutes bailing ourselves out.

At night, when the sky blackens and bursts with stars and auroras, we settle under a blanket on the deck and page through the books Pippa thought to shove on board. An atlas and a copy of *Tamm's Fables*. We wake again with the sun and eat our tiny stash of bread and cheese—a Gregor contribution—and try to figure out where we can next get food. Natasha has declared she's going to become a fisherwoman of great renown.

We haven't found any floating islands yet, but spirits are high.

On the eighth day, Natasha and I sit at the railing, staring at the water.

I rest my hands beside hers. She lifts her pinky so it covers mine.

We sit without speaking for a long time, listening to things other than each other's voices: waves, wind. It feels a shame to break the quiet.

"Do you regret leaving?" I say.

Natasha smiles. "Don't you think the sea wanted us to go?"

I've felt seasick plenty since getting on board. But I have yet to feel that aching, Storm Four tightness inside me since we left Kostrov. Whatever the sea wants to tell me, it seems to have decided I'm listening.

"Probably," I say.

Overhead, then, a sound that's gotten too unusual as of late—the call of a bird. Since Storm Five, it's been a treat, the kind that makes us look up at the flash of wings overhead. The wind spins a spiral above me. In that loosening gyre, a white-bellied, black-beaked bird turns its wings.

I shade my eyes and watch the bird seek horizon. "Are you worried we won't find anything out here?"

Natasha leans farther over the rail like she wants to drink the sea. "At least we will have tried."

Each wave the boat summits sends a spray of mist into our faces. "We could die too," I say. "There's also that."

"Everyone dies sooner or later," Natasha says. She laces her fingers through mine. "Wouldn't you rather live first?"

ACKNOWLEDGMENTS

Apparently, books take a lot of work. Thank you, with every piece of me, to all the people who helped this story come to life.

Thank you, thank you, thank you to Danielle Burby, optimist, hero, cheerleader, and friend. You're the agent of my dreams and then some.

This book had two incredibly smart editors. Thank you to Kathy Dawson for believing in this book and for reminding me to write not just a story, but a story about something. Thank you to Ellen Cormier for adopting me and guiding me through the incredibly strange year that was 2020—I couldn't have done it without you. I'm so grateful to the whole team who made this book a real thing— Samira Iravani, Cerise Steel, Regina Castillo, Tabitha Dulla, Bree Martinez, Rosie Ahmed, Lauri Hornik, Nancy Mercado, and the whole team at Dial and Penguin Young Readers.

To all the badass women I lived with at Stanford and in Outdoor House: To Alexa, for a lifetime of Coupa and for inspiring me every day with your passion for writing. To Halle, for reading an early draft and being my co-flyer. And to Blaire, for telling me my voice could inspire young women out there—you're the one who inspires me.

To Chris, Joey, Martín, and Sophie, the Thimble, the world's darkest apartment—thank you for the champagne, the moral support, and your enthusiasm for pirates. To Wyatt, for your unstoppable love of nature. To Kevin, Fompy, for reading the book I wrote when I was thirteen, a task I would wish upon literally no one. To Gia—nice. To Ariana, for your passion for books of all kinds and the world's best birthday cakes.

I'm incredibly grateful to Rosaria Munda, Rachel Morris, Ava Reid, and Allison Saft for reading drafts of this manuscript, cheering me on, and talking about books with me.

Thank you to the teachers who made me want to write in the first place: Jennifer Baughman, Jan Webb, Susan Walker, and Christie McCormick. You taught me to love stories; to find something meaningful to say and to say it; to speak, write, be, with confidence. Thank you also to the inspiring professors I had at Stanford, and especially to Austin Smith, who read an early, messy draft of this book and helped me figure out where to go next.

I owe lots of thanks to all the family that helped this book (and me) exist. Thank you to the Biggars for welcoming me to Australia and being such enthusiastic, book-loving supporters. Oliver, I owe you a lot of coffees for helping me untangle so many plot holes on our 5k lunch walks.

To Nana, Ga, Gum, Grandma Jean, and Maury. To the Robsons, Knieses, Carmodys, Hubbards, and Strobels, my aunts, uncles, and cousins who surrounded me with books. The best way to make a reader is to read with her, to her, beside her. I owe all of you a whole library.

All the thanks in the world to Aidan. For celebrating every writing victory and helping me through every low—there were lots of both. For listening to me talk about Prelapsarian Eden. For being the other half of my two-person book club. For long road trips with musical singalongs and political podcasts. For drinking coffee on ordinary Wednesdays. IFYA.

To Drew, for always knowing to get me books for my birthday. I look up to you, in part because you're my older brother, in part because you're very tall, but mostly because your pun game is the stuff of legends.

Finally, to Mom and Dad. For reading that story I wrote about otters in fifth grade. For sending me to Iowa. For building me a bigger bookshelf. For Stanford. For always telling me that I didn't have to ask myself if I would become an author—only when. For all the love. For all the words.

JUL 0 8 2021